KT-362-123

CHRISTINE FEEHAN

DARK Legacy

piatkus

PIATKUS

First published in the US in 2017 by The Berkley Publishing Group
A division of the Penguin Random House LLC
First published in Great Britain in 2017 by Piatkus
This paperback edition published in 2018

13 5 7 9 10 8 6 4 2

Copyright © 2017 by Christine Feehan

The moral right of the author has been asserted.

*All characters and events in this publication, other than those
clearly in the public domain, are fictitious and any resemblance
to real persons, living or dead, is purely coincidental.*

All rights reserved.
No part of this publication may be reproduced, stored in a
retrieval system, or transmitted in any form or by any means, without
the prior permission in writing of the publisher, nor be otherwise circulated
in any form of binding or cover other than that in which it is published
and without a similar condition including this condition
being imposed on the subsequent purchaser.

A CIP catalogue record for this book
is available from the British Library.

ISBN: 978-0-349-41652-6

Printed and bound in Great Britain by
Clays Ltd, Elcograf S.p.A.

Papers used by Piatkus are from well-managed forests
and other responsible sources.

MIX
Paper from
responsible sources
FSC® C104740

Piatkus
An imprint of
Little, Brown Book Group
Carmelite House
50 Victoria Embankment
London EC4Y 0DZ

An Hachette UK Company
www.hachette.co.uk

www.littlebrown.co.uk

3/24

Withdrawn

www.hants.gov.uk/library

Hampshire
County Council

Love
YOUR LIBRARY

Tel: 0300 555 1387

Praise for Christine Feehan:

'After Bram Stoker, Anne Rice and Joss Whedon, Feehan is
the person most credited with popularizing the neck gripper'
Time magazine

'The queen of paranormal romance'
USA Today

'Feehan has a knack for bringing vampiric Carpathians
to vivid, virile life in her Dark Carpathian novels'
Publishers Weekly

'The amazingly prolific author's ability
to create captivating and adrenaline-raising
worlds is unsurpassed'
Romantic Times

C016635197

By Christine Feehan

Torpedo Ink series:
Judgment Road

Shadow series:
Shadow Rider
Shadow Reaper
Shadow Keeper

Christine Feehan's
'Dark' Carpathian series:
Dark Prince
Dark Desire
Dark Gold
Dark Magic
Dark Challenge
Dark Fire
Dark Legend
Dark Guardian
Dark Symphony
Dark Melody
Dark Destiny
Dark Secret
Dark Demon
Dark Celebration
Dark Possession
Dark Curse
Dark Slayer
Dark Peril
Dark Predator
Dark Storm
Dark Lycan
Dark Wolf
Dark Blood
Dark Ghost
Dark Promises
Dark Carousel
Dark Legacy

Dark Nights
Darkest at Dawn (omnibus)

Sea Haven series:
Water Bound
Spirit Bound
Air Bound
Earth Bound
Fire Bound
Bound Together

GhostWalker series:
Shadow Game
Mind Game
Night Game
Conspiracy Game
Deadly Game
Predatory Game
Murder Game
Street Game
Ruthless Game
Samurai Game
Viper Game
Spider Game
Power Game
Covert Game

Drake Sisters series:
Oceans of Fire
Dangerous Tides
Safe Harbour
Turbulent Sea
Hidden Currents
Magic Before Christmas

Leopard People series:
Fever
Burning Wild
Wild Fire
Savage Nature
Leopard's Prey
Cat's Lair
Wild Cat
Leopard's Fury
Leopard's Blood

The Scarletti Curse

Lair of the Lion

For Ian Powell,
my Ink Spot, an amazing father,
white Knight and inspiration to me.

FOR MY READERS

Be sure to go to christinefeehan.com/members/ to sign up for my PRIVATE book announcement list and download the FREE ebook of *Dark Desserts*. Join my community and get firsthand news, enter the book discussions, ask your questions and chat with me. Please feel free to email me at Christine@ christinefeehan.com. I would love to hear from you.

ACKNOWLEDGMENTS

There are always so many people to thank, and in this case, more than usual. Chris Tong for his help in my mini-emergency. Thank you for coming through. Ruth Powell for her lullaby; love it so much! Brian Feehan and Sheila English for the endless power hours. I know I wore you both out. Cheryl Wilson for her wonderful edits. I was under the gun and you came through for me. I appreciate you so much. Domini Walker, with me every step of the way as usual. We didn't get much sleep on this one!

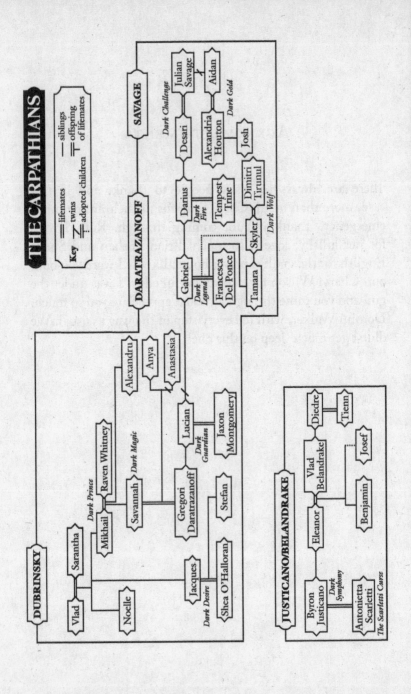

THE CARPATHIANS

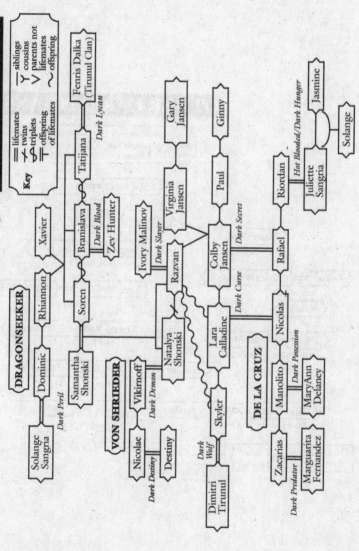

Key
= lifemates
‿ twins
Λ triplets
≡ offspring of lifemates

― siblings
⅄ cousins
V parents not lifemates
∿ offspring of lifemates

DRAGONSEEKER

Xavier

Rhiannon

Dominic

Solange Sangria

Dark Peril

Samantha Shonski

Soren

Branislava

Dark Blood

Zev Hunter

Tatijana

Fenris Dalka
(Tirunul Clan)

Dark Lycan

Ivory Malinov

Razvan

Dark Slayer

Virginia Jansen

Gary Jansen

Ginny

Paul

Colby Jansen

Dark Secret

Riordan

Juliette Sangria

Hot Blooded/Dark Hunger

Jasmine

Solange

VON SHRIEDER

Vikirnoff

Dark Demon

Nicolae

Dark Destiny

Destiny

Natalya Shonski

Lara Calladine

Dark Curse

Skyler

Dark Wolf

Dimitri Trunul

DE LA CRUZ

Manolito

Dark Possession

MaryAnn Delaney

Nicolas

Rafael

Zacarias

Dark Predator

Marguarita Fernandez

OTHER CARPATHIANS

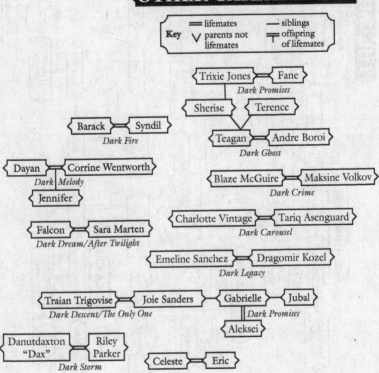

Key
≡ lifemates — siblings
∨ parents not lifemates ⊤ offspring of lifemates

Trixie Jones ≡ Fane
Dark Promises

Sherise Terence

Barack ≡ Syndil
Dark Fire

Teagan ≡ Andre Boroi
Dark Ghost

Dayan ≡ Corrine Wentworth
Dark Melody

Jennifer

Blaze McGuire ≡ Maksine Volkov
Dark Crime

Charlotte Vintage ≡ Tariq Asenguard
Dark Carousel

Falcon ≡ Sara Marten
Dark Dream/After Twilight

Emeline Sanchez ≡ Dragomir Kozel
Dark Legacy

Traian Trigovise ≡ Joie Sanders Gabrielle ≡ Jubal
Dark Descent/The Only One *Dark Promises*

Aleksei

Danutdaxton "Dax" ≡ Riley Parker
Dark Storm

Celeste ≡ Eric

Dark Legacy

1

Emeline Sanchez watched the children playing in the large play yard directly across from her little Victorian home. She liked sitting outside on the wide, wraparound porch where the wind could touch her face. Sometimes, that small touch was the only relief she got from the relentless pain winding through her body every minute of the night and day.

Rain had given the air a clean, fresh scent. The world looked shiny and new, every leaf on the trees a vivid green or silver. Small birds sang to one another, hopping from tree branches to gnarled limbs. They were bright red spots of color, adding to the beauty of the compound. The property was owned by Tariq Asenguard, co-owner of a string of high-end nightclubs. He had a unique piece of property, and she would have loved to live there if things had been different. Tariq was Carpathian, an ancient race with amazing gifts, but they needed to drink blood to survive. She knew they were forced to sleep in the ground during daylight hours and only came out at night. If they didn't find their lifemate in time, many succumbed to the temptation to feel by becoming the vilest of creatures—vampire.

"Emeline." A tall woman with long, dark hair and forest green eyes waved at her from the play yard. "It's a beautiful day."

Genevieve Marten was gorgeous. Model thin. Tall with long legs that went on forever. Dressed in slim jeans and leather boots, she looked far too elegant, even in that attire, to be playing nanny to five children. Emeline knew Genevieve was independently wealthy and had traveled the world, yet she was as sweet as anyone could be, and she'd taken on the job of looking after the children when Tariq and Charlotte couldn't. Emeline was certain Genevieve didn't have a mean bone in her body.

"It is, isn't it?" she called back. For that one moment, Emeline felt normal, like she had a friend and they shared a joyous moment just because it was such a beautiful day.

As she waved, a long tangle of blue-black hair fell around her face and she pushed it back, vaguely thinking she was going to have to cut it soon. She'd always loved her hair, the one feature she thought was attractive about her. But it fell below her waist, and she was just too exhausted to take proper care of it. Merely lifting her arms to brush it, much less wash it, was becoming a terrible chore. She sighed and rested her chin on the heel of her hand, her eyes on the five children running.

She *loved* watching the children. She didn't really know true happiness anymore, but the closest she came was at times like this, observing them playing and laughing, seemingly carefree and happy. They were alive because of her deliberate sacrifice. The sound of their laughter, seeing them on swings and slides and doing normal things, was worth every horrific moment she'd suffered. They were alive. Traumatized, yes, but still alive and hopefully recovering very quickly.

"Come join us," Genevieve called.

Emeline wanted to join them. She even needed to, but she couldn't take the chance. She didn't think Genevieve would turn on her, but there were others . . .

"I'm drinking tea," she said. "You should join me. I baked cookies."

The children had become aware she was out on her porch, something she often did during the daylight hours, even in the middle of a violent storm, but never at night. At night, she stayed in the house, her heart beating too hard, terrified he would come for her. She knew Vadim was coming, it was only a matter of time. He whispered to her sometimes, when she wasn't strong enough to keep him out of her head. Those times were becoming more and more frequent. Emeline often had prophetic dreams. She could replay them over and over, changing small details in an effort to change the outcome of what occurred. Vadim had found her in those dreams, he had found a way to trap her and capture her. She escaped, but he was still with her in her mind now, impossible to get out.

"Emeline!" the chorus of voices called to her. Happy. Affectionate. Although she rarely left her porch, they knew she had their backs. She'd saved them more than once at a great cost to herself. They weren't fully aware of that expense, and she hoped they never would be. They were too young to bear any more burdens than they already did.

"Swing with us, Em," Danny called. At fifteen, he was tall and gangly, his form just beginning to show the promise of who he would become. Emeline knew he had great courage, as well as love for his siblings. He'd kept them together after their parents had died, and when the girls were taken by the

3

monstrous men down in the labyrinth beneath the city, he had gone after them. She couldn't help but admire Danny.

"Not right now, but I have a plate full of warm chocolate chip cookies. And, Genevieve, I also have fresh cranberry and pistachio biscotti dipped in white chocolate."

Tariq Asenguard had taken the children in, become a foster parent of sorts, until the adoptions came through, protecting them with his friends and unique security system—just as he protected her. Emeline was grateful to him, but she knew she couldn't stay much longer.

Danny raced to the porch, leaned down and brushed the top of her head with a kiss, scooped up a handful of cookies and was back at the swings before either three-year-old, Lourdes or Bella, could protest. Bella was his youngest sister. Lourdes was the orphaned niece of Tariq's wife, Charlotte.

"Thanks, Em!" Danny yelled, stuffing one into his mouth whole. "So good." Both little girls immediately held out their hand for one, and Danny obliged them.

Despite his youth, Danny watched over his family with a fierce protectiveness. He was equally as protective of little Lourdes, Emeline, and Emeline's best friend, Blaze. They'd helped him when he thought everything was lost. He was a smart boy, indescribably brave, and he'd begun to emulate the Carpathian males who'd taken them all in. His hair was a little too long, because he was growing it so he could pull it back in a long ponytail like the Carpathian males often wore. He admired Tariq and even walked like him.

They'd been orphans living on the streets, trying to stay together, when the girls had been taken. Danny had refused to give up on his sisters and had gone after them, down into the underbelly of the city—a huge labyrinth of tunnels and rooms, a city below the city. Emeline shivered at the memory. She tried very hard not to think about it, to close the door on

4

the horrors of what had been down there. She first encountered Danny in a dream and then, later, in reality when his sisters had been taken. Despite knowing what would happen to her, she had aided him in ensuring the safety of the girls. She'd seen her fate enough times in dreams, but someone had to get the children out or they would have died in that murky, stench-filled place of nightmares.

She understood street children; she'd been one herself and she knew how much they craved the stability of a close family. She looked around the huge complex, with the buildings, gardens and lake bordering one side, the high fence surrounding the property on the other three sides, and all the amenities the acreage offered. It was still a prison. No matter how beautiful, none of them could safely leave. Not even the children. Maybe especially the children.

"Cranberry and pistachio biscotti?" Genevieve put her book down. She'd gone to the bench under the tall oak where she could keep an eye on the children. "You made them?"

"This morning," Emeline enticed. She wanted Genevieve's company. She needed to feel normal even if it was just for a few minutes. Sometimes, if her focus changed, she could resist the pain longer, not be afraid for just a few minutes and pretend that she would have a life like everyone else. She needed that today—one of the reasons she'd spent all morning baking.

"You can ride my dragon," Amelia offered. She was fourteen, her body already developing into that of a woman's. Her hair was thick and often tousled from her continual roughhousing with her brother. She had beautiful eyes and a killer smile. Emeline adored her and the way she loved her sisters and brother.

Emeline knew it was huge to get an offer to ride one of the dragons. Made of stone, the five dragons—each with a

5

unique color—sat off to one side of the play yard. They looked as if they were statues, just that. Nothing else. Emeline knew that each dragon had been made specifically for one of the children. For their amusement, yes, but mostly for protection. The dragons, crouched so lifelike in the massive yard, could suddenly come to life, spread wings and fly as well as breathe fire. Amelia's dragon was a striking orange and she loved it dearly. Emeline often saw her whispering to it, or circling the long neck with her arm and nuzzling it with affection.

Emeline sighed. She detested disappointing the children, especially Amelia or Liv, the ten-year-old, but she didn't dare chance leaving the porch.

"I'd love to ride your dragon, Amelia. He's beautiful, but I'm enjoying just sitting here, drinking tea and watching all of you." That was strictly the truth. "Come get some cookies. I don't know if dragons like them, but you can feed him one and tell him it's from me."

Amelia giggled and crossed the yard to the house at a much more demure pace than her brother. The Victorian was a smaller replica of the much larger one that was Tariq and Charlotte's home. That house loomed in the background, just beyond the play yard. Emeline always enjoyed looking at it as well. Tariq's main home was a sprawling mansion with the classic semicircular arches, corbel gables, rock-faced square towers, archivolt and transom windows in a ribbon pattern, all classic Richardsonian Romanesque.

Water from the lake lapped lazily at the shore. The sun poured down into it, so that droplets disturbed by fish and birds appeared as dazzling diamonds dripping into the water, causing beautiful rings that spread across the surface. Emeline always found peace in the sound of the water moving. Sometimes she wished she was like Blaze or Charlotte, no longer human but Carpathian, the ancient race of people capable of amazing things. With a wave of their hands they could move water, make it dance, keep that soothing sound up so she could concentrate on it rather than the pain racking her body.

Amelia threw herself into the chair across from Emeline's. She caught up a cookie and leaned forward. "Em, you do know if there's anything at all I could do for you, I'd do it."

God. She loved the children. They were all so amazing. Every last one of them. She was grateful she'd made the decision to go into that labyrinth, the chambers of utter horror, to get them out. She refused to regret that decision, no matter the price she had to pay—and she was paying it every single minute of the day. She forced a reassuring smile. "I know I look awful, Amelia, but I'm getting better." That was a lie. The pain was getting worse. Pain and fear. She kept a close eye on the sky. Sunset was fast approaching and she'd go immediately into the house once the sun dropped out of the sky.

"No, you're not," Amelia whispered. "You're not, Emeline. Please let Tariq or one of the others help you. A couple of the scariest ones are good healers."

Emeline couldn't help the automatic withdrawal, the way her body went smaller. She wrapped her arms around herself, as if she could cloak her body, make herself invisible. The ancient race could heal. She'd seen it. She *wanted* to be able to go to them and ask for help. Anything at all to stop the pain. She shook her head. "I'm fine. I don't need them."

"Are you afraid of them? I'd go with you."

Amelia reached out and touched her wrist and followed the line of bruising up to her elbow. Her touch was light, but it still hurt. Emeline forced herself to remain still. Amelia had been traumatized by the events in the underground city. She didn't need to worry about Emeline when there was nothing she could do. Emeline wanted her to be a child, although, realistically, she knew there was no going back for Amelia.

"It's such a beautiful day, isn't it? I love the rain, but this is gorgeous, everything fresh and shimmering new." She kept her voice light as she casually reached for her teacup, the action giving her a legitimate reason for moving her arm out of reach. When she settled the teacup back into its saucer, she put her hand in her lap, surreptitiously tugging on the sleeve to cover the bruising.

Amelia opened her mouth as if she might say something, but in the end, she just took a bite of the cookie. "These are still warm."

"Right? They're so good. I love them with ice cream."

Amelia scooped up three more. "My dragon's going to love these just like they are. Thanks. Any time you want a ride, let me know, and if you need me, Em, I'll come stay with you." Her gaze dropped to Emeline's bruised arm, not that she could see the discoloration, but she knew it was there.

"Thanks, honey," Emeline said, fighting the burn of tears. "Go have fun with your dragon."

Amelia hesitated, standing awkwardly in front of her, then she leaned down and brushed a kiss across her forehead. "You're important, too, Em. To all of us. You know that, don't you?"

Emeline tightened her arms around her middle, holding it together by a mere thread. She was going to have to risk leaving the compound to ensure Amelia's—and the other children's—safety. She knew when she made the decision to leave that she probably wouldn't survive. "Thank you, Amelia. Sometimes, I guess, we all need a reminder."

She wasn't as important as the children. They deserved a life, and they'd never had it. They were street children, living from one garbage can to another, the older ones stealing to provide for the younger ones. Huddling together to keep warm in the worst of winter. Here, in Tariq Asenguard's compound with the wealthy Carpathian as their guardian, she knew they finally had a home. She couldn't endanger them by drawing the worst evil imaginable to them.

Amelia jumped off the porch and walked nonchalantly back to her dragon. Emeline caught the impression that she wanted to run to the creature, but was trying to act dignified. That made Emeline want to smile when few things could anymore. Amelia went back and forth between being a young teen and a very old soul.

"Emeline." Genevieve's voice floated to her and she realized she was drifting. She did that sometimes, trying to find a place in her head to go where nothing, not even the terrible pain eating away at her insides, could get to her. "Are you certain you don't mind me joining you?"

Emeline raised her head, and it was an effort. She had thought she was holding her own outside, but suddenly she was desperately tired. Everything seemed to be an effort these days, but watching the children play, seeing little three-year-old Bella laughing as her brother pushed her on the swing, was a balm to her. "Of course I want your company, Genevieve." She smiled up at the other woman.

"It's nice to talk to an adult. Charlotte and Blaze sleep all day, and although I love the children, I sometimes think I might pull out all my hair if I don't hear an adult's voice." Genevieve sank gracefully into the chair Amelia had just vacated. "By the time the two of them get up, I'm ready to call it a night." She yawned and poured herself a cup of tea. "It seems I'm turning into an old lady. I want to go to bed earlier and earlier."

Her laughter was soft, inviting Emeline to join in at the

absurdity of a woman her age going to bed just after sunset. Emeline shifted back in her chair so the shadows could soften her appearance. An observant person would notice she continued to lose weight, and Genevieve was observant.

"I don't sleep very well," Emeline admitted. "I play music, but that doesn't always help."

"You need to talk to someone," Genevieve suggested gently. Emeline nodded, agreeing because it was the truth. She wouldn't. Couldn't. But she agreed because she knew Genevieve was right. "Blaze and Charlotte tell me that as well. I don't want to relive one moment of it, not ever again, not even to talk about it."

The incident. That's how she thought of it, trying to minimize those hours in her mind. Make the entire thing just another moment in her history. She pushed at her tangled hair with trembling fingers. For a moment, she couldn't breathe. The pain in her body increased until she writhed on the chair, a low moan escaping. At once Genevieve leapt to her feet and came around the small table toward her.

Emeline held up her hand, palm out, desperate to stop the other woman. "Please. I can do this. I *have* to do it my way."

"Charlotte told me a healer was coming, would be here any day. He's powerful. Also, Dragomir Kozel is reputed to be a tremendous healer—" Genevieve broke off. "Okay, I can't recommend him. Everyone seems nervous around him, including Tariq, and he's the most confident man I've ever known." She subsided, with some reluctance, back into her chair.

At hearing the name of the ancient Carpathian, Emeline pressed her lips together tightly, her heart pounding wildly. She had seen the man striding around the property, his salt-and-pepper hair down to his waist, looking like a warrior out of a movie. His body was roped with obvious muscle, much

10

different from Tariq's sleek look in his suit. She couldn't imagine Dragomir in a suit. Of course she'd secretly watched him, what woman wouldn't? He was rugged, all male, his features grim and scarred, tough, very intriguing.

She'd actually dreamt about him, and that scared her. She didn't dare dream of anyone. She had an enemy that could look inside of her mind when she wasn't being vigilant. Just the thought of that made her want to laugh hysterically. If she went to a counselor and tried to tell them he could read her thoughts, she'd be locked up in a padded cell. No one would believe her. She didn't even have the basic luxury of fantasizing about a man like Dragomir sweeping her off her feet. She knew she would never be able to live with the reality of him, but she wanted to have the fantasy.

Worse, her dreams sometimes came true, the ones that repeated themselves night after night, adding new details with each new dream. She'd continued to have those, even before she'd laid eyes on Dragomir. Always, he died at the end. He saved her, saved the children and died. Because of her. She hid in her house when he was on the grounds because she wasn't ever going to meet him. Not *ever*. If she could avoid that introduction, maybe her nightmares wouldn't become reality.

"You're blushing."

"I am?" She touched her throat and ran her fingers down her chest, shocked that she could feel warmth creeping under her skin. Along with nightmares, she had fantasies about the man—fantasies she tried hard to reject, but they slipped into her mind anyway.

"Everyone gets out of his way," Genevieve reiterated. "Dragomir is dangerous."

"I can see that," Emeline admitted. "Anyone can see it. Believe me, when he's outside, I go into the house." That

11

much was true. She wouldn't take a chance with his life. And now ... she didn't take a chance with *any* of the Carpathian males being around her. Charlotte and Blaze were both Carpathian now. She wouldn't be able to be around them, either. But Dragomir ... any of the ancients really, but Dragomir caught her attention. She couldn't get near him, not without endangering him, her or everyone.

The wind shifted just a little, kicking up leaves and swirling them in small eddies across the grounds. Shadows lengthened, throwing replicas of the sprawling mansion across the ground. In her imagination, those turrets on the ground grew in darkness, reaching out toward her much smaller Victorian. She shivered and shrank back into the shadows, hiding from those reaching hands.

"Em! Em!" Bella's voice drew her attention. Danny had pushed her high on the swing, and she was waving with one hand while clutching the chain with the other.

She waved back at the child, her heart in her throat. "Hold on with both hands, Bella!" she called.

"They really respond to you and to each other," Genevieve observed. "I'm just beginning to break into their circle."

"I was homeless, too," Emeline admitted. She rarely talked about her childhood, but Genevieve was becoming a friend. She had precious few of them. It didn't hurt to explain, especially since Genevieve was so good to the children and sounded just a little hurt. "When the weather was bad, I'd climb up onto the roof of the building where Blaze and her father owned a bar. Their apartment was above it. Blaze would leave her window unlocked, and I'd climb in and sleep there. For a long time, her father pretended he didn't know." She smiled at the memory. "He was a good man."

"So if I didn't have money ... "

"Or an accent," Emeline cut in.

Genevieve laughed softly and then sobered. "I grew up in a very wealthy family. That comes with its own set of prejudices."

Emeline studied her face. Genevieve was truly a beautiful woman. She was always sweet and caring, but at that moment, it was easy to read the sadness in her. She blinked, and Genevieve was smiling again. Hiding. Maybe everyone hid. Emeline didn't know anymore. The thought made her sad.

"Lourdes is a beautiful little girl," she said.

"She's very sweet," Genevieve said. "I suppose I should get back over there. Danny looks like he's had enough of pushing the girls on the swing, and they can keep asking for hours."

"He's a good boy." He was. She was very impressed with Danny.

"Thanks for the tea. I've only got a little while before Charlotte is up and she takes over. I'll have my time off."

Emeline nodded and watched her go back to the play yard. She briefly spoke with Danny, who squinted up at the sun for a couple of seconds and then shook his head. Something about the way he looked up caught Emeline's attention. She frowned, trying to think what was eluding her. The tilt of his head reminded her of something she'd seen several times. It was important . . .

"Em!" Liv materialized right in front of her, a mischievous smile on her face. She flung her arms around Emeline. "I missed you."

Emeline's breath exploded from her lungs at the sudden sight of the little girl. Liv had endured terrible things in the underground city and that had bonded the two of them. At ten, she was years older than she should have been, her childhood ripped away from her. Emeline closed her eyes for a moment, savoring the feeling of love she had for the little girl. To save her life, the Carpathians had converted her, bringing her wholly into their world, so technically, she shouldn't spend time with Liv—it was too dangerous.

"I missed you, too," she murmured. It was true. The child had been healing, put in the ground to allow the rich soil to do its work. Liv looked good, her skin no longer sallow, her eyes no longer haunted. "I thought you were supposed to stay in the ground a few more weeks. And it isn't sunset yet."

Liv shrugged and pulled back. "I feel good and Tariq told me that because I am new and so young I can still walk in the late sunlight. I missed my brother and sisters, and you." She glanced across the yard to where Genevieve was once more settling herself on the bench, book in hand. "They need to see me as much as I need to be with them."

Emeline nodded. "They were very upset, so yes, I think they need to see you, Liv, but not at a cost to you. If Charlotte or Tariq says you need more healing, you do what they tell you."

"Like you do?" Liv said slyly.

She sighed. "I forgot what a little smarty you are."

Liv regarded her with too-old eyes. Emeline blinked back tears. Liv would never have a normal childhood. She'd never be that little girl playing without a care again.

"I'm sorry I couldn't get to you faster," she whispered.

Liv caught her hand and held it tight. "You came. I thought those horrible puppets were going to eat me alive, but you came. You and Blaze saved me."

Emeline wasn't certain it was just the two of them. It had been a concentrated effort. They'd had help. She forced a smile. "Can you tell if Vadim is still able to whisper to you?"

Liv shook her head. "He's gone completely." She tugged on Emeline's hand as if she could pull her up and lead her along the same path she'd taken. "Have them convert you, Em. He won't be able to get to you."

Emeline knew better. She shook her head and looked around, making certain no one else was near. Genevieve was engrossed in her book, looking up only to keep an eye on the two three-year-olds. Danny was pushing the girls so high they were squealing and laughing, calling for more. Amelia watched the little ones with a smile on her face while she petted the stone dragon, occasionally leaning down to whisper in its ear.

"What is it, Em?" Liv lowered her voice, in tune with Emeline, as she always had been.

"I can't become Carpathian."

"Of course you can. They can convert you. They made it so it didn't hurt for me. They can do it for you."

"I wish it was that simple, but Vadim ..."

"He can't get you here, you're protected."

"He still whispers to me. I can't make it stop," Emeline admitted. "He's driving me insane. And the pain ..." She broke off. Liv might be her only confidant, but she was just ten years old, far too young to have to deal with Emeline's problems.

"If you allow them to convert you, they'll take his blood out of you," Liv insisted. "I know it's scary, but I did it. So can you."

Emeline shook her head and pressed both hands to her churning stomach. "It's not the same. It wouldn't work on me."

"Why?"

"Have they explained lifemates to you? Why Charlotte is with Tariq and Blaze with Maksim?"

Liv nodded. "A little."

Emeline took a breath and then said the unthinkable in

15

a little rush, desperate to tell someone, yet afraid to say it aloud. "I think Vadim is my lifemate." She knew he was. He'd told her, laughed horrifically, when he'd taken her blood and forced her to take his. Just the thought of it made her want to vomit. Her throat burned even now, weeks later, and deep inside, the burning continued.

Liv went pale and let go of her hand, stepping back, just as Emeline knew she would. They all would. She was unclean. There was no monster on earth worse than Vadim, and she was his other half. Maybe the Carpathians would even destroy her if they knew the truth. Her friends would turn on her, and she'd be completely alone and unable to defend herself against Vadim's constant attacks.

"That can't be," Liv whispered.

"It is," she said and pressed trembling fingers to her mouth. Covering it. Holding back a scream of utter terror. Sharing the truth hadn't made it easier. She'd admitted it aloud and now the reality couldn't be denied.

Liv regarded her with compassion. "I don't care. It doesn't change who you are, Emeline. He can't have you. We won't let him." She spoke fiercely, making it a vow.

"He's eating me alive," Emeline whispered, knowing Liv, of all people, would understand. It wasn't the scars left on her body from his attack, but the ones in her mind he continued to leave with his whispers. The threats. The taunts. The knowledge that he was there in her head and she couldn't get him out.

"We'll find a way to keep him out," Liv said. "I hear things. I can learn fast. There's a healer coming, and he's supposed to be really good at what he does. And if he doesn't get here fast enough, I can see if Dragomir can help."

Emeline shook her head. "No Carpathians. They would know."

16

"Then I'll learn," Liv said staunchly. "I know I can learn healing."

Emeline found herself smiling. "You can learn anything," she agreed. "Thank you, my sweet girl. I appreciate that you want to help me."

"I watch them. I always have. I remember everything, so it's easy to follow the patterns they make or say the words they do."

A frisson of alarm crept down Emeline's spine. "Baby, you know you can't just go around repeating what they say. Some of their commands are in the Carpathian language and you don't understand that yet. You can't know what they're saying."

Liv shrugged. "I know the results."

"Honey, really, you can't just say things without knowing what they mean. It can be dangerous."

"Everything is dangerous," Liv said. "Knowledge is everything, isn't that what you told me? The more we know, the more we can figure things out."

Emeline sighed. "Now you're turning my own words back on me. At least you listened."

"I always listen to you." Liv hugged her again. "Why don't you go lie down for a while, Emeline? I'm going to play with my brother and sisters before the adults wake up and make us do our studies."

"I will in a few minutes," Emeline agreed. "I like to stay in the sun as long as possible." Once the sun set she had to stay in her house, lock the door and pray she didn't fall asleep. Outside, in the night, were her friends, Carpathians, and they would turn on her the moment they knew the truth about her. In her house, in the darkness, Vadim whispered to her, promising her all sorts of tortures if she didn't leave the sanctuary of Tariq Asenguard's property and come to him. "I know you miss your family."

17

"You're my family, too, Emeline," Liv said solemnly. "But you're right. I did miss them. Look at them"—she waved her arm toward the play yard—"they're so cool."

She laughed, and Emeline was happy to hear the sound was genuine. She hadn't believed she'd hear Liv's laughter ever again. Being wholly Carpathian had helped her immensely.

"I missed my dragon, too. I thought about all the things I'd like to learn to do, and flying my dragon is at the top of the list."

Emeline glanced up at the sky. The sun was fading fast. "You need to wait for Charlotte and Tariq before you try anything like that. You know the safeguards are in place to keep Vadim and his monstrous friends out." She couldn't help the shudder that ran through her body just saying the name. Vadim Malinov stalked her day and night. The thought of him getting his hands on her again, or on one of the children—she couldn't face that. "Wait, Liv."

Liv laughed again, the sound soft and delicate, like musical bells tinkling in the breeze. "Adults always want to make us wait for anything fun."

Emeline shook her head. "That's not true, silly. We love you and don't want anything to happen to you. I know it's hard to live behind a high fence, not to be able to go places and do things other children get to do, but you have other things they don't." That was very true and she needed Liv to see that—to acknowledge it—so there was no chance of the children risking their lives.

"I know," Liv agreed with a small sigh. "We'll fly low, below the safeguards. I doubt if we could get through them anyway."

Emeline didn't like the speculation in her voice. "I know you want to be able to use all the gifts that come with being

Carpathian, Liv, but you have to be patient and allow the adults to teach you. The gifts are powerful and can hurt others if they're misused."

Again, Liv laughed softly, that sweet melody that seemed to vibrate in harmony with Emeline's insides, playing along nerve endings until she found herself listening for more.

"I can't misuse them, Em, if I don't know what they are," Liv pointed out.

"Livvie!" Bella shouted. "Hurry up!"

"Take her another cookie. Don't forget one for Lourdes," Emeline said. She yawned, exhaustion catching up with her. She really should go inside, but it seemed a great effort to gather the teacups back onto the tray and carry it when her arms felt so leaden.

Liv scooped up a couple of cookies for the little girls, glanced at her brother and added several more. "He's always hungry," she explained.

Emeline smiled. "He certainly is." She waved at the little girl. "Go have fun."

Liv leapt off the porch and ran to join her brother and sisters. They gathered together, Danny pulling the swings to a halt while stuffing cookies into his mouth. Several times he glanced up at the night sky as if judging how long they had until sunset—and the adult Carpathians making their appearances. Again, just that simple motion of his head tilting upward reminded Emeline of something important she needed to remember, but her mind felt fogged.

The children ran to the stone dragons, all laughing softly. It was Liv's laughter that she focused on, the sound beautiful to her after all the horrors the child had suffered. She propped her chin in her hand, elbow on the little table, aware her head felt too large, her brain fuzzy. She didn't mind the feeling—at least it was pleasant, and as long as she stayed fixated on the children, she didn't feel the pain clawing at her stomach and the cries of terror reverberating through her mind.

Danny helped Lourdes onto the blue dragon. It was large and scaly, its tail long and spiked. Lourdes sat on its back, her knees gripping hard as she leaned forward to whisper into its ear while she patted the long neck.

He picked up Bella next and placed her on the red dragon. Like Lourdes, she stroked and caressed the stone scales and spikes. Danny wrapped his arm around her waist and whispered in her ear. She nodded several times.

Emeline frowned. Something about his posture, the way his dark jeans looked leaning against the crimson red of the dragon, moved through her mind slowly. Something was there just out of reach, something she needed to catch hold of, but her mind refused to cooperate. The more she tried to grasp the memory, the more it eluded her.

The wind rushed through the compound, stirring the leaves on the ground so once again they rose, this time swirling around the dragons and children. Danny leapt on the back of the brown dragon and Amelia the orange one. They mounted them as if they'd been riding dragons for a hundred years. Emeline couldn't help but admire the way they moved so easily and smoothly, but now that memory was right there, right on the outer periphery of her mind. So close. A nightmare . . .

Liv approached the green dragon, talking softly. Emeline couldn't hear what she said, but the green dragon's spiked tail twitched. The big creature lowered its neck toward the little girl and she petted the wedged head before moving around to climb up the tail. Once seated, she turned her face toward the sky. Clouds drifted overhead. They were gray and massive, stretching out above the compound like a blanket.

Emeline studied those clouds with a little frown. She didn't like the way they blocked out what was left of the sun, and she'd seen them before. The children laughed and called to one another in excitement, the sound of their mischievous voices coming at her as if in a dream, far away, but she was so tired she couldn't rouse herself, even to see what the children were up to.

Her eyelids were so heavy she couldn't lift them beyond mere slits. The sun hadn't set, but she knew it was close. She always went back inside her house at sunset. If she didn't . . . Well, that didn't bear thinking about. Still, there was something elusive in her mind, drifting through like a jarring note in a symphony, something she couldn't quite grasp but knew was important.

Gripping the green dragon with her knees, Liv lifted her hands and began weaving a complicated pattern in the air. Dreamily, Emeline watched the patterns, Liv's hands swaying gracefully in the air. Her murmurs were soft but they carried, as if she uttered commands. Thunder rolled. Dry lightning cracked. The leaves rose like geysers, forming towers high into the air all around the stone dragons. Nightmare. Her nightmares.

Alarm rang like a bell through Emeline's mind. Harsh. Jangling. A shadow moved in there. Dark. Twisted. Gleeful. A whisper. Deep inside her, she heard screaming. Something hard kicked her stomach, raked at her insides. "No." She whispered it, watching in horror as across the play yard, Genevieve's book fell to the ground as she slumped over, asleep.

"No," she whispered again, forcing her mind to work through the terror of that dark force creeping in through the slit that lightning had made between two clouds. The mass above the compound churned and roiled, looking suspiciously like a witches' brew.

The sun sank as the dragons spread their wings and leapt, taking to the air, circling higher and higher until they were reaching for those dark, ugly clouds. "No," Emeline said again and stood. On shaky legs, she ran off her porch. "Liv. Come back. You don't know what you're doing. He's waiting. He's out there waiting."

The clouds glowed orange and red all through the seams of rolling black. Fireballs erupted, spewing like well-thrown grenades at the dragons in the air while others rained down on the compound. Liv had effectively destroyed the safeguards so carefully woven each dawn by the Carpathians. She'd watched and remembered the pattern and had removed them, allowing the monsters access to their home.

The children screamed as the dragons took them higher to get away from the attack, but the fireballs followed, shooting at them, striking the large bodies and knocking the orange and brown dragons out of the sky. They fell, rolling, badly wounded, Amelia and Danny clinging to their respective dragons' necks as they tumbled toward the ground.

Emeline rushed toward Genevieve. She was still out—clearly Liv had cast a sleeping spell—and she was totally vulnerable. She hadn't taken more than three steps when the ground opened up in front of her. On either side of her. Behind her. She halted, terrified. Before her stood Vadim Malinov.

He looked beautiful—handsome, young. He was the epitome of handsome by modern standards, a man who could grace the cover of any magazine. He smiled at her and bowed a low, courtly bow. When he smiled, his teeth were perfect, so straight and white that he probably dazzled the ones he bestowed his smiles on—but not her. She knew better. Her heart pounded and she stood frozen, unable to scream or run. Unable to get away.

"At last, my dear. You should have come to me when I called you. Now you've left me no choice but to punish you."

The smile was gone and he took one step and caught her by the hair, bunching the long tangles in his fist and jerking her head close to his. "You will pay for your disobedience. Every one of those children will die."

2

A whisper of unease ran through the soil deep beneath the earth. That small shudder awakened Dragomir Kozel as he lay in the loam, the rich minerals providing his body with healing and peace. The tendril of evil was barely felt, a slight shifting slithering through the layers of dirt, reaching down, reaching up, spreading like a virus.

Evil had a feel to it. Despite it being such a thin thread, Dragomir recognized that ancient spell for what it was. He doubted if any other Carpathian could feel it. One or two perhaps, but like him, they would be locked beneath the earth until the sun set. In the meantime, that insidious evil worked its malevolent magic, opening pathways beneath Tariq and Charlotte Asenguard's compound. Safeguards were in place, above, below and surrounding, so there shouldn't have been a way in, yet there was no denying that the ground shuddered and flinched away from that snake slithering through the layers of soil.

There had to be a traitor staying within the compound, one weaving spells to weaken the safeguards. Tariq collected humans, children and adults alike, opening his fortress to those in need, and that put him—and everyone else—at risk. Dragomir was patient; there was little he could do until the sun sank from the sky, but he tried to figure out which of the humans worked with the vampires to bring down the Carpathians. Tariq employed a human security force. Perhaps one of them?

Although Dragomir had never been interested in humans, because Tariq surrounded himself with so many, he'd made an effort to be introduced to the members of the security force. In his exceedingly long lifetime, he'd never considered the concept of humans protecting Carpathians. It had always been the other way around. What humans could stand up to a vampire?

Matt Bennett, head of Tariq's human security force, guarded the compound during the day. He had served in the military as a Navy SEAL. Matt had gathered a group of elite soldiers together. Every member of the security force had served their country with distinction. Tariq had trained them to fight vampires. They knew how to kill the undead and were aware that the penalty for disclosing the fact that vampires and Carpathians even existed was death. These were men used to keeping secrets—just about every mission they'd run had been classified.

Tariq had, of course, taken their blood, but Dragomir had done so as well, just to ensure everyone was safe. He was surprised that Bennett stood so stoically, not so much as flinching as the ancient took his blood and examined his memories. Like Tariq, he gave the man a small amount of his blood on the pretense of communicating with him should there be need, but in reality, for Dragomir, it was another precaution. He would always know where the man was and what he was doing. He touched the man's mind. He was using high-powered binoculars to watch the children from his position at the far end of the compound and he didn't like what they were doing at all.

Dragomir made everyone—including Matt Bennett—uneasy for a good reason. He was dangerous. He knew that. He looked at everyone as enemy or prey. Still, there was no excuse that he hadn't gone near the women or children. It was a mistake on his part to dismiss them. He should have carefully vetted them. Someone had weakened the defenses of the compound, and the master vampire, Vadim Malinov, always waiting to strike, had taken advantage.

Dragomir was certain that strain of magic belonged to Vadim. He'd come across his trail several times over the centuries, and there was a particular feel to that of each Carpathian, distinguishing them from others. If a Carpathian chose to give up his soul, he still took his singular composition with him. He had no doubt that this was the work of Vadim Malinov.

He welcomed the battle with the master vampire. His time was long past, and trying to live in a world he didn't understand had driven home the fact that he had been right to secret himself in the monastery, high in the Carpathian Mountains where he couldn't harm anyone. The only honorable purpose left to him was to hunt down the master vampire and rid the world of such evil. Then he could go back to the monastery and keep walls between him and the outside world for as long as it took for him to die—if he could die. He would welcome death. Living an endless, gray existence had taken its toll on him.

Dragomir had wanted to leave Tariq's compound, to have as little contact with any others as he could. Carpathians or humans, neither was part of his world anymore. He didn't belong in this modern world. He'd left the monastery in the Carpathian Mountains for the first time in hundreds of years with one thought—the hope that he could find his lifemate. Now, he knew, even if he found her, his time was already past. He could never live with a modern woman, and she could never live with him. He had stayed too long in a world that had changed beyond every imagining. He had survived countless battles and many mortal wounds, yet in the end, it had been for nothing. Time had been his greatest enemy, and it had defeated him.

He focused on the soil and the way the rich minerals shrank away from the snaking tendril of evil as it made its way through the layers of earth to get to a preordered destination. In his mind, he mapped out the compound, following the shudders and shrinking in an effort to figure out just what Vadim's plan was. The wisp of evil avoided the main house where Tariq and Charlotte resided, but moved beneath the play yard where the children were. The thin tendril became a vine snaking through the soil, branching out, spreading seedpods beneath the play yard as well as around the woman's house. Emeline. He knew *her* name, when he had avoided knowing so many others.

He carefully assessed the situation, building his battle plan. Tariq and Charlotte were away from the compound. They'd gone to San Francisco to spend a little time alone together. Dragomir found it very telling that they were gone and who-ever had weakened their defenses had chosen the time of their absence to make their move. He was the only one, as far as he knew, that had chosen to sleep beneath the compound.

Valentin Zhestokly was gone. His lifemate was far too young to make a claim and he was too close to the edge to be around her. He wouldn't have gone far, but far enough that he might not make it back until the battle was over. Maksim and Blaze, co-owners of the nightclubs and owners of the bordering property, had stayed late overseeing one of the nightclubs and were sleeping beneath it, a good distance away. Who did that leave close?

Afanasiv Balan was a very dangerous Carpathian. Known in their world as Siv, he was extremely dangerous, possibly even more so than Dragomir. He would be a valuable asset, and he'd come at Tariq's call to aid him in setting up the compound. The nightclub owner and Afanasiv had been friends of sorts for centuries. He might be near.

Nicu Dalca had come at Tariq's call as well. Nicu was lightning fast. Few could equal his speed, and in a battle he was sheer, brutal poetry. There was no way to know if he was still in the area or if he'd chosen to leave after the last battle. Ancient Carpathian hunters tended to move on very quickly, looking for the next fight.

Tomas, Lojos and Mataias, the triplets, always traveling together, hadn't been seen for the last two weeks. That meant nothing. They could be close as well. He just couldn't count on them to get there immediately. So, he had to hold out maybe five to seven minutes. In a battle that was a very long time. Extremely long. Vadim would throw everything he had at them.

Dragomir sighed. He would need the human security force. Right now, he couldn't move, paralyzed as he was by the time of day, but he could hear the sound of children laughing and the low murmur of conversation—the woman and a child. *The* woman. Emeline Sanchez. He'd never actually met her, but he realized he should have. He hadn't eavesdropped on her conversations, either—but again, he should have. Even now, try as he might, he couldn't quite catch the sound of her voice, as if she had found a way to shield it. She was a huge

28

question mark because she avoided everyone, including her best friend, Blaze, Maksim's lifemate.

The real reason he'd stayed away, though, was because Dragomir was a little obsessive about her. Not that he'd recognized it until this very moment. He didn't feel emotions, so it should be impossible to be obsessive, yet he now realized he'd been thinking about the woman far too much—and not thinking clearly enough when he did. Especially considering that he wasn't the only one obsessed with the human. Vadim Malinov was as well. And that meant this entire attack was almost certainly about Emeline and Vadim's need to reacquire her.

All during the day the storm had been building. He hadn't seen it, he'd been deep underground in the sleep of his kind, but he'd felt it. Every Carpathian could feel when the earth was disturbed. Thunder rolled, a deep baritone that rumbled for longer than one expected, hard enough that it sent a vibration through the ground.

Dragomir might know his time was long past. He might want to go back to the monastery, where he knew he wouldn't harm an innocent, but he also knew he was an ancient hunter and he would never leave when a battle was imminent.

Vadim was a master vampire. Wholly evil. *That* was part of Dragomir's world. He understood evil. He had spent several lifetimes battling foul monsters. The monastery had afforded him a kind of peace, if a man like him could ever be at peace. What did Vadim want with Emeline? With the children? He knew Vadim had taken the woman and held her for a short time before the Carpathians had rescued her. She kept to herself in the house across from the main one, sometimes sitting on the porch, but most of the time locked behind the door.

He'd thought about her, wondering if she could be the

29

way to track Vadim. From what Dragomir had learned—and he'd made it his business to study the undead—she was the reason Vadim had chosen to remain in an area thick with hunters ... and not just any hunters, but ancients. They were Carpathians skilled so far beyond what the newer generations were capable of, it defied description. Any other vampire—including any master vampire—would have fled. Yet Vadim remained.

The eldest Malinov was reputed to be highly intelligent. He'd embraced modern technology—something Dragomir should have done but hadn't. Vadim had amassed an army, using human male psychics as well as lesser vampires. Carpathians had neglected to think about what those male psychics might be able to do. Clearly, the master vampire was planning something huge and Emeline figured in those plans.

New laughter joined that of the children, distracting him from his thoughts. The sound was soft. Melodious. Edged with a magic. It was simple magic, childish really. So much so, that the moment the spell drifted on the wind, it caught the attention of the spreading malevolence belowground. At once the earth shuddered again, the tremble the smallest of earthquakes, barely felt, more like a ripple of jubilation that raced toward the surface. The ancient malignant spell bound itself to the childish one, feeding power and the whisper of darkness, slowly and inevitably corrupting what the child was doing.

Dragomir clenched his teeth, the first movement his paralyzed body managed when the sun had not yet set. He concentrated next on moving his hand even as he stirred the earth above him with his mind. He had to go very slowly, so as not to alert the spreading vines of evil lurking beneath the ground. He rose inch by inch, toward the surface. He was a big man and displacing that much soil without warning

Vadim's spy was difficult. But he'd learned many tricks in his extremely long lifetime.

Moving the dirt above him and replacing it below him with equal parts at the exact same moment he drifted up to fill the empty space he'd made was all a matter of exquisite timing and touch. He was a warrior, skilled beyond most in every kind of weapon, hand-to-hand and also mind and magic battles, yet he had perfected the softest touch. He'd learned over centuries that a soft touch could be just as deadly as the strongest and fastest strike.

Close to the surface, his skin prickled in alarm. The older he'd gotten and the more kills he'd made, the less he could tolerate the sunlight. He rarely rose right at sunset, knowing just being touched by the rays of the sun, as weak as they might be at that time, was painful and he'd carry burns for several risings after. He had no choice; the moment he could, he would have to rise to counteract whatever plan Vadim had. He was certain the master vampire had been scheming for just such an event, working to make it happen, and that meant Vadim was well prepared.

He waited just inches from the surface, moving his fingers and then his wrists. Moving his toes and then his feet, all the while cognizant of countering the activity so the evil spreading so maliciously through the ground wouldn't detect his movement. He was part of the earth itself and the soil would never betray him. When a strand of the evil got too close to him, the dirt shifted just enough to carry it away.

He didn't know impatience, just the fierce need to go into combat. He began mapping out the surface in his head, finding each person above the ground, needing to know where they were. Five children. Two adult females. All were human with the exception of one child. The children were laughing, unaware of the danger to them. One female was sleeping deeply, put under by the corruption of the child's sleeping spell. It wouldn't be so easy to wake her now. The other female . . .

She was aware of the danger and struggling to wake. She had to be unbelievably strong to fight that spell. She was the target—Emeline. Of course. When Vadim had taken her captive, he'd taken her blood, and now he whispered to her day and night, trying to wear her down and force her to come to him, or at least that was what she had told Blaze. Why would Vadim want this particular psychic woman? What made her different?

Dragomir should have thrown out his rule of not getting close to humans rather than just making an exception for the security team. If he had, he could have solved the puzzle by simply taking the information from her head. Tariq, Maksim and the others had become too soft with the humans, inadvertently giving vampires the advantage. They didn't make decisions based on safety, but rather what the humans would accept in their new, modern world. That made no sense to him, and it never would. One used any and all means possible to defeat evil. There wasn't worry about sensibilities or wording a request correctly so it didn't come out like an order. He sighed. He didn't fit and never would. He defeated evil, and new rules of etiquette be damned.

He sent Emeline a little "push" to counteract the spell. Feeding her a small boost of power had to be done with a delicate touch. He couldn't make it a command because just as he could read Vadim's signature, Vadim would be able to read his. He wasn't certain what was important about the woman, but merely the fact that she had resisted that dark spell enough to try to fight it, that she recognized the darkness woven into the child's spell, meant she was incredibly strong psychically.

Few fought Vadim and won. Emeline's battle with him was ongoing, which meant she'd been strong enough to resist him this long. In his opinion, Tariq and the others should have taken the memories from her, given her blood to reinforce her strength and power. It didn't matter that she'd chosen not to allow them to give her aid. They should have healed her. She endangered the entire community. In the end, if Dragomir didn't stop him, the vampire would reacquire the woman and perhaps destroy everyone else in the compound.

He waited just beneath the surface, rich loam covering his body, sending him signals that told him he wasn't the only one on the move. Evil was also waiting for the sun to set. Even before the last rays had faded, he heard the opening attack. The laughter of children turned to screams. The sound of explosions was loud as fireballs hit the ground all around the play yard. He couldn't wait. The sounds of children crying and screaming in alarm drove him from the safety of the earth. He couldn't leave them to their fate.

Matt, do not give your position away, but get your men in position to aid those in the play yard. I'll tell you when I want you to open up.

Copy that. Matt's voice was devoid of emotion, but firm, indicating a man ready to go into battle.

Dragomir's skin smoked and blistered as he rushed toward the sky and the two injured dragons tumbling toward the ground. How the boy and girl hung on, he didn't know. The dragons, one orange and one brown, were large and they fell end over end, and then rolled like barrels, leaving a trail of blood in the sky. He saw everything on a dull grayish canvas, so that the various colors were identified only from the way he'd marked the variety of gray over the centuries.

On the Carpathian telepathic pathway, he sent out the distress call. *Rise. The battle is on us. Come to us now.*

The clouds flickered dark and then flashed, illuminating with a yellowish-orange glow as lightning forked through them. The glow grew brighter, turned a fiery red, and a mass of whirling hot magma streaked through the sky, raining down on the play yard. One mass barely missed the brown dragon as Dragomir yanked the beast out of the way and floated it gently toward the ground. He caught the orange dragon, removing the girl from it with one arm while he directed the creature to the ground beside the brown dragon. He threw a shield over the boy and girl and their beasts.

"*Don't* put your dragons away until I give the command." He forestalled all arguments with a glare. "Get to the sleeping woman. You and your brother. Drag her if you have to, but get her under cover." He caught the girl by her hair and forced her to look him in the eye. "Do you understand? Wait until I give the command to remove the dragons."

She nodded. She looked terrified, her face white. Her gaze left his face and went to the children above them, small children, not more than two or three.

"I'll get them," he promised.

"Please," she whispered.

For some odd reason that little breathless plea affected him. Nothing usually did. He didn't feel emotion. He didn't even hear the whispers of temptation to kill for the rush, but that soft entreaty stirred something foreign in him, something he didn't recognize, nor did he have time to analyze it, although it was alarming. Chaos reigned all around him. Children screaming, dragons taking them higher toward the dangerous clouds, below him, Emeline running, calling out over and over, her voice penetrating right to his soul.

All around him the fiery streaks fell, seeking targets. He dodged one and realized by the trajectories that they were aimed specifically at the children. Vadim was attempting to kill five human children. Dragomir gave a small push to the teenage girl so that she stumbled toward her brother. He

34

indicated the sleeping woman and turned just as Vadim burst through the ground almost at the feet of Emeline. Vadim was so focused on her that he didn't appear to know Dragomir was anywhere close. Either that or it didn't matter to him, in which case, the entire lot of them were in deep trouble.

Emeline froze, staring in horror at the vampire. He appeared to be perfect by human standards, lean and fit, with flawless pale skin and white teeth. His hair was cropped short and he wore the modern clothes that befitted the time. The expensive suit hung on him as if made for him—and of course it had been.

"At last, my dear. You should have come to me when I called you. Now you've left me no choice but to punish you."

The smile was gone and he took one step and caught her by the hair, bunching the long tangles in his fist and jerking her head close to his. "You will pay for your disobedience. Every one of those children will die."

Emeline's terrified gaze found Dragomir, and then went back to Vadim's face. "I'll go with you. Just don't hurt them."

At the sound of her voice, Dragomir found his eyes watering, burning fiercely as a kaleidoscope of colors burst in front of him, exploding into a whirling wheel of vivid brightness that nearly blinded him. Instantly he was sick and disoriented, his balance off. For a moment he thought it a new weapon Vadim had thought out, and he stopped in midstride, unable to function.

"It's too late to bargain now. Had you come to me any of the thousands of times I commanded you, I would have spared them. Not now. Now you need a lesson."

She kicked the vampire hard, driving her heel into his shin and following it with an elbow to his ribs. It had to hurt. Vadim held her by her hair, but she didn't stop. "I won't let you," she bit out, still fighting.

The words were like a dagger piercing right through Dragomir's soul, slicing it open so all the inky darkness poured out. At the same time, brilliant light rushed in, leaving him shattered. Emotions whirled through his brain, vying to be front and center, a million of them. Shock. Regret. Guilt. Elation. Sorrow. Burning rage.

He couldn't function like this, sick and disoriented with the nauseating colors and the vivid emotions swamping him. "Stop." He whispered the word, but it carried on the wind slashing at them. He couldn't move or think with the terrible burden of color and emotion after centuries of ... *nothing*. It was too much, too soon, too fast. "Stop talking."

She turned her head toward him. Their eyes met, and he felt the impact all the way to his newly healed soul. He had a few moments to contemplate how ironic it was that he would find her now, in the clutches of a master vampire, when he'd finally made up his mind that he could not be the lifemate needed for a woman of this century and could never claim his lifemate.

The sky above them erupted with four vampires. Three went after the children while one dropped toward the Asenguard property. These were Vadim's first line of defense, his pawns. For a short while, newly created vampires lost their abilities to fight as they had as hunters. Vadim recruited them when they were at their weakest. They were given young people to drain of blood, to feel the life drain out of them. The rush was like the high one received from the best drug. It took a year or two before the newly made vampire could begin to draw on his centuries of experience fighting a hunter.

Vadim turned his head slowly to look at Dragomir. He spun around to place Emeline between them, one hand at her throat, his fingernail, suddenly long and razor-sharp, pressed against her jugular. "You know me; you know I will kill her."

He would under normal circumstances, but these weren't normal. "You know me; you know I do not care what you do or who you kill. I have one purpose, and that is to destroy you." Dragomir didn't look at the woman he'd searched for through long, empty centuries. Emeline—his lifemate. She'd kept her voice from him, probably knowing she couldn't live with an ancient such as him. He kept his heart from pounding in terror that she was in danger. He kept his breathing even, as if the possibility of her death didn't affect him one way or the other.

"An innocent? You would allow an innocent to die just to get me?" Vadim spat the words at him, but this time, there was a hint of fear in his eyes. "*Six* innocents? Because they will kill the children. Nothing will stop them. Certainly not *you*." The last was said with a sneer.

Emeline had remained silent, no longer fighting the vampire. She chose that moment to stir, to draw his attention. She looked . . . *ravaged*. Her body was thin, her skin so pale it was almost gray. Her hair was long and disheveled, hanging in tangles to her waist. It didn't matter. She looked like the most beautiful woman in the world to him. He realized the power of the call between lifemates. He would be willing to do anything for her.

"Save them," Emeline whispered. "The children. Please."

If he engaged with Vadim, the children were dead. He could see Liv, the ten-year-old, urging her dragon between the two youngest and the vampires and fireballs raining from the clouds. The child had guts. He had a split-second decision to make and it was a terrible one. His every instinct, honed by more than a thousand years of hunting the vampire, told him to go after the master vampire. He had at last found his lifemate and his instincts told him to save her.

His gaze returned to Emeline's face. Her eyes, so beautiful.

Haunted. Frightened. Determined. The pleading in her voice, on her face, was all about the children. Human children. He'd never really associated with them until he'd come to Tariq's aid. Now, it was either his lifemate, or what she wanted most. The seconds were ticking away.

"Live." He snapped the order and leapt into the sky. *Now, Matt. Take Vadim's head off. It won't kill him, but keep at it. Just do not hit Emeline. Do whatever it takes to delay him leaving with her, even if only by a few seconds. Buy some time. The others are coming.*

Dragomir didn't look down. He shut off all emotion and tried to force his eyes to see in shades of gray rather than in color. The vivid, bright reds and oranges of the fireballs were distracting, making his stomach churn unexpectedly. He avoided the raining fireballs as best he could as he streaked toward the two younger children. They looked tiny on the backs of the dragons, both sprawled forward, arms around the spiked necks, pale faces buried against the scales.

One of the lesser vampires had one side of his face drooping, as if he couldn't quite figure out how to put his mask on properly. He dove at the blue dragon, forcing it to swerve, nearly throwing its little passenger off its back. The child gave a cry of terror as the claws just missed grabbing her. Instead, they raked down the blue scales. The dragon took a swipe with his long, spiked tail. It didn't hit the droopy face, but it solidly hit the second vampire making his way around the dragon to be able to attack the child from the other side.

The vampire shrieked his fury as the spikes opened his flesh and droplets of acid blood leaked out. He lunged toward the child, as if the dragon hitting him was her fault. Vadim had told Emeline he would kill all five children and his servants wouldn't stop until his order was carried out. Dragomir reached the child just as the two vampires simultaneously attacked her, coming in from either side of the dragon. The big beast swung its neck around, the wedged head rushing straight at the vampire he'd already hit with his tail, mouth open, fire pouring out. The flames engulfed the vampire and the undead screamed and plummeted toward the ground below.

The second vampire reached for the child, fingernails long and curved like the huge talons on a harpy eagle. The little girl screamed and screamed, the sound grating on Dragomir as she threw herself to the opposite side of the blue dragon, away from the vampire. Her hand slipped, and she shrieked again as she dropped into space. Dragomir caught her in his arms. Instantly she began to fight.

He didn't bother to reassure her; he didn't have time with two vampires rushing him and the burned vampire streaking toward them. The other two girls were still in danger. He took over her mind, calming her, learning this child was Lourdes and she was three. He forced obedience, shifting her to his neck, so that she hung around him like a necklace, her legs trying to fit around his broad chest. Lourdes clung, a little monkey, but her position allowed his hands and legs freedom to be used as weapons.

He dropped below the two vampires so they smashed together with a wild yell, each swinging viciously at the other as he streaked through the sky toward the second little girl. She looked so scared his heart clenched unexpectedly in his chest. He hadn't ever held a child, or even been near one, not a live one. This little girl was tiny, clinging to the dragon, who twisted back and forth in an effort to keep his rider from being taken.

In the past, Dragomir had come across a village that had been raided and children's bodies were scattered everywhere along with their parents'. He hadn't been able to feel, or remember emotion; now seeing these two little girls and the third one, Liv, the child they'd turned Carpathian, acting so bravely, he felt far too many emotions rushing in, threatening to take over. It could have been overwhelming if he'd let it.

He was ruthless with himself in the same way he was with others. Saving these children and ultimately Emeline was his goal, not figuring out his emotions. Time had slowed down, but he was very aware of the seconds ticking by. Any Carpathian hunter in the vicinity would come. He'd been fighting for two minutes. He only had to hold on for another three to four. But in a battle with a master vampire and his army, that was a lifetime.

Liv, the ten-year-old, turned her dragon to cut off four new vampires who had materialized in the air and were heading for the younger child on the red dragon. Liv's green dragon spit fire, missed the first two vampires but set the one nearest it on fire. The blaze covered one side of him from his toes to his scalp, forcing him to streak toward the ground to try to put out the fire.

The other vampire, the one that had been burned by the blue dragon, dragged himself toward Danny and Amelia, who, below him on the ground, tried valiantly but futilely to wake Genevieve before the vampire could get to them. Vadim dragged Emeline by her hair away from the center of the play yard and out from under the canopy protecting it from the weather. Danny hesitated, torn between trying to help Emeline and obeying Dragomir's orders to get Genevieve to safety.

Matt Bennett took the shot, his aim perfect, the high-caliber bullet tearing into Vadim's skull, shredding it so that it burst apart like a ripe melon. He screamed, even as his head flew apart, the sound rending the air so that the buildings shook. Emeline dropped to the ground and rolled away from Danny and Amelia to draw the vampires away from the two children. Then she was on her feet and running back toward her house.

Vadim howled, his headless body whirling around as his head bounced on the ground, mouth wide open, the sound reverberating macabrely through the compound. He stretched out his arms to call back his shattered skull. The moment it settled on his body, Matt fired, destroying it all over again. The mouth screamed and the headless body pointed toward the "eagle's nest," the tall tower in the far corner where Matt was taking aim at the vampire closest to Danny.

Dragomir had already shielded Matt's position, but he reinforced it before Vadim could retaliate with the bomb he hurled toward the tower. It exploded, fire ringing the tower harmlessly and dropping away. Emeline made it across the play yard before the lesser vampires cut off her retreat.

Dragomir shut off the bombardment of feeling as he commanded Lourdes to move to his left, as he passed the large red dragon, scooping the little girl from the back of the beast. She reacted in much the same way as Lourdes had, kicking and screaming until he cut her off with a single mind command. The moment their minds brushed against each other, Bella relaxed and clung to him just as Lourdes had.

Liv circled him, her green dragon weaving in and out of the vampires. The dragon was extremely fast and able to make incredible turns for such a big beast, almost reversing itself in midair. Dragomir could understand the appeal of a dragon, and if he ever had a child, he'd make certain his son or daughter had such a creature to help guard them.

Liv, drop down now. He gave the child instructions, knowing the vampires could also hear. At one time they had been Carpathian, born into the species just as he was, yet choosing to give up their souls. That didn't mean they weren't able to hear along the common path.

Liv's dragon followed him toward the ground. Dragomir took one small eighth of a second to glance down. He'd been in the air three minutes acquiring both little girls, but thanks to the lesser vampires blocking Emeline's escape, Vadim had caught her again. Below him, he glimpsed the teenagers trying to pull Genevieve from the play yard bench. The boy turned toward the threat of the vampire coming at them, shouting to his sister to run.

Emeline fought Vadim viciously, punching and kicking. There was blood on her neck, trickling down her arm and shoulder. Evidently, Vadim couldn't fully control her mind, or he would have stopped her from fighting him. The master vampire had clearly taken her blood, thinking that would force his will on her. Dragomir's belly knotted at the knowledge, but he didn't have time to dwell on what was happening to her.

Fireballs continued to streak from the clouds, the trajectories straight at each of the children. He had time to turn his back, hunch his shoulders and protect the two little girls in his arms as streaks of white-hot molten fire tore into his shoulders and dripped down his back, creating long grooves. He cut off the pain and kept moving toward the ground below, his gaze on Liv as her dragon dodged the fiery streaks falling around her.

He had a newfound respect for the dragons. It would be good to sit on an animal while he protected children and the beast outmaneuvered Vadim's attacks, dodging the threads of fire raining from the sky.

The boom of Matt's rifle was steady now as more vampires joined the first ones. *Matt, keep your men undercover at all times, tell them to choose their target, aim for the heart. Take out as many as they can.* How many more minutes before he had aid? *Danny, Amelia, get to the grate and call your dragons. Liv, lead the others to it.*

The vampires, former Carpathians, could hear his commands to Liv, and she provided the instructions to the other children. They couldn't hear his instructions to Matt because Dragomir had forged their own path when he'd taken the man's blood. Immediately there was a frenzy as four vampires dove for the ten-year-old. She cried out and bent low over her dragon. The beast spun around in a tight circle, going right through the vampires. Sharp claws scraped the shimmering green scales, leaving a trail of blood in the air. The dragon didn't hesitate, but spun back, his wedged head extended as he bathed the vampires in a steady stream of fire.

They screamed, engulfed in the flames, dropping almost on top of Dragomir as he found the ground with his feet and ran toward the grate, holding the little girls tightly to him. Above him the sky erupted in streams of red-hot magma, shooting down at the children and the Carpathian hunter. He was forced to maintain a shield over Matt to keep Vadim's retaliations from killing him, and additional shields over the children. The threads of dripping lava hit the exposed dragons and just missed him as he ducked under the umbrella of the shield protecting Danny and Amelia.

We can't wake Genevieve, Danny protested.

Leave her. Get to the grate. Get the dragons to follow you.

The two dragons, brown and orange, were hurt and they sat just outside the play yard, their great sides shuddering, heads down, trying to pant away the pain. Danny caught Amelia's hand and yanked hard, pulling her toward the building to the left of the play yard. It looked like a large garage or storehouse. The long wall had no windows, and beneath it, running along the structure, was a long grate built into the ground. As Danny and Amelia raced toward it, the grate popped open, slamming against the outside wall of the storage house. Liv urged her green dragon straight at the hole in the ground the grate had covered. Lourdes's blue dragon and Bella's red one followed her.

Three vampires raced the children and dragons to the opening, their mouths stretched in vile grins, revealing spiked, stained teeth as they spread out, hovering just above the dark pit below them, their backs to the grate. As Dragomir ran with the girls, two vampires rose up in front of him, almost at his feet: one had his hand outstretched in preparation to tear at the ancient's flesh. At Dragomir's silent command, both girls, hands circling his neck, slid around to his back to cling like two little monkeys and he continued forward, driving his fist deep into the nearest vampire's chest. He kept his forward momentum, even as he jerked his arm free, the withered, blackened heart in his fist.

He ran straight at the second vampire. The vampire's eyes widened with shock. No more than a second had passed. The heartless vampire screamed and clutched his chest where black blood spewed. He dropped to his knees, shrieking for his heart.

Danny. Amelia. Dragomir timed his moment, whirling just before he reached the vampire threatening him. He tossed the two little girls into the air, straight at the teenagers. Both had their hands up, and Lourdes and Bella fell into their arms. Danny ran with Bella, Amelia with Lourdes, straight toward that yawning hole and the three vampires waiting for them. Liv led the parade of dragons, although the red and blue ones stayed behind Danny and Amelia.

Simultaneously, as Dragomir leapt into the air, coming down with his fist driving forward straight through bone and sinew to find the vampire's heart, three missiles flew straight

44

to the vampires waiting for the children. Rolling in the air as they flew, flames erupted and they burst through their chests, straight to the hearts, incinerating all three on contact. The vampires stood with their mouths open, shocked looks on their faces, and then they toppled backward. The grate fell, covering the hole, and with it dropped the side of the building, revealing a cavernous lift.

Liv and the injured dragons were swallowed and then Amelia and Danny with the girls and their dragons followed. The grate sprang back up, slamming the wall into place. The entire exchange had taken seconds. Dragomir dispensed with both withered hearts, hurling them to the ground and incinerating them immediately. He turned his head to see Emeline running for her house, with Vadim one step behind her.

3

This had been her worst nightmare, the dream occurring over and over for the last month. Emeline knew she shouldn't run to her house. If she did, the Carpathian known as Dragomir would die. He always died saving her. She'd tried to avoid this destiny. She'd made certain not to meet him, never to speak to him, yet here she was, forced to make a split-second decision. If she didn't make it to her house, Vadim would have her again and there would be no stopping him.

"Don't follow," she pleaded, rushing up her steps. She knew Dragomir would. He was one step behind Vadim. She knew coming after Dragomir was Vadim's army of horrible creatures. Vadim had already weakened her, taking her blood. Her neck burned, a fierce, intolerable pain that spread through her like wildfire.

Vadim waved his hand and her door stuck as she tried to jerk it open. She turned to face him, despair moving through her. Despair. Sorrow. Fear—although she was almost beyond fear. Back to the door, she slid down until her bottom hit the porch, knees up. She already knew exactly how the scenario would play out. Dragomir was on the stairs, and Vadim swung around to face him.

Emeline forced herself to look at the ancient warrior. He was the opposite of everything Vadim was. Roped muscles, scars, waist-length salt-and-pepper hair. He looked rugged. Tough. Scary. He had tattoos drifting up his neck so he looked a little like a modern-day outlaw biker. Vadim, despite his head being blown off repeatedly, always managed to restore his flawless, model looks. At first glance, one would be terrified of Dragomir, not Vadim, and that would be a very big mistake.

Her breath caught in her throat as Dragomir continued right up the stairs toward Vadim. She wanted to close her eyes, but she couldn't. She'd witnessed his death over and over in her nightmare. She always woke up when he went down and she never saw the outcome, only that he sacrificed his life for hers. She felt the least she could do was watch. More—this time, she planned to aid him.

Her hand dropped to the pocket of the long dress she wore. Once before, after continually trying new things in her dreams, she'd changed the outcome of the future. She was determined to do the same this time, or die trying. Time slowed down. Just as she knew it would, the air exploded with more vampires, and as they appeared, the Carpathian hunters joined in the fight.

She knew the children were safe. Genevieve was still out in the open, slumped over the bench in the play yard, but everyone was too occupied with the fierce battle to notice her. Emeline's world narrowed until there was only Dragomir and Vadim. They moved as if in slow motion, but she knew it was really just the opposite. Dragomir didn't so much as hesitate. He came up the stairs leading to her verandah with a steady pace. To her shock, he used a human weapon, one developed by Tariq for his security forces. That was new, not in her dream.

As the missile streaked toward Vadim, the vampire leapt into the air and rushed Dragomir so that the fiery bullets missed him. Dragomir flung the weapon aside as he took to the air to meet Vadim's attack. Emeline crawled across the planks of wood beneath the two snarling opponents to get to the strange gun Dragomir had discarded. Blood dripped down onto her shoulder, and she knew immediately it was Dragomir's. Vadim's blood would burn, a terrible acid, going through skin to bone. She caught up the gun and kept crawling, moving to the far side of the porch and the relative shelter of the wide railing.

"You can't have her," Dragomir said softly.

The words carried to her despite the low tone. The two men were close to each other, fists driving deep into chests. Two primitive fighters going for the kill. The moment she heard those soft, determined words, his statement absolute, her heart fluttered. So did her stomach. She looked up at his face. He had to be in pain. Vadim's talons were digging through flesh to get to his heart, but Dragomir's scarred features gave nothing away. He stared directly into Vadim's eyes, his fist in Vadim's chest.

Emeline pulled her gaze from the two combatants with difficulty, lifting her weapon and turning slightly to face the threat that always came and prevailed in her dream—Vadim's brother, Sergey. He came up behind Dragomir as the master vampire kept the Carpathian focused on him. Before Sergey could reach Dragomir and attack, Emeline rose up onto her knees and pulled the trigger. The gun bucked in her hand, driving her backward. Shockingly, the weapon was hot as the missile left the barrel, rolling, fanning the accelerant so that it burst into flames just before it entered Sergey's body.

She couldn't believe she'd actually scored a hit. It wasn't his heart, but she'd aimed for the chest, the largest target on him. She knew it wasn't a kill shot, but it did drive him away from Dragomir. It also got her Sergey's attention. His lips drew back in a terrible snarl and he slapped the fiery missile away from his body. It left a hole in his chest, flames still licking up his torso.

She steadied her hand and her nerves, placing the weapon on the railing to keep from ruining her aim. She pulled the trigger and a second missile spun through the air. Sergey howled as it struck his stomach, penetrating much deeper than the first. Furious, the vampire dove at her, uncaring of the fiery hole in his body. She bit off a scream and ducked as he raked at her face. The claws ripped at her scalp and snagged in her thick, wild, very tangled hair. The vampire dragged her halfway across the porch back toward her front door before he let her loose to get the burning missile from his body.

The moment she was attacked by Sergey, Dragomir ripped his hand back, taking part of Vadim's heart with his fist locked around it. Vadim screamed, throwing his head back and then forward to crash into Dragomir's forehead. Dragomir fell back, hitting the floor of the verandah. Blood poured from wounds in his chest and neck where the master vampire had ripped at him. In his fist was part of the blackened heart and he kept his fingers closed tightly around the prize.

Vadim, spraying acid-like blood over the flooring, rails and even the side of the house, staggered back and fell, landing almost in Emeline's lap. She dragged the ice pick from under the railing where she'd stashed it after her third dream. She rolled once, bringing her right against the master vampire. He caught her head in his hands as if he might break her neck. Staring into his eyes, she thrust the ice pick into his heart, using both hands and every bit of strength she had. Simultaneously, Dragomir tossed the bit he held into the yard as he called down the lightning, directing it at the little piece of Vadim's heart. Instantly it was incinerated.

Vadim howled, fury overcoming his perfect good looks, now long since vanished. His face was a mask of evil, eyes glowing red. His teeth, sharp and terrible, bit deep into her neck. Pain flashed through her. He wanted it to hurt and he gulped at the blood, even as he pulled the ice pick from his chest and tossed it to his brother. Sergey caught the weapon and slammed it down on Dragomir's thigh, pinning him to the floor as he elongated the blade. His hand morphed into a second ice pick, and he did the same with that blade, deliberately hitting the artery as he struck the other thigh.

Emeline tried to fight, to get Vadim off her, but he held her to him, gulping at her blood while Sergey swallowed the blood spraying from Dragomir's thigh. Vadim thrust Emeline aside without running his foul tongue over the twin marks in her neck, allowing the burning holes to continue to bleed freely. The master vampire crawled to Dragomir, shoved his brother out of the way and pressed his mouth over the wound on the Carpathian's thigh.

Dragomir's eyes met hers. She'd never seen a man more ravaged. The hot threads falling from the sky had burned him over and over. Vadim had shredded his chest and neck and put a hole in his chest near his heart. Both legs were pierced through. He looked tired and pale, the lines etched deep into his face, his scars proclaiming his many battles standing out proudly. He didn't look defeated, only tired.

Sergey turned his head toward Emeline. He licked his lips,

staring at her neck, Dragomir's blood staining his teeth and jaw where it had trickled down. He started toward her, and her breath caught in her throat. She couldn't even scream. She just watched him come at her, aware that the other hunters and the human security force were fighting off Vadim's army and wouldn't come to her rescue.

Dragomir moved then, with sudden blurring speed, catching Vadim by the back of the neck and slamming his head into his leg and then into the floor with shocking strength. He flung the master vampire backward again and was instantly over top of him, his fist driving deep into the vampire's chest.

Vadim screamed, shrieking for his army to come, to kill Dragomir. He fought, pounding at the wounds on Dragomir's legs, lunging forward to bite at him savagely with his sharp teeth, tearing chunks of flesh from him.

Emeline realized she had rolled right over the gun. It dug into the back of her leg. She caught at it in desperation, pulled it out from under her and fired almost point-blank into Sergey's chest. The missile blew him backward right over both Vadim and Dragomir. She fired a second time, straight into Vadim's back.

Sergey scrambled off his brother, yanked him up and kicked Dragomir in the head. Pulling Vadim with him, they stumbled to the stairs where three of their army were just hurrying toward them. Sergey snarled at them to hurry, to kill both.

"Just the hunter," Vadim objected, "but bring me the woman."

Emeline's heart stuttered as Sergey grinned evilly at her and then caught up Vadim, thrust him onto his back and streaked into the sky. She took a deep breath. There were at least two cartridges left. Three vampires. Dragomir wasn't moving. She wasn't even certain if he was alive. She'd altered the course of her nightmare, but as far as she could tell, he'd suffered more, not less.

Her body felt frozen, every muscle locked with fear. She forced herself to take another deep breath and then move. Blood still leaked down her neck to her shoulder in two steady trickles. She felt it and shuddered at the crawling sensation on her skin. It was difficult to move, to force her cramped, frozen muscles to work. She managed to get to her hands and knees and crawled to Dragomir. It was only a very short distance, but it felt like the length of a football field.

She could no longer hear or see the rest of the compound. Her world had narrowed to the three vampires and the help-less Carpathian she'd vowed to save. She put her body over top of his, making certain the vampires would have a difficult time killing him without getting her off him first. That might only buy him a few moments, but every second would count. If she was lucky, one of the other hunters would notice the drama playing out on her porch.

The three vampires gained the porch and spread out, coming at Dragomir from various angles. She couldn't keep them all in her sight, so she chose the two closest to each other to watch. She lifted the gun. "Go away." She hated that she sounded so scared.

One waved his hand to remove the gun. She felt the pull, as if a great magnet had attached itself to the weapon and yanked, but in her mind, she countered the magnet with an opposite one, pushing the powerful compulsive drawing-away. The smile vanished from the vampire's face, and his two comrades looked at each other.

She felt the one coming up behind her. His energy was evil, oily, a filth spreading across her porch and reaching her before he did. She turned and fired a missile right into his chest. Flames raced up his torso and he screamed, sprawling backward, rolling and then jumping off the porch to run. The wind fanned the flames as he raced away.

She felt movement and tried to turn back around to face the double threat, but Dragomir moved then, his arms going around her as he rolled, tucking her body under the weight of his, one hand smoothly removing the gun and firing at the vampire closest to them. He staggered back into the rail and fell backward over it, clutching his chest where the white-hot flames incinerated his heart.

The last vampire was on them, coming down on one knee beside Dragomir as he slammed his fist downward. Dragomir rolled both of them once more, taking Emeline out of the vampire's reach and shoving her away from them as he used his legs as a vicious vise, catching the lesser vampire around the neck and squeezing mercilessly. The vampire thrashed and kicked while Dragomir held him down. Emeline sat up slowly and realized Dragomir was trying to sit up as well in order to get to the vampire's chest.

She hurried over to help him, shoving at his back and then positioning herself there so he could slam his fist into the vampire's chest and remove the heart. She kept her eyes closed tightly, but it didn't stop her from hearing the sucking sounds as he withdrew the blackened organ and tossed it over the railing. Lightning flashed, a terrible whip in the sky lashing out so the fiery tip could incinerate the heart.

The vampire's screams cut off abruptly, and Dragomir shoved the body from him. He turned slightly, caught at Emeline and pulled her close, bunching her hair in his fist so he could tip her head back. "Stay still."

"Don't." She knew his intention. He would try to heal the burning, bleeding holes Vadim had made in her neck. "I'm unclean." The admission slipped out before she could stop it. To her dismay, it didn't deter him.

He tightened his hold on her hair and forced her head back when she attempted to resist. She could have countered magic, or pushed energy, but there was no way for her to counter brute force. His tongue was soothing on the fiery pain. She hated that it was. Hated that he would taste Vadim's filthy blood with its horrid parasites. He would ingest them for her, to try to stop the bleeding.

"I want it to bleed. His parasites are in me, too many to remove. Don't. Please. You'll only harm yourself." God knew, he was already in a bad way. She didn't see how he was still conscious when he'd lost so much blood. It was everywhere, all over her porch, his clothes, her, and both vampires had gulped as much as they could in the time they had.

"Hush," he crooned softly, barely lifting his head. Just enough that with every word, every breath, she felt his lips move against her skin. "Let me stop this right now. Get me into the house and put your herbs and whatever else you deem necessary into my wounds. I'll appear dead, but I won't be. I'll need Carpathian blood." His mouth was once more over the twin wounds Vadim had put in her neck.

"I can't have you in my house," she said, betraying her desperation. "Or any of the Carpathians. I . . ." She felt helpless. Selfish. He was nearly dead because of her. He'd done what she'd asked of him. He'd saved the children and the dragons. He had come back to save her, and he had. Now, he was torn, losing far too much blood. Helping her instead of saving himself.

"Do what I say, woman."

She winced. Now there was authority in his voice. It might be said in a low, velvet-soft tone, but it was pure command. Even Tariq, the owner of the property, didn't give her orders. They all treated her gently, afraid she'd break. Worse, she *wanted* to do as he said for all kinds of reasons, but mostly because he was still alive and she needed him to be. The stroke of his tongue on her skin had been … shocking. Soothing. It wiped out the horrors of Vadim sinking his teeth into her, making her skin crawl and burn.

She glanced over her shoulder toward the battle. The sound of gunfire was loud and once she thought she heard Genevieve screaming. She stood gingerly, her legs shaky, making up her mind. Determined. He was slippery, his blood coating his skin, and so was she, but she managed to pull him a couple of feet across the porch until they were beside the door. She had to let go of him in order to open the door.

She turned back to catch at his arm. To her dismay, there were more of them. Vampires. Surrounding her house. Threatening both.

Did you think I would give up? I will never stop until you are mine. If you don't come to me now, we will kill everyone there. Each death will be on you. Vadim's voice, beautiful and yet foul, moved through her mind like an oily sludge.

She gasped, her hand going protectively to her throat. Could she make herself go with them? Put herself back in Vadim's hands? A shudder went through her body. She should have known that Vadim wouldn't give up. He wanted her, and if she didn't go, Dragomir and every other person in the compound would die.

Dragomir's fingers settled around her ankle like a vise. "Emeline, step back into the house. Leave the door open, but get inside. If they try to get to you, slam the door shut. They cannot enter without an invitation."

She knew that. It made sense. She could save herself. Hide in her house. Watch Dragomir die right in front of her. She shook her head and tried to take a step toward the waiting vampires, five of them. Far too many for a Carpathian, even one with Dragomir's skills, let alone one torn up the way he was.

55

Dragomir flowed to his feet. She had no idea how. None. He shouldn't be alive, let alone standing. He literally shoved her into the doorway. "Stay put. You try to leave and I will have no choice but to stop you."

She glared at him. "They'll kill you. You can't fight them." She took one step toward him, determined to fight with him. If he was going to die for her, then she could do the same for him. Except, she couldn't move. Her foot ran into some kind of invisible barrier. She reached out with a hand and encountered the same thing. She looked up at him, her eyes meeting his. Determination and resolve were in his. She knew he saw despair in hers.

Dragomir turned to face the five vampires. Emeline pressed against the invisible barrier, her heart pounding and her mouth dry. She couldn't stand watching, knowing it was going to be a massacre, but she couldn't tear her gaze away from the big man striding across her porch with confidence.

He was far bigger than she had realized in the confines of the verandah. The blood and scars only served to make him appear invincible, a warrior of old defending his lady. Tears welled up. For him. For her. She wished he was hers. That man, so scarred and torn but standing unbending in the face of evil.

Dragomir moved with sudden blurring speed and she couldn't help but notice how graceful he was, how fluid, like a great lion, bringing down his prey in one easy leap. He was on the first vampire before she could blink, his fist crashing through the chest wall so that his fingers could pry the heart free and toss it aside. He whirled and slammed his bloody arm into the second vampire's chest. Lightning forked across the sky, and he directed it toward both hearts as he turned to face the third.

The third vampire was close, too close, although Dragomir

56

managed to slam his fist deep. He looked exhausted. Tortured. She knew every breath he drew was difficult. He'd battled several vampires, then two master vampires, and suffered several severe injuries, but he kept going. The vampire had turned his body as Dragomir's fist crashed through his chest, throwing the trajectory off just enough that Dragomir had to withdraw his arm and punch a second time, which he did with lightning speed, but that small second gave the remaining two vampires time to join the attack.

Emeline tried to warn him, screaming his name, battering with her fists at the shield preventing her from helping him. Both vampires tore at his body with their vicious teeth, acting as if they might devour him alive. They gulped blood—he had little to spare. Frantic, she battered at the shield and screamed for help until her voice was hoarse. Dragomir remained unbending, like a great lion in the midst of a pack of wild dogs. He didn't move until he withdrew his fist and tossed the heart into the air, where lightning incinerated it.

The moment the heart left his hand, he turned to face both attackers, simultaneously slamming his fists into the walls of their chests. The vampires went berserk, clawing at him with terrible talons, raking deep furrows down his neck, throat and chest. They seemed to want to scrape the skin from his body, tearing it off in long strips.

Emeline wanted to close her eyes so she couldn't see what they were doing to Dragomir, but she couldn't look away. He never changed expression. There was no sign of the pain he had to be feeling, no anger or acknowledgment of any kind that those monsters were tearing up his body with so much glee. One kicked repeatedly at the wound in his right thigh, even as he tore at the hunter with his claws.

Very slowly Dragomir began to retract his closed fists. The vampires became even more frantic. Dragomir didn't even blink at the wildness the two vampires displayed. One went for his eyes, trying to gouge them out. Dragomir moved his head, dodging the claws while he extracted the two hearts. He threw them away from the porch, out toward the play yard. The blackened organs sailed through the air. High. One vampire leapt into the air after them, while the other ran down the stairs.

Lightning lit the sky, a massive display, forks of sizzling whips streaking through the night to strike both hearts before they hit the ground, incinerating them. The vampire in the sky fell at the feet of his fellow undead. Emeline could see five bodies. Lightning kept crackling. The forks spread out and struck simultaneously, turning the five vampires to ashes.

"Let me out," Emeline called. "Hurry."

Dragomir was already staggering. She reached toward him, as if she might be able to keep him on his feet. The movement attracted his attention when her plea hadn't. He glanced toward the compound, where the fighting had all but ceased, and then he waved his hand toward her. She had one hand pressed to the shield and knew the moment it came down.

Dragomir stumbled toward her and went down in the doorway, his weight taking her with him so that he fell inside. She didn't have time to think about a Carpathian hunter entering her home or what secrets he might discover. She crouched down beside him, afraid he was unconscious, but his gaze was fixed on her face.

"Invite me in."

"What? No." She shook her head. Blaze, her friend, had told her it was never a good idea to invite them inside one's home unless one was prepared to let them use their powers there.

He made a move toward the door, trying to drag himself out. She didn't want that, either. "Wait. Just wait. I need to think." She was in a state of full panic.

"No time." He reached up and wrapped a length of her hair around his fingers. "So beautiful. The color. So beautiful."

He sounded delirious. He was bleeding everywhere, but she could see he was still trying to force his body to move out of her home.

"Stop. Stop moving," she demanded, horrified at the trail of blood.

"Going to have to shut down my heart and lungs. Can't do it inside."

Her mind was in complete chaos. She caught his shoulders, trying to keep him from moving back. His hand was still in her hair, connecting them. She felt that, as if a million strands bound them together, yet it was the only thing she had to stop him. She couldn't take one more shoving with his toes and one elbow. She *had* to stop him.

"Okay. Come in. I want you to come inside." Her mouth moved, voicing the invitation even when her brain screamed at her to stop. He couldn't come in, yet she was desperate to keep him there.

His lower lip curved. It wasn't a smile, but still, her heart nearly stopped. It didn't soften the rough angles and planes of his face. He looked like a fallen angel, maybe Lucifer himself. She gently shoved his hair back from where it fell around his face. Grooves were torn there, made by claws. So much blood. So many scars. She knew Carpathians rarely scarred, yet something terrible had happened to this man.

"Can you make it to the couch?"

Something flickered in the depths of his eyes. Humor maybe. "Need dirt, *sívamet*, not a couch." He dropped his hand from her hair and then she had his weight. His full weight, all of it. He was extremely heavy, slumping against her so that she nearly toppled over. She realized he was out.

59

He'd shut down his heart and lungs in order to preserve what blood he had in his body, preventing it from leaking out or spraying the floor around them.

She sat for a moment, his head in her lap, her fingers smoothing back his hair. It was thick and as long as hers, falling to his waist. There were a few places it felt soft, but mostly it was sticky with blood. She sighed. At least he wasn't dead. The children were safe. She could see to his wounds and then find out about Genevieve and the others.

He's dead. Those children are dead. Your friend Blaze is dead. I'll burn that place to the ground.

The vile voice filled her mind and with it came the crashing pain, burning through her veins as if whatever terrible parasites he'd put in her body were determined to punish her for him. Deep inside her womb, she heard the screams of pain, of fear, and she pressed both hands over her churning stomach, wishing she could turn back time. But what would she have done? Allow the flesh-eating puppets he created to devour Liv alive? Tears burned again and she was sick to death of crying. She'd made a decision, and she had to bear the consequences. Her. No one else.

Her gaze dropped to the man lying so still on her floor. She scooted, lifting his head so she could put it more fully in her lap. She knew he was unaware and that made her bold. She sat on the floor with him for longer than she should have.

"Emeline! Unlock the door, Em!" Blaze called. "Are you okay? Open the door."

Emeline took a deep breath. Blaze McGuire was her closest friend. Maybe her only real friend. They were more like sisters, and yet she was so afraid to allow Blaze inside. She was lifemate to Maksim Volkov, co-owner of the nightclubs with Tariq Asenguard. Blaze had been human, but now she was completely in the Carpathian world.

"Emeline, I swear, if you don't open this door, I'm going to break it down."

"You're Carpathian, crazy woman," Emeline pointed out, gently setting Dragomir's head on the floor so she could shift out from under him. "That means no entering without being invited."

"I'm your best friend. Practically your sister. Invite me so I can break down the door."

Despite everything, Emeline smiled. Blaze would, too. She'd break down the door in a heartbeat if she thought Emeline was in trouble. "They know," she whispered softly aloud. "Oh, God, they know and they're going to kick me out of here. What am I going to do?" Tears ran down her face. She wanted to stop them, she was sick of crying, but she didn't have a solution. All this time and she still had no idea what to do. She couldn't stay. She couldn't go. Her tears fell on Dragomir's face and she brushed them off gently.

Dragomir's hand moved, coming up to hers, shocking her. By all rights, he should have been completely asleep, dead to the world. "She is not alone." His fingers settled around her wrist lightly, like a bracelet.

She jerked her hand away, her heart racing. Was Blaze, the one person she counted on to help her, betraying her? "Who is with you?" Her voice shook. There was no way to keep fear from shimmering through the room.

Dragomir's eyes opened. For one moment, she saw pain etched into his face. He took a deep, shuddering breath and was once more expressionless. "Go into the other room and close the door. I'll handle this."

"I've brought a healer with me," Blaze called. "Everyone can feel Dragomir's need."

The relief was so tremendous that for a moment she didn't actually realize the implication. Then it hit her. Dragomir's injuries were so severe other Carpathians could feel them. "Put yourself back to sleep. I'll let them in."

He caught at her before she could get up. "Go into the other room. I'll let them in."

Her heart skipped a beat and then became a drum. She tasted fear. "Dragomir . . ."

"Do as I say, woman. You have secrets. A healer will discover them. *This* healer will discover them. Go now."

"Why are you doing this for me?"

He touched her hair. "Beautiful color," he whispered.

Her hair was a wild mess. In tangles. She wanted a brush immediately.

"Go," he said. "I won't let them near you."

She believed him. He was hurt beyond imagining, but he'd poured steel into his voice and she knew he would do exactly as he said he would. All because he liked the color of her hair? Hardly. It was because he was a good man. The best. He'd appointed himself her shield and he stayed on that course no matter what.

She lifted her chin. Squared her shoulders. It was time to face the consequences. They were hers, not this man's. "I'll let them in. You put yourself to sleep. Whatever he says . . ."

Dragomir moved then, a fluid ripple of sheer power. He stood up, towering over her, reaching down to very gently pull her to her feet. "Do as I tell you." He turned her toward the hallway. "Stay away from the healer until I know if you are safe."

He was implacable, and no matter what she said, no matter that for the first time she was willing to be thrown out of the compound—for him—he wasn't accepting her sacrifice. He was going to force her to accept his.

His finger slid down the path her tears had taken on her

face. She felt that touch as if it had sunk through her skin and impressed right on her bones.

"Emeline."

She nodded, because he'd stand there all day, leaking blood he couldn't afford to lose. She ducked under his arm and headed down the hall to the first bedroom. She stood in the doorway and watched him lift his hand to wave toward the front door, allowing it to swing open. Blaze was framed there for a moment, her long red hair pulled back away from her face.

"Only the healer is invited in," Dragomir said firmly.

Blaze stepped aside and a man moved into the house. Emeline's breath caught in her lungs, trapped until she felt raw with the need for air. He wasn't particularly tall, nor was he short. Power flowed through him, so much that his body couldn't possible contain it all and the energy surrounded him. Like Dragomir, muscles rippled beneath his clothes. His hair was longer in the manner of Carpathians, but to his shoulders, pulled back with a leather cord. It was his eyes that caught her attention. They were a startling blue, rimmed with a liquid silver. They were eyes that would see right through her to her secrets. She was grateful that she hid like a coward in her room.

Those strange eyes swept over Dragomir and then moved past him, the gaze traveling down the hall straight to the bedroom. Emeline stepped back, certain he couldn't see her, but still uneasy.

"You are the Carpathian who betrayed Aleksei with his woman," Dragomir observed. "Ancient, yet young. I do not believe we have formally met."

"There was no betrayal," the man said, clearly uncaring what anyone thought of him, already striding into the room. "Sit before you lose what is left of your life."

Dragomir hesitated. It was the first time he'd ever done so and she instinctively knew he didn't want to be in a vulnerable position, one that wouldn't allow him to protect her. She silently willed him to do as the healer bid him.

"The name is Gary. I am a Daratrazanoff, but was born human." He didn't offer any further information, and Emeline had no idea what being a Daratrazanoff was, or how that was important, only that it was.

Dragomir settled onto the floor, but he turned his body so he could watch the door, the hallway and the healer. She wished she had more of the weapons with the fiery missiles. At least she could protect Dragomir if she needed to.

Gary knelt beside him and, without preamble, allowed his spirit to leave his body and move into Dragomir's. It left the healer completely vulnerable to attack. Blaze had explained the process to Emeline numerous times—how the Carpathians could leave behind all ego, everything to do with them and become pure healing energy. Some were reputed to be far more powerful healers than others. She had heard rumors that they had sent for an extremely strong healer, one they hoped would be able to help heal psychic wounds as well.

She watched closely, saw the wounds on Dragomir's body mend from the inside out one after another. Time went by. She had no idea how much, but it was long. It took the healer hours to repair the damage to the ancient's body. Gary didn't stop until even the rake marks on his face and chest closed. They were still there, red lines to mark where the vampires had ripped him open, but the terrible lacerations and wounds were closed.

The healer came back into his body, pale, weak and clearly disoriented. "We both will need blood, ancient."

Dragomir glanced at Blaze. "He needs blood. I'm inviting you in only to give him blood and then you must leave."

Blaze looked hurt but she came in immediately. Emeline watched her open her wrist with a long fingernail and extend her arm toward the healer. He didn't look at Blaze but studied Dragomir as he fed.

Blaze looked around the room. "Is Emeline all right?"

"Yes."

"She's my friend."

"Then respect her wishes."

Emeline twisted her fingers together, waiting. The healer politely closed the wound on Blaze's wrist, still without looking at her, and offered blood from his own wrist to Dragomir.

"Who are you to her?" Blaze demanded.

"She is under my protection," Dragomir stated and took the wrist the healer offered him.

Emeline's breath caught in her throat. He said it so matter-of-factly, as if his declaration wasn't handing her the world. Why would he do that? Why would he decide to save the children instead of going after Vadim as he wanted to do, just because she asked? Ancients rarely bothered with humans. She'd seen enough of them to last her a lifetime. Mostly, they ignored everyone and seemed only to live for battles.

But they saved lives. She respected the ancients. She respected the Carpathian people. But they would kick her out in a heartbeat if they knew what she was. Who she really was.

The healer gave Dragomir blood, and then Blaze supplied Gary a second time before the man spoke.

"You need to be put in the healing soil," Gary said.

"I will do so when I am ready," Dragomir declared.

Gary opened his mouth, closed it and shook his head. "You will be of no use to her if you die. You aren't out of the woods yet."

"Your reputation preceded you here. I have no doubt I will be just fine. I thank both of you." Dragomir got to his feet with that same graceful way he always moved and led them to the door. "I'll let Emeline know you wish to visit with her," he added.

Blaze inclined her head. "I would appreciate that."

He closed the door and leaned against it. "It is safe, Emeline. We need to talk."

She'd been dreading this moment, but knew it had to come.

4

W hy won't you put yourself in the ground?" Emeline asked. "You need to heal."

"I need to know why you are so afraid all the time. Even afraid of your friend," Dragomir said, no inflection whatsoever in his voice, yet she shivered, aware, without knowing how, that if Blaze had done something to make her afraid, he had no problem removing Blaze and Maksim from existence. He'd appointed himself her champion and would follow through, even if it meant putting him at odds with all Carpathians.

She shook her head. "Blaze would never do anything to hurt me." But she didn't know that anymore. She couldn't be certain.

"Emeline. I have a need, not a want, to know why you're afraid all the time." Again, there was no inflection, but his gaze was very focused. "There is a difference and this is no idle question."

Somehow, it was easier because his voice was so soft, almost gentle, as if he wasn't judging her. She sank into the chair by the window. She was exhausted. He had to be even more so. "If I tell you the truth, you'll want me thrown out of the compound. Vadim will get to me. This is the only safe place I have." The truth came out in a hurried rush.

"You are under my protection, woman. I do not give that lightly. I do not take it back just because circumstances are difficult."

She believed him. He was ... extraordinary. He might sound arrogant and look even more so, but he was an unusual man and he deserved the truth. He had to know who he had committed to protecting. She didn't want to tell him. She didn't want him to look at her with contempt. She wouldn't blame him, but she didn't want to see it in his eyes. In such a short time, she felt as if she knew him more than she'd ever known—or trusted—anyone. That in itself was strange. She didn't trust many people.

"I'm Vadim's lifemate." She just said it. Aloud. Feeling sick, disgusted. She couldn't look away from him, waiting for condemnation.

Dragomir stared at her for a long time. "Woman, you're insane." He gave her what he must have thought was a faint smile, shaking his head as if she amused him. His smile was a very indistinct curve of his lower lip.

She blinked. She'd expected all sorts of reactions, but that was not one of them. She tried a scowl. She'd never been particularly good at scowling, but then until recently, she hadn't been great at weeping, either, and now she was a faucet that couldn't seem to be turned off. "I just told you that I'm Vadim's lifemate, and you're telling me I'm insane. Do you know how difficult it was to admit that to you?"

"What do you know of lifemates?"

She wished he would do something. He stood leaning against the door, looking far too pale, and it occurred to her the healer wouldn't have bothered arguing with him. Gary Daratrazanoff had told him he needed to go to ground, an unnecessary comment—unless the healer was directing it toward her. He expected her to convince Dragomir to go to ground. She couldn't convince him of the truth, let alone of something that was good for him.

"Blaze told me that when a Carpathian male is born, his soul is split and the other half is put into his lifemate's keeping. She will be born again and again if he fails to find her."

"And knowing this you realize there can only be one lifemate. The soul fits together when the ritual binding words are spoken by the male."

"Yes, that is my understanding."

"So if I said the ritual binding words to you, they wouldn't work."

She nodded.

"Did Vadim say them to you?" He looked so invincible standing there, but she could see he was exhausted. She scooted to the end of the couch and patted it. "Please come and sit down."

"Did Vadim say the ritual binding words to you?"

Her hand crept defensively to her throat. "He said ... did ... horrible things. I don't remember any words he spoke to me. I fought him. Everything he did hurt me." She could barely tell him that much, her voice a whisper of raw horror.

Something flickered across his face but the expression was so fleeting she couldn't catch it. "It is impossible for Vadim to be your lifemate no matter what he said or did."

She shook her head. "I know that he is." She was so ashamed. Blaze and Charlotte both had wonderful men. Her lifemate was one of the worst vampires in the history of the

Carpthian world. He'd done terrible things, killed countless men and women. Killed children. Fed live children to his puppets. He was the worst nightmare visited on earth in the form of a monster, and she was his other half.

"You are *my* lifemate, Emeline." He proclaimed it softly, but the vow carried, resonated deep inside her.

She gasped. "No. Don't you dare sacrifice yourself for me or think that will keep everyone from throwing me out. No. I'm going to tell Tariq. I just needed time to come to terms with having to leave the protection of this place. I've already put those children in jeopardy ..."

He straightened from where he'd been leaning lazily against the door. One swift, almost brutal movement. Fierce anger stamped pure aggression onto his face. "*Those children* put you and every other person living in this compound in jeopardy. They are spoiled and lack discipline. I will have a word with Tariq about them, but that is for another time."

"Those children are victims—"

"Vadim nearly reacquired you," he interrupted. "If you thought your life was hell the first time, you would come to know that it wasn't even close."

She shuddered. "I am prepared to confess to Tariq. I don't want anyone else to suffer because of me. Thank you for standing up for me and for the fact that you are so willing to continue, to say to others that you're my lifemate. I appreciate that more than I can say but—"

"So you have no objection if I attempt to bind you to me with the ritual words. My soul to yours, understanding it cannot possibly work if we are not true lifemates. With the full understanding that if it did work, you would be bound to me for all eternity."

She patted the couch again. "If you lie down right here and

rest, then you can say the words to me and see for yourself that they won't work."

"Your hair is black. A true black. No Carpathian can see a true black once he is beyond his two hundredth year. In my case, it was even before that. He only sees color if he is in the presence of his lifemate and hears her voice."

She was very self-conscious of her tangled hair, and he seemed a bit obsessed with her hair. "I think you're over-wrought. Please come and sit down. The healer made it clear you need to be in the ground. I know he couldn't have possibly given you enough blood, and I can't give it to you because my blood is . . . tainted." It was Vadim's blood mixed with a Carpathian's, one he'd held prisoner for a long, long time. Vadim's blood burned and his parasites spread through her body, burning and torturing her, trying to force her obedience to their master. She wasn't about to share her blood with him.

His eyebrow shot up. "Overwrought?" He repeated the word slowly as if he'd never heard it before. "Woman, a Carpathian hunter cannot possibly get overwrought. I just want to give you every possible opportunity to say you do not want me to bind you to me. I know you are my lifemate. I am ancient, and I do not always understand your modern world or the way women act toward their men. I believe it is my duty and privilege, my honor, to make you happy, but I am not certain I am capable of it when I believe strongly that my woman follows where I lead."

She patted the couch again. She wasn't about to say she thought he was delirious on top of everything else. He needed blood and he was obviously exhausted. He'd appointed him-self her guardian and protector, but he was stubborn as hell. His duty, privilege and honor to protect her? Even knowing she was Vadim's lifemate? She changed tactics.

"Dragomir, please come and lie down on the couch. Just

for a few minutes. If you need to slay dragons for me, you can do it later. Although I love those dragons. Ever since the children got them, I've secretly wanted one. I love the idea of having the freedom of soaring in the sky." She smoothed her palm over the cushions. "Please."

His gaze drifted over her face. His eyes were a strange amber most of the time, but right then, they were pure gold. Burning hot, molten gold framed with black eyelashes that were far too long for a man to have. He crossed the room to the sofa and took her at her word, shocking her by stretching out, his head in her lap.

Her breath caught in her throat. It was one thing to have his head resting on her thighs when he was asleep, another when he was awake. It felt . . . intimate.

"You are most certainly *not* Vadim's lifemate, Emeline," he said, closing his eyes as if he was so weary he couldn't keep them open one moment longer. "You are *mine*."

Her heart stuttered at his proclamation. For the first time, there was a bite in his voice, as if no one had better try to take her from him. She wanted the fantasy. This man. One who would want her when she looked like a hag from a horror film. One determined to save the lifemate of a master vampire conspiring to take over the world.

The healer had cleaned the blood from him and repaired his clothing, but even with the hours of work, Dragomir still looked as if he'd been in an epic battle. She couldn't help but smooth back the hair falling around his face. "I wish that was true, Dragomir, but we both know it isn't. I would know. I dream about things that happen. I would know." She knew she couldn't have a man like Dragomir—someone with courage and integrity. She was lost to that world. Lost to any world where there was a good man.

He angled his head and opened his eyes. Her heart jolted.

Pure liquid gold blazed at her. "I do not want you to be upset when the ritual works and you are bound to me. I am giving you fair warning. I *know* binding you to me will work."

"I would be honored to be your lifemate, Dragomir," she said, being honest. "Thank you for saving the children. And me." The last wobbled a little. He had kept her from Vadim. That was worth everything to her. Watching him fight for them, for her and the children, bending his shoulders and back to shelter the two youngest from the horrific burning threads falling from the sky had been so humbling. He was the most courageous man she'd ever known. She was a stranger to him and she knew ancients rarely associated with humans, yet he'd been the one to come for her. To save her.

His unblinking gaze searched her face as if looking for hidden traps. "*Te avio päläfertiilam.* You are my lifemate." He reached up and took her hand, pressing it against his chest, right over his heart. His fingers began to move in slow caresses over her bare skin. "*Éntölam kuulua, avio päläfertiilam.* I claim you as my lifemate."

Emeline felt a shiver go through her. Her body felt hot in comparison to his. That worried her. She knew he needed to be in the healing soil, and the fact that he refused to do so made her anxious beyond her comprehension. "Dragomir," she whispered his name. Fearing for him. "Please do as the healer asked."

"Shh ... Listen to the words I say to you. First, in my language, the ancient language of my people, and then in your language so you understand the enormity of the sacred vows I am saying to you. I am tying us together. Giving you my heart and soul and body. I will take into my keeping your heart and soul and body. You will be safe with me."

His fingers tightened around hers, his thumb still moving until she felt that caress go right through her skin straight to her heart. He had an effect on her she didn't understand. When he spoke his language, his voice was deep, the timbre commanding, vibrating through her body as if he was striking chords in her that were already prearranged and tuned immediately to that frequency. Bonded with him. She was *so* susceptible. She wanted every single thing he said to be true—but she knew it was impossible.

"*Ted kuuluak, kacad, kojed.* I belong to you. *Élidamet andam.* I offer my life for you."

Tears welled up again. The words were so beautiful. He couldn't do that, of course, but she understood why Blaze was so enamored with Maksim. Dragomir brought her hand to his mouth, his lips moving over the center of her palm as he kept declaring his vows to her.

"*Pesämet andam.* I give you my protection."

He'd already given her his protection, and he was so torn up, his body ripped to pieces, yet he refused to take care of himself, refused to go into the healing earth as he should have. She felt the words go right through her skin, his lips brushing the center of her palm, so that his vow sank into her veins. Her blood carried them straight to her heart.

"*Uskolfertiilamet andam.* I give you my allegiance. *Sívamet andam.* I give you my heart. *Sielamet andam.* I give you my soul."

She couldn't stop the tears trickling down her face. Her throat felt raw. Her lungs burned for air. What man could give a woman such a vow and *mean* it? She could hear absolute honesty in his voice. She wanted him for herself with every breath she took, but he deserved so much more. She was a mess. A terrible, hot mess. A man like Dragomir had no business tying himself to her, even if it was only in his mind.

"*Ainamet andam.* I give you my body. *Sívamet kuuluak kaik että a ted.* I take into my keeping the same that is yours."

That lower lip curved again into his almost smile, and she

couldn't help it, she had to touch it with the pad of her finger. A light caress. The compulsion was so strong there was no stopping that little stroke, but his gaze jumped to hers and she fell into all that hot burning gold.

"You have a beautiful body, *sívamet*, and, although mine is a bit torn up right now, I assure you, I will take proper care of you. All the time."

Her heart skipped a beat and then began to gallop. What was she thinking sitting here with this *decent*, honorable man? She made a move to slide out from under him, thinking to run, to keep him from knowing the worst. He thought he knew the worst, but he didn't.

Dragomir rolled onto his side and clamped his arm around her thighs. "Stay still. Listen to me, Emeline. Every word must be said to you."

She shook her head. "Don't. Don't, Dragomir. Not because I don't want it to be true. I do. Every single part of me is saying this is the most beautiful moment of my life, but you can't think to throw away your life. I won't let you. There's Genevieve ..." She broke off. She'd want to kill Genevieve if the woman came near Dragomir. That knowledge shocked her. Already, just because he'd said his vows as if they truly belonged, she wanted it so badly that a part of her was believing he was hers.

"*Ainaak olenszal sívambin*. Your life will be cherished by me for all time. *Te élidet ainaak pide minan*. Your life will be placed above mine for all time. *Te avio päläfertiilam*. You are my lifemate." His thumb slid down the tracks of her tears. "Did you understand me, Emeline? You are my lifemate, not Genevieve. No other woman can possibly be. There is only you for me."

She took a deep breath and let it out. She wasn't going to dissuade him, and he desperately needed to go to ground

75

and heal. If she didn't agree with him, tell him the things he thought he wanted to hear, he would stay there until the sun came up. She stroked a soothing caress over his hair. That beautiful head of salt and pepper that flowed like a waterfall to his waist. She'd never been fond of long hair on a man, but it didn't detract from his fierce warrior persona. Neither did his long lashes or that lower lip she was beginning to fixate on.

"All right. It's done. Now, really, you have to get into the earth and let it heal you."

"Almost. *Ainaak sívamet jutta oleny.* You are bound to me for all eternity. *Ainaak terád vigyázak.* You are always in my care." He turned her hand over and brushed his lips over her knuckles.

The gesture was pure intimacy, sending heat waves through her body. Her heart seemed to have found the rhythm of his. The longer she spent in Dragomir's company, the more she fell under his spell.

"*Now*, will you *please* go to ground?" She needed him to do so. The moment he did, she intended to find Blaze and Maksim and tell them the truth. She had to save Dragomir from himself.

"Not until I remove the parasites from your blood."

"After. Tonight. That doesn't give you much time to heal." She kept her voice low and soothing, because more than her next breath, she needed to take care of Dragomir. She didn't want him out of her sight, but he *had* to heal properly. The healer had made that clear. And no way in hell was Vadim touching him with his disgusting parasites. She was determined to protect Dragomir. It was the least she could do after what he'd done for her. He'd made her feel human again, beautiful and worthy.

"Can you go to ground under my home, so I know you're close?"

She had no idea why the thought of him leaving her made her feel anxious and even desperate, but she needed to make certain he was alive and well.

"I'm going to remove the parasites from your body and heal you. I took Daratrazanoff's blood twice so I would have the strength. It was imperative that I live so I could ensure there is no trace of Vadim's attack left on you. I will remove his parasites and any possible way he can contact you."

She caught his long hair in her hand and leaned over him, burying her face in the thick mass. All along, when he'd been so wounded and torn, he hadn't been thinking of himself or his pain, or even if he would live or die; he'd been thinking of her. Living for her. She could love this man. She really could. But she wasn't surviving for herself.

Emeline straightened and forced her fingers open so his hair slid from her palm. "Go to ground, Dragomir. I have things to do now. Important things." Like pack a bag, pull every cent she'd stashed out of her hiding place and run before the sun set on the next day. "I don't want you to take the parasites from my blood, not until you've spent at least one full day in the soil. I mean it."

"I am unused to women believing they can give orders to their men. Make no mistake, *sívamet*, I am your man. Your ... " He frowned, propping his head up with one hand while he tried to remember the correct word. "Spouse. Husband. We are wed. Our souls are complete. I cannot go to ground when my woman is hurting, and you're ... " He broke off again, his gaze searching the room and hallway. "Who else is here?"

She stiffened and tried to slide off the couch. His arm kept her thighs locked in place, preventing her escape. "No one." Her voice was small. Too small.

His gaze jumped to her face. Those golden eyes refused to

allow her to look away. "I hear a heartbeat. Not mine. Not yours. Fast. Galloping. I thought one of the children, but it's faster, out of rhythm." He frowned. "Painful. As if something is squeezing the heart."

His eyes left hers and began to drop lower. Her lips. Her chin. Her throat. Breasts. She held her breath as his speculative gaze dropped to her stomach. There was no way she could stop the involuntary gesture—she covered her womb with her hand protectively.

Dragomir sat up slowly. Stood. Flowed across the room with the grace of a lion. Turned and stalked back toward her, as if she were the prey. Terrified, she held up one hand, a pitiful defense against him as she surged to her feet with the hysterical idea of fighting her way out of the house.

"Köd alte hän." The guttural words came out like a curse. He towered over her. Close. Their bodies almost touching. "Tell me." It was a command, nothing less. "Sit in the chair over there." He indicated the most comfortable seat in her home with a jerk of his chin. "You tell me everything. *Everything.* You do not leave a single detail out."

She shook her head. The tears were burning behind her eyes. The endless, *useless* fountain she couldn't seem to turn off. She'd lived without hope for so long, weeks of pain and torment, afraid to sleep, unable to eat, terrified someone would learn her secret and force her to leave the safety of the compound.

"Sívamet." His voice softened to a brush of velvet, a stroke she felt over her skin. He cupped her face in his hands. His hands were big and surrounded her with his strength. "I am your lifemate. It is my duty and my privilege to see to your happiness. You must give me the details. All of them. You must tell me what you want. The truth of what you want. I cannot do what is best for us until I know these things."

"You can't help me. No one can help me." She was so damn tired of feeling sorry for herself, but the last thing she wanted was to trap Dragomir into her mess. There was no way out for her. She knew because she'd had weeks to try to find one. "You're like a beautiful white knight in the movies, riding on your horse, or in this case maybe a dragon to save the damsel in distress. Believe me, I know if anyone could do it, you could, but there isn't a solution I can live with."

"There are ways to remove it." Again, his voice was gentle and there was no judgment of any kind. He wasn't trying to persuade her one way or the other, he simply was voicing what she already knew.

"Of course, my first thought was I *had* to get rid of it. A child of the vilest creature on the face of the earth? There was no question. I couldn't stand the thought of it growing inside me like some monster with claws ready to tear me apart from the inside. The pain was so excruciating. I was terrified of what it would be, what horrible thing Vadim had conjured up and put inside of me. Every bad horror movie ever made played through my mind over and over." She was shaking so hard she could barely stand.

He moved into her and gathered her into his arms. His body was large, strong; his arms felt like security, a security she hadn't known ever in her life. He sheltered her against his heart. She could feel it beating, strong and steady, just as he was. He felt invincible.

"You're the most unbelievable man," she whispered, awed by his reaction. He hadn't yelled at her, or accused her of betraying those in the compound by bringing a child of Vadim's into the only small part of the world safe to them. He simply ordered her to tell him everything so he could find solutions.

"Stop crying, *sívamet*. I am unused to dealing with a

woman's tears, and I find yours—unsettling. You aren't alone anymore." He walked her over to the large armchair, sank into it and pulled her onto his lap. "Talk to me, Emeline."

His voice was perfectly pitched. That deep timbre was difficult to ignore, but so velvety it softened the command. He created an intimacy she couldn't resist. She knew it was wrong to sit on his lap, to allow him to be embroiled further into her insanity, but she couldn't stop herself. She had to tell someone, and for some reason she couldn't understand, that someone—the only one she would consider—was asking her at a time when all her defenses were down.

"I made up my mind to get rid of it, but then I heard screaming. Crying. A baby in such pain. I realized she was in pain, just as I was in pain. When I didn't obey Vadim and go to him when he demanded it, his parasites would attack. Not just me, but the baby as well. He tortured her, and she wasn't even fully developed. Not nearly so." She pressed her hand over her womb and lifted her head to look at him. "How can he do the terrible things he does?"

"He is incapable of feeling unless he invokes a strong enough reaction in another. Vampires get high if they kill while feeding. The blood is laced with adrenaline. They can get a rush from someone feeling terror or any strong emotion. The negative emotions are intense. If their puppet eats their prey alive, all of them get a rush. Torturing an unborn child, especially if it distresses you, would be a rush for him."

"Even his own child?"

"He doesn't feel. He cannot feel any attachment."

"Then why go to such lengths to get one?"

His fingers came up to the nape of her neck in an effort to ease the tension out of her. "A tool. He has some plan in mind and children factor into it. Vadim was always incredibly intelligent. All the Malinovs were. He has embraced technology, and clearly Carpathians must do the same if we want to survive in this world. He has a master plan."

Emeline pressed her forehead to his chest, unable to meet his eyes. "I know she's alive, aware, and she's innocent. She didn't want what happened any more than I did. I have to protect her. There's no one else. I don't know how she can survive much longer, not with him torturing her to get to me. I know if the others find out about her, there is a very large possibility that they will want me to leave the compound, and maybe rightly so. I don't know how much control Vadim will gain over her as she grows. I know you can't possibly understand . . ."

"You are not thinking clearly, *sívamet*. The baby will not survive his torture. He knows that. As she grows, his tortures will worsen. Eventually, as you grow to love the child, he will use that against you. He knows you will go to him in an effort to save your daughter."

It was true. Knowing she would end up in the hands of a master vampire, she had still gone into the underground city to save children she didn't know. Strangers. The only thing she had in common with them was that they were street kids like she had been. She hadn't been able to stop herself. Vadim knew her better than she knew herself. Already the baby's piteous cries day and night, echoing through her mind, were wearing on her. She had already considered— and discarded—the idea of giving in and going to him, but as the child grew, so would the connection between them. If Vadim stepped up his torture, what other recourse would she have?

She moaned and shook her head in defeat. "I don't know what to do. I considered ending both our lives. All those women down in the tunnels. Dead. Their unborn children dead. I didn't want to be like that."

"Tell me what happened." His voice was so gentle it turned her heart over. She had never had gentle. Never. She'd been homeless. She didn't even remember her mother and father, only relatives that treated her like a burden. Never gentle until this man.

She closed her eyes and leaned into him, tried to burrow into him, become part of all that strength. She had tried to forget. To put those minutes—not even a full hour of her life—behind a solid steel door in her mind, but she couldn't. Those seconds and minutes were carved deep into her soul and would never fade. She hadn't told anyone, not even Blaze. She couldn't.

The thought of telling it, reliving it ... But she had to. Dragomir deserved to know. He was sticking by her, even going so far as to believe she was his lifemate, mostly, she was certain, so others would believe it. He made her feel cherished, sitting in the chair, on his lap, his arms holding her securely, as if he could keep her safe from evil.

"Vadim had several others with him. They were so hideous. Teeth so pointy and stained with blood. They dug their nails into me, into my arms to hold me. Not like regular fingernails, but these long, thick claws like a grizzly bear." She rubbed her arms, from her biceps to her wrists, feeling those long talons digging into her flesh, right down to the bone. The pain had been unlike anything she'd ever experienced. The wounds deep, burning, as if they'd poured acid into her veins.

"Even so, I fought him. I kept thinking if I fought, someone might come. Someone would help me." The lump in her throat grew until she thought she might choke. "Someone would save me," she whispered, remembering the hopeless feeling she had had when they took her to the ground. "I kicked him hard, really hard, and he just smiled at me." Her body shuddered and she pressed her forehead to his. "I was scared. So scared." Her confession came out in a whisper because she couldn't speak above that mere thread of sound. She didn't want Vadim in the room with them.

"You are safe now, *sívamet*. I am with you, and I am not going anywhere." He rubbed the nape of her neck, his body rock solid, arms strong as they encircled her. "He didn't control you with his mind?"

Another tremor shook her. "He tried. I thought he'd be furious when he couldn't, when I continued to fight him, but he seemed pleased. Why? Why would that make him happy? He tries now and when he can't he is extremely angry. It doesn't make sense."

He framed her face with his hands. "You're strong. Psychically strong. He needed that in a host body. He hunted you because you could resist his compulsions. Now that he needs to reacquire you, it isn't an asset for him. He wants you back and he can't force you."

She searched his eyes. Those strange, golden eyes—so hot they burned. She brought her hands up and tried to put her fingers around his thick wrists. She felt his pulse beat beneath the pads of her fingers. Strong. Steady. So like him. He should be dead, or at least unconscious in the ground, but he was holding her close, like she mattered to him. Giving her a feeling of safety in a world she knew wasn't safe and never would be again.

"They held me down by pinning me to the ground with long claws, almost like ice picks only much thicker. They stretched my legs so far apart I thought they'd tear them off and then they pierced my arms and legs, driving what felt like spikes through my muscles and bone right into the ground. I was surrounded by them, so many." The shaking was impossible to stop, and Dragomir pulled her close again, holding her against his chest, his arms a sanctuary. "I didn't know anything could hurt like that."

He stroked his hand down her hair, and she wished she'd brushed it, that the tangles were gone and she was beautiful for him. He deserved beautiful. It was a strange desire, when she was reliving the worst moments of her life, but the way it felt, that hand moving through her hair, made her want to look her best for him.

"Vadim knelt down, between my legs, and I thought . . ." She touched her tongue to her top lip, her brain trying to shut down to protect her. "He gripped my body right over my ovaries, squeezing, pressing so hard it felt as if he was trying to shove his fingers through my skin. He kept massaging and then he . . ." She turned her face away from him, a sob escaping. She shoved her fist into her mouth.

He immediately pressed her head into his chest, his hand on the back of her skull, fingers in her scalp, creating a soothing massage. "I would not ask you to relive this moment, Emeline, if it didn't matter. I need to know what he did. I can take these memories from you, or ease them to make the burden lighter, but I must know. I do not ask idly."

God. He was so amazing. So perfect. She was desperate to protect him, but she couldn't stop the compulsion to tell him the entire vile story. It was almost as if he were taking part of the pain, the suffering, onto his shoulders and off hers. She pressed her forehead into his chest, staring down at the rows of muscles his tight shirt revealed. Concentrating on them, on the beauty of his body, she continued.

"He was kneeling between my legs and my clothes were suddenly gone. He'd removed them without touching them. I was already feeling so vulnerable, and that made it all the worse. They were all staring at me, grinning macabrely. He put his hand in me." She stuttered over that, her heart pounding. Her mouth went dry. "It hurt. Really, really hurt. Then it felt like he was moving in me, oily and foul, moving through my body, but he was kneeling right there."

"In the same way a healer does? Going outside his body?"

"Maybe, but the healer completely left his body. I could tell. He was pure spirit, pure energy. Vadim was still in his own body." Somehow talking about it with Dragomir being so matter-of-fact, as if it didn't disgust him that Vadim had touched her body so intimately, the way it disgusted her, made her feel stronger.

"He wouldn't risk his body to other vampires. They are not a loyal lot. He couldn't take that chance. Emeline, you're being so courageous for me. I know this is difficult for you, but it helps me understand."

She nodded, keeping her head tight against him. He was her courage. He gave her that when it had been long gone. "He suddenly became gleeful and he started yelling to the others that now was the moment, to hurry. He gripped my body both inside and out, and one of the vampires, one he called Sergey, brought him this enormous needle. The tube was about ten inches long and filled with a dark liquid. I knew. I knew exactly what it was. The needle was very long. He shoved it into my skin, and it burned like hell. Then he began moving it around as if searching for something. There was so much pain."

She closed her eyes and inhaled, needing the scent of him in her lungs. He filled her with strength. "It seemed to take forever. I was so terrified. I felt sickened by what they did. I am so afraid they might have done the same thing to Amelia. She's just a little girl. Fourteen or fifteen. She doesn't really talk about it and I've tried to get her to open up. I know something terrible happened."

"We need to concentrate on what he did to you. We will help the girl once we know how. What did Vadim do next?"

"I was bleeding everywhere. They ... he ... they licked at the blood on my body and between my legs. It was horrible. Foul. Then Vadim sank his teeth into my neck." She brought her hand up and touched the scars there. "He took so much I was dizzy and hoped he would kill me. I knew he wouldn't, but I thought he might accidentally go too far. He was acting so crazy, like it was the best blood in the world—" She broke off abruptly.

"And then?"

She shook her head. She'd told him the worst. The absolute worst. "He forced me to take his blood. He said it was laced with ancient Carpathian blood to make the child survive. I could feel the parasites wiggling inside me. From that moment to this, I can't sleep or eat, and I hurt with every breath I take."

"It makes no sense that he didn't give you a male child. I would think that for his ego, he would have done such a thing."

She was silent a moment and then she sat up and looked him in the eye. "He thought he did. He isn't the only one able to manipulate the human body."

"You changed the sex of the baby?"

Emeline nodded slowly. "Yes, I changed the sex by fertilizing the egg with female chromosomes. He had no way of knowing. I dreamt so many times of what would happen to all of us down in those tunnels. I knew Vadim would rape and impregnate me. He wanted a male child; it was always there in his mind when I dreamt of him."

"Are you telling me that when he had a long painful needle in you and you were surrounded by vampires, nailed to the dirt naked, you had the presence of mind to make certain the baby was female?"

86

There was both awe and respect in his voice. She shrugged. " I didn't know I would be rescued, but I thought maybe if I was able to get out of there with her, she wouldn't be like him."

"Woman, you are amazing."

The admiration in his voice shocked her. She expected condemnation, not praise. Once again, stupid tears burned behind her eyes. She let him hold her, her ear against his heart so she could hear that steady, reliable rhythm.

"I will need the healer to help me, but we must get rid of the parasites. Vadim will be unable to harm you or the child. As for the child, we must get rid of Vadim's blood. That is what is torturing her. I will need to examine her, Emeline. I will not tell you a lie. If she is evil, I will destroy her. If she is not, she will live and be our child."

5

Dragomir took her breath away. Emeline hadn't known there were men like him in the world. She instinctively put a protective hand over her womb. He placed his hand over hers.

"Know this, *sívamet*—this child will be mine. I will take Vadim's blood from you and exchange it for mine. Eventually, over time, she will be ours. My child and yours. My blood will change her cells, her organs, reshaping and repairing any damage. The healer—"

She shook her head. "Just you. Only you. No one else can get near her. I wouldn't trust them to keep her safe." Just the thought of anyone trying to harm her daughter after what the baby had suffered was enough to make her want to run.

"This will not be easy, Emeline. We need a delicate touch. The healer knows I will kill him if he attempts to harm her. He has the blood of Daratrazanoffs running in his veins so it won't be easy, but I have been on the earth a long, long time. My experience is ... great."

She continued to shake her head. He caught her chin and held it firmly, forcing her to meet those golden eyes. "Emeline, you are my lifemate. I told you the kind of man you are dealing with. This is best for you and for our child. I know you are frightened, but you have to trust me to protect both of you and to know what you need."

"We can wait," she said desperately. "You're not at full strength. You need blood. He'll need blood. We have to wait. Vadim is leaving me alone. He was angry at first but he's quiet now. Go to ground, Dragomir." She didn't know what she would do. Just thinking about leaving him, or him leaving her, was suddenly terrifying. Still, she had that need to make certain he got everything he needed to heal. She didn't know how he was awake and alert.

"Vadim is leaving you alone because his wounds are very severe. It will take him some time to heal. Now is the time for us to do this because we won't have to fight him. He will be asleep in the ground."

"Where you should be," she pointed out, feeling like a broken record.

He brushed his thumb across her bottom lip and a million butterflies took wing in her stomach. All at once she couldn't breathe. He stroked across her lip again and she wanted to moan. Men had kissed her and her body hadn't reacted. She was in pain, suffering from the inside out with the blood and parasites of a vampire running through her veins, making her feel unclean and so exhausted, yet the moment he touched her with such a small gesture, her body came alive.

"I am going to summon him now."

She shook her head but didn't look away from those brilliant eyes. Holding her breath. Fighting not to cry. Trusting him, not just with her life, but the life of her unborn daughter, a baby no one was going to want. *But me,* she murmured to the baby. *No, us. We want you. We'll take care of you and love you.* She kept looking into Dragomir's eyes as she nodded slowly.

His expression changed subtly. His lips softened. So did his eyes. "My woman is extremely courageous. I appreciate that trait in you. Thank you for giving me your trust. It will not be misplaced."

"Maybe you should ask him to bring Blaze. If anyone would help us, it would be her. She can give blood again."

"There is uncertainty in your mind, Emeline. I can hear it in your voice. I would kill a woman if necessary, but I prefer not to. You are correct. We will need a blood supply. Perhaps her lifemate?"

He would kill for her. Kill for their child. She had the feeling he was prepared to call any number of ancients he knew to give them blood. And he would. He would do what he considered best for her. She had seen the way the others talked about Vadim and the possibility that he might be attempting to bring children into the world. They considered it an abomination. She was terrified they would view her daughter that way.

"Can we let Blaze come first, and if she is okay with everything, ask her what she thinks Maksim will do or say and if we can ask him to come?"

He nodded slowly. She had the feeling he wanted one of the others, but he didn't say any more. She felt the energy in the room as candles sprang to life and a combination of healing scents filled the air. The lights went off, plunging the room into darkness so that the red and orange flickering flames were the only relief. The drapes over her windows were heavy, blocking all light from the house. She'd done that deliberately. Her eyes burned in the sun, and she didn't want anyone to see her clearly.

The knock came almost immediately. Emeline took a deep breath, her hands going to her hair. Before she could ask for a minute to try to tame the tangles, he ran his hands over the length, all the way to the ends, smoothing and cleaning her hair so that it shone brightly. A wave of his hand gave her a long thick braid that hung down her back.

"Is that better?"

She nodded. "Thank you, it was really bothering me."

"I need to take a small amount of your blood and give you mine, just so we have the ability to speak telepathically on a path that is intimate between the two of us."

She recoiled instantly, nearly flinging herself out of his arms. "No. Not with the parasites in my blood. No. Absolutely not." She would do anything to protect him. *Anything*.

He studied her expression for a long time and then he nodded. "Stay here while I let him in. While he is in the house, please do anything I ask you without argument. If I say leave the room, do so immediately. I will be at a disadvantage in a fight if I have to worry about where you are." He brushed his lips over her hand again. "Do you understand?"

"Yes." She did. She didn't have to like that he would put himself in jeopardy for her, but there would be no arguing with him. Well, at least no winning the argument.

He set her very gently on her feet and stood, towering over her. She watched him walk to the door. She couldn't tell that he'd been in a major battle just hours before and that it had taken half the night to heal him. Power clung to him and as he moved, it seemed to be distributed throughout the room. Flames flared as he walked by the candles, reaching toward the ceiling and flickering brightly.

Dragomir resisted the urge to glance over his shoulder to look at his woman. Her fear was palpable. He wanted to soothe her, to reassure her, but he had no idea how the healer would react to the child in her womb. *His* child now. His daughter. He should have taken blood from Emeline, but he'd already pushed her very far out of her comfort zone, and he could see it on her face that she would have fought him. She was very resistant to compulsion. The childish sleep spell wouldn't have worked at all on her if she hadn't been so exhausted.

Gary Daratrazanoff stood in the doorway, Blaze one step behind him. Behind her was Maksim, her lifemate. He didn't look happy and Dragomir didn't blame him. Emeline wouldn't be summoned anywhere without her lifemate going to ensure she was safe.

"Thank you for coming. We have great need of a healer. *Great* need. We will need blood. A good amount of it. Maksim, I must ask you to wait outside until Emeline talks to Blaze. It will be difficult for her."

Maksim and Blaze exchanged a long look. He finally nodded his consent. Dragomir stepped back to allow the healer and Blaze entry. Blaze went immediately to Emeline and took both her hands. Gary remained standing beside the door, waiting. He didn't look like a man easily shaken.

Emeline moistened her lips. "I can't go through telling that again, Dragomir. I prefer you do it." She had dropped into her favorite chair again, too shaky to stand.

Dragomir stood behind her, his hands on her shoulders to steady her as he quietly told them what happened to her, including that the same may have happened to the young girl, Amelia. As he told them, he watched them closely, not only for visual cues how they took the news, but feeling for any ripples of hostility. He had subtly spread the receptors through the room, drifting in the air with the scents of the candles.

"You're pregnant? With Vadim's child?" There was horror

92

in Blaze's voice. "Emeline, you should have told me. You shouldn't have tried to do this alone."

"You were able to make certain the child is female?" Gary asked. His first question. He watched Emeline closely, his strange eyes burning over her face.

She nodded. "I didn't think he would want a female as much as a male, and if we got away, he would lose interest. I don't know." She pushed back the few tendrils of hair falling around her face, showing them her exhaustion. "I honestly don't know what I was thinking, I just acted instinctively. Something told me to do it and I did. I could at least control that."

"An extraordinary feat, especially considering Vadim would be using compulsion on you as well as forcing his will physically. Later, when you feel up to it, we will need to know exactly what his delivery system was like. Perhaps you can give us the image in your head. Or at least," he added when she looked horrified, "give it to your lifemate."

Blaze shook her head but before she could deny that Dragomir was Emeline's lifemate, the healer continued. "By now, the parasites will have found every hiding place in her body." Gary switched his attention to Dragomir.

"I'm particularly concerned with the baby's heart," Dragomir said. "If you listen, you can tell that each beat is painful. The child can't last with this kind of torment."

"Are you certain you want the baby to survive, Emeline?" Blaze asked. "She might always be a reminder of what happened to you."

"She wants to live," Emeline said. "We went through it together. We've been through the pain he inflicts together. I won't abandon her."

"I need to look and see what we're dealing with."

"I will enter with you." Dragomir didn't bother to tell the

healer that he was a dead man if he made one move against Emeline or the baby. He reached over Emeline's shoulder and took her hand. "I will reassure the baby."

Emeline's fingers tightened around his. She didn't look at him, and he knew she was holding herself together by a thread. He was proud of her, and by the end of the healing session he would make certain they would form a telepathic bond no one else could hear—including Vadim. When the master vampire woke from his sleep, his favorite punching bag would be out of his reach.

Vadim will fly into a rage when he awakens and cannot hurt her. He will definitely retaliate. The girl must be checked.

You know if he has planted a spy . . .

I am aware. I have told her there is a possibility we cannot save the child, but we are going to try. He was firm on that. His lifemate had fought to save her daughter. He could do no less nor would he allow the healer to do less.

"Blaze, what do you think Maksim's attitude toward Emeline and the child will be? Emeline is very fragile. We need his blood but not his condemnation." Dragomir pinned her with a hard stare, hoping she got the message that retaliation would be swift and brutal.

"Maksim loves Emeline," she said. "Of course he will do anything he can to help." Her chin went up. "Why would you care one way or the other?" It was a challenge.

"Blaze." Emeline sounded horrified. "He saved my life. He saved the children."

"Emeline is my lifemate," he said firmly.

"But that's imposs—" Blaze broke off under his continued stare.

"The night is fading," Gary said. "Forgive me, but I have very ancient blood running in my veins. I cannot yet take the dawn light easily."

Neither could Dragomir, and he was already exhausted. They still had several hours, but they would need every one of them. He wished he could send Emeline to sleep.

Blaze hurried to the door to allow Maksim entry. Clearly she had told him what was going on, because he positioned himself beside the healer to donate blood when needed. Gary didn't wait. He shed his body with astonishing speed, his energy so strong the light was blinding in the muted light of the room. Dragomir followed him.

Emeline's bloodstream was packed with parasites, streaming through her body, hiding in cells and surrounding the baby and placenta. Gary didn't hesitate. He began driving the parasites out of Emeline, leaving the child to Dragomir.

Emeline's blood circulated through the baby, so the healer was right to try to clear her blood first, but the child was in pain and struggling for survival. Dragomir surrounded her with his spirit, sending her reassurance as he moved into the tiny being. Her heart was clogged with the parasites. Every time they moved her body thrashed in pain, her heart hiccupping. Dragomir's light moved to her developing brain. The parasites were fewer there, much fewer, but they were beginning to increase in strength. They washed through and some remained, building a nest.

He attacked them first. *Little one, hold on. We will get rid of these things causing you pain.* He wasn't good with children, but he felt sympathy for her. More than just sympathy, but he thought that might be a reflection of what Emeline felt. He worked carefully, meticulously, driving the parasites from the tiny brain, all the while looking for any anomalies and abnormalities. He took his time, even though he felt urgency to aid the child.

You're being so brave, little one. So very brave. You are like your mother. She was. She was stoic and courageous, just like

95

Emeline. He moved through her brain, over and over, leaving little pieces of himself behind. Her little brain absorbed his spirit, his energy, the bright light that shone from his innermost soul—the light Emeline had given him, so that he became a part of her. Satisfied that her brain was developing normally despite the torment from Vadim and the continual assault of the parasites, once he knew every last one was gone, he moved to her heart.

The heart was so clogged it seemed almost impossible for it to continue beating. It was clear to him that Vadim was setting up to kill the child. Why? He was still trying to acquire Emeline. Was it possible Vadim realized the baby was female and Emeline had managed to thwart him on the sex? Was it possible the baby was resisting him in the same way Emeline was? Whatever the reason, the heart was laboring because Vadim had ordered the parasites to clog the chambers. They scurried away from the light, some clinging in desperation to the walls.

The vile little parasites sickened Dragomir. He found himself pushing emotion away. He hadn't remembered how feeling could be both a blessing and a curse. The longer he worked, the more he felt for the child and the more he didn't want to leave her alone. He had no idea how much time had passed but he was only a third of the way through her heart when light edged along the outside of it.

He wanted to protest as Gary moved through the tiny child. She was barely there, just developing, but the healer had no emotion, no sympathy. He was what Dragomir needed to be. Still, even knowing that, even knowing the child *had* to be vetted to discover whether she was a potential weapon Vadim could use, Dragomir wanted to stop the healer from examining the baby. It took a tremendous amount of discipline to stay still and let the Carpathian do what he needed to protect the others.

We must return to our bodies and be replenished.

The healer's light was dim, his voice the same, but there was a single weary note in it. Dragomir couldn't let himself think about exhaustion. It was wrenching sliding back into skin and bones, the pain overwhelming. It took seconds to block it out, but those seconds were pure hell. He breathed through them, his head down, his body slumping against the back of the couch Emeline rested on.

"Dragomir."

Just his name. Her voice was breathless. Filled with tears. He knew he must look like hell. He'd been maintaining a façade, making certain the repairs the healer had made looked far better than they were. Several of his wounds had been extremely severe, bordering on deadly. He was almost desperate for blood. He needed an ancient. One from the monastery. He had a long way to go before he was finished. Even with Maksim and Blaze donating, it wasn't going to be enough.

He lifted his lashes to stare into the healer's strange eyes. Such a mixture. The blue was light, almost silver. Strange. Disconcerting. Eyes that saw far too much. Gary's skin was so pale it looked almost translucent. The ancient shook his head and turned toward the wrist Maksim held out to him.

"Dragomir?" Blaze held out her wrist.

He took her wrist politely, his mind reaching for the one ancient he'd known as a young man. Afanasiv Balan was close. Others nearby included the triplets—Tomas, Lojos and Mataias—and Nicu Dalca as well. Valentine Zhestokly was gone. Dragomir could recall him, but not soon enough. He had known the men on and off over the centuries, but he wasn't as close to them or as sure of their support as that of those in the monastery. None of those that had been in the monastery with him were sworn to the existing prince.

He needed the men who would have his back no matter what Carpathian politics were at present. Sandu had been in the monastery nearly as long as he'd been there. He had followed Dragomir to the States and was somewhere close by. Where some said Dragomir had ice in his veins, Sandu was thought to have fire.

I have immediate need, Sandu. A war is coming and my lifemate and I are at its center. He sent the call on their private path. He politely closed the laceration on Blaze's wrist, afraid of taking too much blood from her.

"She is holding strong, Emeline," he said aloud, turning his head to look up at her. She looked so scared he took her hand and tugged until she tumbled into his lap. His arms closed around her. "The healer examined her as did I." *Ferro, I have need of you.* Ferro was a question mark, but he was close and his loyalty would be to those of the monastery. Ferro was the tallest of them, with wide shoulders and strange, iron- and rust-colored eyes. He rarely spoke and was a man few ever challenged. Dragomir couldn't recall a single time over the centuries that Ferro had been defeated in battle. *I have found my lifemate and we are in great danger.*

He waited for Gary's verdict, knowing the healer would tell the absolute truth about the child. As much as he wanted to protect Emeline and the baby, he couldn't risk allowing Vadim to gain any foothold in the compound—or have any power over Emeline.

"I examined the child," Gary said.

The moment he spoke, all eyes were on him. Emeline put both hands over her womb. Dragomir covered her hands with his as if they could protect the child from Gary's findings. Emeline leaned her head back against Dragomir's shoulder and pressed her lips against his ear.

"If you cannot save her, be merciful when you do it."

Not the healer. She expected him to be the one to end the child's life. He already thought of the baby as theirs. Emeline's child with him—not Vadim.

"Have no worries," Gary said. "It will take time. You must be patient, but her brain shows no abnormalities. We can continue to check, but both of us examined her carefully. We still have much work to do."

Andor. If you hear me, I have great need of you. There is a war coming. If the healer could drive out the parasites from mother and daughter and replace their blood with that of ancient Carpathians, Vadim would be wild with rage. *I have found my lifemate and we are in great danger. Reach out to Petru and Isai and Benedek.*

"Are you saying you think you can drive out Vadim's servants? You can keep him from hurting her?" Emeline asked.

"We are hoping to keep him from harming either of you." Dragomir looked up at Maksim. "I have sent for ancients, men from the monastery. Their blood is ..." He shrugged. "Should they come, please let them in. They will watch over us while you and your lifemate attend to the young girl."

"Amelia," Emeline supplied. "Blaze, check her closely. Take her away from the men and ask her if they did to her what Vadim did to me. Something terrible happened. She came to talk to me a few times. She claimed she was talking to Charlotte and it helped, but I don't believe her. I don't think she told them the truth. Let her know that Gary and Dragomir can help her. Or Tariq and Gary."

"You think they might have done something like this to her? Impregnated her?" Blaze was clearly shocked. "She's *fourteen*."

"Age wouldn't matter to a vampire," Gary said. "They are incapable of feeling emotion. More than likely, she was terrified. Her terror would have given them the rush they needed.

99

They feed on the fears of others. That's why they torture before they kill. If she was very, very scared, they would have tried just to increase her fear."

Blaze looked at her lifemate. He touched her cheek gently. "Go, *o jelä sielamak*, see to her. The moment the others come, I will aid you."

Blaze nodded once, leaned down to brush the top of Emeline's head with a kiss and hurried out. Maksim looked after her and then sighed. *You realize, Dragomir, that many Carpathians may reject the idea of a child with any DNA from the Malinovs.*

I am very aware. Dragomir knew he sounded grim. He felt grim. He was preparing to go to war with his kind, should they try to harm his lifemate or her child. He would have destroyed the baby if it was in any way evil, but it was innocent. *She is female and has only light in her.* Vadim couldn't twist the child into something he could use as his tool.

Dragomir turned his head to study Gary. The Carpathian looked utterly impassive. He had traveled great distances, something that had to have worn him out, but it didn't show on his face. He had taken part in the battle to drive the vampires out of the compound, yet that didn't show, either. He'd spent hours healing Dragomir and more with Emeline, yet he simply sat waiting.

The Daratrazanoffs were a line of warriors with a connection to the prince's line. They always acted as second-in-command to the prince. They were renowned as fighters and healers both, a natural balance that aided the Carpathian people when one was near. Gary had been human, which meant that to be accepted as a true Carpathian, he would have been taken to the sacred caves where the spirits of the ancestors could be called. To bring him fully into their world, he had to die and be reborn, his soul split in half at that moment of rebirth. Somewhere in the world a child had been born with his other half.

Dragomir couldn't imagine what it would be like to carry the burdens of all those ancients that had come before him. Men battle scarred and weary. Men who had never found their lifemates. It was bad enough to carry one's own burden, but to take on the burdens of so many? He would be the age of the oldest of the Daratrazanoffs. He would know every single skill and fragment of knowledge each of those warriors possessed. That in itself could be a tremendous burden.

"It is time," Gary announced.

Dragomir nodded. He caught Emeline's chin in his hand and turned her head toward him. She'd been burrowing into him, her thin body shivering. At least Vadim wasn't aware of what they were doing or he would have been fighting them, using her pain and suffering against them. Emeline's eyes were wide with shock. With fear. With all the negative emotions a man never wanted to see on his woman's face.

He brushed his mouth over hers. Lightly. Needing to reassure her. His emotions were still a little overwhelming being so new and intense, but with Emeline, he was grateful he felt them. He didn't want her to ever feel the way she was feeling in that moment. He tightened his arms around her and lifted her back up onto the couch.

"It is going to be all right, Emeline. Blaze has accepted the child. So has her lifemate."

"He has reservations," she clarified.

"We are losing the night," Gary said.

Dragomir sent him a warning look. He knew they weren't going to remove all the parasites this night. They would have to face Vadim's wrath the next rising—unless he was injured so badly that he remained asleep. He was going to take the time to reassure his woman.

"It doesn't matter if he had reservations," he said, keeping his voice gentle but firm. "She will be loved and protected."

Gary sighed as if even explaining was difficult. "Ivory Malinov is one of the bravest, strongest women I have ever met. She holds all the light of the world in her soul. She shines brightly and is one of the greatest treasures of the Carpathian people. A fierce warrior and a gentle woman. Ivory is Vadim's sister."

The relief on Emeline's face made Dragomir want to thank the other man, but Gary shed his body fast, leaving just a shell behind, his speed reminding them all that they were racing the dawn. Dragomir followed him, leaving behind his shell, his spirit moving freely, white-hot energy flowing through Emeline's body.

He could see that the healer couldn't possibly remove all the parasites. Vadim had made certain Emeline was flooded with them. He wasn't taking any chances on losing her. *Do you have a plan?* He began burning the wiggling creatures with the intense heat of his spirit. Most fled in front of the light, or tried to hide in cells or along her bones.

We can trap them between us. It won't get all of them in the time we have, but if you find a good place to sleep and heal, tomorrow we can use you as a filter.

Dragomir wasn't certain what that meant. *I'm listening.* His light moved into position opposite the healer's so they could prevent the parasites from escaping.

You will remove her blood. All of it. While you remove it, we will supply her with our blood. The parasites will go into you and you will destroy them by pushing them out of your pores. We'll burn them as they come out. It's a nasty, ugly business and will look like something out of a horror movie. It would be best if you put your woman to sleep. She isn't going to want to see.

Dragomir would wait to talk to Emeline before he made

102

that decision. *I am not certain she is so easy to put to sleep without her consent. If that were the case, the sleeping spell would have worked on her.*

They burned several of the parasites and then moved over a few inches. The creatures had tried to embed themselves in her ribs to keep from being seen or removed.

Vadim is a master vampire, Gary pointed out. *Not just a master vampire, but one that is ancient and has schemed and battled his way to the top of the food chain. In other words, he is extremely powerful. For your woman to resist his compulsions and continue to fight him, she must be very strong. Once ancient blood flows in her veins and she is fully Carpathian, she will be even more so.*

Dragomir waited to hear what Gary meant. Of course Emeline would grow in power. Her gifts would be stronger. *She* would be stronger. Where was the ancient healer going with his observations?

She will be turned when we take her blood and give her ancient blood. So much of it. You must do the initial exchanges. It will not be easy on the child, but as your lifemate grows in power, so will her daughter, Gary said.

There is a child here, Liv, a ten-year-old who Tariq was forced to turn. All Carpathians gathered and they did so joined together beneath the main house where Tariq has brought in rich soil. By all of them joining together, they were able to minimize the girl's pain. It would be best if we do the healing and turning there. We can ask others to aid us.

They had to spend a long time just in that small area. *Are they reproducing?* Dragomir asked.

I believe so. At a rapid rate, too. Vadim took measures to ensure that your woman wouldn't escape him. He wants her, Dragomir, for more than a vessel to carry a child.

He was prepared to kill the baby, Dragomir mused. *Her heart was clogged with the parasites. He would have ordered them away from that organ. There were a few in her brain. If he was monitoring the child as well as Emeline, it is possible Vadim realized it was female and he was planning on retaliating because Emeline managed to outsmart him.*

She did more than that. She ruined his plans. Just for that alone, he should want to kill her. Anyone else would have been dead. You wouldn't have gotten to her in time. Vadim has handicapped himself by letting all of us know he wants your woman alive.

Dragomir didn't like the sound of that, or the speculation in Gary's mind. *What are you planning?*

I am not a strategist, but it occurs to me we have something Vadim wants very, very badly.

Dragomir considered what it would take to end the healer's life. It would happen if he deliberately endangered Emeline to lure Vadim in. *That means he will come at us with everything he has.*

Better to convert her immediately. Her and her daughter.

My daughter. Our daughter. I will saturate the child with my blood.

That is admirable, but you know her brain is already developing and she will always have the ability to think like a Malinov.

The Malinov line is known for intelligence and fierceness in battle—and that includes their women, Dragomir pointed out. *You said so yourself.*

He had grown much weaker. The battle wounds as well as exhaustion were catching up with him. He needed blood and the healing earth. That would leave Emeline unprotected all during the daylight hours. By now, the compound would probably know she was pregnant with Vadim's child. Tariq would be arriving home any moment and he wouldn't be too happy with anyone. His time alone with Charlotte had been important to him. Tariq and Charlotte would have to be underground, but what was to stop him from utilizing his human security force?

We are too close to the dawn. I must get to ground. There was no inflection in Gary's voice, but Dragomir felt the regret.

They had worked steadily, but the more of Vadim's taint they destroyed with their combined light, the more the parasites seemed to reproduce. Dragomir left Emeline's body and went back to his own. To his relief, Andor, Ferro and Sandu were waiting. Maksim was already gone to help Blaze with Amelia.

Andor stepped back away from Gary, his odd, rust-colored eyes assessing the healer. Sandu's eyes burned a deep red through the relentless black. He stepped closer to Gary, a clear threat. Obviously the ancients recognized him from the healer's encounter with Aleksei, a member of their brotherhood.

"Give him blood," Dragomir said, once more collapsing on the floor beside Emeline's couch. "He more than earned it, and he'll work even harder on the next rising."

He betrayed Aleksei, tried to take his lifemate.

There is more to that story than meets the eye. Aleksei is happy. We can ask questions later. The important thing is, I need this man to help me keep Vadim from destroying my lifemate from the inside out. Dragomir pushed memories of the battle and everything that had transpired after, including how Gary had come to his aid, into the minds of the three ancients.

With some reluctance, Sandu extended his wrist. Gary gave him a faint smile, his strange eyes wary, his body, exhausted as he was, on alert. Dragomir couldn't help but admire the man. He was surrounded by four very powerful ancients, but he was ready and willing to take them on if they pushed it.

Dragomir laid his head back against the couch just as Emeline slid to the floor, drawing up her knees, leaning

105

against him. She felt soft and warm, while he was cold, his temperature telling him he'd been out of his body too long. He reached with one hand to clasp hers, enveloping her small hand in his and bringing it against his chest.

"You were gone so long. I was worried about you."

She didn't ask if they had been successful, only said that she was worried for him. He couldn't remember a time someone had worried for him. He tucked her hand over his heart and took the wrist Ferro practically forced against his lips. It was difficult not to gulp the ancient blood. The moment he took it in, it began to work its magic, spreading through him quickly, infusing his cells and organs with rich, life-giving energy. He felt power rushing through him, filling him again when he'd been so spent.

The moment Gary had taken his fill from Sandu, he rose. "I will return at sunset. We should be ready for a fight, Dragomir."

"A fight?" Emeline echoed. "What does that mean?"

Dragomir didn't like that she sounded frightened. He closed the laceration on Ferro's wrist and put his arm around Emeline. "Thank you, healer. We will be ready."

Gary gave an old-world, slight bow and was gone, shimmering one moment and then disappearing, leaving Dragomir alone with his woman and three of the men he'd spent years locked away with, men so dangerous they *had* to be locked away in order to keep the world safe.

"Thank you for coming. Emeline, my friends—brothers, really—Sandu, Ferro and Andor. These are men you can always rely on. Always. They will guard you and have your back. We must go to ground, and we will do so close to you . . ."

She made a sound, and he felt the tremor go through her body, but she nodded, not voicing her fear that once she was without his protection, if there was objection to the child, Tariq could send his security force to remove her.

"Before we go to ground, we will weave a safeguard that is impenetrable, keeping everyone out. They will not be able to get into the house, or harm your home in any way. It also means you cannot leave. I don't want you to be afraid if you must remain in the house. It is for your protection and also the protection of the child. The house will not allow even the children or your women friends inside. We cannot take chances with the baby."

Emeline dropped her free hand to her cover her womb.

"You will be safe. We will keep you safe." He made the declaration firmly, in the way he stated an absolute. She couldn't help but hear the resolution in his voice. He stood, flowing to his feet, taking her with him, and setting her aside. Each of the men faced a different direction and they began to weave the safeguards no man alive other than those that had been in the monastery had a chance of getting through. When they were satisfied that the protections they'd woven together were strong, the three ancients bowed as Gary had, ready to take their leave.

For the first time, Emeline looked up at the three men. "Thank you for coming. I really appreciate it."

It was Sandu who inclined his head, and then the three men disappeared, retreating as the sun began to rise.

"You still do not fully believe we are lifemates, Emeline, but this day will prove to you that we are. It will be difficult for you not to be able to reach me when needed, but know I am close and will come to you," Dragomir said. "Try to sleep as much as you can."

She gave him a faint, you-are-a-little-nuts-but-I-like-you-anyway kind of a smile.

"I'm going to give you blood."

She recoiled involuntarily, shaking her head and wrapping her arms around her middle for protection.

He couldn't let her get away with it as much as his heart wanted to. "You need my blood, and so does the child, *sívamet*."

She swallowed hard and then moistened her lips with the tip of her tongue. "What does that mean? What you call me? *Sívamet*. What does that mean?"

"My heart. You are my heart."

She looked at him a long time, staring into his eyes, searching for something. He didn't hurry her, although he felt the burning rays of the sun on his skin, when they weren't penetrating the heavy drapes. She nodded slowly, evidently finding whatever she had been looking for.

"I like that. I shouldn't encourage you, Dragomir, but I like that someone thinks I'm their heart."

"Do you want me to aid you? To make it easier?"

Again she nodded slowly, never taking her eyes from his. He reached for her, circling her wrist with his fingers, a shackle, a protection. Very gently, he pulled her to him and leaned down to brush kisses down the side of her face. The corner of her eye. Her cheekbone. He loved that line. The corner of her mouth. He loved her mouth. The shape. The way her bottom lip curved and her top lip formed a perfect little bow.

She shivered in his arms, relaxing into him. He kissed his way along her ear. That perfect little shell he found intriguing. His tongue made a little foray, tracing the lines there. That earned him another shiver, and her body melted into his. The feel of her in his arms was unlike anything he had ever known. She fit. She belonged.

His body came to life, a hard, painful pleasure that took him by surprise. Need flowed through his bloodstream, a hot, urgent demand centering in his groin. It was a beautiful, perfect moment, one he would never forget and would treasure for all the rest of his time. Emeline in his arms, holding her against him while she melted into him, making them one.

He kissed his way down her throat, his lips tasting her soft skin, finding her pulse beating, beckoning. His own pulse quickened in response. Matching hers. Finding that exact rhythm. It was so beautiful. Moment by moment. Each brush of his mouth. His teeth reacted, lengthening while his body hardened more, becoming a savage ache. Now his blood thundered in his ears and pounded in his cock. Deliberately, he scraped his teeth back and forth against her skin right over that sweet sound of her heart so it beat into his mouth.

She gasped. Moaned softly. Music he'd never heard but found he loved. He needed more. He scraped his teeth a second time. She moaned again and moved restlessly against him, pressing her lower body into him. Her hips rocked subtly so that her belly rubbed enticingly over his thick cock. The action sent streaks of lightning ripping through the waves of heat in his bloodstream.

He sank his teeth deep. She cried out. Arched into him. Her breasts and mound rubbed against his body until he thought he might go mad with sheer pleasure. Her blood tasted exquisite. He knew he would ingest the parasites, but the moment he was out of her sight, he could rid his body of them. He could only think about her taste, an aphrodisiac, an addiction he would never be rid of. He had to be careful not to take too much. She would be alone in the house without him. Without anyone. He didn't like it, but it was the safest way possible for her until she was fully in his world.

He lifted his head reluctantly and closed the wound with his tongue. He kissed his way around her throat, back up to her chin, and then brushed his lips over her mouth. That perfect mouth he found impossible to ignore. It was fast becoming his obsession. He thought about it far too much.

"That didn't hurt," she whispered against his chest. "It felt ... erotic. Intimate. Beautiful."

"*Te avio päläfertiilam*. You are my lifemate, Emeline," he whispered, opening his shirt. He lengthened one fingernail and opened a line across his chest. "My blood is for you. It will make you stronger. It will bring the baby one step closer to being fully my child. Drink."

She leaned her head toward his chest before he gave her the command to distance herself from what she was doing. For one moment, he hit a barrier of some kind, a natural protection she had in her brain. He felt her indecision and then she gave him the gift of her trust. The barrier tumbled down, and her lips were on his skin. Soft. So soft. The whisper of movement was nearly his undoing.

He hadn't expected the way his body would react to her mouth on his skin. Her tongue slid along that seam where ruby drops of his blood welled up. His body went up in flames. Electricity danced over him, so that little sparks seemed to go off in his brain. His cock jerked with urgent need. The world dropped away until there was only the two of them, locked together, her mouth taking from him what she needed, her body edgy, impatient to be with his, his arms holding her to him, one hand cradling the back of her head. The moment was etched into his brain.

So many firsts. All perfection. All sensation. The beauty of having a lifemate was beyond anything he had imagined in all the hundreds of years he had sought her. He thought about how he had decided to go back to the monastery because the modern world and the women in it had seemed beyond his reach, yet here she was in his arms, better than any fantasy he had ever imagined. He knew he had to share that knowledge with the others so they didn't make the mistake he almost made.

Gently he stopped her feeding, catching her chin in his hand and lifting her face so he could take her mouth, kissing her, removing all signs of blood from her lips and teeth. She came out of the dreamlike state he'd put her in, kissing him back a little tentatively. He didn't push it further, although every cell in his body screamed at him to do so.

"I have to leave you," he murmured, his mouth against her throat.

"I know. I don't want you to go, but I know you have to. Dragomir, thank you for fighting for me. You are the most incredible man."

"Thank you for just existing, Emeline. I am not dead. If you have need of me, reach for me in your mind. Our exchange ties us together. I will hear you and answer if at all possible. Don't try to leave, and don't be beguiled by anyone calling to you. Not the children and not your friends. Someone cracked open the doors to allow Vadim in. It wasn't just Liv, although she played a huge part in the conspiracy. We don't know who we can trust."

She nodded, clinging to him. "Be safe, Dragomir."

"I will be close," he promised. It was difficult to leave her. Her eyes swam with tears, which made his heart hurt, but he had no choice. The sun was climbing and his skin was burning. He brushed one more kiss along her cheek and was gone.

6

E meline stared out the window, counting the minutes until the sun set. It had been the longest day of her life. The worst. She had tried to sleep, but she couldn't keep her mind still. Over and over her brain insisted on tricking her, telling her that Dragomir was dead. He lay in the earth, the soil over him, covering his terrible wounds, wounds he hadn't fully taken care of because of her. He'd spent so much time trying to save her, in the end he'd sacrificed his life.

She didn't understand what was happening to her. She'd never paid serious attention to any man. Now she couldn't think about anything or anyone else. She'd spent a good deal of time pacing. Then she showered and washed her hair. She was weak enough that she had to sit twice, but she was determined that when next she saw him, her hair wouldn't be a tangled, horrible mess. It was a little shocking to run a comb through her hair after washing it and have not one tangle snag the wide teeth. Dragomir. He had done that for her.

Three times during the day, she had found herself with tears streaming down her face. She needed to touch him. To see him. She was desperate for any kind of contact with him.

Outside, the play yard was silent. The dragons were back on guard, five of them, made of stone, standing vigil, but the children were nowhere in sight. A breeze kicked up leaves and swirled them in the air.

Genevieve had knocked, and then called her on her cell when Emeline hadn't opened the door. She was shocked that Emeline was pregnant and wanted to know how to help. Emeline didn't know how she could. Genevieve couldn't bring Dragomir to her. She followed his orders and didn't allow anyone in.

She spent part of the day trying to find food or drink that her stomach could handle, but she'd been sick from the time Vadim had taken her prisoner, and that only seemed worse now. She could barely manage to sip water and keep that down. Mostly, if she did more than wet her parched mouth, she vomited.

She rocked back and forth, trying to soothe herself. The baby had been very quiet, with very little movement, as if she were sleeping right along with Dragomir. She rubbed her stomach, happy that her daughter was finally comfortable enough to sleep. She knew eventually the parasites would attack her, but Vadim hadn't issued that order, so they left the baby alone. That was Dragomir, too. He'd done that.

She tried to rest, but she couldn't lay down or relax. She closed her eyes and reached for him, giving in to need and the sorrow building in her. She had always lived her life on her own terms, and it was difficult to need another—but she did, desperately.

Dragomir. I don't want to disturb your sleep, but I can't seem to function without knowing you're alive and well. I know it sounds stupid when it's only another hour until sunset, but I can't relax. She waited, her heart in her throat. Her body was still, her lungs refusing to draw in air until they burned.

I am here, close. Right beneath you. There is a chamber beneath the house. Tariq must have put them in for safety reasons. This one is quite large and runs nearly the entire length of your home.

She closed her eyes, drawing in air as relief flooded her. He was alive. Close. Right beneath her. She sank down onto the floor, and ran her hand over the hardwood. She loved the gorgeous pattern, a huge moon in the center, with stars scattered around the room, formed by beautifully cut wood. She would change the furniture if she lived there permanently. She'd begun to think of the house as hers. It was the first real home she'd had in her life. Blaze's father had sent her to France when there was trouble, but she returned when she found out he'd been murdered. In France, she'd had a tiny apartment, but no one was there, not even Blaze, so she had been very lonely.

Has the soil helped?

Yes. The healer is extremely powerful. I doubt I could have aided you and the baby without him.

You could have died, Dragomir. Just acknowledging that truth made her heart skip a beat and then begin to pound. *He saved your life. You should have gone to ground immediately, and you know it. Your wounds were horrendous.*

Then I am more than grateful to him. Every minute I am alive is a minute I can spend in your company. Are you ready to acknowledge that I am your lifemate?

There was faint humor in his voice. She wasn't feeling the least bit amused. "No. I think you're the best man I've ever met in my life, and that's saying something because I loved

114

Blaze's father and thought he was until I met you. I think you're trying to save me from myself and from everyone else."

Kislány kuŋenak minan, you are going to continue to deny the truth, but it doesn't matter. I am your lifemate and I will watch over you no matter what. Did you rest?

For a moment, she considered hedging, but she didn't want to lie to him. She'd done enough of that by not telling him she was pregnant from the moment she first saw him. *No, it was a difficult day. If you had known I was pregnant with Vadim's child, would you still have rescued me?* She chewed on her lower lip, wishing she hadn't asked, terrified of the answer. She was fairly certain she would hear the truth. She was beginning to hear nuances in voices.

I am your lifemate, Emeline. I will always come for you, no matter the circumstances. If you believe nothing else, believe that. When she didn't respond, he said, *My friend Aleksei is lifemate to a woman who was begging another man to take her away with him. Now Aleksei and his lifemate are together and happy.*

Emeline frowned. *Aleksei's lifemate was in love with another man? That seems . . . wrong. What were the circumstances?* She was genuinely interested, but even more, she wanted to keep him talking.

I do not know much, only that the woman had not been born Carpathian as we all had believed and that the healer who aided me was the other man. He was human also at one time. He was subdued by the prince of the Carpathian people and Gregori, the prince's second-in-command. It took them both to keep him restrained.

How sad for everyone.

There was silence for a moment. *I understand that you would have sympathy for this man, but I would not want you to develop feelings for him.*

She frowned, tracing a pattern onto the hardwood floor

115

with her finger. *I don't think you have anything to worry about. He makes me uneasy.*

What is it about him that makes you uncomfortable?

She realized she was writing Dragomir's name on the floor over and over. *He looks at me as if he knows every secret I have or will ever have. I think he knows about the loaves of bread I stole from my aunt's store when I was eight.*

You stole bread?

I was starving. I tried to clean houses, but my aunt was kind of a jerk and she didn't really want me in her house. She said I could sweep the floor in the store and clean all the glass cases. Unfortunately, she didn't come to pay me or give me food, so I took two loaves of bread. Nothing has ever tasted so good.

There was a long silence again, so long Emeline could hear her heart beginning to beat too fast. He had to keep talking to her. She needed the sound of his voice to ground her. She traced the letters of his name on the floor three times before he spoke.

Why didn't your aunt come for you?

She sagged a little with relief. *She drank a lot. By that I mean every single night, an entire large bottle of vodka. I don't think she remembered me.*

Is she still alive?

There was a bite to his voice. A hint of menace that made her shiver. She moved back against the couch where he had sat the morning before. *No. She died fairly young. Her liver didn't hold up.*

How very fortunate for her. This time there was no mistaking the threat. *What happened to you? Who took you in?*

She drew up her knees and circled them with her arms, hugging herself. *No one. I was a street kid like Danny, Amelia, Liv and Bella. Maybe that's why I had to save them. And the baby.* She put her hand over her stomach protectively. *I never*

116

had a home or brothers and sisters. Well, I had Blaze. She was always good to me. She let me climb in her bedroom window and sleep there whenever I wanted to. Her father let me stay and paid for classes and schooling. Even dance. He was a good man.

I will be rising soon, Emeline, Dragomir said, *and then we will remove the remaining parasites from you and the baby. What we are going to do will seem scary. You must trust me implicitly. I know that is asking a lot when you barely know me, but I swear to you, I will keep you safe and do what is best for you and the baby.*

She wanted one night without scary. One night to just breathe. She'd told the truth about being Vadim's lifemate and about carrying her child, and so far, no one had thrown her out of the compound. They knew the worst. Maybe they would ask her to leave, but she knew that Dragomir would go with her. She wouldn't go alone.

We have to do this tonight? But she knew they did. She was in bad shape. She couldn't eat or sleep. He would take one look at her and know.

Yes. Vadim will fight for you. We must get every single one of his tormenters out of you and the baby. It will take all of us to turn you without pain so the baby will survive.

Turn me? Like Charlotte and Blaze. She bit her lip hard. She knew she was well on her way. She probably was more vampire or Carpathian than human. *The baby, Dragomir. She's suffered enough. Blaze and Charlotte told me it can be extremely painful.*

Vadim's parasites had flooded her heart. He was going to kill her. I do not understand his plan for you or why he would attack the child he put in you, but he will make another attempt on her life if we don't do this.

She frowned, trying to piece together just why the master vampire would go to such great lengths to impregnate her and then decide to terminate the pregnancy. *That doesn't make*

117

sense at all. She glanced out the window and watched the sun dip down toward the horizon. *The sun is beginning to set.* She couldn't keep happiness from her mind and knew he saw it. It didn't matter. He would be there soon.

I must feed and then I will be right there. Tariq is back. I will meet with him first. We won't have much time. I need your consent, Emeline, to speak on your behalf and make decisions. I will tell you what the plan is as we make it.

I should face him. Apologize for not telling him the truth and for bringing the battle right into his compound.

Those children let in evil so they could play.

She winced at the hard, unyielding voice. He was angry. He might not show it, but deep down, he was. She *felt* it in his mind. *Dragomir.*

Give me a few minutes.

She dropped her head into her hand and took a deep breath, wishing he was there with her now. Wishing she really was his lifemate. But she knew better. Street children like her didn't get the gorgeous, courageous man, the sweet one, the one who would take on a baby along with its mother. No, they got the villain, the monster. And she got the worst monster on earth.

"But not you, baby," she whispered aloud. "You're going to be loved. Very, very loved."

Dragomir read her thoughts, because now that he was in her mind, he couldn't quite let go. He wanted to go to Emeline and reassure her, to find a way to make her see that he was her lifemate, that he would never leave her, but there was too little time. He switched from his intimate path with his lifemate to the more common path of the Carpathian people. *Tariq, I must meet with you immediately. I am hunting for sustenance, but will return in a few minutes.*

Come to the house.

118

Dragomir left the compound. Sandu, Ferro and Andor fell in with him, taking to the sky as birds. They had hunted many times together, long before they ever made the decision to go into the monastery. Their flight took them a distance from where they slept. It was ingrained in them to hunt away from the places they frequented.

Deep within the bird, Dragomir puzzled out the strange emotion bothering him. Hurt. Emotional hurt. He knew physical pain, but he had never experienced emotional pain until his lifemate had restored feeling in him. The pain of destroying friends and loved ones ran deep, holes in his soul he knew he could never repair. Intellectually, one might say the person he loved had died when they'd made the choice to turn vampire, but that didn't stop the pain of having to terminate the corrupted shells of those who had once been friends.

This hurt was different. His lifemate refused to believe she was his. Even after tying them together—and she felt the effects, she just didn't recognize them—she wouldn't believe it. Why? He turned that over and over in his mind as the four of them circled above a back road where three men dressed in business suits had parked their cars. Clearly they waited for someone else. With the advanced technology of cameras on cell phones and seemingly everywhere, the Carpathians had to coordinate their confrontation. The blitz had to be fast and simultaneous, all keeping their prey from using cell phones, cameras or any technology. They simply made certain none of them could be seen from the road, not the hunters and not the prey.

Three dropped down, Sandu, Andor and Dragomir, while Ferro kept watch above, staying in the form of a bird. They each picked their prey, materialized behind them and took control of their minds. Dragomir sank his teeth into the neck, taking in the life-giving fluid. He knew he needed more time beneath the ground to fully heal, but that would have to come later. He was about to engage in the battle of his life, and this time he had something to lose.

Emeline. His woman. Had she been born Carpathian she would have recognized all the ties between them. Those differences she felt would have been instantly attributed to their bond. But she wasn't Carpathian. She had been born human. She might know of their world, but she had never experienced it. She'd never had a family. She'd been thrown away by her relatives.

She had thought she was sacrificing her life for the children in that underground city Vadim had created, but instead, he had other plans for her. That had blindsided her. Her precog dreams only took her so far and the outcomes weren't always what she thought they would be. That was probably why she didn't trust that her bond with Dragomir was real. She didn't believe because she couldn't let herself believe. He would have to put aside hurt feelings and get her there. She needed kindness. She needed to be cherished. She needed to know he would always be there for her. He would find out the things that mattered to her and give them to her.

Politely, he closed the wound on his prey's neck and helped him to the ground so that the man sat against his car. Then Dragomir took to the sky. Minutes later, they found Ferro his quarry then headed back to the compound.

Tariq Asenguard was a good man. More, he was an intelligent one. Others had thought him strange with his interest in humans, yet he had assimilated into the human world far better than most. He used their technology and began researching ways to advance it. He had amassed a fortune, bought land and established a business. He had a way of blurring facial recognition so anyone checking could never quite identify him.

Tariq had shared his knowledge with the ancients, transferring all he'd learned about the advances made while the ancients had been locked away from the world. Not only was he intelligent, he was generous. His lifemate had been human, and she seemed as generous as her man. Perhaps talking to her might help ... if they both agreed to allow Emeline and the baby to remain. The compound was the safest place for her. Tariq had been building up the number of hunters, and with that came the protection of many.

Vadim had elected to stay in the area when common sense and his centuries of experience should have urged him to leave. Was Emeline really that important to him? The child wasn't the reason he kept trying to get her back. He had directed the parasites to the baby's heart, knowing they would eventually kill it. So, what made him so determined to recapture Emeline that he would not only remain in a territory inhabited by so many ancient Carpathian hunters, but also openly attack their compound?

Tariq waited just outside the door to his home, Maksim on one side of him, Mataias and Lojos on the other. That meant Tomas was somewhere near. Dragomir would bet his life that Afanasiv Balan, one of the ancients who had briefly stayed in the monastery, was also close. Afanasiv had been a good friend of Tariq's growing up and they had remained close, yet he was a member of the brotherhood.

"*Én jutta félet és ekämet*," Tariq greeted in their ancient language, stepping forward to clasp Dragomir's forearms in the way of warriors.

Friend and brother. That greeting told Dragomir everything he needed to know. Tariq would have chosen another salutation if he was opposed to having Emeline in his compound.

"Bur tule ekämet kuntamak." Well met, brother-kin, was Dragomir's choice of greeting.

"Thank you for saving the children," Tariq said, stepping back. "They are confined for the moment until we decide what to do about the situation." While he spoke, his sharp gaze moved over Dragomir, assessing the damage to him. "Tell me what you need."

"We must drive the rest of the parasites out of my lifemate and the child. Vadim flooded her with them and they torment her continually. She was able to direct the fertilization and carries a girl. I do not know if Vadim became aware of that and chose to kill the child, but he was close to his goal. He will fight us for her. I must convert Emeline as soon as we rid her body of his parasites, and that means the child will go through the conversion as well. They cannot feel pain or the baby will be lost."

"You and the healer vouch for this child?"

"We examined her carefully. She is female and therefore cannot hold darkness. She will have my blood and her developing organs will be from me. Essentially, she'll be my child, but there will always be that part of her that is Malinov. They are highly intelligent and fierce fighters. She will be an asset to our world."

He felt like he was fighting for his child in that moment. The baby had gone from being Emeline's child and therefore his responsibility, to being just plain his. His child. *Theirs.*

Tariq nodded without hesitation. "I gathered the richest soil I could find and brought it back little by little. It lies deep beneath this house. Bring her there, and we will all gather to aid you. We are still learning, but we seem to be able to do so much better controlling pain and convulsions when we're together."

"Will the others welcome us here?" Dragomir was blunt. "If not, after she is converted, I will take her and we will go."

"As long as the compound is mine, she will always be welcome here," Tariq said. "Naturally there are some with concerns, but we refuse to give anyone up to Vadim, not the child and certainly not Emeline. Your word and the word of the healer are good enough for us." He indicated Maksim.

Dragomir knew Maksim had established the nightclubs and compounds with Tariq, but clearly Tariq was the acknowledged leader.

Dragomir. There was panic in Emeline's voice. *He is attacking us. The baby . . .*

He whirled and took the distance between the houses, half flying, half running. Sandu, Andor and Ferro flanked him instantly.

Come to me, sívamet. I am right outside. He gained the porch.

She flung open the door, doubled over, her eyes wide with pain and shock, her breath coming in ragged pants. She alternated between putting her hands over her ears and over her womb. "He's talking to me. Taunting me. Telling me what he's going to do to me." All color had leeched from her face. She swayed there a moment and then her knees buckled.

Dragomir swept her up in his arms before she had a chance to fall. Cradling her close, her pushed his mind into hers. At once, he encountered that barrier that partially shielded her from commands and compulsions. *Let me in fully, Emeline.*

I can't. He will get in.

Dragomir heard the echo of Vadim's harsh laughter. The sound was ugly, a jarring note that hurt the ears. His voice, when he spoke, was just as grating. *I am already in. I am her lifemate, and you cannot keep me out as much as you try. You cannot drive me out. You can lie, give her blood, try to confuse her, but my claim is first and she is mine.*

123

Aloud, he said, "Emeline. *Sívamet.* You are my heart and soul. I need you to trust me. We knew he was going to fight us. That was a given. Let me in fully." He kept his voice calm and soothing.

She turned her face against his chest, both hands gripping his shirt, her eyes closed tight. "He said he would hurt you. He told me the terrible things he would do to you. Because of me." Her body shuddered and then shivered over and over in pain.

Dragomir carried her over to Tariq's home. The Carpathian held open the door and waved him inside. The ancients followed. Tariq led the way through the hall and downstairs to a basement filled with woodworking projects, including carousel horses. They crossed to a section of floor Tariq opened with a wave of his hand. Below, Carpathians had gathered, several men and a couple of women.

Cement borders surrounded the huge healing grounds. Just beyond the cement were the wooden boards cleverly constructed to make up the walls beneath the basement of the house, yet between every so many support beams were cracks to allow the moonlight in. Above the grounds were raised platforms surrounding them so the Carpathian people could gather for ceremonies.

The soil gleamed, a dark, rich loam. It glittered with minerals from the light provided by the flickering flames of scented candles. Dragomir searched the surrounding platforms until he spotted Blaze. He knew exactly who had set everything in motion and he gave her a nod of his head to acknowledge her. She stood beside Charlotte, Tariq's lifemate, and she looked frightened. He understood even more than she did the enormity of what they were attempting as he had seen the overwhelming number of parasites in Emeline's blood.

Emeline cried out and twisted in his arms. Dragomir's

brows drew sharply together. Her pain was increasing. Vadim's parasites were at work, torturing her, and he couldn't take it. Not one more minute of her indecision when he knew, ultimately, they had to stop Vadim now.

"I am no longer asking, Emeline. I demand that you allow me into your mind." He could push past the barrier but it would cause her pain, more than she was already in. He never wanted to be a part of her suffering, even if it was to save her from the torments of Vadim, but he would if necessary. Modern rules didn't always make sense to him. She suffered. He could stop it.

Emeline lifted her head, her eyes drowning in pain and despair. She searched his face, then nodded, and that fast the shield went down in her mind. The moment she gave him full access, he built a defense so strong in her mind that Vadim's voice couldn't possibly penetrate to her.

He also did his best to protect her from the pain of the parasites biting her bones and scoring wounds in her organs as they bored holes and wiggled inside to gnaw with their teeth. So many were back; they had reproduced during the day in anticipation of their master's commands.

Dragomir floated to the expanse of deep, rich soil below them. Gary was already there. Dragomir sank down, placing Emeline beside him. Instantly the healer shed his body and entered Emeline's. Dragomir brushed kisses across her eyelids and then followed the healer.

The Carpathians began a soft chant, the lesser healing chant, and the lullaby for unborn babies.

Tumtesz o wäke ku pitasz belső. Feel the strength you hold inside.
Hiszasz sívadet. Én olenam gæidnod. Trust your heart.
I'll be your guide.

Sas csecsemőm, kuňasz. Hush, my baby, close your eyes.
Rauho jone ted. Peace will come to you.
Tumtesz o sívdobbanás ku olen lamt3ad belső. Feel the
    rhythm deep inside.
Gond-kumpadek ku kim te. Waves of love that
    cover you.
Pesänak te, asti o jüti, kidüsz. Protect, until the
    night, you rise.

The song was sung to unborn infants, created when so many had been lost. Dragomir loved the beauty of it, that all the Carpathians would sing to their child to try to save its life.

I have a special death planned for you, Dragomir. One that will take a century. You will feed us. Feed my children. You will be nothing but fodder for those stronger and better than you.

There was something both soothing and incongruous about hearing the lullaby at the same time as the jarring, ugly voice of Vadim's taunting. Dragomir didn't bother responding to his threats. The vampire had no idea what they planned, and he wasn't about to tip him off.

Dragomir sent his spirit to examine Emeline's brain first. There were no parasites, which gave him a measure of reassurance. Vadim wasn't taking the chance of damaging her. Of course, once he knew for certain he was losing her, he would likely turn on her and do everything in his power to kill her. To help protect her from that possibility, Dragomir built a heavy shield around her brain, one he was certain the parasites couldn't penetrate. He did the same with her heart and lungs, then her ovaries and womb. Gary was doing the same for the baby, once he pushed the parasites from her little body, back into Emeline's.

It is time, Gary said, when they had completed building their shields.

Daratrazanoff? Vadim made the name sound like a curse. *Do you think you possibly can take on a Malinov and win?*

Gary made no reply. Dragomir admired him even more for ignoring the master vampire as if he were a mere nuisance, far beneath his notice. The two withdrew from Emeline's body and each returned to his own.

"I'm going to take your blood now, Emeline," Dragomir said gently. "Just like when we were alone. I will be removing quite a lot of it, which means your blood will have to be replaced. Sandu, Andor and Ferro will take turns giving you blood."

She recoiled, shaking her head. "I don't think I can do that."

"I can aid you," Dragomir said. "If we are going to save the baby and you from Vadim, this is the only way. Once I take your blood, I cannot give you blood. Not at first. I'm the filter. I will ingest the parasites ... "

"No. Absolutely not." She scrambled to her feet. "You are not going to take his vile, poisonous worms into your body."

He reached out and caught her wrist. Gently. So gently. His thumb slid over the back of her hand in a soothing caress. "I did so before I left you at sunrise this morning, *sívamet*. They are already inside me. I can rid my body of them a little at a time, and that's what we're going to do. The danger is that you will begin to convert before we are ready. If you have any way to hold out, please do so." As he spoke he drew her back to him. Patiently. Slowly. Inexorably.

"I don't want this for you," she protested in a whisper of despair.

"Of course you don't." He pulled her down to his lap once more. "I'm going to distance you from all of this so it is easier on you. Gary will send his spirit back inside you and begin destroying the parasites. He'll be there when they make a concentrated attack on the baby." When she started to protest again, his voice turned stern. "Emeline, you promised to trust me."

She took a deep breath and nodded. Immediately he wrapped her in his arms, unwilling to give her more time to worry or object. Gary shed his body and once more entered hers. Dragomir sank his teeth in her neck as he distanced her from the action. Even as the parasites in her blood burned his tongue and throat, her taste was exquisite. Vadim couldn't corrupt that. Dragomir stayed anchored in her mind, shielding her as Vadim shrieked his rage and ordered his creatures to attack.

Gary countered, burning large groups of the parasites as they swarmed toward her heart. Dragomir drank down her blood, drawing as many of the parasites into himself as he could. The flesh inside his throat and mouth blistered as the foul microorganisms stung and bit at him in a frenzy. Their poison spread through his bloodstream, racing though his veins and saturating his cells. His muscles seized. His organs cramped, sending pain lancing through his body.

The parasites spread to every part of his body, and now they were systematically targeting his own vital organs. And still he drank down Emeline's blood, willing Vadim's foul creatures to enter his body in order to spare her. His breath grew labored, his heart slammed against his chest, a hoarse shout lodged itself at the back of his throat, held back only by his will.

Enough. Get rid of them, Gary ordered.

Beating back the horrendous pain, Dragomir slid his tongue across his lifemate's skin, closing the small wounds left by his bite. He set her from him and strode to the edge of the healing grounds where the cement wall was the thickest. He forced the worms from his blood, pushing them through his pores. They burned and bit, fighting to attack him, to kill him, Vadim's commands making them vicious. He made certain they dropped on the cement slab. Andor called down the lightning to incinerate the creatures, bringing it through the cracks in the wooden wall Tariq had designed for just such an occasion.

Dragomir took a deep breath, pausing to gather his strength and shore up his inner defenses before turning back to Emeline. Andor followed, staying close.

Sandu met him halfway there and extended his wrist. "That healer is thorough."

Dragomir sent him a look, something between a reprimand and admiration. "You're monitoring the healer? How?"

"We sent a little spy in. This is your daughter. Your woman. We don't know much about him other than he tried to take Aleksei's woman."

"Unforgiving just a little bit?" Dragomir prodded. Granted, he'd been more than a little suspicious of Gary himself until the healer had worked so hard to save the lives of Emeline and all the others who'd fended off Vadim's earlier attack.

"O jelä peje teräd," Sandu said. "Take the blood and hurry."

Dragomir did as the ancient suggested, practically inhaling the sustenance. Sandu's blood was like a punch of sheer power, filling him with strength. He murmured his thanks and sank down beside Emeline.

She slipped her hand into his, surprising him. In spite of the shield he'd put around her to distance her from what was taking place, she was still very much aware. "Are you all right?"

"Better than all right." He wrapped his arms around her again and sank his teeth in a second time.

This time the parasites were waiting for him, rushing to

attack, flooding his bloodstream and heading directly toward his heart.

Andor, I have need. He didn't stop ingesting her blood; instead, he took more, doing everything he could to draw the microorganisms out of Emeline and into him.

Andor shed his body and entered Dragomir's. He moved instantly to guard Dragomir's heart, using the white-hot blast of energy to burn as many parasites as he could. The vile things ran from the light. Some tried moving around it, attacking Dragomir's heart from every direction. Andor was fast, blasting them in a long semicircle, but there were so many of them. Dozens found purchase and began burrowing through the outer layers of heart muscle.

Enough, Dragomir. You need to purge them before they manage to clog your heart, Gary said. *I need blood. The moment I leave they will attack the child. They are trying every way they can to get around me, even sacrificing themselves so others can fling themselves at her heart.*

Ferro, Dragomir directed. *You're up.*

Ferro shed his body without hesitation and entered Emeline's. The healer was back, and this time he sagged to the ground, clearly worn from his fight to keep the parasites off the baby. The fact that Gary was weak told Dragomir time was passing. He closed the small punctures on Emeline's throat and took a step. The parasites attacked, coming at every organ, using teeth and spitting acid in every direction. He stumbled, his insides burning. Pain burst through him with every bite the parasites took.

He was an ancient, familiar with pain and suffering in all its forms, but even against his millennia of experience, this was sheer agony. He knew the attacks were aggravated by the vampire's command, but Emeline had borne this torment for days … weeks … without aid of any kind. Her strength left him equal parts stunned and humbled, and more than a little angry.

She'd borne this—this torture—alone. He'd not been there to shield her from it, and no one else had done so.

"Dragomir." Fear burst through him. Her fear for him. He held up his hand to stop her from moving. Afanasiv was there beside her, trying to give her blood. Tariq gave more to the healer.

"Emeline. Stay there." He poured command into his voice and forced his body upright, forced himself to ignore the fact that it felt as if someone was taking a blowtorch to his insides.

She hesitated and then subsided, sinking back onto the ground, accepting Afanasiv's extended wrist. Again, she didn't ingest the blood and Dragomir sent another command, this time with a harder push to distance her from the necessary act. He didn't move until she bent her head and gave in to his order.

It took every bit of discipline he had to cross to the edge of the dirt. He flowed over the soil rather than expending physical energy on walking. He couldn't let the parasites escape to get into the ground. This time, Maksim was waiting to incinerate Vadim's creatures and replenish Dragomir's lost blood.

While Dragomir forced the parasites from his body, pushing the infected blood through his pores, the gathered Carpathians continued singing the lullaby for the baby. They sang of peace and strength, of love for her, urging her to hold on, that they were there for her, waiting for her. He found the song soothing and hoped the baby did as well.

It took a great deal longer to rid his body of the parasites, and he was cognizant of how much effort Andor had expended to shield Dragomir's most vital organs. Maksim incinerated the expelled parasites as they tried to rush for the soil. He was thorough, making certain not even one escaped. Dragomir drank the powerful, ancient blood Maksim offered, then hurried back to Andor's body to allow his spirit to reenter. Both men slumped to the ground. Immediately Nicu and Lojos were there to give them blood.

Gary politely closed the wound on Tariq's wrist. "He's up to something. We're making progress. We've gotten rid of most of the parasites in the bloodstream. He's got a few hiding that we'll have to ferret out, but I can feel his rage, and he's trying to get them to reproduce faster. Fortunately, I think we've got a good deal of the ones able to reproduce. Vadim's pulled back and that's bad for us in terms of getting rid of the parasites."

Dragomir regarded Emeline's pale features. She was lying on top of the soil, her eyes closed, but he could feel her mind trying to assess what was happening to her and the child. "I feel it, too. He'll strike hard when he does."

"No parasite is attacking Emeline's brain or heart," Gary said. "Just the baby's."

"And mine," Dragomir said, frowning. "If he isn't trying to kill Emeline, which doesn't make sense, then the baby must be protected. He'll try to hurt Emeline through the child. Emeline must be protected, as well, because if he can't rid her of the baby, I fear he'll do something else to harm her—maybe try to kill her." That didn't feel right. Even if the baby was gone, he feared Vadim wanted Emeline for some purpose. Not wanted. *Needed*.

Gary turned his strange eyes on him. Dragomir knew his own eyes were different, as were Ferro's and Sandu's. It hit him then. Gary was *truly* an ancient with all the knowledge and power of those in the monastery. He had the experiences in battle, the kills of his ancestors, the burdens they took to their graves, all of it. He didn't even have the relief of temptation, those dark whispers to take blood until the rush came. To kill their prey and just *feel*. Instead, there was—nothing. Like the ancients in the monastery, he lived in a gray void of nothing. He belonged in the brotherhood.

"Take her blood and give her yours," Gary said.

Emeline was about to go through the conversion, and the healer knew it was important to Dragomir to have her last moments as a human be about the two of them. He nodded his thanks and once more took her in his arms, holding her close to him while the healer shed his body.

"It hurts," she said softly, pressing her body close to his, melting into him. "What is it doing to you?"

"I can shut down pain. Stop worrying about me. We still have the conversion to get through." He nuzzled the top of her head, aware of time slipping away from them.

The sound of Carpathians singing the lullaby filled the air with a soothing peace that was a counterbalance to the vicious attacks the few remaining parasites continued on both of them. Despite the urgency, he wanted to just hold her for a moment—to block out all the pain and blood for her and allow her a moment of respite.

He swept back her hair. "You're being so brave, Emeline. I can't imagine what this must feel like for you." For the first time that night, he thought to go into her mind further, to smell and experience what she was feeling. She was wide open to him, without any barriers.

"Don't," she said softly. "Feel what I do when you're holding me. Safe. Cherished. Those are the things I concentrate on, not the rest of it. You're risking everything to save me."

His heart clenched hard in his chest. He leaned down to press his lips against her pulse, feeling her heart beat into his mouth, taking that rhythm into his heart. He touched the spot with his tongue, scraped over it with his teeth. "*Sívamet andam*. Do you know what that means, *sívamet*? It means I'm giving you my heart. You are the only one to have it. It is in your keeping for all eternity. I would never take someone's lifemate. I am an ancient and my honor is all I have. All I have to offer you. I know Vadim keeps saying he's the one, but choose me. Make it a choice, Emeline. If you cannot yet feel the ties binding us, make me your choice."

"Every time. With every breath," she said instantly, reaching back to circle his neck with her arm. "You will always be my choice."

"*Sielamet andam*. I give you my soul. You gave me back light. Hope. You will always be home to me, Emeline. It will never matter to me where we are, as long as we're together." He sank his teeth in her neck, this time, not distancing her. Letting her feel the erotic bite. The flash of pain followed by pure pleasure.

She cried out and then rewarded him with a small moan that told him she was feeling what he wanted her to. Her body moved restlessly over his. Deep inside he felt Vadim hiss his building rage. He was like a snake, coiled and waiting for an opportunity to strike. Dragomir gathered her closer protectively, allowing himself to savor the taste of her blood. Nothing Vadim did could diminish that for him. He would always be addicted to her taste.

You'll never have that again, he whispered on the Carpathian telepathic path. He didn't care that the others heard him taunt the master vampire. An enraged vampire made mistakes. Vadim was not ever getting Emeline in his hands again. He ingested the rest of the parasites. Before she took his blood, he would remove them from his body, so that she would get rich, ancient blood to strengthen both her and the baby.

134

He brushed a kiss over her pulse and then swept the punctures closed with his tongue. "I will be right back to give you the exchange."

She smiled at him. "They're gone, aren't they? I feel different."

Gary had once again entered her body to help herd the rest of the parasites into Dragomir. He emerged, as grim-faced as ever, but he was triumphant. "They're gone," he stated. His eyes met Dragomir's, reaffirming his conviction that Vadim hadn't put up a hard enough battle at the end. The question was, what was he planning?

Dragomir brushed a kiss over Emeline's forehead and once more made his way back to the edge of the healing grounds. Every step of the way, the parasites bit, scoring his bones and ripping at organs. He forced his body upright, standing tall.

The outside night poured in through the crack deliberately left for the Carpathians to call down lightning, or for each to pull what they needed from the night. Sandu was with him this time, ready to incinerate the vicious creatures attacking his body. Dragomir stared out the crack into the dark. The sliver of moon was beginning to expand, a hot, bright crescent in the sky. Lightning forked, Sandu charging the air.

The slight breeze shifted, touched Dragomir's face as he forced the wiggling, fighting parasites through his pores. He concentrated on making certain not a single one was left behind. Andor aided him, his spirit shining his white-hot light everywhere, so none could hide. He drove them while Dragomir all but shoved them through his pores. He didn't look down at the parasites but rather outward, into the night. He was leading Emeline there. The night would become her world. Their world.

She had chosen him without hesitation. She was ready for the conversion, placing all her trust in him. That humbled him. Lightning zigzagged across the sky and then Sandu directed a sizzling whip straight at the parasites. Dragomir caught an odd faint scent, something he'd smelled before. There was a hint of conspiracy about it. He leaned toward the crack, moving to one side to get the breeze on his face.

The whip of lightning crashed through the crack. Instead of the precise hit on the parasites, it swung in a wide arc, seeking Dragomir.

7

Sandu leapt out of the way of the whip of lightning. More crashed through the crack, swinging around in the air like sizzling snakes seeking a target. Gary threw his body over Emeline's, taking her to the ground, while the ancients scattered in every direction. Each took a corner, ducking as the lashes bit into the ground, slamming all around Dragomir.

In the midst of the chaos, the parasites had to be watched so that none slipped into the ground. They all knew that the high mage, Xavier, determined to drive the Carpathian people into extinction, had developed microbes to infect the soil and cause miscarriages in the women. They couldn't risk that taint spreading here.

Emeline's cries nearly drove Dragomir mad. Every instinct he had—Carpathian, ancient and lifemate—pressed him to get to her at any cost. To protect her, ease her transition into her new life and protect their child. As he turned toward her, lightning whips lashed all around him, striking the ground, shaking the entire house and healing grounds as they sought him.

Emeline needed his blood. He felt the first pain blossoming in her body, a blowtorch taken to her insides—the start of the conversion. She needed him desperately. They had given her so much Carpathian blood, the transformation was imminent.

Sandu, I must get to Emeline. The lightning strikes are directed at me. You must seize control from Vadim and his spy.

As he sprinted back toward her, Sandu wrested control of one of the wildly flailing whips to incinerate the parasites. Several of the wriggling creatures leapt off the cement wall in an effort to gain the safety of the soil, but Sandu had the presence of mind to dive beneath them so they landed on his body rather than in the earth. The parasites tried to burrow into him, desperate to live, to carry out their master's commands. Sandu kept moving, driving his heels into the dirt and launching himself to the cement barrier. He swept the parasites off his chest and lashed the whip right across them, incinerating them.

Lightning cracked across the healing grounds, running along the ceiling above them, springing out from a main fork to strike at the chanting Carpathians above the grounds. The bright light illuminated the dark, rich soil, so that one could see the minerals sparkling throughout. The whips were nearly blinding, so bright, forcing the Carpathians to cover or close their eyes against the white-hot energy. The moment they did, the whips danced, slapping at the grounds, the upper balcony and all around Dragomir.

Dragomir, using the preternatural speed of his kind, rolled beneath the lightning whips and then dove over them in somersaults that had him back on his feet running. No one could take to the air in molecules; the electrical energy was too strong. Hair stood up all over his body as the whips continued to strike. The ground should have been the deadliest place to be as the arc current spread out in a circle from each strike—and there were dozens of them—but instead, the ground itself was protected.

When he was nearly to his goal, the whips went into a frenzy, slamming all around him, making it very clear that he was the target. He hesitated for a moment, continuing to time the strikes, dodging them, testing as he inched closer to Emeline. Sparks rose over and over from the healing grounds as lightning struck, but it couldn't arc through it, spreading out to do more destruction, because powerful safeguards protected the healing earth.

As he neared her, the strikes lessened and came at him from behind or sideways. Not one hit near where she lay, the healer's body stretched over hers, his hands plunged into the soil, aiding the safeguards. Andor and Ferro were on either side of her, their bodies, and the safeguards woven with Gary, protecting her from harm.

They couldn't protect her from the conversion. The three men tried to lessen it for her, hoping to keep the baby from letting go, but Emeline needed Dragomir—her lifemate. That bond had forever sealed them together. A woman could go through the conversion without her lifemate, but he knew it would be much more difficult for her.

He knew the exact moment Tariq and the healer made the decision to strike back at Vadim. He knew it was the combination of the two; no Carpathian could fail to recognize the decisive Daratrazanoff touch. Even as he shielded Emeline, Gary wove his power with Tariq's and the two struck at the wielder of the lightning. As they did so, Sandu took back complete control of the whips of lightning. It was a three-pronged attack, the two ancients' strike concentrated, and unexpected, not one hint of their communication with each other spilling out. That told Dragomir that Tariq and Gary had a past connection he knew nothing of.

The moment Sandu had the lightning back under his control, Dragomir was on the ground beside Emeline, dragging her into his arms almost before the other ancients could relinquish their guardianship positions. "I'm here," he said, stroking back her hair. "Look only at me, Emeline. I will not leave you or the child." He caught her chin and forced her head around, away from the display of power and into his eyes. "Look only at me, *sívamet*."

She reached out to trace the road map of scars on his rugged face. She had first thought him striking but too rugged to be considered handsome. Now, she looked at him and found him gorgeous, the best-looking man she'd ever met. More, he was just plain the best of the best of men. She let herself fall into that hot, liquid golden pool of his gaze. It should have burned, but instead she felt cleansed. She had been tainted by evil for so long she hadn't thought she could ever feel this way again.

She stroked his face, traced one of the many scars, her touch loving, but she couldn't help it. He'd given her back more than just her life. He'd given her courage. He'd given her hope. Somehow, despite her looking her absolute worst, despite evil permeating her body, Dragomir still had seen her—the person under all of that.

"I am falling in love with you so fast," she murmured. "I don't want to do that to you, and there aren't any strings, but just know it's there. It's so deep inside me now, so much love for you." She ignored the fiery pain bursting through her body. She could do that because she was melting into all that glittering gold. Because his arms were around her and his chest pressed tight against her body. Because he was Dragomir and always standing for her. She had to give him the truth. "I've never felt like this before, given my heart to someone. So much love, so many threads binding us together, it's terrifying and beautiful at the same time."

It was a confession, one of love growing deeper by the moment. She truly didn't want him to feel obligated to love her back, but she was so tied to him now, she wasn't altogether certain how she would survive his leaving her.

"I want the strings," Dragomir murmured, reaching down to trace a line along the heavy muscle of his chest. "As many as possible. You are the only one, *sívamet*. Your heart is safe with me. Feed now. My blood is clean. I am an ancient and strong. This will get you and our baby through the conversion safely." He paid no attention to the chaos that had been going on just moments earlier. She was his entire focus. He was in her mind and could feel the beginnings of the change in both her and the baby.

He cradled the back of her head in his palm and pressed her forward until her mouth was against his chest, even as he distanced her from what she was doing. She was still aware, but he took all human abhorrence from her so she only saw the beauty. Only tasted the essence that was Dragomir. His blood ultimately was hers. His body was hers. Everything he was belonged to her.

He felt the first tentative touch of her tongue. His body reacted unexpectedly, a strong, hard jerk as if waking from a long sleep. He'd had that reaction before, but this was even stronger, more urgent. The first caress of her tongue sent a burst of pleasure rushing through him. Her declaration of love sank into his bones, wrapped around his heart and pierced his soul like an arrow, settling there for all time.

He wrapped his arms around her tightly, holding her to him, throwing his head back as she drew more and more of

141

the ancient blood from him. He felt the rush in her as the blood hit her system, as it flooded her organs and moved through the placenta to the baby. Even as his blood gave her strength, it swept through both mother and child, fueling already saturated organs to speed up the change.

You know me now, he said to the child. *Please accept this offering of my blood to make you strong. I offer it with my protection and this promise—to cherish you, to love you, to always protect you. Be strong for us, for your mother and me. Once the conversion is complete, you will both, mother and daughter, be wholly in our world. You will always be my daughter, close to my heart. Be strong, little one. Stay very strong and know I am with you. The healer will be with you. Listen to the song our people sing to you. It is for you, all of them helping you to hold on. All of our people waiting to meet you when you come to us whole and healthy.*

In response, he felt a faint flutter in his mind, as if the baby had reached out for him, trying to connect back. At the same time, just as he could feel Emeline's pain, now he could feel the child's. *Healer. The baby.*

Gary immediately shed his body and entered Emeline's to help ease the baby's transition into their world. Dragomir had lost count of the times Gary had given blood or shed his body to fight for the child against Vadim's attacks. The man had to be immensely strong to continue, but Dragomir believed in him now. The healer was a Daratrazanoff through and through, willing to pay the ultimate price if necessary to save the child. Dragomir would always be indebted to him.

The chanting around them continued. Half the Carpathians sang the lullaby and the other the healing song, all in the language of the ancients. The Carpathian hunters had regrouped and were now surrounding Emeline and Dragomir, shouldering the pain as much as each of them could to help ease the mother and child into their world.

Dragomir monitored them closely. He knew the moment he had to stop Emeline from taking more blood. He would never forget that soul-destroying second in time when she transitioned from feeling him, his love, his caring, building that addiction to his taste, the pleasure great enough to drown out the alarming and painful changes in her body, to pure pain. Nothing but pain.

Emeline tried to pull out of his mind to spare him. In agony from the twisting, dying organs, she still attempted to put him first—to spare him the pain of what she was going through. She hadn't told anyone about the agony of Vadim's parasites eating at her day and night, and he realized her reasons hadn't just been to protect herself from the possibility of being thrown out of Tariq's compound, it was about keeping the others from being harmed by the master vampire. She didn't dare have any of them attempt to cleanse her, give her blood and especially not take hers. He refused to give up his connection with her.

Please. You've done enough for me.

This is for all of us. You. Me. The baby. We're in this together, Emeline. All three of us. What you feel, so must I. What our child feels, so must I.

Her breath caught in her lungs and then came out in a sob. Her body twisted in his arms and he laid her down in the soil, shielding the sight of her from the Carpathians, not because he was modest, but because he knew she was. He stripped her clothes from her with a single thought. Her body temperature was rising and the barrier of her clothes to the cool air was a terrible burden.

That only serves to make me love you more, Dragomir. She whispered the declaration into his mind. She gave him the reassurance of their intimate connection when she should have been conserving her energy for the next swelling wave of agony. *Thank you for accepting my daughter. I want us to give her a name now.*

The wave hit and her body convulsed. He felt the healer easing the baby through it and wished he were the one. The moment he had the thought, both mother and daughter reached for him, connecting mentally, as if he was the one easing their way. He breathed with them. Sent them strength. Held them close, sheltering them as best he could. He was grateful for the Carpathian people surrounding them, just as determined as he was that the baby wouldn't die.

He stroked caresses over Emeline's forehead, his fingers twining in the thick mass of midnight black hair. He loved every strand. She was beautiful to him, more beautiful than he'd ever conceived. He realized she'd made an effort, showering and washing her hair when she'd been too weak, almost, to stand. She'd done that for him even knowing what was in store for her. Blaze had told her just how difficult the conversion was on human women. She had known what she was facing.

The wave subsided and Emeline opened her eyes, her long lashes framing all that true violet. No one really had violet eyes, but she did. His woman. He brushed a kiss on her forehead. "I'm so proud of you."

Blaze told me to relax and embrace the change. That breathing and relaxing would make it easier. I mostly worry for you and the baby. Do you have any names you think are beautiful? I couldn't make myself name her when I thought he would win.

Staring into those violet eyes, he could only think of one name. "*Carisma* means *gift.* You have given me the greatest gift a woman can give her man. We can call her Carisma when she is being our sweet girl. No doubt she'll have your fire."

I don't have fire. I just go my own way.

We go together, sweet Emeline. He didn't tell her that when she kissed him, he felt her fire. It was deep and passionate. She definitely ignited for him, and more, she made him ignite.

He could feel the swelling pain building before it was there in her eyes and in the lines of strain around her face. This time she pulled her knees to her chest and turned away from him, vomiting repeatedly to expel the human toxins. He swept the toxins away as fast as possible, keeping the air around her clean and fresh.

When the long wave subsided, she didn't turn back to him. He felt her humiliation. He didn't understand it. Expelling toxins was part of the process, but the fact was she was uncomfortable, and he needed to ease that for her.

"No one can see you but me," he assured her. "The healer has all he can do with keeping our daughter safe. For us, this is part of bringing you into our world, and we celebrate each step toward your entry."

She touched the tip of her tongue to her upper lip as she turned her head to look at him. *Thank you. This is difficult, but I am happy I'm moving us closer to you.* She took a breath and tried a tentative smile. *Carisma. I like the sound of that. Calling her a gift sounds beautiful. I think of her as a gift, something inno-cent and beautiful created in a moment of evil. I want the world for her, Dragomir. I want a home and happiness. Love filling it. I want her to have one of those stone dragons Tomas, Lojos and Mataias made for the other children. I would love for us all to soar through the sky together and point out stars. Her childhood and life are going to be so different than mine ever were.*

"She will be well loved, *sívamet*," he assured, and once more reached out to the child. *Laña—daughter—are you holding strong for your mother and me? The healer is cradling you in his arms, easing your way into our world. I hold both of you, mother and child. Do you feel me with you? Do you feel her? We surround you with such love. Hold strong for us.*

Again, he felt that small flutter in his mind and knew it was his daughter. He tasted the word—*laña*. Daughter. He had never had much of a family and the memory of the one he'd been born into was dim. Now he had a lifemate and daughter. *We wish to call you Carisma. Your mother and I consider you a gift, a precious treasure we are honored to love. Carisma means gift. Does this name suit you?*

That little flutter came again. An awareness. The child was reaching out as best she could and he took that as a yes. He had the impression of fear, pain, courage—a little fighter, then. She was stealing his heart, that little presence struggling for her life. He would always be indebted to the healer. Always. For eternity. He knew Gary's lifemate couldn't possibly be old enough yet for him to find as he'd only been recently born again as a Carpathian, but if he could aid the healer in holding on over the next few years, he would do so.

The waves were starting again, and this time the pain was even stronger. The chanting and song also swelled in volume, and more Carpathians joined the ancients in shouldering the agony of conversion. He felt the women in the mix, working to aid Emeline and the baby, to keep them safe and as far from the pain as possible. No one could stop the convulsions, or the body's purge, but the combined strength and power of the Carpathian people distanced both mother and child from the agony, allowing them to get through that violent wave.

Dragomir gathered Emeline to him, opening the earth in the richest spot he could find. He would place her in it the moment he could safely command her and Carisma to sleep the healing sleep of their people. Until then he needed to hold her—not for her, but for him. He nuzzled the top of her head, the shadow along his jaw catching in her thick hair. He loved those silken strands, every single one of them, and she

146

had a lot of hair. It was the color that had caught his eye, all that midnight black.

"You're almost there, *sívamet*. We're so close."

"What happened? All the lightning. It was terrifying. I couldn't see much because Gary threw me to the ground and covered my body with his. Beneath me, I felt the ground sizzling, almost like it was fighting back, but I knew it was him—Vadim. I knew he was attacking you. He kept saying he was going to kill you and the baby."

The little catch in her voice, almost a sob, made his heart clench so hard it hurt. That catch was there for him. He couldn't remember a time when someone worried about him enough to cry. He brushed at the tears on her lashes, wanting to kiss her. Wanting to tell her the things welling up in his heart.

"The baby is safe. I'm safe. He can't talk to you anymore."

"He took my blood." She sounded ashamed, as if somehow, she could have prevented it.

"He did. But your blood isn't the same, Emeline. We used me as a filter and removed every drop of your blood. It was replaced with the blood of the ancients. He can try to talk to you, but your blood will resist his invasion. When we replaced your blood, we replaced Carisma's blood as well. He cannot harm either of you."

"He'll be so angry," she whispered. Her lashes fluttered and then went down, covering the welling pain in her eyes.

He took a deep breath as if he could breathe air into her lungs as the next wave arrived. He shared her mind. He felt the fire blazing through her organs, an endless, agonizing flame. She didn't make a sound. He was aware of Gary, taking that heat, deflecting it from the baby. Both ancients held fast, trying to shield mother and daughter as the conversion raged through them.

147

Dragomir knew he'd never given much thought to love. He'd thought about his lifemate often. He'd been obsessed with finding her for centuries, but he'd never considered what he would feel when he found her. Not love. Not this overwhelming, *terrifying* feeling that shook him to his core. He hadn't known love could be felt through one's entire body. That it could manifest itself physically.

Emeline's body twisted, convulsed, her temperature raged, an alarming heat radiating from her body.

Gary. She's like a furnace. Is the baby burning up? Dragomir was alarmed at the heat burning through Emeline. *I am doing my best. Her temperature must come down soon. She must die and be reborn, but this heat has to affect the baby. What happens to her when Emeline succumbs?*

She is either strong enough to hang on through those vital minutes, or we will lose her.

He detested the detached way the healer gave him the facts. He knew the process, what it entailed, but he had been looking for reassurance, hoping Gary could perform a miracle and make certain his daughter came back when Emeline's body surrendered to the conversion. She was rolling with it, breathing through it, not fighting, but she wasn't surrendering. That knowledge hit him hard. His woman wasn't just giving in to the inevitable. He waited, breathing away her distress, his. He matched her laboring lungs, her struggling heartbeat, and waited for her to recognize it.

It didn't take long. The moment the wave subsided, her lashes lifted and she rubbed her palm along his thigh. *What are you doing?*

She kept choosing the more intimate telepathic method of speaking instead of the human one. She interspersed it with speaking aloud, but it was rare in their communication here, in the Carpathian healing grounds.

"What do you mean?" He waved his hand to bring in a cool breeze, mindful of the cracks running around the structure, woven in to allow the night to spill onto the healing grounds. He kept his heart and lungs completely tuned to hers, and slowly, painfully slowly, he began to take over for both, giving her more air in little increments so she didn't notice. His heart slowed just a bit, just enough to keep hers from racing.

Why are you wheezing? Why is your heart so fast?

"Because you are wheezing. Your heart is beating too fast." Her lashes fluttered, drawing his attention. He brushed a kiss on her forehead because he couldn't stop himself. "Why are you prolonging your agony? Give in, Emeline." His voice was demanding. If she didn't of her own free will, he would have to take over and he didn't want to do that, but she was leaving him no other choice.

The baby.

"She needs her strength. The longer this goes on, the less she will have. The less you will have. You'll be drained and so will she."

I don't want to lose her.

"The healer is with her. I'm with you and can feel her. Trust me again. You've given yourself to me. Trust me with our child."

The tip of her tongue touched her bottom lip in an effort to moisten it. He took care of the dryness immediately, annoyed he hadn't thought to do it earlier. When the convulsions had started, he had waved his hand to tidy her braid, keeping most of the long length away from her body, knowing the heavy weight would hurt her skin, but he hadn't considered that her raised temperature and the ridding her body of toxins would dehydrate her.

Her lips curved into a sweet smile that shook him. *You can't think of everything. You were a little busy. And you didn't tell me what was going on when Gary threw me to the ground.*

"Vadim took control of the lightning we used to incinerate the parasites. He must have a spy here, a traitor inside the compound working with him. There is no other explanation. That's how the safeguards were lifted."

She frowned. *I thought Liv did that so the children could fly their dragons.*

It was a sad state of affairs that he found her frown adorable. He rubbed his finger lightly over it as if he could erase it when he didn't really want to. He wanted to commit it to memory so when he pulled up images of her in his mind, it was there.

"I felt the thread of evil twisting beneath the ground. The safeguards had been in place beneath the ground, yet evil tainted the soil. Liv couldn't have done that. It had Vadim's touch to it. I can recognize the signature of the master vampires, the ones I've chased or encountered throughout the centuries. That had Vadim's mark all over it."

She turned her face up toward his with an obvious effort. Her eyes, a deep violet that reminded him of twin amethyst gems, looked up at him with a clear reprimand. *You don't believe Liv is tainted?*

"She is Carpathian. She opened up the compound and allowed the vampires access, but there was another working behind the scenes to make it all happen. Liv needs to be punished, to be shown just how bad the situation could have been. Any death would have been directly on her shoulders. Every injury. If Vadim had reacquired you . . . " He broke off, feeling that—the near miss. He could have lost her. "That girl has a lot to answer for."

She's only a child.

"She's Carpathian, Emeline. There are consequences for every mistake one makes in our world. Let go for me. Do it now, with this wave. I feel it coming and I want you to give yourself to me. To our life."

The baby . . .

He tightened his hold on her, afraid if she waited too long neither would be strong enough to make it into their world. "She will be fine. *Sívamet*, you need to trust in your strength and your love for her. She's a fighter. Give her the chance to live. Let go for me."

The next wave hit her before she could answer him. She caught her breath, looked up at him and deliberately followed the rhythm of his lungs. He took her hand and put it over his heart, holding her palm tight against his bare chest. She pulled her knees to her chest, but kept her hand over his heart, her eyes staring straight into his.

He saw trust. Complete trust. It was a gift, a precious one, and it humbled him. *I've got you, Emeline. I will always be with you.*

He was in her mind and saw that first acceptance of their true bond. She was tentative, reaching to touch his mind. She could, he was open to her. She was his lifemate and he refused to hide his past from her. Not even now, when she was making that connection. She was aware of Carpathians and what they were. Predators. Every single one of them. She would be one as well. Her touch might be tentative, but it was intimate, even in the face of her physical distress. His body stirred, an inappropriate reaction when she was suffering.

Never inappropriate, she whispered into his mind.

He fell hard. Fast. So deep he was out of breath. Every beat of his heart was for her. She was—extraordinary. All those weeks she had suffered Vadim's attacks, his parasites hurting her, over and over in an attempt to force her into compliance with the master vampire's wishes. She'd held out. She'd kept her baby alive even when Vadim turned his attacks to it. Now, when her insides were dying and being reborn, when she was suffering because of him . . .

151

Silly man. Not because of you. This is my choice. Keeping the baby was my choice. Defying Vadim was my choice. You are my choice.

Her body writhed, twisted, was lifted up, jerking, as he held her to him to keep her from slamming down. That didn't matter to her. Her mind was peaceful. Serene. She'd chosen, and her choice was him. Dragomir Kozel with his road map of scars on his face and the tattoos carved, rather than inked into his skin. His vow—to her.

Tell me. I need to feel your touch.

There was a catch in her voice. One that told him she was hurting beyond measure, even with all of them helping to bear her burden.

Not beyond measure. Talk to me. Tell me what those symbols and letters mean. It helps to distract me, and I really want to know.

He rocked her, more to soothe himself than her. Stroking back her damp hair with long caresses of his fingers, he told her using the more intimate form of communication because his explanation belonged only to her.

A few of us believed it was cowardice to suicide. We were at the end, monsters growing worse by the hour, and we wanted—no, needed to keep our honor. We wanted to wait for our lifemates, to hold true to our course. The trouble was . . .

The twisting fire in her body slowly eased and her long lashes lifted. She reached up to touch his face, drawing in air for both herself and the baby. *The trouble was . . .* she encouraged.

He was a big man. Tall, like most Carpathians, but with heavier bones and muscles. She wasn't petite by any means, although thin from her ordeal, but she seemed very small held up against his heavier muscles. His protective instincts were working overtime as he gathered her back to him. "Only once more, *sívamet*, and I can send you into our healing sleep. You and Carisma did well."

Tell me.

He sighed. He'd hoped to distract her, but she refused to let it go. His woman had a mind of her own, and she would get her way with him. Easily. That didn't bode well for him, but he understood why it had been ridiculous for him to think his time was over—that he couldn't live with a woman from this century. As her lifemate, he would do whatever it took to make her happy.

He felt her stir in his mind, soft feminine amusement. "Within reason, woman. You are my heart and soul and I protect my own. You will not always agree with the way I choose to do that, but as my lifemate, you will do your best to see to my happiness."

This lifemate business is a two-edged sword. Now tell me. Already I feel the next wave building and it is the worst yet. I need to hear your voice. In my head. Talk to me so I can concentrate on how mesmerizing you sound. You provide me with all sorts of fantasies I can hang on to when things get really rough between us.

"Things? What things? I intend to provide you with a life without *rough*."

She smiled up at him, but the building wave reached higher and higher, crashing through her internal organs. He felt Gary's white-hot spirit, a ball of pure energy, shudder and dim with the assault as he surrounded the baby and took on the growing wave of pure fire racing through their bodies. Dragomir was in Emeline's mind and he felt the pain the way she did. The Carpathian healing chant swelled in volume. The women's voices sang the lullaby, trying to give the baby strength to hold on through the last transformation. All of them connected to share the pain, easing it enough that hope-fully mother and daughter would get through it.

Be strong, Carisma, for your mother. She fought for you. Fight for her. Fight for us. You are not alone. You have all of us waiting for you. Prepared to love and defend you. He didn't know the slightest thing about babies, and all he knew of children was that parents spoiled them and didn't teach them the things that would keep them safe.

The softest touch in his mind held a trace of that feminine amusement he knew was his woman laughing at him.

Tell me. Those scars.

On my face or body?

The ones you call a tattoo.

Dragomir sighed. He couldn't deny her anything, let alone a simple explanation that wasn't really so simple. "I cannot tell you what it was like to live centuries in the darkness. Not even darkness." He ran his fingers over her hair, those silken midnight black strands he loved. "Gray. A gray void. No feelings, none, Emeline. Just the battle and the kills. Men who had been my friends. Watching everyone that had been in my childhood turning from lack of one thing—finding a lifemate."

The wave was almost at its peak. He tightened his hold on her, bringing her front to his, so that her breasts pressed into his chest. He cradled the back of her head in the palm of his hand, feeling every ragged, labored breath she took. Every wheeze. The inevitable struggle for life. "At first there is the whisper of temptation. Soft at first, then as time passes, that whisper becomes the only thing one hears. Kill. Terrorize. You will feel the rush. You will *feel.*"

To his shock and dismay, Emeline's mind stroked caresses in his. Soothing. Comforting. In the midst of the pain, she still thought of him first. There was a persistent burning behind his eyes—one he'd never felt before.

Keep talking. Hurry. I need your voice. It keeps me centered. Grounded. I can do this if I have your voice.

I thought that whisper was the worst of what could happen and

I learned to live with it, to ignore it. Time passed. So much time. And then even that was gone. There was no whisper of temptation, only time moving and no letup in sight. I was growing weary, and that is a dangerous time for a Carpathian hunter. Every battle, every kill, takes its toll. So, those like me got together, and we found our place in the monastery. Alive but not. Dead but walking. We found a gatekeeper, one close to his time like us, but unwilling to meet the dawn. His job was to keep us from killing anyone. His job was to feed us.

He fed all of you? What a good man.

No one had ever called any of them a "good man." Most ran from them, and with good reason. Every one of the monks was dangerous to mankind.

Those nights were difficult. To get through them, we practiced fighting, pairing off most of the hours to engage in hand-to-hand or weapons training. Sometimes one of us had to take on the rest of the brotherhood.

One man against so many. Her breath hitched and she exhaled a long wheezing rush of sound like a ragged whisper.

He loved her beyond all imagining. She made him feel such a wealth of emotions, all centered around her. *The ink embedded into my skin was carved deeply by my brothers in the monastery. We took vows, and were a brotherhood, but those vows weren't said to a higher deity, but to the ones holding our souls. The ones keeping us safe. Ones like you, Emeline. Those vows were made to our lifemates, not anyone else.*

He'd meant every word of those vows he'd taken to become what he was—a part of that brotherhood. *The first line is Olen wäkeva kuntankért. That translates in your language as staying strong for our people. The second line is Olen wäkeva pita belső kulymet. That means, staying strong to keep the demon inside. We all know we have that demon. It is powerful and at any time could consume us or those around us. The third line is*

Olen wäkeva—félért ku vigyázak. That is our most important line and the one we repeat when the demons are too close. It means staying strong for her. The last line is very simple but it says it all. Hängemért.

He knew his voice had changed. He knew that last word was said with reverence. It always was. *Hängemért means only her. It is simple, but it is everything. You are everything to me. You always have been. I lived a life of honor for me, but also for you. There is only you. None came before you and none will ever come after you. There is only you.*

The terrible wave was receding and her breathing changed, became less labored. She needed respite. She needed the healing soil. He checked her, every part of her, and then checked their daughter. Gary had kept her shielded enough that as her little organs changed, she had hung on through the terrible, painful transformation.

Dragomir pushed back strands of damp hair from her face. She was sweating blood. There were dots of it on her forehead and smears on her body. He opened the earth right next to them, making it deep. Seeing the shimmer of rich minerals made his heart a little lighter.

This is the scary part. Buried alive.

Her voice tried to make light of it, but he felt the undertone of horror. *You will sleep and the baby will sleep. When you wake, you will be out from under the soil. On your rising we will practice opening and closing the soil until I know you are always safe and feel confident in your abilities.*

He brushed a kiss across her mouth. He, as always throughout her ordeal, had swept away the dots of blood on her forehead and the smears on her body. All toxins were gone and the air was sweet-smelling and fresh. Still, she turned her head away.

I am not clean.

You are very clean. I will put you under before the next wave starts. I'll sleep beside you this night. He waited for her consent. It was a long time coming.

Her gaze clung to his and then finally she nodded. He reached out immediately to the healer. *It is time.*

I agree. The child is ready.

Dragomir touched his daughter lightly, just to make certain. She was sleepy. Weary. She needed the ordeal over. Gary was back in his body, slumping to the ground. Immediately Tomas offered him his wrist and the healer gratefully took it.

Dragomir kissed Emeline again and sent mother and daughter to sleep. They went under without a fight. He floated into the deep hole with Emeline in his arms. He was gentle as he placed her carefully in the soil before rising again. One wave closed the blanket of rich dirt over her. He turned as Sandu offered him his wrist. His gaze found Tariq's.

"We need to find the traitor aiding Vadim. We need to do that now, before they have another chance to strike at us."

8

All trace of civility was gone from Dragomir's face. There was death in his eyes and he didn't care who saw it. Centuries fell away until there was only the vicious predator stripped of all mercy, all hint of kindness. There was only the killer left, the one that hunted—and prevailed. He looked like what he was, ruthless and implacable.

Tariq nodded, his face as grim as Dragomir's. "I agree. We need to find out just who is aiding Vadim and how. I will do that, *ekäm*. You must feed and then go to earth to heal."

Dragomir shook his head. "My lifemate was nearly taken by a master vampire, one who raped her mind and invaded her body. He tortured her for weeks. The traitor allowed Vadim and his army access to this compound, putting every single man, woman and child, human and Carpathian alike, in danger."

Tariq nodded a second time. Maksim moved up to stand on Tariq's left. Gary took up a position on his right. Tomas, Lojos and Mataias flanked them. Dragomir understood the men were protecting Tariq, although Tariq didn't seem to notice the others surrounding him. He was the acknowledged leader. Those guarding him were making a statement. Dragomir wondered briefly why Gary was throwing his support behind Tariq, but at that moment his reasoning didn't matter.

As soon as the Carpathian hunters lined up behind Tariq, the ancients made their move. Sandu moved to Dragomir's right and Andor to his left. Ferro, Afanasiv and Nicu flanked Dragomir. Afanasiv and Nicu both had the same tattoo as Dragomir, drifting down and across their backs. The two had left the monastery, but they had joined the brotherhood. They were ancients, experienced in every kind of battle, shockingly fast, infinitely powerful. Brotherhood trumped friendship every time.

Dragomir hadn't asked for that allegiance, not in the issues he had with safety at the compound, but the others had decided to make a show of force and solidarity with him. Emeline wanted to remain in the compound, and for her safety and that of the baby, he knew it would be best. Creating a division wasn't what he wanted, or what Emeline needed. That didn't matter right at the moment. He had to shut down every threat to his lifemate. It was his duty, his right, and more than anything else, *his* need.

Tariq let his breath out in a long sigh, not looking at any of the other ancients, his entire focus on Dragomir. "I understand. Charlotte is my world as Emeline is yours. You know that every woman is cherished by the entire Carpathian community and equally as important. I will examine every member of my security force, the older couple—Donald and Mary Walton—and every other person living on this compound. I intend to get to the bottom of this tonight."

Dragomir pinned him with a steady, challenging gaze. His

eyes were pure gold, glittering with menace and the promise of violence. "My woman is pregnant. The baby was in grave danger, her heart clogged with Vadim's poisonous filth. If the healer had not been here, Vadim would have forced Emeline to return to him, using the threat of killing her child. This traitor allowed that threat to become a very real possibility by allowing him to use the lightning during the healing and conversion."

Again Tariq nodded. "I understand the anger you must be feeling."

"Rage," Dragomir corrected. "Ice-cold rage. I invoke my right as her protector, as her lifemate, to hunt those putting her in harm's way." His voice was pitched low, a hint of savagery deepening the timbre. Still, as softly as he'd spoken, his words carried to the Carpathian people ringing the healing grounds. A hush fell instantly. Dragomir was well within his rights. He could hunt—and kill—anyone threatening his lifemate.

The invocation of Dragomir's right as Emeline's lifemate was a formality no one in the Carpathian world could dispute—not even the prince himself. It was a body blow to Tariq, who hoped to take care of it himself. Charlotte came up beside him, slipping her hand into his, looking up at the leader there in the compound.

"What is it, Tariq? What does that mean? Surely we all want to find out if someone is betraying us."

Tariq understood exactly what was in Dragomir's mind. Centuries past, children were raised by the community. It was a necessary way. If one's lifemate was killed, the other followed, leaving behind any children. The children were left bereft, but by having everyone participate in raising them, they were able to carry on. Each warrior could aid in sharing battle experience with the children. When the child did something wrong, the punishments were severe. Every consequence of their action was life-threatening—to the child or someone else, so the repercussions were equally harsh.

"It is your right, Dragomir," Tariq agreed. "I ask that you make an effort to understand these children. They were raised human and in a different century."

Dragomir didn't take his gaze from Tariq's, not for one moment. He didn't blink. He focused completely. "You know it is one of them." He hissed the accusation, a soft, piercing spear of sheer anger. "You know."

Charlotte gasped and put a defensive hand to her throat, but she glanced up at the mask that was Tariq's face and subsided instantly.

"I suspect," Tariq corrected. "There is someone, that much I'm certain of. None of my security force has been near the vampires long enough for Vadim to gain control. Genevieve hasn't, either. The Waltons aren't even on the vampires' radar. The children are the ones he had down in the underground city long enough to put them under his control. But they are traumatized children, Dragomir . . ."

Swift impatience crossed Dragomir's face. He waved away Tariq's caution dismissively. "I am tired of the excuses all of you make for them. These children wield power. One of them was brought into our world. She must abide by the rules of our world, just as every other Carpathian child has done. The other children have chosen to stay here, within the safety of your walls. They enjoy that safety because of the ancients safeguarding them. That means they fall under the rules of our world."

"There is no mercy in you," Charlotte whispered. "They are children."

"They brought evil into the compound," Dragomir said. "They allowed a master vampire to come into this place of

161

safety, and they endangered my lifemate. As it was, she has been tormented every hour of her existence by Vadim Malinov, and someone here aided this monster in torturing her."

There was steel in his voice, steel in his heart. He turned abruptly away from Tariq and started across the wide expanse of the healing grounds. "Call them out of their home. They will stand for punishment and inspection." It was a decree. His invoking the ancient law of their people had given him every right and Tariq could do nothing but comply.

Behind him, he heard Charlotte begin an argument with her lifemate, begging him not to allow Dragomir near the children. She feared what he might do. She should fear the repercussions of such a grave offense. It angered him that Tariq hadn't done more than confine the children to their home. Genevieve watched over them, which to him was laughable. She had succumbed to a sleeping spell already, so the children knew they could manipulate her.

"They may decide to fight for the children," Sandu murmured.

Dragomir glanced at him, his features set and hard. He knew every scar on his face showed, every line depicting his many battles. "You do not have to accompany me."

"I believe you are right in what you do. More than right. I will admit I know little about the human world, but these children live in our world. That means they follow the rules. They can't have human rules and get away with a slap on their hands when we are dealing with life-or-death matters."

"Then what?"

"Your woman lies beneath the earth and must remain at least for the night. Possibly longer. If we start a war and must leave this place, she will remain behind."

Dragomir shook his head. "I thought of that. If there is a war, we must be the ones to keep this place. She needs the healing soil. The one that must be taken out before all others is—"

162

"The healer," Sandu said. The others nodded solemnly in agreement.

Dragomir sighed. "He is good, too good. Strong. He holds the memories of many ancients. He is programmed with the knowledge of their battles and experiences. It is a heavy weight to bear, but it also makes him a deadly opponent. Clearly he has given his protection to Tariq. I think Tariq makes a good leader and is needed here, but those children are his weakness."

Dragomir led the way outside and went straight to the side of the house where the cracks had been strategically placed in the wooden walls to allow the Carpathians to call down lightning when it was needed. He crouched low and sniffed the air, the wood and the dirt surrounding the flower beds. Flowers had wilted, some stalks yellow and drooping. The signs of lightning were right there, right where he was scenting that elusive odor he knew he'd caught just before the first lightning strike. The person who had given Vadim control when safeguards would have kept him out had stood right there, staring into the healing grounds, seeing Emeline, seeing him. She had allowed Vadim, *aided* him in attacking Dragomir's woman. His lifemate. His child. This girl would pay.

Tariq had called the children out of their house and they came slowly, holding hands, looking both guilty and remorseful at the same time. Tariq and Charlotte stood to the side of the play yard where the children had gathered to hear what Tariq had to say. Dragomir strode into the center, between Tariq and the children, shocking them. Alarming them.

Danny stepped forward, pushing his youngest sister, Bella, toward the fourteen-year-old girl, Amelia. "Thank you for saving out lives, Dragomir. We know we messed up. We wanted to fly the dragons and we should have waited until Tariq said it was okay."

Dragomir crooked his finger at the boy. Danny glanced at Tariq, but Tariq remained stoic. The boy shuffled forward a few steps, putting himself in jeopardy.

Maksim and the healer are behind us. Tomas and Lojos to our right. Mataias is to your left. I do believe they have us boxed in, Sandu said.

"Tariq, if you do not want a war, send your guardians elsewhere," Dragomir said. "We can keep this to the finding of our traitor, or we can make it something else altogether."

Tariq frowned and lifted his head, looking left and right as if seeking. "I didn't ask them to attend. You were invited to this compound and I have not rescinded that invitation, nor do I intend to. You are needed here, as are the others. Vadim has declared war and we have to stop him. You are well within your rights to demand punishment for the children. They did open us up to an attack, and that could have ended badly. More, *all* of us want to find the traitor. That's imperative. I trust that you will remember these are my children. As you love Emeline and your daughter, I love these children. I also know they must learn what their actions could have caused."

Dragomir respected the man even more. Tariq was a born leader, a diplomat, but he was a hunter through and through. He understood language and words. He understood that by giving Dragomir carte blanche to punish his children, he was also tying his hands—just a little.

Danny straightened his shoulders and crossed the cement patio to stand right in front of Dragomir. "I lead my family, my sisters. If one of them did something, I will take the responsibility for it and the punishment."

A collective gasp went up from the girls. Ten-year-old Liv shook her head and ran toward her brother. "It was me. I did it. I opened the safeguards so we could fly the dragons."

Even as she stumbled over the last words of her confession,

Dragomir waved a casual hand toward the child and she stopped in her tracks. She looked horrified. Terrified. The air shimmered for a moment and then a man materialized beside her. Valentin Zhestokly stood to the right and one step in front of the child, his body shielding hers. He didn't say anything, but he looked grim. Liv ducked her head, not looking at him or Dragomir. She looked as if she might burst into tears any minute.

Dragomir knew the expression on the child's face—one of absolute remorse—should have moved him, but it didn't. Emeline's silent cries were in his head. The sound of the baby screaming in helpless pain echoed through his mind.

"I accept that you are responsible for opening the safeguards and allowing the evil into the compound," Dragomir told her. "You knew what you were doing, didn't you?"

She nodded, lifting her head up so she could look him in the eye. "I did."

"You knew that the vampires waited outside the compound." He made it a statement. The children had laughingly referred to their new home as their prison. They had a roof over their heads, food day and night, playgrounds, movies, every luxury Tariq could give them, and every pleasure, including swimming in the lake.

Liv looked confused. "I didn't think they could get here so fast. There were so many. They were everywhere."

"Did you know that we lost two members of our security force?" Dragomir was relentless.

Danny turned as if he might help his younger sister, but Dragomir waved his hand and, like Liv, the teenager couldn't move forward or back.

Charlotte gasped and pressed a hand to her mouth, looking toward her lifemate. Tariq shook his head at something she said telepathically, but he didn't protest.

"Those men had families."

Valentin placed a hand on Liv's shoulder, but he didn't do other than that. Dragomir admired him. The man knew what Dragomir planned. It was a tactic they often used with Carpathian children.

He waved his hand again and replayed the screams of the unborn child. "This is my daughter. Vadim is torturing her and she is yet to be born." He allowed her to hear the cries of the families of the two men killed in their defense. "These people, mother and father, wife and children, will never hold their loved ones again."

Tears streamed down the child's face, but she remained standing, looking at him. Waiting. Knowing. He gave it to her then. "My lifemate, suffering the pain of what he did to her." He allowed Emeline's screams, the ones she kept so silent, to be heard by Liv. Then he did what all Carpathian ancients had done before him. He played out the scenarios of what could have happened: Emeline being taken. Danny, Amelia, Bella and Lourdes dead on the ground in front of her, their dragons dead or dying from the many wounds inflicted on them. The sounds of the battle, the screams of the children, explosions, fire, chaos reigning. She saw it all. He made certain Danny and Amelia saw it as well. Only the three-year-old was spared.

The three children sobbed, eventually putting their hands over their ears to try to block out the sounds of what nearly had happened.

"Do you understand now?" Dragomir asked Liv. "Do you know why the rules are in place? The elders don't put them there just to hoard their power. The rules keep everyone safe."

"Why are you doing this to us?" Amelia burst out, tears tracking down her face. "Those things didn't happen."

"They didn't happen because I was alerted to the danger

and took care of it. Would you like to see my back where the threads of fire Vadim created burned through my skin to the bone?" Dragomir demanded.

Liv shook her head, sending her older sister a quick glance of sympathy. "I'm so sorry, Dragomir. I would never want to hurt Emeline. She's been one of my best friends. She saved us." The last was said in a whisper, on a hiccup.

"Emeline trusts you. Tariq trusts you. We all do. You betrayed that trust to have fun. Just for fun." He let that sink in.

Liv was silent for a long time, staring up at his face with too-old eyes. "You're right, Dragomir. I didn't think of the consequences, only that I wanted to fly my dragon. I couldn't wait." She took a deep breath. "I wanted to show Danny and Amelia what I could do so they would want to be Carpathian, too. I should have thought it out first. What can I do to help the families of the two men who died?"

"They are dead. There's no bringing them back from the dead. Their families will have to go on without them," he said, driving reality home to her. "I would say those deaths were on your shoulders," he began.

Charlotte shook her head and took one step toward the child, but Tariq's firm hold on her arm stopped her. Valentin shifted a little bit closer to Liv, but he remained silent. Liv's tears streamed unchecked down her face, but she didn't look away from Dragomir, accepting her responsibility for all that had taken place.

Dragomir shook his head. "But you are not wholly responsible. There is another among you. One you trust. One you believe in. He—or she—whispers in your ear to get you to do Vadim's bidding. He—or she—is his pawn."

Danny scowled at him. "We've all been examined. Tariq took our blood in order to monitor us and we all consented." He sounded belligerent. Challenging.

He turned his gaze on the boy. "One of you managed to hide from Tariq with the aid of the puppet master."

Danny turned to glare at Tariq. "I can't believe you are allowing him to accuse us like this. Do you believe I'm tainted? Or Amelia? Maybe Bella. Maybe a three-year-old is running around doing Vadim's bidding."

"This time"—Dragomir circled his prey—"this time, the person came to wreak havoc in the healing grounds. Was someone gone from your group? Even for a few minutes?"

Danny couldn't turn to watch Dragomir. He could only look forward toward the house—toward that little break in the wood where someone had crouched and took command of the lightning when it was called down to aid Dragomir in getting rid of the parasites.

"We were all in our rooms, doing what Tariq asked us to do. He grounded us. That meant we didn't talk to one another or interact because we were supposed to spend time alone contemplating our mistakes." That was said defiantly. His voice said he knew the punishment didn't fit the crime. "He was going to talk more to us about what happened and assign a punishment then."

"Healer." Dragomir called to Gary. He wasn't going to do the examining. He didn't want the women to say he had planted evidence in the traitor. Blaze, Charlotte and Emeline had been human and their thinking was human. They couldn't conceive of children betraying them, certainly not children they loved. "I ask that you examine each of these children for evidence that Vadim has used them as his puppet."

Gary, of course, had the right to refuse, but he had aligned himself with Tariq. He'd placed himself in the position of being second-in-command, just as all Daratrazanoffs had done before him. He wouldn't refuse. It was in the best interests of the compound to find the traitor, and Gary wouldn't be emotional one way or the other over children. He was incapable.

The healer materialized beside Danny. His strange ice-blue eyes appeared more silver than blue, moving over the boy. "Do you give your consent for a search?"

"If I say no, would it matter?" Danny said bitterly. "I'm not a traitor. I would never betray Tariq or Charlotte, let alone Emeline. I know what Vadim put her through, and I know it happened in order for us to be saved. *All* of us. Emeline sacrificed for us."

"Will you do less, then? Do you have her courage?"

Danny's jaw tightened. "I have courage. I don't think what you're asking me to do takes courage. I know you won't find anything. I don't like the accusation, but search away."

Daratrazanoff didn't waste time; he shed his body and entered the boy's.

Amelia lifted Bella into her arms. "Is he going to search the baby, too?" She didn't look at Dragomir, but rather at Tariq.

Dragomir answered. "Unless someone confesses, all of you must be searched."

"We all *were* searched," Amelia pointed out. "Tariq, you searched us yourself. This isn't right. First you let him make Liv cry and then you just stand there while he's mean to us. We all love Emeline. Why would we try to hurt her?"

Dragomir waved his hand and she stopped in her tracks when she would have turned to take the child back to their home. He stalked around her in that same circular pattern he'd made around Danny, scenting the air, hunting. He had a well-developed sense of smell, one he needed when tracking the vampire. The familiar scent reached him. One of grape and vanilla, and the elusive odor of burnt grass. He moved closer. It wasn't the baby, but the girl. He was certain of it.

Still, he moved away from her, shifting his gaze—and the breeze—toward Sandu.

Sandu inhaled deeply, drawing the poisonous truth into his lungs. He nodded, an almost imperceptible movement, but Tariq was sharp, once more underscoring why he was the chosen leader. He caught the small communication between the two ancients.

He strode over to Dragomir. "Tell me." It was a command, nothing less.

Dragomir had a split second to decide if he wanted to go to war with this man. "Go to the side of the house and smell the scent there," he encouraged. "And then smell the one here."

Tariq glanced at Valentin's expressionless mask. The ancient gave nothing away. He simply stood in front of the child who one day would be his lifemate. There had been another child, a girl adopted by Francesca, one of the Carpathian women. It was discovered early on that Dimitri was her lifemate. Like Valentin, he stayed away to make it easier, but returned if there was trouble. Valentin would protect his lifemate with his life.

It was Liv who answered her sister. "This isn't about us, Amelia, it's about the Carpathian world we live in. Someone aided Vadim. I'm sure it isn't me, but I want them to examine me just in case. I need to know it isn't me."

"You already know," Amelia pointed out. "And now they're accusing us once again. Why can't they take our word for it? We don't like knowing there's a traitor any more than they do. Why does it always have to be one of us they accuse? Why can't it be one of them?" She hugged Bella tighter to her. "Danny's right, it's insulting."

Liv shrugged. "The healer is confirming, Amelia, that's all. We did open the safeguards. It was wrong and foolish of us. I think this is a small thing for them to ask of us."

Amelia scowled at her little sister. "I hate it when you make sense."

"Give me Bella," Charlotte said. She held out her arms.

Amelia couldn't help the triumphant look she shot Dragomir. At least her baby sister was going to be spared. He didn't deign to answer her. Just the fact that she'd handed the baby over, drawing attention to the child, made him suspicious. He glanced at Sandu, who nodded. Tariq turned to look at Bella as she clasped her little arms around Charlotte's neck. There was speculation in his eyes when he turned back to Amelia.

Gary emerged from Danny's body, his spirit moving back into his own. He swayed but remained upright. Tomas offered him blood. The healer took it before he gave the verdict.

"The boy is clean of all parasites."

"Examine Bella next," Tariq said, voicing the demand unexpectedly.

Amelia tried to swing around but she couldn't move, couldn't take a step toward Charlotte to regain possession of the child. Gary didn't waste time. Once again he shed his body and went into Bella's. Charlotte held her close while Amelia glared at the Carpathians.

"This is so stupid," Amelia said. "A baby? You think Vadim chose a little baby to rush outside when we were all supposed to stay inside. Where was Genevieve? She always watches Bella."

"I believe the last time you wanted to go flying you sent Genevieve to sleep," Tariq answered. "That's enough, Amelia. We're going to get to the bottom of this tonight."

Amelia fell silent, but clearly she was still angry. Dragomir would bet his last dollar from the considerable fortune he'd amassed in his lifetime that the girl was the one Vadim had used to take over the lightning whip used to try to kill him.

Gary emerged almost immediately. "There are parasites in this child's blood."

Tariq closed his eyes. Dragomir shook his head. "It isn't her."

"No, it can't be her," Gary confirmed. "I found a fresh entry wound on her thigh. It was up high and cleverly concealed, but someone pushed a needle into her and shot her full of parasites. It is so new, they haven't had time to take root in her bloodstream. I have to clean them, though, or she'll suffer. He could kill her. Direct the parasites to clog her heart as he did with Emeline's unborn child." He addressed his statement to Amelia.

The teenager looked horrified. Dragomir watched her closely. Either she was the best actress on the planet, or her reaction was genuine.

"Get them out of her. Right now. Get those things out of her. They're horrible little wiggly worms with teeth." She tried to go to her sister, but Dragomir refused to allow her to take a step.

"Who do you think could have done this, Amelia?" Tariq asked gently. "There was only you, your brother and Liv."

She shook her head. "Genevieve was there. The vampires were all over her last night. Dragomir, you saw them. When you were helping Danny and me, you had to have seen them."

Dragomir replayed the images in his mind. Amelia's orange dragon had been wounded and was spinning out of control. Danny's brown had been in real trouble as well, not able to stop its plunge to earth. Had he not interfered, both dragons and both teens would have been lost. He'd directed Danny to aid Genevieve, to get her out of the play yard to safety. In his mind, he slowed down the replay so that he saw everyone. Genevieve was slumped over on the stone bench, her head on her book, hair blowing in the wind. She was oblivious to the danger, the vampires following their chosen leader—Vadim.

Vadim had Emeline a distance from the stone bench where Genevieve lay sleeping. Danny had started to wake Genevieve, shaking her repeatedly. Amelia aided him. Dragomir had turned his attention to Vadim, his ultimate challenge. Out of the corner of his eye, he continued to observe the drama unfolding by the bench.

Genevieve didn't seem able to wake up. She didn't respond at all. Danny seemed to be directing Amelia to pick up Genevieve's legs, which she did, but she dropped them, tripping over a tuft of grass in the yard. It was then that Vadim directed a couple of lesser vampires toward the children, not Genevieve. He remembered that distinctly. He told Emeline he was going to kill all the children because she hadn't cooperated. He had not included Genevieve in the threat.

"I do not recall vampires going after the woman. They chose you and Danny as their targets," he said, his voice betraying his thoughts.

"They did. She was on the ground and Danny kept trying to wake her."

"You told Danny to run," Dragomir persisted. "But you didn't run. You turned to face the vampires, and both followed Danny. Neither came after you."

"That's crazy. You were fighting Vadim. You couldn't possibly have seen what took place," she objected.

"We are taught from the time we were children to record every battle so we can replay it and improve for the next fight. I have the recording in my mind."

"Well, your recording is flawed. I tried to help Genevieve and then I gave up and ran to the safety of the underground chamber where the dragons were being held. That was the drill, Tariq's orders. Outnumbered, we get to the safety room. That's the rule." She sounded just a little smug.

"That's convenient for you."

As he spoke, a tired-looking Gary returned to his body. He was pale and weak. He actually staggered and almost went down, but Lojos eased him to the ground and then extended his wrist to him. Dragomir noticed that this time Amelia stared at the mouth over the laceration. Clearly the sight fascinated her. A single drop of blood ran down the back of Lojos's hand and dropped almost in slow motion to the ground. Amelia's gaze followed it.

"Amelia." Tariq's voice was soft. Gentle. But it held a command.

Amelia seemed mesmerized by the drop of blood, staring at it as it lay in a perfect circle on the ground. Dragomir subtly enlarged it. Not much, but the ruby drop was nestled in the nearly black dirt, rich loam Tariq had on the property to grow his plants and trees—to heal his people.

"Amelia." Tariq's voice sharpened.

She licked her lips and reluctantly tore her gaze from the crimson drop of blood showcased by the rich dirt.

"Did one of the vampires touch you?"

She blinked rapidly, her face closing down. "You know they did. Blaze examined me. I'm not pregnant like Emeline. I didn't let them put their disgusting child in me. That baby is *vampire*, just like its father. Dragomir can pretend all he wants that he's the baby's father, but he'll never be. How do we know it wasn't the baby attacking him? The baby could have tried to kill him. Did you ever once think about that?"

There was a long silence. Amelia looked around her. "I'm just saying what everyone else is thinking. You accused me, so my entire family has to be searched, but we can't even speculate that the baby did this?" There was pure defiance in her voice. She looked to Lojos. "What about you? Do you worry that the baby is a Malinov? I've heard all of you use that name. You know she's his baby, yet you all act like it doesn't matter."

"It doesn't," Gary said before Dragomir could respond. "Vadim targeted the baby for death. He can't turn a female child, and he knows that. He might use one as his tool, but if the baby was unborn, he'd have to force the mother to carry out orders."

Amelia changed the subject the moment he spoke. "How is Bella? Did you get them all?"

Gary nodded. "I did. They hadn't had time to burrow deep or hide themselves, so in comparison to Emeline and the baby, this was relatively easy. She has no memory of Vadim or any other vampire."

"You looked in her memories?" Amelia's tone was accusatory.

"Yes," Gary said. "I looked back over the last few hours. She was playing in her room when you came in, Amelia. You walked right past Genevieve, who once more had succumbed to a sleeping spell. I know it was a spell because every use of magic has a signature. The spell surrounding her was Vadim's."

"I just thought she was asleep," Amelia defended. "How would I know what Vadim's signature looks like?"

"You picked her up and swung her around. She laughed and snuggled into you." Gary stood up and walked right over to her. "That's when you did it. You injected her thigh. All the while you were laughing and joking. If she felt anything, it was a tiny pinch. You kept playing with her so she wouldn't get suspicious."

Amelia shook her head. "I wouldn't do that. I would *never* harm my own sisters." Both hands curled into fists. "You can't possibly think I would inject parasites into a toddler.

Into Bella." She crossed her arms over her chest and stared in a kind of horror at Tariq. "I didn't, Tariq. I don't talk to Vadim. I really don't. I would never let evil into our home. I love it here. Danny and the others are happy. So am I. I don't want to leave." Words tumbled out, running into one another as she denied all charges.

Her voice rings with truth, Tariq sent to Dragomir.

There is more than Vadim in this. We face multiple vampires, not just one. She opened the earth enough to allow Vadim to send his dark magic. Vadim has a sliver of Xavier, the high mage, in him. With that sliver come his darkest spells. It was Vadim directing the lightning strikes at me. He did it through this girl.

Dragomir wasn't about to let it go. Amelia had allowed Vadim to influence all of the children, but in particular, Liv, the ten-year-old. Blaze hadn't found parasites in her blood, so how was Vadim controlling her?

"Check me, then," Amelia demanded of Tariq. She refused to even look at Dragomir. "I want you to. Check my blood. I know I didn't do something like that."

"You did," Dragomir said softly. "Vadim found a way to control you."

"That's not true," she denied. "Tariq"—she turned to her guardian—"I swear, it isn't true. I would never hurt my little sister, or Emeline. Either one of them. Where would I get a needle filled with parasites? Tell me that."

"When I went up to get Bella and Lourdes," Dragomir said. "He had plenty of time to give you whatever he wanted to give you. You were out of my sight. Danny had run for safety. You were supposed to be right behind him, but you weren't. Was she, Danny?"

Her brother frowned and then shook his head, his eyes sliding away from the Carpathians to find the ground. "I can't remember. Everything happened so fast."

Gary moved then, slowly getting up and moving toward Amelia, who backed away, ran into the barrier Dragomir had set up and turned as if she might try to run. He sent her a sharp reprimand. "Hold still. I'm going to ensure you have no parasites."

"Wouldn't I feel them?" Amelia looked as if she might burst into tears.

"Amelia." Tariq simply said her name. His voice was loving. Persuasive. It carried a soft command, one that ensured his order would be carried out.

She subsided immediately. Gary didn't waste time on the niceties. He shed his body and entered the teen's. No one spoke. Amelia trembled continually. Dragomir knew he should feel bad for the girl, but he was absolutely certain she had influenced her younger sister Liv to remove the safeguards and open the compound for Vadim's invasion. Emeline had nearly been taken, and if the master vampire had been allowed to get his hands on her again, there would have been little chance of ever getting her back.

Dragomir felt Amelia's gaze, her hatred of him. She stared at his throat as if she could strangle him. He felt a burn there. It was slow, as if the temperature in one spot increased. At first, waiting for the healer's verdict, he paid little attention to the fact that a human teenage girl despised him. It was beneath his notice. As his throat became more uncomfortable, he realized it was her doing. She hadn't taken her eyes from him.

He sent a her a perverse grin, one without humor, one challenging her to do her worst. She lifted her chin, her eyes narrowing. He felt her hatred, a tangible thing. Because he was a hunter, he never focused solely on one threat but kept every sense flaring out in order to see the larger picture. Tariq was watching Amelia intently. Charlotte turned Bella so the child was unaware of anything happening, all the while keeping up running chatter with her.

Something flickered inside Dragomir's throat. The tip of a flame burned along the inside with a delicate touch. Too delicate for a teenager.

Gary chose that moment to emerge. This time it was Tomas stepping close to offer his wrist.

"The girl is clean of parasites," the healer said and bent his head to the laceration and the ruby drops beading up.

9

Dragomir leaned one hip against the wall and studied the healer's face. He looked worn, but his peculiar-colored eyes were shrewd and assessing as they compared observations. Tariq had sent the children back to their rooms, reiterating they were still grounded. Tariq, Dragomir, Gary and several of the ancients gathered together in the main house.

"She's tainted," Dragomir said. "I don't care if you didn't find parasites."

"Unfortunately"—Tariq's breath came out in a long, slow hiss of anger—"I have to agree. She's a child and she's already been traumatized by Vadim, now this. I don't know how she's going to recover."

Dragomir bit back what he would have said and instead silently observed Tariq. The man had genuine compassion for the teenager. He could see beyond her betrayal to the person underneath, one clearly being directed by a being far more

179

powerful. Tariq was a leader because he cared about those under his protection. Dragomir realized that was what made him someone to follow. He had compassion. He knew Amelia hadn't betrayed them on purpose, she was being forced to do a master vampire's bidding. Dragomir hadn't looked beyond the damage done to his lifemate and their child.

"I agree that she's tainted," Gary said. "I could feel evil residing in her, but I couldn't find it, and believe me, I looked."

"She came after me." Dragomir touched his throat. He still felt the effects. "Her touch was delicate, a master's hand."

Tariq raked his hand through his hair in agitation. "How can you get rid of his presence if you can't find it? Gary, you're our best shot at this. If you can't get rid of him, no one can."

"I have to figure out how he's doing it first. If he discovers we know about him and are looking to get him out of her, he may kill her," Gary answered. "It's best to go slow, but remember, she can't be trusted, not for a moment. You will need eyes on her at all times."

Tariq shook his head. "The risk is too great. She could harm one of the other children. Look at what she did to the baby, Bella. Charlotte is still worried about the child. She's taken her to Lourdes and the two little ones are playing with Blaze and Charlotte watching over them, but Amelia could be forced by Vadim to strike at one of the others."

"It's a big possibility," Dragomir agreed. "Vadim swore to Emeline that he would kill those children. What better way to do it than force one of their siblings to commit murder?"

Gary nodded in agreement. "I think his first target will be you, Dragomir. He has to know you're the biggest deterrent to his plans for Emeline. That's the other thing we need to figure out. Why does he want your lifemate so badly?"

"Can we use her?" Sandu asked. When Dragomir unfolded his arms and took a step toward the ancient Sandu shrugged his wide shoulders. "The girl. Amelia. Can we feed her information to draw Vadim out? Maybe something about Emeline."

"Use her?" Tariq's voice was a whip of anger. Any other might have winced, but like Dragomir, Sandu was in the brotherhood for a reason. The tattoo drifted across his back, letting the others know what he stood for. He was impervious to anger or any other emotion.

Sandu nodded. "Information flows both ways. If we can't take the chance of Vadim knowing we're aware that she's his spy, reporting every conversation, every weakness the compound has, any data he desires, then we can reverse that."

Dragomir had to smile at the ancient's use of the word *data*. He was taking in everything, absorbing the history of the planet and the new technology like a sponge. They all were. It was necessary to survive. Sandu seemed especially confident in computers, software and technology. Once he'd been given the information, his mind grasped it and demanded more.

"I have to agree with Gary's assessment," Andor said. "The child will be sent after Dragomir. And Sandu's right, if we can't get him out of her, then we need to use her. She'll make a good weapon."

"She's a little girl. A teenager," Tariq snapped. "Quit thinking of her as Vadim's spy. Whatever he's done to her, she can't stop."

"And the longer he's influencing her, the less chance we have to reverse his effects," Gary pointed out.

Dragomir tried to reason out what his lifemate would be thinking in the situation. She loved the children. She'd put them first from the beginning, before she'd ever met them. They were strangers, creeping into her dreams night after night until she figured out just how to save them. The first few dreams she'd had had been unsuccessful and the children had died, but each night she'd changed her responses in the dream until she'd chosen the right actions to keep them from being killed and getting them free of Vadim.

"She dreams. Emeline dreams. She's a strong psychic, able to resist Vadim's compulsions. She remained alive and kept the baby alive when all those other women we found down in the underground city died. They hadn't been able to withstand the torment of Vadim's parasites. He might want her for either reason or both." Dragomir still hadn't gotten over the sight of those dead bodies carelessly thrown aside like so much garbage. Vadim had been trying for some time to find a woman who could carry his baby.

Tariq rubbed the bridge of his nose. "Charlotte mentioned this to me. She said Emeline can share her dreams, that when they were together and Emeline dreamt, Blaze had the exact same dream."

"Wait a minute." Gary paced back and forth across the room, all pent-up, restless energy. "You told me about the machines down in the underground. The computers and how they were tracking hunters and sending out alerts to leave an area if a hunter arrived. He's using widespread communication with his army. It doesn't matter that they're a world away, they just have to have access to the Internet. But the Internet can be hacked. We have a few weapons on our side. There's a kid, a Carpathian. His name is Josef and he's brilliant with computers. He can do just about anything with them. He's the one that got the Morrison database for psychics. He's on his way here. In any case, it would be interesting to know if Emeline's dreams can be shared by several people at the same time."

Icy fingers of fear crept down Dragomir's spine. "Could he force her to dream?"

"He didn't when he had her," Gary said.

"He had her less than an hour," Tariq said. "We were hard on his heels."

Dragomir found himself swearing, using his ancient language, wanting to hit something hard. Emeline had a talent of dreaming and one didn't think much about it. But Emeline didn't just dream; she had prophetic dreams. And she could change the course of events by continually dreaming the same dream over and over and changing details in it, until the dream itself changed. She could literally figure out how to best others every time. She would be a huge weapon in Vadim's arsenal. She'd gone for psychic testing and she'd been off the charts. Vadim had realized her potential immediately.

"I'll talk to Emeline and see what she thinks is possible. She must have some idea of the scope of her talent. I don't want Amelia anywhere near her." Dragomir was adamant on that.

"You're going to have trouble with that," Tariq said. "Amelia was cultivating a relationship with her. They shared a similar experience. In truth, we were all playing right into Vadim's hands by trying to get Amelia to talk to her. We thought it would be good, they both could open up to each other about what had happened to them. Once they started talking, Charlotte had hoped to bring in a professional. In the end, Amelia talked to Charlotte, not Emeline, but I fear she didn't tell the entire truth."

Andor scowled to show his displeasure at the idea. "We can't mix with humans to that degree. A counselor?"

"We have an experienced counselor," Tariq said. "She's in London at the moment, but she is wrapping things up and will arrive in a week or so. If she doesn't work out, there is another in South America we will try. These women and children have the right to feel whole again. If talking to a professional works, then that's what we'll get for them."

"What are we going to do about Amelia?" Dragomir brought them back to the problem at hand. "Because she isn't getting near Emeline, and that's going to alert Vadim that his plan isn't working."

"Not necessarily," Gary mused. They all turned to look at him. He wore a faint, humorless smile. "You made your dislike of her apparent already. Vadim knows you're at odds with Amelia, that you don't like her."

"She's smug."

"Vadim is smug," Tariq corrected.

Dragomir shrugged. "Right now, she *is* Vadim. Everything that comes out of her mouth is because he's her puppet master and is controlling her."

"It's important that you understand Amelia is a victim in all this. She's being controlled, it isn't her choice." Tariq was adamant.

"She can fight him. Not allow him to swallow her whole."

"She's fourteen, Dragomir, and not Carpathian. She is without shields of any kind. She was taken before Emeline was and subjected to Vadim's form of rape. He also managed to invade her mind somehow." There was a clear reprimand in Tariq's voice.

Dragomir shrugged. While he could acknowledge that Tariq made a good leader, and he could even find compassion for the girl, he couldn't find it in his heart to agree with the man on this particular subject. The bottom line was simple: Amelia wasn't getting anywhere near Emeline. He hoped they could save the girl, but he wasn't risking Emeline.

"If we have conversations in front of Amelia about how we didn't find any parasites and you must accept that verdict, that she's clear of all evil. If all of us argue with you, Vadim will think the split between you and the rest of us is going along happily for him. It makes sense that you don't like her and would want to keep her away from Emeline," Gary pointed out. "Vadim will love the fights you have with your lifemate over him."

"Great." Dragomir knew Emeline wasn't going to like any of this.

"We should feed Amelia some small bit of information that requires activity on his part, just so we can be certain," Gary said.

Tariq sighed. "I guess it's necessary, but I don't like it."

"A location of a lair?" Sandu suggested. "We're going out hunting now. Andor found some possible activity in Cuyamaca Rancho State Park. We were going to check it out. She can overhear us talking, making plans to raid it."

"That's a pretty big target to give up," Dragomir protested. "One of Vadim's lairs?"

Sandu shook his head. "No, the safeguards were pathetic. No one was home, but we think they'll return before sundown. In front of Amelia we can say we'll be waiting for the vampire when he rises on the next day, but we'll get him tonight."

"Vadim won't have a chance of finding out until it's too late. He'll send someone to aid the vampire against the hunters and we'll get them as well. Vadim won't know that we killed the original vampire the night before. He'll just know he'd better be careful with the elite hunters in the area." Gary turned his head, those slashing silver eyes meeting Dragomir's.

They were both eager for the hunt. Men like them didn't sit around talking. They weren't diplomatic. They left that to the leaders, like Mikhail, their prince in the Carpathian Mountains, and Tariq, the acknowledged leader here in the United States.

"It is best if we test our theory before condemning Amelia,"

Tariq acknowledged. "I believe Vadim has found a way to control her, just as all of you do, but I would prefer proof."

"We can set a trap for Vadim," Dragomir said. "Using me as bait."

Tariq glanced up sharply. "You have a lifemate. Emeline's been through as much as she can take. You have a daughter. Both need you."

Sandu nudged him, a psychic nudge, not a physical one, but it was the same, only others couldn't see it. *He means keep your ass home. Perhaps your woman could find a broad leaf and fan you.*

Terád keje, Dragomir responded mildly, telling his friend to "get scorched." *Life as you know it is going to end.*

You're soft now that you have a woman. I will bet that the moment she cries because she cannot see this girl, you will give in and the teen will move right into your house.

Dragomir turned cold golden eyes on his friend. There was nothing remotely humorous about his reaction. *I will kill that girl before she gets near Emeline,* he vowed. He glanced toward the house where the children were.

Not yet, Sandu said. *If it needs to be done, I will do it for you. You cannot afford to have your name attached to her death. Your woman and the rest of the community would find it difficult to forgive you.*

I have the right to keep my woman safe.

You need to spend a little time at the computer. The days are long past where we kill our enemies and are glorified in song.

Dragomir frowned. *You were glorified in song?*

Of course. My deeds were great. Weren't yours?

My deeds were great, and yet no one glorified me in song. Köd alte hän. Darkness curse it, Sandu. That's just not right. There must be some mistake.

Andor nudged him next. *Pay attention. Tariq is sharp, and he's watching you two. He knows you're up to something. You*

186

planning to kill that girl? Because if you are, I'll do it. You do have a lifemate you have to think about.

Do I look like I'm going to kill her? Dragomir asked, exasperated.

"I want all of you to remember, Amelia is my daughter. I have taken her and her siblings as my children. I would track any man who harmed her to the ends of the earth."

"Do I look like I'm going to kill a child?" Dragomir snapped aloud. He had an expressionless mask for a face. There was a multitude of scars, but he didn't show what he was thinking.

"Yes." Tariq looked him in the eye. "That's exactly what you looked like. You also look as if there might be a few others willing to help."

"Were you ever glorified in song?" Dragomir asked abruptly.

Tariq's brows came together. He looked at Dragomir as if he'd grown two heads. "Yes. Of course I was. Several centuries ago. Weren't you?"

"*Köd alte hän*, darkness curse it and all songs glorifying the lot of you." Dragomir pushed himself away from the wall. "I've had enough. I'm going hunting."

It was all he could do to keep from answering Tariq's grin. Humor was still new to him. Abruptly he turned away from Tariq. The man had the right to protect his family—the same right Dragomir had. Dragomir knew he'd kill any man threatening his lifemate or his daughter. Despite his diplomacy, despite looking as if he had been born and raised in the current century, Dragomir had no doubt that Tariq would hunt him down if he harmed Amelia.

That knowledge would never stop him from doing what he considered right. Dragomir liked Tariq—more, he respected him. Tariq wasn't blind to the fact that Amelia was tainted. Frowning, he regarded Gary. "You said we had to figure out

187

just how Vadim is able to use Amelia as his spy when she has no parasites in her."

The others had all turned to go separate ways, but at Dragomir's question, they all turned back to listen.

"I have an idea or two," Gary said. "None are good."

"Let's hear them," Tariq said.

Gary shrugged. It was more of a shoulder roll. His shoulders were wide; his muscles, once sleek and strong, were now more defined, rippling loosely beneath the material of his clothing. "Xavier, the high mage, could take splinters of himself and place those splinters in very unlucky people. The splinter was actually a true part of him so he could take over the body and see and hear what was happening around his chosen vessel. Xavier is dead, but two of his splinters remain behind and the common consensus is that those splinters reside in Sergey, Vadim's brother, and in Vadim himself."

Tariq's breath left him in a long, slow hiss. Dragomir froze in place. Sandu leaned his palm against the wall, allowing it to take his weight.

"What are you saying, Gary?" Ferro was the one who asked. Ferro was quiet and rarely spoke, so the sound of his voice was disconcerting, adding to the building tension between the ancients. "You believe that Vadim knows how to splinter himself and would introduce slivers into others? He could have spies everywhere."

"There is danger in splintering," Gary cautioned. "It diminishes the man performing the magic. It leaves him weaker, his power less. He must bring the splinters back to him. That's imperative. If we were to find those splinters, remove and destroy them, he would never get his full capacity for magic back. That's what happened to Xavier."

There was a small silence.

"Having said that," Gary continued, "being in possession

188

of Xavier's splinters gives Vadim access to the knowledge Xavier had."

Tariq glared at him. "You didn't think to tell us this before?"

"Before what?" Gary asked, his tone mild, but there was a curious menace to it. Those silver eyes slashed at Tariq. "I haven't exactly been idle since I arrived."

Tariq gave a small, courtly bow. "Forgive me, Gary, I am so worried about Amelia and knowing this hasn't helped."

"At the moment, Amelia is a valuable asset to him. He can hear and see everything she does. He can attack his enemies using her. He doesn't have to worry about the safeguards because Amelia is already in the compound. She brought him in with her. He most likely hadn't even considered putting a child in her. He knew from experience that she was too young and fragile. He needed her to have those memories so the one of him entering her body and leaving a small but extremely valuable piece of himself behind wouldn't be noticed."

"We all saw the 'rape' in her mind," Tariq said. "Not the fact that he entered her body in the way a healer might. What happens if Amelia is killed? If she dies?" His voice was low. Anguished.

For the first time, Dragomir put himself in Tariq's shoes. If that were his daughter, how would he feel? What would he do? Knowing a piece, even just a splinter of such evil was in his daughter would be horrifying. The parasites did Vadim's bidding, tormenting Emeline and the baby, but they hadn't been so evil that they could take over the bodies. The splinter of Vadim was powerful. Evil. A part of him. That part allowed him to take total control of the vessel.

Dragomir found his compassion for Amelia was growing. She wouldn't be able to fight Vadim's influence. She might fight off the parasites that tormented her, refusing to give in to the pain or their sway, but what human could defeat the power of a master vampire?

"If Amelia dies, does the splinter die with her?" Tariq persisted.

Gary shook his head. "The splinter would look for a host. It would abandon the dying body and find another. That's what Xavier's splinters did. They also try to get back to the original brain they were taken from. So each hop from host to host would take them closer to their ultimate goal."

"With the splinter gone, will Amelia return to her true self?" Dragomir asked.

Gary frowned and rubbed at his temple with his thumb. "She should. But she's very young. These attacks on her will stay with her. I'm inclined to think she will need counseling."

"If I was to turn her," Tariq persisted, "would the splinter abandon her then?"

Gary shook his head. "You are not thinking logically, Tariq. This is your daughter. You're too close to the situation. Vadim is vampire. Originally, he was Carpathian. The death of the human body in order for the Carpathian body to be reborn would not kill it. If anything, the splinter might grow more powerful. Vadim would have access to everything she learned of us. Of the healing grounds, of resting places, of every weakness this compound has—and there are many."

"Many?" Tariq's eyebrow went up. "We have thought of nearly every contingency. Every way they could attack us."

"You are under attack," Gary insisted. "Your own daughter is being used against you. The biggest weakness the compound has is *you*. Your heart. You take in these abandoned people and collect them like others collect wine. You have a security force made up of human Special Forces soldiers. Every one of them has seen too much combat and is ready to implode. You have an elderly couple, the Waltons, wandering around holding hands as if they're in a musical. You have four street kids, all traumatized by what they've been through. You have a woman, unmarried, no lifemate, but by any standards beautiful, watching those children, and she doesn't have a clue they can put her to sleep at will. You have a three-year-old child, the niece of your lifemate, whose father was murdered by a vampire and who has been uprooted several times avoiding them. Carpathians do not live this way."

Dragomir had to agree, but he also disagreed. "That's all true, but he's created a safe zone here, one where Carpathians and humans can live together without fear."

Gary shrugged. "I didn't say I thought it was too risky, only that it is a flawed system. There are weaknesses and they have to be addressed if all of you want to be safe."

Dragomir noticed the healer had said "all of *you*." He hadn't included himself as if it didn't matter one way or another that he was safe. It hadn't to Dragomir before he'd found Emeline. He knew it still didn't to Sandu, Andor or Ferro. He looked around at the other ancients. So many without lifemates. The burden of an entire species fell squarely on the shoulders of a very few couples.

"Emeline wishes to remain here. She wants to have a home here near her friends," Dragomir said. "She will go with me if I choose to leave, but she would much rather be here. I would like to buy property bordering this one and add to the compound. I would also like to go through the entire compound with you, Gary and Tariq, to see if some of these weaknesses can be addressed."

Tariq inclined his head. "I'm grateful you wish to stay. Blaze would have a difficult time without Emeline. Already, Maksim has said, she's been very sad that their relationship has deteriorated. I'm aware it was necessary, or at least

191

Emeline thought it was, but it is difficult for a Carpathian male to see his lifemate unhappy."

Dragomir was instantly aware Tariq was warning him. It was imperative he keep Emeline from Amelia, but Emeline wouldn't be happy about it. "I understand, or I'm beginning to. Still, I can do no other than what my nature dictates to me. Emeline must be out of the line of fire. Healer"—his thoughtful gaze rested on the man—"is it possible that if we try together, we could rid this child of the splinter?"

"We have no idea of the location. He would know before we did that we were close. If he thought we were there to extract the splinter, he would attack and kill her."

"We do have a location. The splinter must be in her brain. It is directing her actions."

Gary frowned in contemplation. "I still don't see how we could sneak up on it."

"Divert his attention," Sandu said. "Go in to heal her and check it out."

"I will think on this," Gary said. "In the meantime, before the night fades, I need to hunt."

Dragomir agreed. "I need more blood as well. The night is fading and the healing soil will be welcome."

"I will plant the story with Amelia," Tariq said. "Give me the location of the lair."

It was Ferro who supplied it, pushing the information into Tariq's mind. "We will hunt near there and take him down when the sun is rising."

Tariq shook his head. "That's cutting it too close. Do you have a death wish? You'll fry in the sun."

Sandu shrugged. "I've fried before. We all have. As old as we are, with not so much as a whisper to tempt us, it is the sun we defy. Our defiance comes at a high price."

"Yet you still take the chance."

"We are hunters first," Andor pointed out. "Hunters hunt. There is little left for us. Hunting is something we can do."

Tariq nodded. "Go, then. It will be natural for me to visit all the children before we go to bed. I'll have Charlotte with me and just out of Amelia's room, where she can hear. I'll let slip the plan to attack the lair at first rising."

"You will need someone at least a little resistant to Vadim's compulsions watching her. Otherwise the children aren't safe. Vadim might use the opportunity to force her to kill one of them," Dragomir said. "I know that's not something you want to think about, but it is a very real possibility and one I think Vadim would choose. He would want the girl to know what she was doing, but be unable to stop herself."

Tariq nodded. "I hoped he would wait, fearing she might get caught and then she'd be of no use to him."

"Hoping when lives are at stake is a poor choice," Gary said. "Find a reason to lock her up." He pushed away from the others, closing down, the weight of his ancestors on his back and in his mind. He strode away from them without another word, his movements fluid, his body rippling with muscle beneath the thin material of his clothing.

Dragomir watched him go, sadness settling. Eighteen or twenty years in Carpathian time was nothing, a blink, no more—or it was centuries of endless waiting for a lifemate. Sandu, Andor and Ferro were at that other end. Gary was clearly there. It mattered little that he'd been reborn into their world; the ancients had poured themselves into him and now he carried every single one of their memories. The man was living in hell. Twenty years would be more than a few lifetimes for him waiting for his lifemate to grow up.

"How many men do you have working for you? Human men that you can trust."

"There are twenty in my security team that I trust. I've taken their blood so I can monitor them at will, but more than that, I've looked into their minds and the men I see are honest, loyal and capable. I respect them," Tariq said. "There are a few others but they're relatively new and I'm not certain of them yet."

"How many there?"

"Another seven. I've taken their blood, know they live by their word, but haven't seen them in battle against vampires. The first time human fighters see the undead in action, especially in their true form, it is ... disconcerting. That's when I know whether they'll be able to handle it. I wipe their minds clean if they can't. These are good men and valuable assets."

Dragomir nodded. He had never considered drawing humans into their fight. Humans had always seemed very vulnerable. Tariq had always had the reputation of being fascinated by them. He spent a great deal of his time with them. He'd studied them, and now, he surrounded himself with them. He fit into their world with ease.

Dragomir wasn't the kind of man to dismiss an idea just because he wasn't comfortable with it. He'd seen the security force in action and they'd helped tremendously. They hadn't flinched in the face of the enemy, and Vadim had brought a strong force with him. The weapons they'd developed were impressive. Matt Bennett had been a huge help in the battle with Vadim.

"The Waltons. I've seen them on the property," Dragomir admitted, "but I avoided them. Who are they? Are they capable of defending this place?"

Tariq smirked a little, his warning to Dragomir of the answer. "Both were in the service. That's where they met. They lived for years together as survivalists. They can handle guns and, in fact, have quite an arsenal in their home now. They've lived on the estate for a few years, before the children. They were gracious enough to say they would help with defense."

Dragomir had to admit, Tariq hadn't just gathered a group of humans and brought them under his protection without thought.

"You didn't have problems convincing them vampires exist?"

"They were already aware. No one believed them."

Dragomir nodded. "I see. Still, you realize, even with training, these people will always be at a disadvantage. Vampires can easily take over their minds."

"Not with shields in place. I got the idea from the De La Cruz family in South America. They have ranches in various countries and human people, people loyal to them, take care of the ranches in their absence. The families know about them and protect them during daylight hours. The family members, throughout generations, began to be born with natural shields. I thought it would be a decent idea to gather my own force."

Dragomir had heard of the families protecting the De La Cruz brothers. He hadn't considered the idea good or bad. Now, he thought this was another reason why Tariq was a leader. His thinking had far-reaching consequences. He'd planned for his human army. He'd bought up land. He'd gathered other like-minded Carpathians and they had begun the task of setting up compounds in other places, much like the stronghold of the prince in the Carpathian Mountains.

"Perhaps I was wrong about your weakness, Tariq," he ventured, still not quite convinced. Yet, he couldn't have kept the vampires from inflicting a terrible blow on the compound without the help of the security force. There were too few Carpathians and too many vampires in the United States. It was a big territory to cover. Matt Bennett, the head of the security force, had delayed Vadim enough for Dragomir to complete his task and return to confront the master vampire. He'd even managed to get a piece of Vadim's heart and that had to have weakened him just a bit.

Tariq inclined his head at Dragomir's observation. "Perhaps," he agreed. "On the other hand, I have found my love of humans is both a strength and a weakness. Thanks to the prince, we do know some human women can be converted. Those of us who did not find their lifemates, century after century, still can have hope. That soul is reborn again and again until we find her or we go into the next life. There are women out there, human and Carpathian, protecting the soul of a hunter."

"We left the monastery because three women came together and gave us hope. They told us that our lifemates were waiting in this century for us. I am not certain I really believed them at the time. I may have needed to believe them, but I was skeptical. Then I heard Emeline's voice, and my world changed from darkness to light. I hope that finding Emeline continues to give the others hope that they might find their lifemates, too. Like me, they don't think they belong anymore. We are ancients, and while we locked ourselves away, the world moved forward without us. Women moved forward as well. We don't understand them."

Tariq sent him a small grin. "No one has ever understood them. They only ask for partnership. They are intelligent and their opinions matter. They are intuitive."

"These are things I know, but partnership? What does that mean?"

"She will want to walk at your side, not behind you."

"I assume you mean that literally rather than figuratively," Dragomir said. He was aware of the others in the brotherhood paying close attention to the conversation.

"Both."

Dragomir shook his head. "That's where you lose me. What is wrong with wanting to protect my woman? My every instinct is to do just that. She carries life in her. She's light to my darkness. She's everything good in the world."

"To us. We know what we lost. We know a world without women and children. That drought has never happened to them. Even the women no longer know their own worth. We know they are more precious than the greatest jewel, but others don't understand and treat them as less than animals. They are possessions, not cherished partners."

"Emeline will not like me treating her as a cherished woman?" He was more confused than ever. "I know no other way. I am incapable of any other way."

"She will like that part. Just not the part where you lock her up when you don't want her talking to Amelia."

"And Charlotte?"

"She won't like that, either. I will do my best to distract her, but once she realizes what I'm doing, she will voice her opinion rather strongly."

There was a note of amusement in Tariq's voice. Dragomir still didn't understand, and he sensed this was an important subject. "You don't seem to mind your woman getting upset with you." Emeline's tears would kill him.

"There is little I can do about it, Dragomir. She will want to be with Amelia, to try to help her, and I will forbid it knowing Vadim could strike at us through her. I won't risk Charlotte. She won't understand, or she'll pretend she doesn't because going to Amelia and helping her is worth the risk to her. It isn't to me and never will be. Risking Emeline won't be worth it to you. You can't control Emeline's reactions any more than I can control Charlotte's."

Tariq shrugged. "The bottom line with your woman is

this: you can try to explain your position in a logical manner, but remember, it's *your* logic. It's *your* emotion—fear—that is driving you. Her logic will be different, but no less real. In the end, you will do what every male Carpathian must do—you will protect your woman. She won't like it, but she'll accept it because she has no choice. Your comfort level during that time will not be the best, but it will pass and your woman will be safe."

Dragomir nodded. "I think I understand. What is the use of explaining if she won't listen?"

"Always explain. She deserves an explanation. Your relationship cannot be a dictatorship."

Dragomir sighed, something in his heart twisting hard. "I do not want a dictatorship, but where I lead, my woman goes. I don't know, Tariq, I may have tied her to me far too fast. I was trying to convince her she wasn't Vadim's lifemate. Honestly? I still don't know if she's entirely convinced. But she's tied to me now, and that may be worse than a false belief. If what you say is so, then she will detest being my lifemate."

"You've been her lifemate all along. She seems to have fought for you. She didn't run."

"That's different."

Tariq threw back his head and laughed. "Go feed, my friend and brother. Emeline will be fine. She has been in our world. Blaze is her best friend and sister. They talk. Blaze is a warrior, Emeline is not. Blaze is suited to Maksim. Emeline is suited to you. My Charlotte is perfect for me. That is how it works. You will do your best to make her happy, and she will do her best to make you happy. Go, Dragomir, before you talk yourself into running for the monastery. I can assure you, most modern women, if you act like you don't want them, will shrug their shoulders and take their hurt in the opposite direction."

"I would not run from her. If I returned to the monastery, she would go with me."

Tariq laughed again. "Go start our little charade. Feed and then destroy the lair and hopefully any vampire you find in it. I will check on the children, isolate each of them from the others and make certain Amelia cannot escape the gilded cage we put her in."

Dragomir took to the sky with Tariq's laughter echoing through his mind. Sandu and Andor flew on either side of him. Ferro, Afanasiv and Nicu flanked him. He wanted the others there, Petru, Benedik and Isia. He sent out a call to the others in the brotherhood, hoping they would come. He wanted them to see that he had a lifemate and they were right to search for theirs.

10

Dragomir fed well, knowing he was heading for a fight. The lair that had been found was a good distance from the compound, in the Cuyamaca Rancho State Park. There were more than one hundred miles of hiking trails. Camping sites and picnic areas made it a smorgasbord for vampires. Up in the highest peak, a crack appeared in a large jutting boulder. It was barely a half of an inch wide, but ran about five feet long in a jagged pattern almost to the very foot of the boulder.

He stood facing it, the other ancients spreading out, feeling the air, the ground, listening and scanning. There was a compulsion embedded in the rock face that warned people away from the area. Anyone feeling it would just turn and leave. That had alerted Andor to the fact that the lair had to be close.

Anywhere one went in a forested area, there was the continual drone of insects. Here, it was eerily silent. There was a feeling of impending violence, of an unseen watcher. The ground shifted subtly under his feet, a built-in snare just in case the compulsion to leave didn't work. He crouched low to run his hand along the soil.

There is something here. A trap beneath our feet. It feels like the ones used a few centuries ago by the Astors. Fridrick and Georg. They had a few kin that ran with them as well. When the Malinovs turned, they also chose to give up their souls. Do any of you recall the others in this family and the traps they preferred to use?

The brotherhood had long ago formed their own telepathic paths. They didn't need to use the more common Carpathian path—the one any vampire would hear. The sun hadn't set, so any vampire inside the lair would be still bedding down and setting more safeguards.

They liked to use the local habitat so everything always looked natural, Afanasiv answered. *There were at least three others. Cousins, I think. My memory is dim.*

Karl, Leon and Raban. They all went from the Carpathian Mountains to Germany. They took German names to fit in, better to terrorize the people there, Ferro added to the bank of information.

Dragomir ran his hand, palm down, with exquisite gentleness along the top of the soil. There was no grass. He found a small, withered bush just to the right of the boulder. The plant had shrunken away from the foul, unnatural being that had trampled the dirt near it. He felt something, a small electric shock almost, leaping toward his palm. None of the other ancients had boots on the ground. Only Dragomir had allowed his feet to touch the soil.

They used insects. Swarms of them, stinging and biting. They enhanced the beetles or whatever it was they found in the earth, giving them poisonous venom and nasty stings, Nicu added. *They have scorpions here. He could use them. Enhance them.*

That would be like any of the Astors. They liked drama,

Dragomir said. *Be ready, let's see what he has.* He stood, walked first left and then right, paced back and forth, so that the vibrations would disturb the insects and trigger the trap.

Behind you. The warning came from Sandu.

Dragomir took to the air, turning to see the ground erupting with hundreds of scorpions. They rose to the surface, climbing on one another, covering the soil so it looked like a living, moving carpet. Tails raised high, stingers in position for a strike, they were agitated, looking for prey. None of the ancients moved. They knew that the trap had to have been triggered multiple times by wildlife in the area. The vampire would expect his allies to feed. He wouldn't be suspicious because something had disturbed his first line of defense. Still, one might expect him to check since the sun hadn't yet risen.

Dragomir and the other ancients shimmered into transparency and then disappeared, becoming nothing but molecules in the night air. They waited, aware of the minutes ticking away. Dragomir was certain there would be no going back to the compound before the sun rose. That meant he had to rely on Tariq to keep Emeline safe from Amelia. While he waited, he replayed everything the Carpathian had said to him. Tariq might love Amelia, but he wasn't blinded. The sliver of evil Vadim planted in her would take her over. It wouldn't be Amelia trying to harm the others, it would be Vadim. Tariq wouldn't give in to sentiment, not even for his lifemate.

A steady stream of yellow vapor slipped out of the crack in the boulder, just as a small mule deer stepped close to the swarm of scorpions. They rushed at it. The deer shrieked as one stabbed it with its stinger. Others tried to run up its legs. The deer whirled around and ran a few feet only to drop. At once the other scorpions were all over it. The yellow vapor retreated into the crack, clearly satisfied.

Dragomir moved back into position at the boulder, while the others spread out, all in the air, keeping their boots from touching the surface and adding to the frenzy taking place just a few feet away.

Anyone remember the safeguards the Astors relied on? Even if they've changed them, they will use the base form. They were always on the lazy side, Dragomir said.

You remember, Sandu said. *You're testing us, like you always do, being an ass.*

Someone has to keep you sharp.

I believe I kept you sharp in the training area.

Sandu was correct, he had taught all of them many lessons with various weapons, over and over. He was incredibly fast. Not as fast as Nicu, who moved like lightning in a fight. It was almost impossible to see him because he moved so fast he was a blur, but Sandu could anticipate almost every move an opponent would make.

Dragomir was grateful he had the ability to find humor in everything again. He'd forgotten humor and how much it could change one's mood. Sandu was telling them all the strict truth. A fact. But the play on words made it humorous without the ancient meaning it that way.

I sent for the others. Benedik, Petru and Isia, Sandu added. *I had forgotten what it was to chase the vampire, and a war is shaping up here.*

I did as well, Andor admitted.

The others nodded and Dragomir had to smile. He had also sent for the others in the brotherhood. *It scares me that we all think alike.*

We've been together too long, Ferro pointed out with a small shrug.

Dragomir got back to the task at hand. *They always used the first safeguard, Alycrome taught us.* Alycrome had been the high

203

mage for many years before Xavier, his son, had taken over. Alycrome had insisted they follow their instincts and develop safeguards of their own, but many had problems completing that task. Weaving strands was easy enough; making them complicated, so difficult that others couldn't unravel them, was something else again.

Dragomir and the other ancients lifted their hands into the air and began a reverse of the oldest safeguard known to their people. It had been a simple one, not at all complex like the ones used in the centuries following. Sure enough, as their hands and fingers played out the symbols, the air around them once more shimmered and the barrier was revealed. It lay heavy around the boulder, a wide net blanketing the rock, preventing anyone from entering.

The next layer looks simple enough, Ferro said. *That's just a retaliation spell. It's barely finished.*

Dragomir looked at the weave moving in and out of the first strand, the foundation of the spell. It was sloppy work. Someone had thrown it up hastily. These vampires hadn't been chased by hunters in a long while and they were feeling safe. Secure. Vadim had given them that false sense of security.

Classic seven weave, Ferro volunteered. *Not well done and nothing original.*

Ferro was right. It was ridiculous that the vampire had even bothered to safeguard the area. Dragomir took the next two strands down. The ancients surrounding him scanned the air continually, looking for hidden traps. That was always the worry. The vampire had made it easy to draw a hunter in.

He glanced uneasily at Sandu, who shook his head. *I think he's really that careless. I don't feel or see anything out of place.*

Dragomir took the next two strands down. One remained. It floated in the air, looking like a string of knots.

Rosary, the ancients identified simultaneously. The weave

had been taken from the prayer beads in the thirteenth century. Now it was called a rosary weave by those practicing to remove the safeguard.

Dragomir began to undo each knot slowly. Waiting. Watching. He just couldn't believe that the safeguards set were so careless. *When we go in, fan out. He could be anywhere.* He was uneasy, but he figured it probably had to do with the way his skin prickled in alarm, telling him the sun was close to rising.

Do you get a sense of who constructed the safeguard? Andor asked. *You ran across them from time to time before they turned, Dragomir.*

Dragomir hadn't liked them. But then, he'd lost emotion earlier than some of the others and by the time the Astors and Malinovs arrived, he was already an experienced hunter.

I think Leon. It feels like his signature.

Yellow vapor suits him, Sandu said. *Whiny little brat. Always causing trouble and running from the consequences. When I heard he and his brothers turned, I wasn't surprised. I never ran across them after that. Figured they avoided me.*

Everyone avoids you, Dragomir pointed out. *They avoid all of us.*

With reason, Afanasiv said.

No one spoke again as Dragomir took out the rest of the knots. Once the safeguards were down, he wasted no time in streaming through the crack. The others followed him. The crack opened into a narrow corridor. The sides of the small cavern were lined with cracks running up from floor to ceiling. The ceiling wasn't high. Had he been in his normal form, he wouldn't have been able to stand up straight.

The corridor narrowed again until a slight man or woman could have moved sideways through it. Three times there were narrow alcoves, just rounded spaces carved out of the rock by water that had long ago disappeared. Dirt had fallen from the sloping walls to the floor.

Sandu materialized in the small space, bent over, crouching low to examine the floor and run his hand up the side of the wall. *Go. I'll make certain this one is clear.*

Ferro took the second space, which was much smaller than the first one. His wide shoulders scraped on either side of the walls, but, like Sandu, he took his time exploring.

Nicu waved the others on and stayed behind to scrutinize the walls and floor of the third alcove. It looked as if someone had tried to form a grotto in the boulder. This was deeper and smoother, but there was also suspect dirt lying in crumbles all over the ground. It was easy to see where it had rolled off the sides as if something had disturbed it recently.

Dragomir kept going through that narrow corridor. Behind him, Afanasiv and Andor followed. Afanasiv stopped abruptly and materialized, his large frame taking up a good portion of the hallway. He was forced to bend over, and his shoulders didn't fit, so he also had to turn sideways as he crouched down to examine the floor. There was a large fracture zigzagging down the center of the passageway. All around it was dirt and debris. A few rocks. Nothing lay in the crack itself. No dirt at all. Dirt should have been caught in the fissure, but there was none. Afanasiv ran his finger down the fracture until he got to a tiny piece of rock that looked as if it had fallen in the crack, but the crack had formed around it.

I've got something, he said.

Dragomir stopped moving forward. He materialized beside him. The two barely fit in the narrow space.

Andor streamed past them. *I'll check out the rest of this passageway and come back.*

Dragomir concentrated on the fissure in the floor. It had

been there for centuries. No vampire had constructed it, but they could easily have taken advantage of it. Even though they were in darkness, with a mountain on top of them, a barrier between him and the sun, he still felt the burn as the sun began its first journey.

Let's get this done. You ready?

In answer, Afanasiv waved his hand to open the crack. It widened a mere half inch. As it did, the entire boulder above and around them creaked and groaned. Dirt ran down the sides of the cavern to land on the floor. Dragomir was already streaming through the crack, Afanasiv behind him. They were used to traveling in complete darkness. They were used to tons of earth overhead. More, hunting vampires was what they were most comfortable doing.

Below them was space, lots of space. The boulder hid a cave beneath with no outside entrance. The cool air hit their bodies, feeling good after the heat of the narrow corridor. Dragomir knew instantly they weren't alone. Vampires had a stench to them. They were undead, their bodies often decomposing before they could figure out how—or bother—to overcome that little stumbling block.

The stench indicated the lair was used often—or by multiple vampires. The latter would be highly unusual, but then, he didn't discount the idea simply because in the past it hadn't been done. Vampires were vain and selfish. They wanted glory. They didn't want to share their victims. On the other hand, their biggest drive was to stay alive. Vadim had somehow connected with that drive and he'd built himself an unusual army. These vampires used modern technology, and they worked together. They had an acknowledged leader.

We're not alone, he warned. *One, possibly more.*

The attack came out of the darkness, a fireball that lit the world around him, exposing the cave to his vision. He instantly mapped it, committing every curve, every rock, the ceiling, floor and surrounding walls to memory even while he dodged the fireball and dropped straight down toward the vampire rising out of the ground.

It was Leon, and he wasn't alone in the chamber. Leon called out, and three spouts of fresh dirt rose into the air like giant plumes. In the dwindling light of the fireball, Dragomir recognized two of the three. One called himself Ravenous. He must have turned quite recently because he was disheveled and shaky as he came out of the ground. The second one he recognized was named Eugen, and he also must have turned recently. Both had been a few centuries younger, but they'd been impressive hunters.

Leon must be the master vampire, or at least moving in that direction. He gave the information to Afanasiv even as he drove straight at Leon. Leon squawked and hurtled a spinning spear of fire at him, dodging to the left and disappearing behind a large rock.

He wishes he was a master vampire, Afanasiv said. *Collecting pawns doesn't make you good in battle. Leon and his brothers perfected the art of running away.*

Dragomir had to agree with the ancient. Truthfully, though, he'd been out of the game for a while. His recent battles were the only experience he'd had since he'd entered the monastery. Yes, they'd kept up their practices, and they'd shared battle strategy and what they knew of various Carpathians and vampires, but he hadn't had actual practice in a while.

He pursued Leon, expecting an attack, but Leon circled around toward Ravenous and Eugen. *Do you know the third one?* He had some information on the other two and he imparted it immediately to Afanasiv. He shared the lesser vampires' weak sides, which weapons they favored, which battles they'd fought

208

in, everything he could remember. Dragomir couldn't remember his past, growing up as a child, but he remembered battles. Wars. Weapons. He pushed what he had into the ancient's mind. It took no more than a couple of seconds to arm Afanasiv with everything he knew about the vampires.

The third one is called Kaiser. He was a hanger-on with the Astors. I'm surprised you don't remember him. He's a tricky devil. Well versed in warfare. My guess, he's been with the Astors, running interference for them for centuries. Watch him. He's probably the most experienced and the deadliest.

The spear had been thrown with such force it embedded into the wall of rock, throwing light through the chamber. Kaiser's lips were drawn back in a savage grimace as he saw who he faced. If he chose to stay and fight, he would be fighting two ancients with fierce reputations, with little help. If he ran, he would be chancing burning alive as the sun rose. He didn't have any good options.

Kaiser raised his hand and waved it toward the spear. It dropped to the ground and as it did so, the flame was extinguished, plunging the cavern into darkness again. Dragomir had no trouble seeing in the dark as a rule, but there seemed to be a thick veil covering the space, one difficult to penetrate without light. He waved his hand and light burst throughout the cave. Kaiser was nowhere in sight.

Leon flattened himself against the ceiling near the opening. When he realized Dragomir could see him, he screamed to his three pawns to attack while he crawled along the ceiling to the crack. Dragomir smacked his hands together loudly and the fissure closed with a clap of thunder, sealing itself, preventing Leon's escape.

Afanasiv dropped down fast, driving his fist into Ravenous's chest, fingers reaching through bone and sinew, talons scraping away flesh to get at the heart. He tore it from the vampire's chest and flung it to the floor of the chamber. Ravenous abandoned tearing and biting at the ancient to dive after the falling heart. Afanasiv waited until the vampire's outstretched fingers nearly connected before sending the fiery spear rolling right through the withered, blackened organ. The flames were white-hot, bright orange red, spilling glaring light across Ravenous's face. His lips were pulled back in a soundless grimace of sheer strain as he desperately tried to force his long, bony fingers into that fire to retrieve his heart.

Leon crab-walked down the side of the cavern, his features, too, illuminated by the fiery spear incinerating the lesser vampire's heart. He didn't appear as fearful as he should have. The cave filled with the sound of a drumbeat, a call, Leon sending for reinforcements. That told Dragomir that there were other pawns in the web of underground caves. That didn't matter since the other ancients, he was certain, were already dispensing justice to those vampires.

He followed Leon's every move, matching the steps like a dance partner, he on the ground, Leon coming down the side of the cave. Leon's eyes flared, went bright with excitement and adrenaline, a red flame flickering in their depths. Dragomir took that as his warning, spinning to meet the attack of Kaiser. The vampire came at him with dozens of replications of himself surrounding Dragomir. The ancient ducked low and went under the wall of Kaisers, somersaulted and came up behind the one he was certain was the real flesh-and-blood vampire. He'd chosen that one simply because, just once, the eyes shifted toward Afanasiv. It was a small thing, but it was telling.

He caught the head between his hands before the vampire could spin around, wrenched with his enormous strength, snapping the neck bones and tossing the body to one side.

Leon waved his hand at the replicas, giving them a kind of life. Each of the bodies, and there were a dozen, turned to face Dragomir.

Afanasiv darted toward Leon as soon as Ravenous's heart was fully incinerated. It took much longer than the mere second with a lightning whip, but the way the cavern was formed, they had little chance of bringing the lightning down to them. He improvised, heating the fiery spear as close to the temperature as possible.

Leon, as if directing a symphony, had both arms in the air and tossed his make-believe army in front of the Carpathian hunter. They rushed him, wicked talons reaching for his chest and face, trying to gouge out his eyes and get to his heart.

Dragomir kept to his task. If he could incinerate the heart, all the replicas would drop. Kaiser's head flopped to his right and then fell back, a grotesque parody of what once had been a Carpathian male. Kaiser didn't seem to need his head to maneuver. He reached up to right it, smiling insanely at the ancient as he did so. The moment he straightened his head, he launched himself into the air, flying at Dragomir's face, scoring with his talons across his eyes to try to blind him.

Dragomir was stoic, accepting the pain and the injury as he slammed his fist into the vampire's chest, using Kaiser's own momentum to penetrate the armor of the bones and muscle. Blood running into his eyes, he stared straight into the vampire's as his fingers closed around the heart and he began to extract it.

Behind him, Leon divided his army, sending several after Dragomir. They crept up behind him as he began to withdraw the heart. Kaiser fought hard, raking Dragomir's chest and leaning forward to bite chunks from his shoulder, trying to reach his neck and the pounding pulse calling to him.

Dragomir suddenly spun, forcing Kaiser around as well,

the heart in the ancient's fist, using his chest as a pivot to bring them both around. The attacking replicas raked talons down Kaiser's back, tearing through his flesh to bone. The vampire screamed in agony as he was struck from behind, and Dragomir ripped his heart from his body. He tossed the heart into the air and followed it with a spinning, fiery spear.

All replicas and Kaiser leapt into the air to try to get to the heart. Leon waved his hand to send the spear off course, but Afanasiv launched another right behind the first one. Dragomir followed with several more. Some pierced the bodies flying toward the now-dropping heart. One went straight through Kaiser. He was closest to the withered organ, stretching to reach it. The spear penetrated his back, right at his spine, and came out his abdomen, flames engulfing him.

The spear flying behind the first hit the heart dead center. By the time the spear hit the ground, ashes were already falling to the earth. The replicas faded from sight as Kaiser's body, in flames, dropped to the floor of the cavern.

There was a moment of silence. Leon stepped out from behind the rock where he'd taken refuge again. He smiled at them. "It has been a long time since I saw either of you."

"If you're stalling for time, Leon, you can forget it. I brought others with me. They are hunting your pawns right now." Dragomir was very aware Leon probably already knew that when they hadn't come to his aid. The master vampire was stalling, but his hope was that dawn would break and leave the ancients helpless. They were old and had too many kills to be able to sustain being out during even early morning hours, at least not without severe repercussions.

Leon shrugged and casually touched the rock. One finger. Two. He tapped as if nervous, but Dragomir wasn't fooled. He didn't wait to see what Leon was going to do; he started forward. The cavern trembled. The floor buckled. Dirt ran down the walls, first trickling and then in a steady stream. Overhead, the ceiling creaked and groaned. Dragomir continued his forward momentum as giant fissures appeared in the ceiling.

Scorpions poured out of the rock and swarmed up his legs, viciously stinging with poisonous tails, the strikes penetrating his calves and thighs to inject their venom. Undeterred, he slammed into Leon, his fist hitting the solid wall of the master vampire's chest. Great chunks of rock rained down on their heads. Around them the mountain shuddered and shook as if a great seismic event was occurring.

Afanasiv groaned under the weight of the ceiling as it fell. He stood in the center of the cave, legs wide apart, knees slightly bent, both arms raised, hands palms up to keep the tons of rock from coming down on top of Dragomir as he fought to extract the heart from the master vampire.

Leon calmly raised both hands, his nails lengthening into sharp daggers. He slammed them into either side of Dragomir's neck, burying the nails deep, piercing the artery on both sides. Dragomir didn't waver, not even when Leon slowly pulled the nails loose so the ancient's blood spurted out. Leon opened his mouth to catch the treasured blood. He gulped as his army of scorpions swarmed up Dragomir's thighs.

Get it done, Afanasiv snapped.

It wasn't easy extracting the vampire's heart. His blood was acid, burning through skin to penetrate bone. It felt as if each individual finger was burned off. Dragomir couldn't feel the heart, only excruciating pain as he closed his fist around what he perceived to be the organ. He cut off all ability to feel and kept pulling.

Leon was bathing in blood, rubbing his face in Dragomir's shoulder like a cat might, lapping at the blood as it ran down the neck and shoulder to the chest. He smeared it on his hands and licked his fingers. He didn't appear to notice that Dragomir's fist had retracted from his chest. When several scorpions made their way up to Dragomir's chest and the blood there, Leon waved them away, so they fell off the ancient's body and retreated back to the base of the rock where they'd crawled from.

Dragomir staggered and went to his knees, the venom and loss of blood taking its toll. Leon caught him and eased him to the ground, almost embracing him, holding him close as he licked and sucked at the blood, a frenzy of need, a euphoric high. Dragomir opened his fist and looked down. The heart pulsed there, black and withered, but alive. It jerked in his palm, ready to spring back to its master. Leon was close, but Dragomir shifted slightly, as if offering his neck and the hideous wound there.

Leon made a sound, a kind of greedy triumph. Dragomir tilted his hand and allowed the heart to drop to the ground and roll a few feet from them. His sight blurred. In the midst of the pain, he was all too aware of the sun climbing into the sky. His skin hurt, began to smoke and then blister. Leon didn't even notice his own skin was smoking and blisters were forming just from the presence of the sun. It mattered little that they were underground, the presence of the sun still was felt. Soon the paralysis of their kind would strike all of them.

Dragomir sent a spear from above, spinning straight down so that the point penetrated the center of the heart and flames engulfed the organ. Leon lifted his head, clearly shocked. He smiled and petted Dragomir's head. "You're dead, too. You know that, don't you? I've killed you." He was still smiling as the second spear hit him.

Dragomir crawled away from the deadly flames, but he

didn't get far. Weakness hit. His legs felt useless. He rolled over and stared up at the chunks missing from the ceiling. Afanasiv cautiously allowed one hand to drop so he could begin to weave a holding spell.

Above their heads, the rocks began to reconstruct the interior ceiling. Immediately Sandu and Andor floated down into the cavern.

Sandu crouched beside Dragomir, whistling softly. "You're a mess," he greeted.

"I know." There wasn't much more to say.

Ferro joined them, and it took all of them healing and giving blood, pushing out venom to try to keep Dragomir from succumbing to the vicious wounds. All of them had blisters rising on their skin when they finally gave up working and went to ground for the rest of the day.

Dragomir woke just before sunset. For the first time in his life that he could remember, everything hurt. His body protested the slightest movement. He lay still, absorbing the feel of the soil cocooning him like a warm blanket. He knew he needed the healer. His wounds had been mortal, but he counted himself lucky. Leon, for all his idiocy, was a master vampire and he had endless skills. He hadn't had a taste of ancient blood in centuries—clearly Vadim hadn't shared Val's blood with his lesser underlings. The moment he gulped that first mouthful of ancient blood, his greed overtook all else.

Dragomir knew that was one of the biggest downfalls for master vampires. It wouldn't work on Vadim because he'd used Valentin for years, caging and feeding off him. That blood had been ancient and Vadim wouldn't succumb to the high it would cause in others. Still, it was a difficult way to defeat a vampire, allowing them to inflict mortal wounds and try to drain their opponent dry. He used his mind to move the earth above him. At once he felt the coolness of the night air. Sandu, Andor and Ferro had worked hard on Afanasiv and Dragomir while Nicu cleared the cavern and marked out all the best places one could find healing soil. Dragomir was alone in the chamber where Leon had taken refuge.

He moved slightly, his body stiff. His legs were on fire. His neck throbbed. His arm, right up to his bicep where he'd slammed his fist into Leon's chest, was burned and painful. He was starving. *Starving.* At that moment, he was grateful he had found his lifemate. No human would have been safe for him to feed from in the state he was in had she not been anchoring him.

Dragomir? I am dreaming, and you are in need. I can't find you and the healer won't allow me to wake and go to you.

He stiffened. His heart nearly seized. Carpathians didn't dream. Well, as a rule they didn't. Throughout history, a few had reported having nightmares, but no one took the phenomenon seriously. Now, his woman, the one Vadim wanted for her visions, could continue to dream after she'd been converted. He didn't know which was more extraordinary—that she could dream or that she could reach out to him in her sleep beneath the earth.

Are you dreaming that I am in need of you? I will always be in need of you, lifemate. You are most important to me.

There was a small silence. He pictured her little frown. He found himself smiling instead of checking his body for levels of pain.

That is a good play on words, but I know you're injured and those injuries are severe. If you allow me to wake, I can send the healer to you.

The healer will soon be on his way to me. I am sending for him. He loved being in her mind. He loved the way she thought

216

of him. Her worry for him. He wanted to be with her. No, he needed to be with her.

Why didn't you send for him on waking?

We have set a trap and if I call to him on the common path, everyone will know I am injured. I am needed to fight, not be bait. I took the healer's blood, but he didn't take mine.

She was silent a moment. He was in her mind and could feel her trying to sort out what that meant.

There must be an exchange to forge a unique telepathic link between two people. Her exhaustion beat at him. He didn't want her to keep talking—or dreaming.

I can't help my visions. This one was of you in a cave and you were being attacked by insects. Scorpions, I think.

He touched his legs, burning with a fire that shouldn't have been there.

You lost a lot of blood.

The pads of his fingers found the puncture wounds in his neck. They felt raw. The rake marks down his back where talons had flayed his back open stung.

Your eyes.

His eyes hurt like hell. He touched the laceration that ran across his both eyes and his right temple.

You are not healing as you should. The earth and the ancients tried to heal you, but they cannot. I dreamt this, Dragomir. My visions are real. I know there is something that horrible vampire did to you, something you're unaware of.

Dragomir took a deep breath and let it out. *You're dead, too. You know that, don't you? I've killed you,* Leon had told him. Stated it. Dragomir thought he meant no one could heal him or give him blood before the sun rose. Ancients could endure. They did endure. Even burning, the members of the brotherhood did what was necessary to save their own. Leon meant something else, something altogether different.

217

I need to know exactly where you are. I can reach Blaze and she can reach the healer. Tell me now, Dragomir.

They know. We set a trap. Tell him here. He sent her the coordinates. Maybe they were both wrong, but he didn't think so. He'd never felt like this. He couldn't move. He didn't want to move. Lethargy had crept into his mind. His body felt like a furnace. He forced himself to lift his head enough to look down at his legs. They were swollen and blackened.

He is on his way. Her voice was soothing.

A cool breeze moved through the cavern and flowed over his face and body. *How did you do that?*

We are connected to each other through my vision. I can change things that have not already happened. I know where you are, I have the picture in my mind and I just added to it.

She made it sound so ordinary, as if anyone could do such a thing. His woman. Well worth the wait. Well worth all those centuries of nothing.

He knew the exact moment when the sun went down, giving the Carpathians back their world. Sandu, Andor and Ferro joined him immediately, shocked that he hadn't risen when they had.

"Nicu and Afanasiv have gone out to hunt. When they return, we'll go," Andor said. "This doesn't look good, Dragomir. I have not seen this before."

"Leave it to Leon to actually find something no one else has done when he's always been so lazy about everything else." Dragomir attempted humor. "The healer is on his way. Be ready. Vadim will send others the moment they can rise. He will not want to lose Leon and his pawns."

"Eugen escaped, Dragomir. He will go to Vadim and tell him we're here," Andor pointed out.

"Eventually. But he won't want to admit he abandoned Leon. He will have found a resting place close. The dawn was breaking when he fled. There's still a good chance Vadim will send a few others to aid Leon." Dragomir closed his eyes, waiting. Feeling Emeline. She held the connection between them in her dream until Gary Daratrazanoff materialized beside him.

Be well, she murmured and faded from his mind.

At once he felt bereft, his mind seeking hers automatically. There was only a void where she had been. She was in the deep healing sleep of their kind—and she needed to be. He just wished he was right there beside her, his body curled around hers.

"Have you seen this before, Gary?" he asked.

The ancients retreated, all but Sandu. He waited in the shadows on the pretense of giving the healer blood should he need it. In truth, he needed to feed every bit as much as the others, but he stayed behind to protect Dragomir and the healer in case Vadim's men got through.

"I know of it, yes."

Which wasn't the same thing. Along with battle experience and all the negatives Gary had endured from the ancients pouring into him, he had their healing experiences. He shed his body and entered Dragomir's without hesitation or any thought of himself.

It took time. Time enough that outside, a battle had raged. Vadim had sent three more vampires to catch the Carpathians between Leon and his pawns and the ones Vadim ordered to fight. The ancients made quick work of them and brought blood back several times to feed Dragomir, but mostly to keep Gary from succumbing to exhaustion. He worked for hours until finally he deemed he had gotten rid of the poison that had found its way into the bones. The scorpions had stung over and over, puncturing the bone, making tiny holes. Those holes were deep and the venom went right in and spread.

It hadn't been easy, but Gary had managed to turn the tide and rid Dragomir's body of all venom. With ancients surrounding them, Dragomir and Gary returned to the compound, Dragomir to the healing grounds to finally lie beside Emeline. No one knew where Gary chose to sleep, and no one made the mistake of asking.

11

Emeline woke in a bed in her home. She was dressed in a soft gown, red with red roses embossed throughout the material. Before she opened her eyes, she realized she felt no pain. None. She inhaled and drew the scent of Dragomir into her lungs. He always smelled wild. Dangerous. Delicious. She would recognize that scent anywhere. Sliding both hands protectively over her unborn child, she smiled without opening her eyes.

"You're here with me."

"Where else would I be?" The deep timbre of his voice slid over her skin like a caress. "Open your eyes for me." He always spoke softly. She loved the way he did that. His soft was commanding yet gentle.

She lifted her lashes, her gaze moving over him a little anxiously. She knew every wound on his body. She'd seen them in her vision. She'd experienced the battle with the vampires as if she'd been there. That world was so far removed from the

221

one she'd been born into. She thought she was tough being a street kid, but Carpathians were on an entirely different playing field. She would never have had the courage to go there if it hadn't been for Dragomir.

He laid his hand over hers. "Gary checked the baby, and she's doing fine. I'm going to feed you. She needs blood every bit as much as you do."

She winced at the word. *Blood*. She didn't like the image, and she knew he used the word deliberately to get her used to the idea. She took a deep breath and sat up, looking down at the gown. "Did you do this for me?" She smoothed her hand over the silky material. "It's beautiful. It feels beautiful." She reached up to touch her hair. It fell in a thick braid down to her waist. "You thought of everything."

"You'll get used to taking my blood, *sívamet*. It will feel . . . erotic . . . to you."

Her stomach did a slow somersault and a flutter started somewhere deep. Everything about Dragomir was erotic to her. His scars, the raw line across his eyes that told her he'd nearly had them taken out. The long salt-and-pepper hair that fell like a waterfall, every bit as soft as her own hair. That chest of his and his back with the tattoos drifting across muscle.

She found her courage. "Tell me what to do." She wasn't certain she could do it, but for him and her daughter, she would try.

He rewarded her with a smile. "You don't have to do anything. I'm going to help you."

"Does Maksim help Blaze?"

"I don't know. I don't care, either. We make our own rules. We do what we're comfortable with. Come to me, *hän ku kuulua sívamet*." He pulled her gently into his lap.

In all her imaginings, even her wildest, she never had considered she would like sitting in a man's lap. She couldn't

222

remember ever sitting on anyone's lap, even as a child, but Dragomir made her feel safe and secure.

He drew the side of his nose down her neck, a long slow sweep, skin against skin. For some reason, that small gesture made tension coil in the pit of her stomach and flutters grow in her sex. She moistened her lips with the tip of her tongue. His lips followed the same path as his nose, a long, slow caress that started at her earlobe and continued down to the pulse pounding in her neck. Her heart beat faster in anticipation.

As much as she wanted to be afraid of what he was doing, it was erotic. The way he held her. The way his mouth moved over her skin. His tongue sliding over her pulse. Lingering. His teeth scraping back and forth so gently. Barely there. Back and forth until she couldn't focus on anything but that movement. The feeling. Her stomach did another slow roll. Her sex clenched. Her breasts reacted, nipples hardening beneath the gown.

She closed her eyes in anticipation. Waited. His hands slipped over her gown, slid to the back and then she felt the gown glide over her breasts. Cool air hit skin. She looked down and saw her breasts exposed, the gown under the soft mounds, pooling around her waist. All the while his teeth continued that teasing, tugging, nipping. Each sting sent liquid fire arrowing straight to her sex.

Her breath came in ragged pants. With every pant her breasts lifted and fell. One hand cupped her chin, the other her left breast. The feel of his palm cupping her soft flesh was exquisite. His thumb, brushing back and forth over her nipple, sent invisible sparks leaping over her skin. She felt boneless, her body melting into his.

He trailed kisses both openmouthed and closed from her neck to her throat. His teeth nipped and scraped, keeping her body on edge. His mouth moved down her throat to the

223

curve of her breast. She hadn't expected that to feel so sexy. Every nerve ending flared into life, came alive and centered entirely on him.

The hand at her breast tightened possessively. He tugged at her nipple roughly. She was sensitive and the little bite of pain shocked her. Teeth sank deep, right at the top of the curve of her right breast. That was more than a sting, more than a bite of pain. It was a flash that took her breath, immediately giving way to something altogether different. Pure pleasure. Sinful pleasure. So erotic she couldn't think beyond giving herself to him.

Her arms cradled his head and she stroked his hair. He drank, pushing into her mind to share how taking her blood felt to him. His cock hard and full. Pulsing for her. Throbbing. Jerking with each strong pull of her essence into his mouth. She tasted better than the finest wine ever could to him. He was addicted to her taste. Obsessed with it. His body was on fire for hers. The wicked things in his head he wanted to do were right there, easy for her to see.

Emeline wanted to try all of it with him. The more he shared the way his body reacted, the more her body needed. His hands stroked her curves, traced her ribs over and over down to her waist. Then his tongue swept across her breast, closing the two puncture wounds. His hand anchored in her hair, pulling her head back and his mouth was on her, tongue slipping in, sharing her taste.

The craving was there instantly. She knew part of it was his craving for her blood, but it was also hers. She wanted blood. Needed it. It might be abhorrent to think about, but the hunger was there. She shifted in his arms, her hands locking at the nape of his neck. She kissed him over and over. Hot, delicious kisses. Sexy. Wild. A little out of control. She wanted to be out of control with him. She wanted him that way—so into her he couldn't think—because she was that way about him.

She was the one leading the kisses now, her mouth moving over his, her tongue dancing with his. Her hands pushed at his shirt, wishing it was gone, and it was. Just like that. There was bare skin beneath her palms. She kissed her way along his jaw, feeling that shadowy bristle. That made her thighs tingle. She'd seen that image in his head, his mouth between her legs, those bristles inflaming her nerve endings even more. She wanted that. She wanted everything from him.

She nipped his chin with her teeth, scraped them down his throat. She paused for a moment over his pulse, feeling it in her mouth. Feeling the answering beat in her sex. She was dripping for him now. Feeling empty. Needing him to fill her. Complete her. She kissed along the fierce lacerations on his chest. Nipped the heavy muscles of his chest.

His cock was raging now, and she wanted to feel that. She turned to straddle him, the silken gown bunched up around her waist. She wore no panties and her bare bottom slid along his thighs as she leaned forward to keep her mouth pressed to his chest. The lengthening of her teeth shocked her just a little, but the call was too strong.

Tell me what to do. I need you right now.

His hand came up to cradle her head. *Your instincts are just fine. I'm going to lift you up. You're so ready for me.*

She was. She wanted him with every breath she took. She wanted his blood. She wanted his mind. She wanted his body. *Mine.* He gave himself to her. He'd said the words. His heart and soul. His body. She was claiming every square inch of him.

She licked along the heavy muscle of his chest, right over the pounding pulse. She heard it so clear, that beckoning sound. Strong. Comforting. Arousing. His hands went to her hips and he lifted her, held her so that his cock nudged her entrance in demand. She licked a second time, hunger beating at her. Did she need his blood? She *craved* the wild flavor of him. She remembered exactly what he tasted like.

Dragomir's fingers bit into her hips, but it was Emeline who impaled herself on his cock. She drove down hard, unable to stop herself. Her breath left her lungs as he filled her, pushing through tight muscles, stretching and burning her feminine sheath. She flung her head back, gasping for breath as pain and pleasure mixed together.

There is so much more.

The devil tempting her. The sound of his voice triggered a hard clenching of her sex around his thick cock. Just that little movement bathed his shaft in liquid heat. She felt his pleasure, the way her sheath surrounded him, grasped at him like a scorching-hot silken fist. He held her still, when she needed to move.

Let your body adjust to me, to my size. Concentrate on other things.

Again, his voice triggered a spasm, her body clenching his hard, dragging him deeper when he wanted to be still. She nearly sobbed with her need to move, but one hand was back cradling her head, pushing her toward his chest.

That heartbeat was there like a beacon, calling to her. A summons. She couldn't resist. She leaned forward, rocking her hips on his cock as she sank her teeth into his chest, right over that steady drumbeat. His taste exploded in her mouth. So perfect. Addicting.

All for you, sívamet.

That whisper in her mind was as intimate as his cock stretching her body. She had never felt so much pleasure. There was a sting, too, a burn, but that added to the heightening of her passion. She felt his love, so dark, and his lust, so sharp and terrible, mixed together like some forbidden aphrodisiac. That was his blood. That was the taste of him. Dark and forbidden. What he was doing to her body felt wicked and sinful. She rode him, his hands forcing her to move the way he wanted, the way she needed. Her breasts mashed against his chest, nipples rubbing his muscles with every movement of her hips.

She couldn't stop feeding, or moving. She ground down on him, made tight circles as she went up and down, riding him as if he was some wild horse. She lost herself in the feeling, in the need and hunger. The feeling was beautiful. Terrible. Glorious. She would never get enough. His hand slid between his chest and her mouth. A silent command. For a moment she thought to resist him, but his cock swelled, stretching and burning the tight muscles of her sheath, and she couldn't think straight. She let him take over by sliding her tongue instinctively over the small punctures on his chest.

Immediately she threw her head back, grinding down, rising and sinking on him. She didn't want that to end, either. She wanted to live there with him, sharing the same skin, the pleasure spilling through her like a diamond comet streaming across the night sky. Pure and perfect.

You're so beautiful you make me cry. She whispered the truth into his mind. So intimate. She knew he saw her. Every sin. Every fantasy. Everything she was. She wanted him to know because he'd given her so much. He'd believed in her when others might have thrown her out for carrying the child of a Malinov. He had made that impossible. He had tied himself irrevocably to her, when she claimed to be the lifemate of a vampire. *I'm so ashamed I didn't know the truth. I just couldn't believe someone like you would ever be for someone like me.*

It would still take her time to believe it. She felt vulnerable and terrified at the same time. She was given a miracle. She didn't get those. People like her were lucky to get through life with food in their bellies and a roof over their heads. She had Dragomir now, but she felt that at any moment he could be ripped away from her.

I'm not the beautiful one, Emeline. You are. I look at you and can barely breathe. He moved then, tipping her back on the couch so that she lay on the cushions, and he was over her, her legs on either side of his hips, spread wide for him. He was exquisitely gentle as he moved in her, going deep, over and over, settling them both back to a slower burn.

I need more. She felt helpless under his weight. She ran her palms down his back to his buttocks, digging her fingers in to try to force him to go faster and harder. She slid her legs around him, hooking her ankles, taking him even deeper.

He smiled down at her. *Slow is good. You'll like this.*

She was so close. That force gathering in her. So tight. The tension coiled and coiled until she wanted to scream and claw at him for more. Still, looking up at him, at his face, so scarred, so beautiful, so *hers*. She hadn't known she was capable of so much feeling. The strength of her emotions shook her. Scared her. No, terrified her.

Emeline had always relied on herself. She didn't trust others easily. In her life, there had been Blaze and her father. No one else. Now, her world had narrowed to this one man. She barely knew him . . .

His mouth brushed kisses over her eyes. Trailed more kisses along her cheekbone to the corner of her mouth. His tongue traced her lower lip, teased at the seam, and when she parted her lips for him, he kissed her again. Over and over.

You know me, Emeline. You know me better than any woman can know a man. I give you everything. I trust when you look into my mind, that you will see the good with the bad.

He kept kissing her until she couldn't think. Fire burned

228

through her. His body was still in hers. He just lay over her, his hips cradled by hers, his mouth wreaking havoc with her senses, his cock a steel piston, stationary, stretching her tight muscles until she felt every breath, every beat of his heart right through his shaft.

That look doesn't belong on your face. You have no need to fear, Emeline. You're in good hands.

As he spoke so intimately in her mind, his hips slowly pulled back. She gasped and caught at him, trying to keep him close. He surged forward, filling her, taking her breath, blurring the edges of her mind. He knelt up slowly, his cock shifting inside of her, so that her muscles clamped down hard around him. The friction was incredible, taking away her ability to think clearly. She could only feel. Only need more. He was right, her body was in good hands. It wasn't her body taken over by his that alarmed her. She could give him her body, and would, as many times as he wanted her. The pleasure was too intense, unlike anything she could have imagined. It was her heart in jeopardy.

Your heart is just fine, Emeline. I am its keeper. I have given you mine and trust you to take the utmost care of it. Do you think I could do less for the woman who matters more to me than life itself?

There it was. She could see into his mind, read him as easily, in that moment, as she might a book. He meant what he said. Her heart was safe. Now she just had to convince herself she was worthy of him—and that was going to be the difficult part when it had been drilled into her since childhood that she was worthless.

Feel, Emeline, don't think.

His hips moved again and a streak of fire raced through her body, leaving her gasping. It was impossible to think when he moved, and she gave herself up to the moment, letting him sweep her into another realm.

Fire burned. Flames spread through her veins, rushing to every part of her body. He caught her hips in a firm grasp and began to move faster, harder. Just what she craved. Needed. Hungered for. That terrible coil inside her gathered tighter and tighter. His face was a mask of sensual carnality.

The tension in her built and built until she was thrashing under him, her hips rising to meet his every thrust. Her lungs burned for air. Every cell in her body was alive and focused on him, on the way their bodies came together, and that coiling tension terrified her. It had to stop.

Emeline was beautiful. Utterly beautiful. Dragomir stared down into her eyes. Dazed. Long lashes fluttering, her breasts jolting, stomach muscles rippling with every hard thrust of his cock. That raw sensuality that colored her features a soft rose. Her lips a dark red. He breathed out and watched her lungs take in that breath. That small action sent more heat flashing through him. His cock swelled. Lightning struck as her eyes dilated, sizzling through his body, a fiery whip of shocking pleasure.

Her lips parted on his name and there was another strike. Every move of her hips, the way her muscles rippled around his shaft, gripping hard with scorching heat, the friction as they came together. Her breath came in ragged pants; there was panic in the beauty of her gaze. She was skating so close to the edge but wasn't going over, not surrendering to him, to their passion, to the inevitable loss of control.

Every move of her body produced more lightning strikes until there was no holding back. *Now, sívamet. Let go and give yourself to me. Surrender, Emeline. I will never let you fall without catching you.*

Her helpless gaze clung to his as he shifted his angle and rode along that sweet spot, hard, heavy strokes. Her eyes widened. She expelled her breath and he breathed in his name.

Soft. Reverent. So beautiful, that whispered name. *Dragomir.* On her breath. In his lungs. Binding them together. All the threads between them, soul to soul, mind to mind, body to body and now breath to breath.

The music of her ragged breaths rose, a crescendo. Her body clamped down like a vise on his, surrounding him with scorching fire. So tight it was strangling him. His own breath hissed out of his lungs, a harsh accompaniment to the melody of hers. He felt a dark force gathering in him, the pleasure so intense it bordered on pain. Gathering, moving, rushing. A hot, explosive release. All the while her tight muscles clamped down, gripped and stroked. It was a kind of sweet but brutal harmony, dark and forbidden, perfect and terrible. He never wanted it to end.

Emeline clutched at Dragomir's arms, those hard, defined muscles that seemed to be everywhere. His body didn't have an ounce of fat. She was a mess and he was ... perfect. Everything he did or said was perfection. She'd just jumped him. She'd been so out of control. She hadn't been able to stop touching him. Stop making demands. She'd all but forced him ...

Dragomir burst out laughing. He blanketed her body with his, letting her take his weight as he framed her face with both hands. He was heavy, and she couldn't quite catch her breath, but she didn't care. She loved him lying over top of her. She couldn't help her reaction. His hands, holding her face with such exquisite gentleness, allowed her to look up, to meet his gaze when she really wanted to hide from sheer embarrassment.

He was beautiful. That face. All male. All perfection. She was lost without him. She knew that. She had no idea what she could bring him in return for giving her him, for his making her his choice, but she was determined to find a way to even their relationship.

"*Forced* me? I'm still in your mind, *sívamet*. You can't think things like that with a straight face. I want you every moment of the night, or day. There is no forcing me. I will have to remember there are certain rules in place in society or I would be pushing you up against the trees outside, the front verandah, the play yard. Wherever we were walking together."

He allowed his heavy cock to slide from her body and she wanted to protest. He filled her body the way he filled her heart. Without him, she felt empty and alone.

"Never alone, Emeline. Never again. You are in my mind, the way I'm in yours. Whenever you have need of me, in any way, even if it is just to touch me lightly, to know I'm always here, you have the capacity to do so."

"I drank blood. It was the most beautiful, erotic thing I've ever done." The confession slipped out of her, her darkest shame. Her gaze slipped from his because she couldn't let anyone see what was in her soul, how she wanted to repeat the experience over and over. The craving was there. The insatiable hunger.

"Look at me, *sívamet*."

His voice was so gentle it turned her heart over. How did he manage that particular tone? It didn't just sound that way to her ears, his voice caressed her skin, moved over her body, inflaming her senses. She loved the way he sounded. She wished his cock was still in her, stretching and burning and bringing that intense fire.

"I don't think I can."

"You need to breathe and I'm heavy. I'm going to sit up and put you on my lap." Even as he said it, he didn't give her a chance to protest. She worried about their combined cream spilling out of her body, ruining the couch, but it was gone as he lifted her and put her on his lap. She was naked in his arms, and she felt more exposed and vulnerable in her mind and heart than with her body unclothed.

"Now, Emeline, look at me."

This time his gentle voice included that note of command. Sometimes, when she heard it, like now, she wanted to disobey just to see what he would do.

Dragomir laughed softly. "I see I am going to have an eternity of my woman challenging me. Do not worry, *sívamet*, I welcome the skirmishes."

The notes of joy and happiness in his voice allowed her to look at him. She couldn't help smiling. It didn't matter that she had taken his blood and enjoyed it or that she had been the sexual aggressor in the beginning, he was happy. She wanted him that way. The lines in his face had softened and he had laughed. *Laughed*. He barely smiled, almost as if his mouth didn't know how to form that upward curve, but he was laughing. She felt the way he was happy. Deep inside, she felt that and knew she'd given that to him. Everything else melted away for her and she hugged that tightly to herself.

"I can't believe I have you here with me," she whispered and turned her face into his throat, nuzzling him. Inhaling. Tasting his skin with her tongue. "My life was pain and terror. You took away his voice. You gave me hope that my daughter would survive and others wouldn't shun her. I was terrified and alone, and you changed all that. You brought beauty and hope back into my life. Thank you for that, Dragomir. I swear I will spend every minute making you happy."

He bunched her hair at the nape of her neck in his fist and gently tugged until her head went back and she found herself looking into his golden eyes. "You gave me back my soul, Emeline. You gave me life. The scales are more than even. Much more. Still, having you make me happy sounds good, especially since I am very aware I am not an easy man."

A frisson of alarm slid down her spine. Small. A cautioning. An awareness. She frowned. He'd warned her before. He

233

looked scary. Outside, around others, he acted scary, but he'd never been anything but gentle with her. "You've said that before. What do you mean?"

Slowly, she sat up on his lap, pulling herself reluctantly out of his arms. If they were going to talk, she was going to have the armor of clothes. She looked around for her gown. It was a beautiful gown. Dragomir had given it to her.

"I made it for you."

Her eyebrow shot up. The gown was beautiful, in material and design. "How? Are you telling me you can manufacture clothing along with everything else you can do?"

He nodded. "I wish I didn't have to tell you the truth because I like the way you look at me, as if I can do anything, but actually, Emeline, you can manufacture clothing for yourself or anyone else. When you rise with the sinking sun, you think about being clean and what clothes you want to wear for the night."

She felt a small smile welling up. "What? No shower? I was looking forward to showering with you. That can be . . . sexy."

"Show me."

The growling demand sent another shiver down her spine, but this one was delicious. Fun. Sensual. She did her best, picturing the fantasy she'd had more than once. Maybe a few too many times. Him lifting her, her legs wrapped around his hips. The water running down over both of them. Her mouth on his cock. His mouth between her legs. It was embarrassing, yet she *wanted* him to see the things she'd thought about long before he claimed her.

While the scenes played out in her head and he saw them in detail, more, he *felt* them, his cock grew hard and thick. She felt the hot pulsing against her bare buttocks. If they kept this up, neither was going to be able to resist the other. They wouldn't dare go out in public. She moved deliberately, sliding her body over him in a slow, sensual massage.

"I see the benefits of a shower," he said.

"Good." She slid off his lap, down to the floor. "I'm glad you're wise enough to see some of the things humans do can be very beneficial." She caught his knees and tugged.

Dragomir obeyed her silent urging, allowing her to widen his thighs so her body could fit between them. "I have seen, over the centuries, many men sitting while their women knelt on the floor at their feet. I always thought it was strange, but I can see there is advantage in that as well."

She smirked at him. "It's good you're willing to learn, Dragomir."

"Very willing."

He circled the base of his cock with his fist and did a slow, sexy slide. She couldn't take her eyes off him. He leaned back just slightly, and the tension he always carried in his shoulders and face was gone. Those scars on his face were softer and his jaw wasn't so strong. He was beautiful to her, just like that. All male, his cock in his fist, so sexy her heart pounded and her sex clenched hard.

She couldn't help herself—the temptation was irresistible. She leaned forward, her hands on his knees, and licked at the flared head. A shudder went through his body and pleasure flooded her mind. She loved that she could feel what she was doing to him. She saw herself in his eyes. He found her the sexiest creature on the face of the earth. He loved watching her body, the sway of her breasts, the hardness of her nipples telling him she loved what she was doing.

He watched intently as his cock disappeared, engulfed by her mouth. He loved the way her lips stretched over his girth. He liked watching her tongue lick up his shaft and dance under the crown of the head. Every movement of her mouth brought scorching heat rushing through his body, centering in his groin.

She felt everything he felt, and her body reacted. She was giving him paradise. She liked that she could take everything from his mind and replace it with—her. With heat and flames. With passion and fire. With sheer pleasure. It was an indulgence, something he'd never experienced. She loved that she could give that to him. She loved the moment he couldn't think clearly, yet he was still gentle, even while his hips moved just that bit out of control.

She knew she was giving him a kind of ecstasy he never expected from her. Complete giving. All for him. Everything for him. She loved the way her image was in his mind, branded there, her kneeling on the floor, hands on his knees, her lips around his cock, eyes on his while her breasts swayed and brushed his body with every movement. She was burned into his mind. That picture. That feeling.

The picture of him above her, the look on his face and the feeling in his mind were burned in her memories for all time. She knew she was just as addicted to this moment as she was to taking his blood or having him in her. She would always crave giving him this, the feeling, the image. She felt him swell, grow hotter. Then she was tasting that wild Dragomir flavor that was unique to him. All for her.

His groan was deep, and one hand went to the back of her head, holding her there, her mouth gentle on him now, her tongue lapping up every drop that had leaked. His breathing had gone ragged and his entire body shuddered with pleasure. She'd given him that. Satisfaction was a beautiful thing.

She stayed there on the floor, looking up at him. Her man. When had that happened? How? She might never feel she deserved him, but she did know, just by the way he saw her in his mind, that he would always be happy with her.

"We were talking about something but I can't remember what it was," she said. "I got distracted. I hope you don't mind."

"Not at all." He watched her tongue lick at her lips as she sank back onto her heels. "You're the most beautiful woman I've ever seen. Throughout the centuries, I've seen quite a few women, but none of them compared with you."

The wonderful thing was, being in his mind, she knew the compliment was sincere. He honestly felt she was the most beautiful woman in the world. He was nuts, but that was all right with her. She smiled up at him, because he made her happy. She couldn't believe how he had changed her life in such a short time.

"I had dreams of you, Dragomir. First, daytime fantasies like the shower, and then I was horrified when I began to dream that you died trying to save me. I dreamt of Vadim coming and you were lying on the floor of my living room, wounds everywhere, so much blood gone, and I thought you were dead."

Her heart hurt just thinking about it. There was a huge knot in her throat, one she couldn't swallow. The idea of his death because of her had weighed on her.

"I didn't want to ever meet you, and I went into my house the moment night came so there was no chance that you would try to save me—and yet you still did."

"You ended the dream with me lying on your floor." He reached out and caught her hair in his hand, tugging gently.

She nodded. "I couldn't go past that moment, with you lying without a heartbeat, no air in your lungs and your blood soaking into my floor. Because of me."

"Had you forced yourself to keep going—"

"No." She shook her head, uncaring that the action caused her hair to pull at her scalp. "I couldn't. I tried to save you, Dragomir, but you just wouldn't let me."

"Good thing, too." He leaned down to brush a kiss on top of her head. "Your dreams interest me. Tell me about them."

"I've always had them." She nuzzled his thigh because she couldn't help herself. His body was warm and hard. It was hers. He'd given himself to her. All that he was. She liked sitting on the floor, her body between his legs, surrounded by him. There was safety in it. There was also the heady realization that this man was hers and anything she did, any way she touched him, he was fine with.

"I started having dreams when I was fairly young. I really didn't notice at first, but somewhere along the line I realized that some of the places I went to I'd already dreamt about. Once I was paying attention, it wasn't only places, but what was happening in my dreams, taking place in reality days or weeks after. That was terrifying to a child. I thought maybe my imagination was causing things to happen. When you're alone and scared and hungry, people can be cruel. In retaliation, I would think bad thoughts about them and if I dreamt about it later, I was so terrified I was making bad things happen to those I didn't like."

"*Sívamet.*" He murmured it softly. The hand in her hair was soothing and gentle, stroking caresses down the silk of her hair.

She wasn't used to compassion, and tears burned behind her eyes. Joyful tears. She'd never known what that was until that moment. Dragomir changed her perspective on everything.

"I would dream something bad, and if it hadn't happened, I would treat the dream as if it would happen. I'd call it up every night, changing little details. I found I couldn't change what happened, but I could modify it. I could change the way I reacted. So I'd play the dream over and over in my head and change little things until I could change the outcome of the dream. Most of the time, the dream didn't spill over into reality, but the times it did, I was ready and I knew exactly what to do."

"Tell me about having the dream where you went down into Vadim's underground city."

She felt her brain shut down. She didn't want to relive that nightmare ever again. Not even for Dragomir. She shook her head.

His palm cupped the side of her face, his thumb trailing over her high cheekbone. "I wouldn't ask you if it wasn't important, *sívamet*. I am here with you. He can't get to you or our daughter. You're safe now. Detach yourself and just tell me the dream. Tell it as if it remained a dream."

For him. Emeline knew she would do anything for him, even things that were difficult for her. If he wanted or needed this from her, she would tell him. He hadn't offered to help distance her from the dream, so she knew he wanted her complete version.

"The dreams started years before it actually occurred. My dreams don't always happen in real life, even the recurring ones, so I never know what is real or not. I wasn't certain, at first, if that particular dream would happen, although it was vivid and night after night I dreamt it. One day I came across vampires killing in an alleyway and I knew they were real despite everyone I told wanting to lock me up."

She looked down at her hands. They were shaking. "The dream reoccurred over and over. The girls were taken down into the city. Liv was eaten alive night after night by Vadim's puppets. Blaze and I couldn't stop it. We couldn't save her in time. Amelia was taken by the vampires and they drained her of blood and left her dying in a corner. Bella . . ." She broke off, pressing a trembling hand to her mouth. "They eventually fed her to the same puppets that ate her sister. And Danny was used for days as food for the vampires. Blaze and I went into the tunnels nightly to try to change the course of what happened. We did little things at first and found what tools

239

we needed. How fast we had to run, what would be behind a door when we got to it. I repeated the dream night after night and shared it with Blaze."

"How did you share it with Blaze?"

Emeline frowned. She hadn't thought about trying to explain that. "I can do it easily. I could do it with you. I think it's the same way we get into each other's minds."

Dragomir sat straight abruptly, the action causing her heart to jump. His eyes went from lazy and languid to sharp and demanding, the gold going bright and hot, glittering with intelligence. "You can get into people's minds? Anyone's? You could do that before you were converted?"

She chewed on her lower lip until his finger rubbed along it, easing the bite, making her conscious of what she was doing. "I don't think I get into people's minds. It's when I'm dreaming. I can reach out to anyone around me."

"If I were connected at that time to others, all those in this compound, could you share your dream with them all?"

"Of course. It isn't like it requires tremendous effort on my part. I reach out, just the way I do when I want to connect with you. If Blaze was a distance away, it would be more difficult, but if you were connected to her, or Maksim, and I shared with either one of you, the dream would be easy to give her as well." Her voice rang with confidence because she *was* confident.

He nodded. "How would Vadim know this about you? He did, didn't he? When he had you prisoner, he had to have mentioned it."

She nodded, keeping her eyes fixed on his mouth. She hadn't told any of them, not even Blaze. No one. She had been terrified that whatever Vadim wanted her to do, the Carpathians would either kill her to keep her from doing, or want it for themselves. She had told herself numerous times that was a leftover fear from her childhood—that no one wanted her, the woman, only what she could do for them.

"He did ask me. I refused to answer."

"Even when he tortured you and tried to get the answer out of you. How did he know?"

"I went to the Morrison Psychic Center for testing. I put down that I could share my dreams. It was so stupid of me. I thought it was for fun, like those psychics at fairs. I kind of thought it would be funny to have a real ability but to pretend I didn't. It was the worst mistake of my life and started everything."

"I'm grateful for your mistake. I wouldn't have you had you not made it."

12

The water on the lake was like glass. Emeline had never been on it, or even on the dock around it. She found it was peaceful and gorgeous. All of her life she'd been drawn to the night—until she'd gone into that underground city and realized that monsters were lurking in every shadow. Walking hand in hand with Dragomir gave her back a sense of peace and serenity to the night. He kept her tucked in close to him, her fingers threaded through his, and he took her straight to the lake.

She loved the way the moon appeared silver in the dark sky. Stars were scattered overhead as if thrown haphazardly, yet they formed unique patterns. The sounds of insects and frogs added to the beauty of the place. "I can understand why Tariq chose this place to build," she said. "He has everything. The lake and the woods, yet he's close to the city."

"It's also easily defensible. Maksim owns the property to

the south, and I told him we'd buy up as much of the property toward his east as possible."

"You need a lot of money for that," she cautioned.

"I have lived centuries. Even before I entered the monastery, I had wealth. Most Carpathians do. You learn what is needed and you acquire it."

"Good to know. I don't have a penny to my name. Not really. I work, so I have a bank account. Or rather I did work before all this vampire nonsense, but I didn't acquire actual wealth."

He looked down at her, waited until she looked up and smiled. "You've acquired it now. You can have anything you want. Go anywhere you want."

"I want to go out on the lake. In a canoe or the rowboat. Or the paddleboat. I've never done either one and the minute I saw the lake and the boats, I knew I wanted those experiences."

"I think we can do that tonight. How is little Carisma feeling? She making you sick?" He stopped abruptly and took a step in front of her, forcing her to stop as well. He put both hands over her tummy.

"She's feeling good," Emeline said. She couldn't help but smile. The baby seemed happy and content. She kicked and stretched a little, the feeling as if butterfly wings brushed her insides, but there was no sickness at all.

Good evening, little Miss Carisma. This is your father talking to you. I hope all is well. I am going to take your mother out onto the lake and I would prefer that you didn't make her sick. You'll like the feeling—it is almost like the rocking chair your mother says you enjoy.

Emeline laughed, the sound shocking her. It was carefree. She'd never been carefree. She hadn't known what it was like not to worry where her next meal was coming from or where she could safely lay her head down at night. Those fears were ingrained in her and stayed with her even after she could work and rent an apartment.

"I love that you talk to her."

He looked a little embarrassed if that was possible with his too-male features and his expressionless mask. She couldn't help smirking. "You're so caught, Dragomir. You only pretend you're a tough guy."

He caught her arm at the elbow and began walking along the dock, back toward the small canoe tied up there. "You worry me, Emeline, that you choose not to see all of me. You have never looked into the things I have done for my people."

"The things you were forced to do to keep our world safe?" She stole a quick glance at his face.

"The things I *chose* to do. I was born a predator, *sívamet*. I am still a predator, and I will go into the next life a predator. You cannot mistake me for anything else." He stepped into the canoe with complete balance and reached up for her.

His grip was strong and comforting as he put her on the end close to where the canoe had a backrest. It curved at the top in the traditional sense, but clearly Tariq had designed the canoe for comfort.

She worried a little that Dragomir kept insisting she wasn't seeing everything about him. Of course, she wasn't, but she did see what mattered most. He was kind and courageous. He devoted himself to her. He accepted her baby without hesitation. What was he referring to over and over?

She settled on the floor of the canoe and watched him settle opposite her and take the oar in his hand. One strong pull had them gliding fast out over the water. The sensation took her breath away. She loved the quiet of it and the feeling of moving over the wide expanse of the lake. The

244

color of the water was different depending on where the sliver of moon shone, or the depth and the darkness. The farther out they got from the lights of shore, the darker the water appeared.

"This is beautiful," she whispered, looking up at the stars, one hand trailing in the water. "Thank you. You've given me so many experiences I never thought I'd ever have. I appreciate every single one of them."

"I love giving you things you want, Emeline." Another powerful stroke took them gliding farther away from the shoreline.

Her gaze jumped to his face and then drifted over his chest and arms. He was hers. All that unadulterated male beauty was hers. "I love knowing you're mine." She felt a little shy telling him, but at the same time, she wanted him to know. That was more important to her than revealing her embarrassment. He deserved to know what he meant to her.

"Do you feel safe with me?"

"That's an odd question. Of course I feel safe with you." She wrinkled her nose at him, wondering where he was going with that line of questioning.

"Then why are you gripping the edges of the canoe until your knuckles have turned white?"

She looked down at her hands. He was right, she was gripping the edges and her knuckles *were* white. She absolutely loved the teasing note in his voice. "I'm hedging my bets."

His eyebrow shot up. "You do know I could float us out of the water, turn upside down and still keep you from falling."

She didn't like that matter-of-fact way he asked. "I am certain you can, but I prefer that we stay in the water, exactly as we are meant to."

"*Humans* are meant to. They don't fly. We fly."

"This part of 'we' is just trying out canoeing and enjoying it. Flying can come later. I watched the children on their dragons and was a little envious, I won't lie."

"The beauty of being Carpathian is you can do both. You can fly by yourself in any form you choose, and you will be able to fly a dragon if you really want to do that."

"I do." She drew up her knees cautiously and one by one pried her fingers from the side of the canoe so she could wrap her arms around her legs and settle her chin on her knees. "Do you remember the first time you ever flew?"

Dragomir shook his head. "Memories faded over the centuries. Even after getting my emotions and colors back, I don't remember much from my childhood. I can remember every vampire and how they fight, what their preferences are in lairs and safeguards, but I can't remember my mother's face."

He sounded crushed by that, but his expression hadn't changed. She realized he often refused or more likely didn't recognize an emotion that was sad or negative. He didn't dwell there. He felt them, but he didn't identify with them. Emeline couldn't make up her mind whether she thought that good or bad.

"I don't think about my parents much," she said, needing to give him something back. "I didn't really have family. Maybe that's why I fought so hard to keep Carisma. I heard her screaming in pain and I just couldn't hate her. She was an innocent caught in Vadim's ugly world." She rubbed her chin on her knees and then put her head down, staring out at the water. "He does that, you know—he hates innocence and does his best to strike at it."

There was a small silence. Two more powerful strokes of the canoe sent them parallel to the shore. "I hadn't thought about that, but you're right. That's exactly what he does."

"He's determined to kill the children, Dragomir. All of them. He targeted them for some reason as well. It wasn't just because he knew it would draw me into the underground city, either. He had a reason he went after those children. I tried to find out about their talents, but then I realized if I knew them and Vadim was in my head, then he would know their talents as well, so I stopped asking. They don't let others in easily, but Blaze, Charlotte and I are closer to them than anyone else here. Probably I have to include Tariq in that as well. Still, I don't think anyone knows what they can do."

"Valentin would know. Liv, the little girl, is his lifemate. What is in her mind, he knows."

"I didn't think of that. I thought he left."

"There was that trouble with the lightning when we were converting you. He came back to protect Liv."

"I don't understand how he would know she was his lifemate. She's too young. I thought it had to do with sexual maturity."

"That plays a huge part," he admitted. "Sometimes being in close proximity over time can make a man aware his lifemate is near. His colors fade but don't altogether leave him. His emotions don't completely disappear and he has a sex drive. One that won't go away. I've heard all kinds of things that tip off the male. Most don't have those luxuries. Valentin most likely discovered it when Vadim brought the child to him to take her blood. Vadim had kept Valentin starving for so long, he thought when he gave him a child, Valentin wouldn't be able to resist killing her. It was Vadim's poor luck that he handed Valentin's lifemate to him."

"What will Valentin do?"

"He will watch over her until she is of age. What else can

he do? She's too young to claim, nor would he ever consider it." Dragomir shrugged his broad shoulders and gave more powerful strokes of the oar so that the canoe slipped over the water easily.

Emeline realized he was keeping along the shoreline for her, recognizing that, although she loved the water and what they were doing, she was nervous. She licked at her lips. "I don't know how to swim. I never had the chance to learn. I was more of a dancer."

Dragomir's look wasn't one of shock or judgment. His eyes had gone soft and his incredible mouth curved in that sweet smile that always shook her. "Now you don't have to worry about it, *sívamet*. You are Carpathian. You can swim, fly or dance up to the stars."

Her breath caught in her throat. She *loved* dancing. She lost herself in dance. "Blaze's father paid for dancing lessons for me. I was homeless, crawling in his daughter's window at night, and he paid for my dance lessons. That was better than eating regularly, although he let me raid their fridge and cupboards whenever I wanted."

"But you didn't." He set the oar across his lap, his focus completely on her.

She shook her head. "I didn't trust easily in those days. He was a really good man, but I didn't dare wear out my welcome. At first I was very young, and the streets were intimidating. Then I grew up and there was an entirely different set of obstacles."

"You still don't trust easily."

"It's difficult to believe you're for real," she admitted, her hand moving in and out of the water, as if she were dancing on the surface with her fingers. She'd given him her body and her heart. She was fairly certain she wouldn't survive without him, but he was right. There was a part of her that didn't trust that he'd stay. Maybe she'd never be able to trust that he'd stay.

"I'll stay. And if you really want to dance in the stars, we'll do that, too."

"Any time you want to go dancing in the stars, or the clouds, or on the pier, I'm ready," she assured him.

The sound of childish voices drifted on the wind and made Emeline smile. She hadn't seen the children yet and she missed them. She turned her head toward the sound. The boat glided over the water as the oar cut through it, powered by Dragomir's strength. She made out Danny with Lourdes on his back. Bella ran beside them, calling out to him that it was her turn. The scene was familiar to her. Danny gave the youngest ones rides all the time. It was the two littlest ones' favorite pastime.

Liv had a book in her hands and walked with Amelia, talking softly; the sound carried on the slight breeze, but the words were lost. She was animated as she talked to her sister, occasionally stopping to make a point. Amelia took the book from her when Liv's wild gestures threatened to send the book skittering across the lake.

Amelia indicated the ground, and Liv crouched low, searching for a moment. She picked up a rock and sent it skipping across the surface of the lake. Amelia followed suit. Both girls laughed.

"I love to see them like that," Emeline said. "Sisters are so wonderful together. Do you want more than one child, Dragomir?" She rubbed her palm protectively over the place the baby was nestled and safe.

He frowned, and her heart clenched hard in her chest. "As many as you want." His gaze remained on the children rather than on the lake.

She sat up straight, her hand going protectively over the

baby. "Dragomir? Do you not want children? Because if you don't . . . " She trailed off. She was having a baby. If he didn't want children that was a big problem. Huge.

"Of course I want children. Why would you ask me that?" He dipped the oar in the water and they went soaring over the glassy surface.

He'd frowned, and she'd panicked. That was another testimony to the way she felt about herself. Unworthy. Not good enough for him. For someone to really love her or want a life with her. *She* was going to be the problem if she didn't watch it. What man liked a woman who was afraid every minute that he was going to leave her?

"Emeline." He said her name softly and her gaze jumped to his. His eyes had gone that molten gold she loved, as if it was melted and hot. "I want you any way I can have you. Children. No children. You're always going to be my world. There is no other and there never will be. I know you have a difficult time understanding the concept of lifemates, but you'll get it eventually. I would tell you to stop worrying, but I can see that won't help."

"I'll try, Dragomir," she promised. "It's just that for a moment I thought maybe you didn't want children, and I do. I want it all. The family, the home, the man who adores me just as much as I adore him." She ducked her head, her gaze going to the water, anywhere but facing that penetrating stare. "I want you to want that same thing. Especially the children."

"I want the same thing," he assured. "The more girls we have, the more lifemates we give to the Carpathian people."

She rested her head back, letting the gentle sway of the water lull her. "I never thought about that. How a child we have might save one of the males of the Carpathian race. All those women . . . " She broke off and closed her eyes, shaking her head as if to get the sight out of her mind.

"Those women?" he prompted.

"In Vadim's underground city. They were psychics. He told me they were, but not strong enough for his purposes. The bodies were piled up, and I could see half-formed babies, some fully formed, all dead. When those women died, they were lifemates, weren't they? Lifemates to some of the hunters waiting."

"More than likely. The loss was felt deeply. The souls will be reborn but there is no way of knowing if the hunters can hang on that long. That was part of Vadim's plan. If he takes the lifemates away, destroys them, more hunters will turn, helping him to create a larger army."

"If they know they'll be reborn . . . "

"There is no way of knowing when they will be reborn. What century. Where. The world is a big place, and some of these hunters have held on for centuries. When there is nothing to hold on to but honor, it can be very difficult."

She studied his face. He had suffered. It was there in his harsh male features. Dragomir would never have been called handsome in the traditional sense of the word—his features were too angular and male. Almost brutal. But he was beautiful and sensual. The scars on his face and body added to his appeal. He looked dangerous. Walking into a room, she knew he would command attention and scare most people. Maybe all of them.

"I hate that you had to wait so long."

"You are worth every moment of that wait." Sincerity rang in his voice.

She turned her head toward the shore where the children were playing. "Listen to the frogs. So many. It sounds like they're gathering for a frog concert."

"Noisy little things," he observed. "If I'm going to take you dancing in the stars, we need better music."

251

She liked the sound of dancing in the stars. For the first time, she allowed herself to fully relax. She tipped her head up and studied the constellations scattered overhead. The sky looked beautiful, so dark it was nearly blue, the stars and sliver of moon hot and glowing against that backdrop. There were a few drifting clouds, but they looked inviting rather than threatening.

More childish laughter caught her attention, and she turned her head to see the Waltons standing with Danny, talking to the two youngest. Mary Walton carried something cradled in her arms. Her husband, Donald, had a large gun slung around his shoulder. She sat up so fast she nearly spilled into the water.

"What in the world?" She stared at the couple as they laughed and talked with Danny. "Dragomir, they're carrying guns. Both of them. They're the sweetest couple. They live in the boathouse. I've never been in it, but the children tell me it's really nice and homey. Why in the world would Mary be carrying a gun? Or Donald, for that matter. They could hurt themselves."

"My understanding is they know how to use them. They're both efficient at it."

"I suppose they're protecting the children. I hate that Bella and Lourdes have to see that. And poor Liv. She's only ten, and she had those terrible creatures of Vadim's tearing at her, eating her alive. If it weren't for Valentin, she never would have made it out of there. I couldn't have saved her, nor could Blaze. It was Valentin."

The sound of the frogs increased and, along with them, the crickets started. She found herself laughing softly. She almost couldn't believe anything could make her laugh, not when she'd been thinking about Vadim's underground city and the atrocities he'd committed on men, women and children there. The frogs and crickets added a magical reality to the night.

"Listen to them. Any minute I expect them to burst into song."

"They are singing," he said. "Dance with me, *sívamet*. I believe I have pulled enough information out of your mind to lead you in a waltz." He put the oar down and the canoe glided by itself over the water to the dock nearest the Waltons' boathouse and away from the children. It was darker and more secluded.

He stood up, balancing easily, and held out his hand to her. She hesitated. They were still in the canoe and if she moved wrong, they could both fall into the water. He might be right—that she could swim—but she didn't want to test his theory there in the dark.

His white teeth flashed at her and his lower lip curved into the soft, intriguing smile she found herself watching for. "Emeline. Really? You think I would allow you to fall into the water? Especially since you're afraid. That would be cruel. I'm capable of great cruelty, but never to the woman I love. Give me your hand." He held out his hand to her.

Her heart went crazy, for him or out of fear, she wasn't certain which, but it beat like a drum out of rhythm. She placed her hand in his and allowed him to pull her to her feet. The canoe didn't so much as rock. That was all him. Looking out for her.

He moved then, shifted his feet, took them into the air so that her sandals hovered just above the canoe. His arm went around her back and he brought her hand up. His frame was superb, as good as any of the professionals she'd danced with. She put her hand on his shoulder and allowed him to pull her into his body. Close. Closer than she would ever have allowed any other dance partner.

His body felt wonderful. Strong. Male. Pure Dragomir. No other man could ever make her feel the mixtures of things he did. Or give her the intensity of emotion he gave her. She felt safe and sexy, beautiful and intelligent. He listened to every word she said. Gave her strength and made her hope—believe—even if it was just for a few minutes.

Dragomir enfolded Emeline into his arms, guiding her body into the shelter of his. If dancing was what she loved, then he would be an expert dancer, guiding her up through the air toward the stars. The song that was playing over and over in her head played in his as well. He brought the music to life, hearing the beat in her head, feeling it in his body.

Below them, on the ground, the children continued to play together, Liv and Amelia skipping rocks on the lake, Danny and the little girls talking with the Waltons and Genevieve, who had joined them. The scene seemed surreal. He didn't care about any of them right in that moment. Only Emeline and her happiness.

They moved together in perfect rhythm. Dancing was like making love, he decided, his body guiding hers through the intricate steps as they danced up unseen stairs, going higher and higher until the clouds drifted past them.

He allowed her to step on one, ensuring that to her it appeared a fluffy white floor. He whirled her out and brought her back into him. All around them the stars shone brightly. Their cloud drifted across the sky as they danced to the music, her body moving in rhythm with his. He always was in control, yet when he was with Emeline, his body refused to listen to his commands, taking over, rebelling. Swelling with urgent need. She couldn't fail to feel his cock, hard and aching, pressed so tightly against her stomach.

"I love that you want me, Dragomir," she whispered. Her head was against his chest, her ear over his heart. "I want that always. I want to know when I walk into a room, you're aware of me. I'm always aware of you."

The sound of her voice whispering against the immaculate suit jacket he wore ratcheted up the hunger beating through him.

"From the first time I saw you in the yard with the others, I thought you were the sexiest man alive." She turned her head so her chin dug into his chest and her eyes were on his. "I daydreamed of you. I fantasized about you. I dreamt of you at night. Before Vadim's attack and certainly after, I never thought about sex. After I saw you, it was all I could think about."

She pleased him with her admission. She didn't have to tell him, but she gave that to him. Just handed him that gift as if it were nothing. She was very shy about their relationship, more so than about their sex, yet she gave him a piece of information that was a little embarrassing to her.

"You didn't share your dream with me."

Color crept into her face. Her long lashes fluttered. "Well. No. That was private. I wasn't about to share the kinds of things you did to me."

"Good things?"

"In my dream they were good things. In reality, I'd be afraid. We already went up in smoke together. Can you imagine if you were getting creative?"

"I plan on being very creative. Do you have a problem with that?" He nuzzled her neck. His teeth tugged on her ear.

"No. I'm just saying we could set the world on fire."

"Show me." His voice had lowered to a sinful, wicked temptation.

She shook her head. "We're dancing."

"We have this cloud to ourselves, *sívamet*," he pointed out.

She couldn't help but laugh at the absurdity of it. Of

255

course they had the cloud to themselves. No one danced in the clouds. No one danced surrounded by stars. Leave it to Dragomir to give that to her.

"We have too many clothes on for me to show you anything," she said. Already her blood had gone hot and rushed through her veins like a torrent of fire. Her center had gone liquid with need. She tasted him in her mouth and wanted more.

Immediately, just as she'd known he would do, their clothes were gone in a blink of an eye. The hand that had been on her back slid down to cup her buttocks. His fingers kneaded and stroked, sending heat waves through her.

"Show me," he commanded.

She would have done anything for him. His cock was heavy against her stomach, and she wanted it inside her. Right that moment. Her hand slid up his hip to find that thick girth. She wrapped her fingers around him and bent her head so she could lick at the pearl drops leaking there. He tasted as good as she remembered. She stepped out of rhythm and then had to straighten to keep in step.

He never stopped dancing with her, keeping up the rhythm of their bodies moving together. It was not only beautiful to her, but sexy. With every movement, her nipples slid across his chest, sending streaks of fire aimed straight to her center.

His hands cupped her buttocks, pressing her mound tightly against him. She couldn't stop her hips from riding his thigh. It felt so good. He always felt so good. She was lost in the sensations his body created.

"If you don't show me, little rebel, I am going to have to wake you up."

"Mmm." She wouldn't mind him waking her up. She let the various ways he could do it play through her head. She didn't have a lot of experience, but she read books. Tons of them, and there were many books that had erotic relationships, ones that intrigued her.

His hand came down hard on her bottom, startling her out of her fantasy. His palm rubbed and heat spread through her center. She pressed closer to him. "All right. Before you get too comfortable, I'll show you." She pushed the image into his head.

He was behind her, hands on her hips, taking his time, controlling her completely. She couldn't move or she'd fall. He held her up with one arm, forcing her body over his forearm, so her head was down and her bottom up in the air. He teased her, first with his hands and then with his cock, making her plead for him, making her so needy and hungry for him she had gone mindless. She wanted mindless. She wanted sexy. She wanted him to make her feel out of control.

At once he spun her around, his hands hard on her body, the sheer strength and speed making her heart clench hard and fear pound through her body straight to her sex. Excitement and trepidation mixed together. She knew he could read her emotions and that he monitored them, but she hoped he would realize this was what she wanted, this mixture of emotions.

His arm was an iron band around her waist as his other hand slowly pushed her head down so she hung over his arm. She should have known Dragomir would take creative license. She found her upper body hanging over a padded bench. Her breasts swayed in the air and her hair spilled to the soft cloud. She stared through the layers of cloud to the lake far beneath her, her heart pounding. The position left her feeling very exposed and vulnerable.

Biting her lip, she started to pull up. Instantly his hand

came down hard in warning on her bottom, a stinging pain that morphed into heat as he rubbed her buttocks. Then his hand was between her legs, fingers sliding over her clit, circling, tugging and then moving away. Her breath came out in a ragged burst. He repeated the entire sequence, started with a swat on her other cheek. His fingers were relentless, moving in her. Around her. Then his tongue with there, lapping at the cream spilling from her body.

She couldn't catch her breath. There was no way to know what he would do next. Hit her bottom with his hand? Devour her with his tongue? Use his teeth? His fingers? She closed her eyes and gave herself up to the wicked, sinful sensations he created. She hadn't known anyone could feel so much or so intensely.

The tension in her built and built until she knew the tsunami was going to overwhelm her. She would get close, so close, right on the edge, and his fingers went away. He took his mouth from her. She couldn't help the whimper escaping, or pushing back with her hips, trying to reach his hands. His mouth. His cock. She *craved* his cock. She needed his touch. Oh. God. His mouth. She absolutely needed his mouth. She'd take anything from him, but he had to do something. She moaned and bit out his name between her teeth.

His hands came back, but not on her sex. He was under her, his mouth on her left breast, pulling strongly, sending waves of fire sizzling and crackling through her veins. His finger and thumb were on her right nipple, tugging, rolling, dancing in a kind of rhythm with the pull of his mouth. So hot. So incredible. She could barely think with the sensations pouring through her.

It didn't stop. His mouth was on her breasts, but she felt his hands moving on her bottom again, that quick hard

258

swat, the rub that spread the heat, the sensation of his finger pushing into her tight folds. His mouth. Tongue devouring her. Teeth scraping along her clit. Then there was his mouth at her breasts. The twin sensations took her right up fast.

She screamed in frustration when everything stopped. Only her harsh breathing could be heard, a loud ragged dragging of air into burning lungs. He caught her hair and pulled her head up; at once his cock pushed into her mouth. Grateful for something, anything to distract her, she closed her mouth around him and she suckled hard. Her tongue danced and stroked. He held her head still, following the images in her head, his hips pushing into her.

"That's it, *sívamet*, take me all the way."

His voice was harsh with need. The sound encouraged her and she poured herself into the task of making certain he felt as much urgency as she did. She tried to reach his cock with her hands, but found she couldn't move them. Somehow they were pinned under the bench. His mouth was at her breast, pulling strong, teeth tugging on her breasts, his cock pushing into her mouth. Then she felt his mouth at her sex, tongue and teeth driving her right back up.

The tsunami hit hard, sweeping her over the edge, her entire body feeling the ripples, her breasts, her mouth, her thighs, and her sex all rippling with the powerful quake. It seemed to go on and on. She opened her mouth to scream, but his cock was there, demanding she keep suckling. She couldn't catch her breath, especially when she felt him, the broad, flared head pushing slowly into her entrance, forcing the invasion when her tight muscles tried to prevent him. She was slick, dripping with her need of him, and nothing could prevent her greedy body from not only accepting him, but pulling him deeper. It didn't matter that she was tight, her muscles gave way.

Then he was everywhere. Dragomir behind her, pounding into her. Below her, his mouth on her breasts. In front of her, filling her mouth with heat and fire. With the addictive taste of him. It was too much, overloading her. She came and came. Over and over. One orgasm ran into the next.

Honey. You have to stop. I can't. Not again. But that was a lie. Her body tipped over the edge again, gripping and milking his cock, determined to take him with her. She didn't want him to stop, but if he didn't she'd lose her mind. The pleasure was too intense.

The grip in her hair tightened until there was a bite of pain. Reluctantly she lifted her eyes to his. His hips surged forward, burying his cock in her scorching-hot channel. Burying his cock in the heated depths of her mouth. *Look at me. See me. I'm in you. Surrounding you. Yours. Always yours in every way. I will bring you pleasure beyond your imagination. I will keep you safe. You will have the things you want in life because I love you that much and I can give them to you.*

She felt the swelling of his cock in her sheath, pushing at the tight walls, creating a friction that sent fire coursing through her. In her mouth, his cock matched, pulsing and throbbing, and then she felt the hot release jetting into her, deep, so deep it splashed along the walls of her sheath, triggering another hard orgasm. In her mouth he erupted as well, pouring down her throat, giving her that taste that was only his, only for her.

She lay over the bench, unable to move, completely worn-out. He was behind her, his hands on her hips, his cock still buried deep, gliding gently, soothingly. She found she could move her hands and she put them out in front of her, stretching while she licked at her lips, feeling as if they were coated with him.

"Why do you always taste so good?"

His hand rubbed her bottom and then he slowly, with obvious reluctance, pulled out of her. "I taste the way you imagine me to taste. Let me help you sit up."

She didn't want to move. "You took creative license. Big-time."

"I put my own stamp on it. I gave you those sensations, each of them, and chose where I would be and where you would feel me. It can make our sex life interesting."

"If it gets any more interesting than that, I won't live through it. That was crazy sexy." She felt his hands on her waist and she let him lift her onto his lap. She looped her arms around his neck and buried her face in his chest. "I think you wore me out."

"You're Carpathian. Breathe, *sívamet*."

"How did we not fall through the cloud to the lake below?" She stared down. Through the cloud's thin layer, she could see the that little sliver of moon shining invitingly on the lake's surface. It didn't seem possible that such a short time had passed. She was certain they had been having sex all night, but everything was the same. The lake. The moon. The children. Only she was different.

She lifted her face to look up at him. To trace those beloved scars on his face. He'd given her so much. Nothing had prepared her for this night. Canoeing on the lake. Dancing up to the stars. Sex in the clouds. Wild, crazy sex that shook her to her core. Not because it was wild and crazy—and it had been—but because she felt love in every touch. Every stroke. Hard, gentle, brutal, exquisite, it had been a beautiful declaration of love. For her. She knew it. She felt it in her heart. He'd filled her with him. Surrounded her with him. He meant what he said when he'd told her he was in her.

"I'm so in love with you," she admitted softly, her eyes burning with tears. "So very much in love with you I can barely think straight with it."

He framed her face with his hands. "That's a good thing, Emeline. Your heart is in safe hands."

"I know." She was beginning to know, daring to start to believe.

13

Dragomir brought Emeline safely back to the dock and settled her feet there, holding her until he knew her legs were steady. He'd deliberately used the marina closest to the boathouse and away from where Amelia and Liv were skipping rocks. He glanced over at the two girls. Amelia was watching.

He wrapped his arm around Emeline's waist, tipped up her face and kissed her. Hard. Possessively. Wet and deep. She melted into him instantly, her body going soft and pliant, her arms circling his neck. He loved her mouth. It was always so responsive. His kisses. His cock. Her mouth loved both and she showed that to him every time.

"I like your creativity," she whispered. "I intend to explore every inch of you when we're alone."

"In the middle of a crowd we can be alone," he informed her with a wicked laugh.

She pulled back just enough to look up at him. "How?"

"I could take you right here, remove every stitch of your clothes, carry you to the picnic bench and pound into you. No one would see unless I wanted them to."

"So, in the nightclub? We're dancing and you could do that?" A frisson of pure desire slid down her spine. Her sex clenched. She shared both with him, pushing her reaction into his mind. Instantly his body reacted as well.

"I can see that dancing is something that gets you in the mood."

"I'm always going to be in the mood around you, but yes, dancing does it for me."

"Then we're visiting a nightclub really soon. You can wear something very sexy for me."

She stood on her toes so she could press a kiss to his throat and then scrape over his pulse with her teeth. The action sent heat coursing through his body. His cock stirred again.

"For an old-fashioned man, you've taken to modern clothes nicely."

"I realized they have their uses. Although I still object to your undergarments. They seem silly. Sexy when you're wearing just them, but otherwise not at all useful when I want access to you."

He caught the image of a very short skirt, black bra and sheer blouse in her head. He waved his hand and clothed her in the outfit. "Nice. But still doesn't make sense." He waved his hand again and removed the bra and panties. At once his hand slid up her thigh to caress her bare bottom. His other hand found her nipples through the sheer material.

She shivered and pushed into his hands. He liked the way she was so responsive to him. He liked that she didn't protest his hands on her, that she welcomed his stroking caresses. She was so perfect for him.

"Would you want other men to see my body?"

His gut knotted at the thought of other men near his woman. Times were different, but he was still primitive. "I told you, they wouldn't unless I allowed it." And that wasn't happening.

She bit at his jaw and then licked the sting. His body tightened. His cock jerked. Pulsed. Strained hard against the material of his trousers. He loved his reaction. He *felt*. Actually felt.

"Do you know what an exhibitionist is?" There was a teasing note in her voice.

"Of course." She wanted him to believe she was one just to see what he would do, but he knew better.

"So if I told you I was one and wanted to go to a club dressed like this, would you allow other men to see me?"

He kissed her again. Hard. "You're not. I know everything about you. What you like, what you don't like. What you want to try but are afraid, so we're going to try, but slowly and gently so we can stop if you don't like it. You like the thrill of having sex in public places, but you have no desire to be seen or get caught."

She nodded her head in agreement. "I wouldn't like other men to see me. But still, what would a lifemate do?"

"If he was okay with it, he would allow her to be seen; if he wasn't, he would walk in with her, making it appear as if she was seen. Either way, she gets her way. Lifemates are compatible. They make each other happy. If one has needs like that, chances are very good the other would as well."

The frogs took their chorus up a notch, calling to one another, serious about their symphony. The crickets sounded off, trying to rival them. Dragomir waved his hand and she was once again in her long gown. She looked ethereal and elegant. He liked the look. All her looks, including the one with the transparent blouse. He was beginning to think he could live in these times with the technology and the women wanting to be partners.

He dropped his arm around her shoulders and started her walking in the direction opposite the children. She didn't protest, or seem to notice. She leaned her head into him and wrapped one around his waist.

"Every step I take, I can feel you inside me."

"You're sore?" He scowled and stopped, pulling her tightly against him. "I should have checked and healed you. You're very small and we had vigorous sex ... "

She burst out laughing. "Vigorous sex? Is that what you call it? Honey, we had great, amazing and awesome sex. The best sex *ever*, in the history of the world. I'm *deliciously* sore and I don't want you to take that away from me. I love the thought of feeling you in me with every step I take. It's very sexy."

His heart turned over. It hurt. Hearts didn't hurt because you loved someone too much, did they? Because his did. It was a physical pain and he rubbed his palm over his chest to ease the ache. There was no easing it, not when she was looking up at him and he knew all that beauty was his. Inside, where it counted, she was everything a man could ask for. Her outside body was perfection. As near perfection as a woman's body could get. He knew by human standards, Emeline was considered beautiful. By his standards, she was beyond all measure.

Something moved in the grass. A gopher peeked its head up from a hole in the ground. The sliver of moon sent a beam right down to the lawn, spotlighting the little creature. The tip of its nose glowed with a strange white star. He looked around the lawn and saw several white stars shining. Ten. Twenty. More. They rolled out of the holes and stood on their hind feet. Not gophers. Something else.

"Emeline, we're going to float to the house." *It is starting. Get to Liv.* He called to the other Carpathian hunters waiting.

"What is it?"

Overhead an owl screeched. The trees around them shook, the limbs sagging under the weight of hundreds of birds settling on the branches.

"Another attack. I need you safe in the house. Once you're under cover, I can aid the others."

Emeline turned back, trying to pull away from him. "The children."

His hold on her didn't loosen in the slightest. He kept moving them toward the house, refusing to let her struggles soften his resolve.

"Dragomir," she began.

He took her to the front door, yanked it open and thrust her inside. "You are to stay." He waved his hand at the doors, and then in a circular motion, sealing every door and window. Even if she tried to use her Carpathian abilities, she wouldn't be able to leave the house. He caught a glimpse of her furious little face and then he turned and streamed out into the yard.

Vadim wouldn't make the mistake of exposing Amelia, but he had threatened the children, and he would want to show Emeline he could get to them, even with the Carpathian hunters around. With their added safeguards, it didn't make sense that Vadim could strike, even with his splinter in Amelia. They had safeguarded the children, allowing Amelia and the others to come together as they often did in the evenings, but the hunters remained especially vigilant. Liv was with Amelia. Nearest to her. She was Carpathian and a lifemate to one of the hunters. She would be his first target.

The birds took wing, flying low, a heavy migration, so heavy the air seemed to groan and there was little to breathe.

They flew at the children, the Waltons and Genevieve. Pecking, ripping at them with beaks and talons. Dragomir threw a hasty shield over them as he burst past them. He saw Tariq materialize and with him the healer, Maksim, and the triplets, Tomas, Mataias and Lojos. Dragomir's job, along with the other ancients, was to get to Liv and Amelia.

He winged his way over the lawn filled with creatures that should have been gophers but had morphed into something altogether different. The mutations flung their bodies at the hunters, swarming up legs, hurtling themselves onto arms and backs. Biting ferociously. Their giant teeth tore large chunks of flesh out of the Carpathians while the birds circled and came back for a second assault. The timing was perfect, the mutated creatures keeping the Carpathians occupied with their terrible teeth while the birds regrouped and circled, darting in to try to tear the little ones from Danny's hands. He had dropped to the ground, covering both little girls with his body. Genevieve covered him, adding a second layer of protection.

The mutated gophers bore through the ground to get at the children, forcing Danny and Genevieve to stand, each protecting a child, vulnerable now to the attack from the birds. Tariq and Gary laid double protection over all the humans, so that the birds battered at an invisible barrier and the mutated creatures threw themselves over and over at the shield.

Tariq used a torch, throwing flame across the lawn, incinerating as many of the gophers as possible. Most ducked into the holes and came up behind him. Gary caught them with his flamethrower. The ones he didn't get went back into the holes, regrouping as the birds made a third attack.

Dragomir saw the ground moving, a solid green-brown carpet and realized it was the frogs. They hopped to the girls, covering them, weighing them down, taking them to the water's edge. Amelia screamed and beat at them.

"Take my hand. Get my hand." She reached frantically for her sister. Their fingertips touched, but Liv was pulled away from her.

The sheer numbers of frogs carried the smaller girl into the lake. Amelia threw herself into the lake, diving, coming up, looking around hysterically and diving again. Dragomir dove straight down into the water from above, right over the spot Liv had disappeared. He could see the girl being dragged, her little body thrashing as thousands of frogs of all shapes forced her body toward the floor of the lake.

Amelia dove under again and this time they met beneath the water, staring eye to eye. The frantic, desperate look slowly faded, replaced by silver eyes. Glowing silver eyes. Eyes filled with hatred and triumph. Amelia swam straight at him so fast her body was a blur in the water.

Out of the corner of his eye, he spotted Valentin swimming at an angle to reach for Liv. The frogs used sticky hands, feet and tongues to hold Liv to the lake floor. As Valentin approached, large bullfrogs leapt on his back, impervious to his spells and waving hands. He kept swimming toward Liv. Fish surrounded Valentin, cutting him off from her. They darted in, huge mutations, teeth grabbing and pulling, in a feeding frenzy.

Dragomir timed Amelia's attack, spinning to one side and clipping her hard as she rocketed past him. Vadim had shown his hand. He had to know Dragomir would recognize the girl was possessed. They'd stared at each other. He'd revealed himself to Dragomir. He planned to sacrifice Amelia to make his try at the children. That worried Dragomir. If Vadim was willing to lose his spy, he was planning something much bigger.

To his shock, he felt Emeline moving through his mind, searching for the way to undo his command to safeguard the house.

Stop. I cannot concentrate when I worry about you. The girl will die. He was trying to save the teen, mostly because Emeline cared for her but also because she belonged to Tariq. That and he wouldn't allow the vampire to harm one more child if he could stop it.

He half expected Emeline to fight him, but she didn't. He felt her there in his mind, watching, but she remained silent.

A large mutated fish hit him from behind just as Amelia's body jerked to a halt and then was spun around. She came flying at him, this time with her body contorted, her face a mask of twisted hatred. He stared into Vadim's eyes. They were silver rimmed with a red glow. The teen slashed at him with a knife she must have had hidden in her clothing. The blade slipped under his arm, the tip dragging a slice down his ribs as he wrapped her up, one hand catching her wrist to force her to drop the knife.

Her hand opened, and as the knife fell toward the lake floor, a fish caught it in its mouth and rocketed toward Dragomir, blade facing him. He had his hands full trying to subdue the teenager, their bodies turning one way and then the other. It was Emeline who hissed a warning.

At the last second, with her warning burning in his mind, Dragomir thrust the teen from him and turned to face the fish. The blade bit into him as he batted it aside with his forearm. Instantly he knew the edge had been treated with a concoction of Vadim's.

Get out now, Emeline. I may have to kill her. Do you want to see that? Do you want me to live with the knowledge that you witnessed, even shared in a kill? She *had* to leave. To be safe. It wasn't safe in his body with poison spreading. He spun to face Amelia, his heart heavy. He knew Vadim intended to kill her. If he thought Emeline was watching, he would do it in a sick, twisted way that hurt the teen as much as possible. *Sívamet, you have to go. Please.* The burn down his ribs increased until it was almost impossible to block the pain, but the one along his forearm was like a wrenching, excruciating hole that seemed to be spreading. He didn't bother to look; it wouldn't matter what he saw. He had to prevent Vadim from abandoning Amelia in the lake. To do that, all the vampire had to do was kill the teenager.

Dragomir could see Amelia had come to the realization that the vampire was in her, forcing her to do things to the people she loved. There was desperation behind the eyes Vadim had taken over. She tried to fight for supremacy, looking toward Liv, her little sister. Twice she turned toward the drowning child to try to get to her, and both times, Vadim forced her back to face Dragomir.

Liv and Amelia are the targets. He's striking at the children, he told the hunters, even as he swam straight for the teenager. *If he kills Amelia, his sliver will be impossible to find. He'll attach to a fish, or a frog, and it will make its way back to him. How did he get in? Amelia didn't let him in. She couldn't, not with the safeguards we wove around her.*

Ancients were everywhere, swimming to save Liv, sweeping the frogs and fish from Valentin, circling Amelia so she had no way to escape. Dragomir saw it in her eyes, that moment of realization that Vadim was going to kill her. That he would drown her before he would allow her out of the lake.

Save yourself, Dragomir. I want Amelia alive, I do, but I can feel the poison spreading through you. Get out now. Let the others save her. Get out of there.

His heart clenched hard in his chest. He knew what it cost Emeline to say that to him. She loved the children. She'd sacrificed her life for them, endured torture and continued to safeguard them. With all that, she'd chosen him, taking the

271

chance that one of the other hunters might not reach Amelia if he abandoned his task.

There is no choice, Hän sívamak. I cannot allow this child to die. Please, wait for me and know that I put you above all others always. It wasn't enough if it was a final good-bye, but he had to let her know how much she meant to him, how much her choice meant to him.

Amelia hurtled herself through the water, determined to gouge out his eyes. Dragomir caught her around the waist and kicked hard at the fish and frogs leaping onto his back to tear at his flesh. The water around him turned red. The mutations were after Amelia now, in earnest, trying to keep her from Dragomir. She fought the hunter, tearing at him with her fingernails, punching and kicking, frantic to get away. Then she went quiet, opened her mouth and gulped lake water. At the same time, she inhaled.

He gripped her hard around the waist and shot out of the lake up into the sky. He turned her upside down so the water was forced to drain out of her as he took her to the dock. The birds screamed when they saw him and circled around to begin the attack on him. He threw up a shield and started pumping her lungs and stomach to rid her of the water.

The moment it began to trickle out of her mouth, he turned her on her side. All the while, his hand was over her pulse, making certain she stayed alive and Vadim couldn't escape. The birds went insane, screeching as they dive-bombed. Each vicious creature the master vampire created and manipulated turned its assault on Dragomir.

Dragomir knew they were too close to the lake. Too many of Vadim's creatures surrounded him. If the vampire was successful in killing Amelia, his sliver could escape her body and had a very good chance of returning to him.

I have immediate need. Amelia must be transported to the safe room with my body. I will be inside her trying to keep Vadim from killing her.

He would have to leave his body behind, unprotected, but she didn't have the time it would take to get her to the safe room.

He heard the soft echo of Emeline's cry. *No. No, don't do this.* The wrenching pain in her voice nearly shattered him. He sent as much emotion to her as possible, giving her his heart as he shed his body, leaving it vulnerable to Vadim's mutations.

Amelia's mind was the real battlefield. Vadim wanted her dead before they contained her. The sliver of evil commanded her lungs to cease breathing. Dragomir forced the air to continue in and out of her. He felt the anger as the master vampire realized he wasn't alone in Amelia's mind. The force of the undead's rage, coiled and ugly, hit him hard. Waves of turbulent sound bounced through Amelia's head, high-pitched, painful. Vadim tried to drive Dragomir out of the teen while he went after her heartbeat.

In the midst of the waves crashing into him, driving his spirit time and again away from Amelia's lungs, Dragomir suddenly realized the frantic drumming of the girl's heart had ceased. He immediately stimulated the heart, forcing it to beat and pump the precious blood through her body to her brain.

He was aware of Tariq there, carrying the body, moving fast, the healer and others surrounding him. Sandu was there, carrying his body with the ancients guarding him. They took them through the house where the children lived, rushing deeper into the walls where the safe rooms were built in. Each room was off a child's room, and once they were inside, would be in the ground surrounded by safeguards where no one or their monsters could reach the children.

Amelia's body was laid out on the bed. Dragomir's body

was on the floor beside the bed. Gary shed his body fast and entered the fray. *Tell me*. It was a demand, nothing less.

He is striking at her heart and lungs, desperate to kill her so he can get out. If you can take over keeping her alive, I will hunt him.

The poison he put in your body is lethal. You would have little time, but by shedding your body, it shut down your heart. The poison can't spread.

That was one consolation, although Dragomir hadn't given a thought to what was happening in his body from the knife cuts. He hadn't had time. *Is Liv alive?*

Yes, Valentin and the others pulled her out of the lake. She is strong, that one. Valentin commanded she breathe underwater and she did. Without a single lesson.

Do you hear that, Amelia? Liv is alive. All the children survived. You cannot allow him to defeat you. There was no response, but Dragomir didn't expect any.

The girl was in a comatose state. There was no fighting Vadim and winning. She was human. She was a teenager. She couldn't process the kind of evil inside of her. He had deliberately allowed her to see him, to know that she was the one causing all the trouble, the one trying to kill Dragomir and Emeline. Vadim wanted her to want death. To seek it.

Gary was an ancient healer with the knowledge and experience of an entire line of healers. He was also a hunter with that same lineage pouring their experiences of battle into him. He was fast and he moved through the teen's body, repairing each massive problem Vadim began. Aneurisms, strokes, lungs filling with fluid, Vadim tried them all, while the healer rushed to repair or stop the damage.

Dragomir was quiet, looking for a pattern in the attacks on Amelia. There always was a pattern. Always. No one could help it, and an ancient vampire such as Vadim least of all. He'd developed a huge sense of self-preservation over the centuries and he would keep to the things that had always worked for him. Vadim knew he had to kill the girl to free the sliver. However, if he didn't kill her, they might not find the sliver in her and the Carpathians wouldn't kill her—to them she was an innocent child. Why had Vadim outed her as the spy? Why would he do that?

Dragomir had already dimmed his spirit's light in order to move through Amelia's brain looking for that tiny little discolored spot that would be Vadim's sliver embedded there. The vampire needed a base from which to conduct his attacks, which meant he must be in the brain. The sliver couldn't move around. It would get lost in the bloodstream and be carried away too far from the brain to be of any use to Vadim.

Dragomir examined each portion of the brain with slow, meticulous care. Xavier, the high mage, had been the first to embed slivers of himself into others so he could see his enemies and fight from a distance. Vadim and Sergey both carried a sliver of the high mage in them, allowing them to use his spells when they needed them. None of the Carpathians were particularly adept at finding the slivers because, until now, Xavier had been the only one using such a forbidden technique.

Dragomir went through the entirety of Amelia's brain and found nothing. There was no dark spot he could see. Nothing that seemed off to him. He had a moment of doubt. Was he wrong about where Vadim had to be to direct her heart and lungs to shut down? He had concentrated his efforts in the brain stem. He'd looked everywhere throughout the brain, but he had been certain Vadim would have chosen the brain stem for his sliver to reside.

The cerebrum controlled action. He'd had to control Amelia's movements when he had taken on the lightning in the healing grounds, and again when she fought Dragomir underwater. He had just started to move around the brain toward the cerebrum when Amelia's body convulsed. Nerve cells fired in massive bursts, lighting up areas of the brain as the electrical charges spasmed. Dragomir spun around to study the brain stem under the fiery glow of the electrical charges.

There it was. He was certain. The tiniest little curved splinter, barely discernable, lying in a shallow crevice of the cerebrum. Dragomir floated closer, keeping his light as dim as possible. The electrical charges sputtered and slowly died out as the seizure eased. Dragomir moved with infinite slowness, coming into position above Vadim's sliver.

I think I've found him. Keep his attention centered on you, he said to the healer.

Gary responded by using the white-hot light of his spirit to build a shield around Amelia's heart, effectively stopping Vadim from giving her a heart attack. The little spot wiggled just once, and then waves of rage and hatred burst through Amelia's brain. Dragomir didn't wait. He dropped right over the splinter and shed his spirit's light on the dark, destructive piece of himself Vadim had placed in the teen.

At once the splinter began to smoke, to blister. It tried to escape by attempting to burrow, but that allowed Dragomir to get even closer, wholly incinerating the tail of the tiny sliver. Rage filled the brain, and Amelia's body came up off the bed and was slammed back down. Once. Twice. Again and again. Tariq caught her and held her against the mattress. Dragomir was certain he heard Emeline sob.

The moment that small sound echoed through his mind, Vadim's splinter erupted into a mass of cruelties. He sent agonized pain after pain through Amelia's body. He knew he couldn't save his splinter, and he wanted Emeline to suffer. So, he tortured Amelia, causing as much pain as possible to the teenager, all the while fighting to stay alive, skittering from one crevice to another, trying to get Dragomir to miss and burn the sensitive brain tissue instead of the splinter.

Emeline suddenly comprehended that Vadim was aware she was in Dragomir's mind and he was punishing her through Amelia—that her presence had added to the horrors he visited on the teenager. She slipped further away, into the back of Dragomir's mind, hoping to ease the girl's suffering, although her lifemate could have told her it was too late. Vadim was going to hurt the child as much as possible in hopes of hurting the woman who cared for her.

Dragomir stayed distant from all of it. He had one job, and that was to destroy the splinter Vadim had placed in the girl. It couldn't escape. He'd burned half of it but as long as there was anything left, it could cause harm. He followed that wiggling little thread relentlessly. Each time his light passed, white-hot and bright, over it more smoke and blisters arose. He could hear Vadim's screams as the master vampire felt the death of that tiny piece of him. He would be diminished in power. The loss of that part of him was critical. Dragomir had already taken a piece of his heart. Now, this loss would further weaken him.

Dragomir reached for the vampire, using the common link between Carpathians. *Your brother will be the one everyone must look to. You are defeated by a teenage human child. With the loss of this splinter, you lose power and all those following you will be aware of your diminished capacity.*

He was poking the tiger, but he wanted the other vampires and especially Sergey Malinov to know Vadim wasn't invincible. In the past, vampires were too vain and selfish to stick together. The Malinov brothers had been the ones to accomplish what no one had ever done—they'd formed their own army of vampires. Even other master vampires were talked into joining with the Malinovs. That was unheard-of and boded ill for the world.

The Carpathians were playing catch-up with the vampires. The Malinovs had put a plan in place centuries earlier and had the patience to carry it out. Vadim was a huge part of that. If Dragomir could discredit him and cause doubt among his followers, it would be all to the good.

Amelia's body convulsed again, this time a long, violent seizure. The bursts of electricity aided Dragomir in finding Vadim's sliver as it skittered up the brain, looking to slither into the bloodstream. He pinned it down with a concentrated flow of white-hot light, refusing to allow it to get away. Another section incinerated and dropped off, turning to ash. Vadim howled with pain and rage.

She will suffer as no one has ever suffered.

Dragomir didn't respond to the threat, although he didn't like the confidence in Vadim's voice. By all reasoning, the master vampire should have left the area. There were too many hunters. He had to know that the hunters would do what they did best. They were going to track him and kill him. Not just him, but a good portion of his followers. Still, the vampire stayed. Whatever he needed from Emeline was so important that he refused to cut his losses and retreat. Vadim also had managed an attack on the compound when they all should have been safe.

This child won't be able to take much more. Her body is going into shock, Gary warned. He fended off the attacks, but he couldn't stop her body's natural reactions.

Dragomir followed the last tiny segment of Vadim's sliver. It was miniscule, but it was still dangerous. He didn't dare allow it to escape his light. He just had to get close enough . . . The sliver tried to take refuge in a layer of neurons, desperate to conceal itself. He knew he had it then. He didn't wait, but sent a burst of white-hot light straight into the tiny bit of matter, burning it until it was nothing but ash.

Thunder crashed across the sky, rolling through so strongly it shook the compound. Outside, the last of the mutated creatures converged on Emeline's house, trying to find cracks to slip through. The birds went for the chimney. They flew into the windows over and over, pecking wildly to try to break the glass. The little gopher mutations covered the porch while the frogs attached themselves to the door and sides of the house.

Dragomir slipped out of Amelia's body back into his own. Pain blasted through him. He looked down at his arm to see it blackened, blistered, the skin sloughing off.

Emeline gasped. *Let me come to you.*

It's what he wants. You can't leave the safety of the house until all the creatures have been dealt with. The children are safe. That's what matters.

Not to me. You matter to me. I have to come to you.

Gary materialized beside him, swaying with weariness. Andor immediately extended his wrist to allow the healer to feed. "You have to shut down your heart and lungs. I've seen this poison, Dragomir. It is ... difficult. The same as the poison used by Leon. Xavier created this, not Leon, and Sergey or Vadim must have accessed his memory of it. It will eat through muscle and bone if I don't stop it. Shut down now." There was a bite to Gary's tone, as if he was weary of having to tell others what to do all the time—especially more than once.

Tariq dropped a hand on Dragomir's shoulder. "Thank you for saving Amelia. I'll take care of Emeline."

"The house is covered with Vadim's creatures. He's up to something, Tariq. Amelia wasn't his big gun. She was always expendable. He didn't want to lose the sliver, but he was willing to give it up. You know he isn't finished. He has something far worse in store for us. It's already here. And how did he attack us? How did he get through the safeguards?"

"Dragomir." Gary's tone was a warning.

He wondered vaguely if the healer would try to force him to sleep before he could make Tariq and the others understand the danger was worse than ever to the compound and people residing in it.

Please do what he asks, Emeline whispered in his mind. *Please, Dragomir. For me.*

Women. They were a curse. He had duties. His honor demanded he aid Tariq and the others, but his woman . . . She broke his heart. How could he refuse her? Not when she was silently weeping and so scared. For him. She had Vadim's mutated creatures trying to break down her doors and windows, trying to chew their way to her, but she was thinking only of him.

He looked up at Sandu. Sandu nodded. Dragomir did as Emeline asked and shut down his heart and lungs, allowing the healer to enter his body. Sandu followed on the pretense of learning about the poison. The brotherhood backed one another up at all times. They knew little about Gary. He was a dangerous hunter and a skilled healer, but there was death in his eyes and a layer of coldness only the ancients from the monastery recognized. He belonged with them, behind those high walls where they couldn't do damage to others. He didn't have the code inked into his back reminding him that they lived by honor. They lived for their people. They lived for the one. He needed that reminder.

Sandu watched as the healer tracked the path of the poison. It appeared a long, dark ribbon winding its way through Dragomir's body, toward the heart. It was thick, like sludge, and it moved with infinite slowness. Everything it touched turned dark and discolored. The outside flesh was blackened and blistered, but inside, the dark muck burned deep trails along bone. When it touched a vein or artery, it burned through it, cauterizing the wound.

If you're going to be in here with me, get to work. I have to repair the damage to his body, the veins, arteries and anything else this has touched. You destroy it.

Sandu stared at the healer's white light. How did one stop that slow stream of death? It burned everything it touched, so it stood to reason that burning it would do no good.

How does one destroy it? I've never seen it before. He shared the image with those in the brotherhood.

You haven't seen it because it was originally Xavier's concoction. Sergey was always very interested in poisons and how they affected the body. If I had to guess which brother, Vadim or Sergey, accessed Xavier's memories, I would say Sergey. This is a mixture of an ancient poison developed by the high mage. It is extremely dangerous, even to the one wielding it.

Yet he had the girl put it on the blade of a knife. The water didn't damage it.

No, it wouldn't. The poison is too thick. As he explained, the healer was working to repair the damage done to Dragomir's veins. *This poison is made in darkness. The spells cast over it are of darkness. The ingredients are those found only at night in the deepest part of the forest, in the darkest soil.*

Sandu continued to share with the others everything the healer said. *So, light kills darkness. That's what you're saying to me.*

Gary didn't bother to respond. Sandu positioned himself at the end of the stream where it hadn't managed to spread yet. He shone the white-hot light of his spirit over the darkened sludge. The brown stream shuddered and then slowly shriveled everywhere the light touched it.

Can this be done outside his body, on the flesh that is being eaten away?

It is the only way to stop it. One must shed the body, become the spirit and destroy the stream that is slowly devouring Dragomir's outside body.

Sandu made certain his brethren heard every word and was satisfied when Afanasiv began the work of healing Dragomir from the outside in. It took the three of them several hours and quite a bit of blood to stop the poison, destroy it and repair the damage. By the time they were finished, it was close to dawn.

The ancients returned Dragomir to Emeline's house. Maksim and the triplets had destroyed Vadim's creatures. Charlotte, Blaze and Genevieve settled the children down in their beds with the Waltons watching over them. Tariq and Ferro took Amelia back up to her room and made certain she was in a healing sleep.

It was Sandu who opened the floor of Emeline's house and showed her over and over how to open the earth and close it. He floated Dragomir down into the healing soil. Emeline managed to float down on her own but she landed a little harder than she would have preferred. Wrapping her arms around Dragomir, she filled the dirt in around their bodies, burying his head, but leaving her own outside the cover of dirt. She couldn't quite make herself bury her body entirely.

"I can do it for you," Sandu offered.

She shook her head, her arms tightening around Dragomir beneath that blanket of soil. Her breathing was coming too fast, her heart beating too hard.

Sandu ignored her, waving his hand to put her to sleep and then covering Dragomir and Emeline with the richest soil possible. He opened the earth above them, prepared to take on any enemy threatening them. Emeline was a Carpathian woman. Dragomir's lifemate. She was also the vessel carrying another female child. That child held the fate of a Carpathian hunter in her hands. No one would harm her on his watch.

Spreading out beneath the house, Ferro and Andor took refuge in the soil. One to the right of Dragomir's resting place and the other to the left. Afanasiv and Nicu slept beneath the house as well, one under the porch in the front and the other under the porch in the back.

When the sun came up, only the security company moved in the bright light of day.

14

melia's so far away, none of us can reach her," Dragomir told Emeline as he gathered her close to feed her. "Tariq is hoping you'll try. The healer thinks she doesn't want to come back. She knows Vadim used her to try to kill me, her sister and the other children. She knows he used her to try to reacquire you. Charlotte and Blaze have tried. Gary has tried; so has Tariq. Danny is at her bedside along with Liv, but nothing is working."

They had to have the conversation about Dragomir imperiously preventing her from helping during the attack, but right then he sounded so distressed over Amelia that she couldn't help reaching up to link her fingers behind the nape of his neck as she fed. He tasted delicious. Perfect. Truthfully, she was just thankful he was alive.

You throw yourself into battle without thinking of the cost to yourself, she pointed out. *It's terrifying, Dragomir. You almost died. That poisonous knife could have killed you. So many things could have killed you last night. You don't weigh the consequences; you just do whatever it takes to save the day.*

She had woken with her heart pounding and the taste of fear in her mouth. She'd been disoriented, reaching for him, afraid she'd lost him. He'd promptly proven to her that he was alive and more than well, his body moving in hers, sending streaks of fire radiating through her until she couldn't think straight. He'd gone to feed, and in his absence, that same frightening feeling she'd woken with had consumed her. She hadn't wanted him out of her sight, which had made her feel needy and dependent.

His hand stroked caresses down her hair, hair that she'd woken with free of tangles, he'd still brushed it—because he loved to, he'd said. She was certain it was because *she* loved it. She'd gone to sleep in the ground and woken in her bed. Naked. His mouth on her. His hands so gentle she'd felt the burn of tears. After, when they lay together, holding each other, he'd talked to the baby, his mouth against her stomach, sending waves of love and reassurance.

"I am a Carpathian hunter, Emeline." His voice was as gentle as his hands had been, so at odds with the way he fought. With her, he was the complete opposite of the man she saw battling the vampires. She hadn't found a shred of emotion in his mind when he'd been in the lake, not even for Amelia. Now, with her, he was all emotion. Gentle and thoughtful. "I hunt and destroy the undead."

She ran her tongue over the two tiny holes in his chest, tasting those last delicious drops. She loved everything about him, everything about the way he touched her, the way he tasted, the man that he was, but she was beginning to think there was a lot about him she didn't know. She had access to his mind, his memories, everything he was. Dragomir didn't limit her ability to see him, not even his violent past, yet she hadn't probed. She didn't want to.

"I know you've always done that. Hunt vampires. I also know you're a huge part of keeping everyone here safe," she conceded, looking into his eyes. Those strange, golden eyes. "But the way you throw yourself into battle as if you have nothing to lose, as if you don't care that you might lose your life, is terrifying to me."

"I don't know any other way." He didn't blink, and her stomach did a slow roll. He looked wild. Dangerous. All predator.

She turned his statement over and over in her mind. "What you're saying is you will continue to battle vampires the way you've always done it."

His gaze remained fastened on hers. She felt captured there, a prisoner. There was no looking away. They were locked in a battle she didn't understand. It was as if he was holding his breath. Waiting. They stared at each other for what seemed forever.

"Dragomir, tell me."

He was so still. Holding himself together as if at any moment he might shatter. That was so unlike him. He always had such confidence in himself. Confidence bordering on arrogance.

"There is no other way to fight the vampire and win."

Again, his tone and expression gave nothing away. Nothing. He still waited, held himself too still, as if the axe would fall any moment. She was missing something important, something she needed to address immediately. She bit down on her lower lip, her heart beginning to beat out of rhythm with his. The moment that happened, he took her hand and pressed her palm to his chest, right over his heart.

"I need you to tell me what's wrong." Emeline whispered

it. She did. She detested seeing him so upset. It hurt to see him so ready to believe ... What? That she would be so upset with him that she would reject him? That didn't make sense, but the nagging feeling stayed with her.

"You're angry with me."

"I'm not." She wasn't. How could she be? He'd saved Amelia, even when she told him he was her choice and even implied if he had to choose, to save himself.

"*Sívamet.*"

The endearment washed over her. Through her. His heart. He'd told her what it meant, and she loved when he called her that. It wasn't just the endearment, it was the way he said it, the tone, that soft caress to his voice. He meant it when he called her that.

"You are angry with me because you think I go into battle without thinking of you and our child. You are angry with me because when I went into danger, I refused to allow you to accompany me."

She opened her mouth to protest, but had to close it. He was right. He was *so* right. She hadn't wanted him battling the vampire when he could have been killed. He'd been horribly wounded more than once. She also was angry on behalf of all women that he would lock her in a house while a battle raged outside.

"Okay, yes," she conceded. "But I don't understand why you're so upset that I'm angry. It happens between two people when there is a misunderstanding."

He shook his head, his thumb sliding over the back of her hand. "There is no misunderstanding, Emeline." His voice was gentler than ever. Sad. There was sorrow in his eyes. "I have no choice. To come home to you, I must push you and our child from my mind and fight the way I always have. If I am divided, my thoughts with you, fear in my mind,

I wouldn't stand a chance against the undead. I know no other way."

Her heart hurt. A physical pain. She forced air through her lungs. She wasn't weak. She had tied herself to a man who would always be on the front line. Always determined to keep those around him safe. That was who he was. If she loved him—and she did—she had to accept that in him. She also had to accept how he kept himself safe.

She touched her lower lip with her tongue, soothing the tiny bite mark she'd made earlier. She didn't like him throwing himself into battle with no thought for his own life, but if he said he had to fight that way to survive, then she had to find a way to accept it. He hadn't looked away from her. Not once. She felt him moving in her mind. That was intimate, the way his mind brushed over hers, so gently, the way he touched her skin, that was the way he touched her mind.

"I understand, Dragomir. I do. I'll do my best not to worry too much." Like that would happen. "I love you. When a woman loves a man, she worries. I can't stop that."

He brought her hand to his mouth, still looking into her eyes. "And the other?"

Emeline realized immediately it was "the other" he was most worried about. "I realize you are from a different time where women didn't have rights and their men looked after them—"

"Carpathian women have always had rights," he interrupted. "They are cherished. Treasured. We know how capable they are."

"Blaze and Charlotte go with Tariq and Maksim. They are at their side when a battle comes."

"That affects us how?"

He seemed genuinely puzzled. She sighed. "Dragomir, I can't be locked up."

"You wouldn't have stayed where you were safe."

If she were honest, she wouldn't have stayed in the house. She would have tried to help in some way. She wasn't like Blaze, a warrior woman. She never had been. But she went her own way and made decisions for herself. She'd been doing that since she was a very young child.

"Maybe I wouldn't have . . . "

"You wouldn't have," he said. "There is no maybe, Emeline. You would have rushed to help those children without thinking of the consequences to you, the baby, or to me."

"It has to be my choice."

For the first time he looked away from her, but not before she caught that terrible sorrow deep in his eyes, as if she'd just shattered his world. She curled her palm around the nape of his neck. "We're talking it out, Dragomir. That's what couples do."

He shook his head. "There is no talking it out, Emeline. I am centuries old. There are things about myself I cannot change. One of those things is my need to keep you and our children safe. I have to know that before going into battle. You think it is reasonable to put yourself and our unborn child in harm's way. I do not."

"So because you're bigger and stronger we do it your way?" She tried to keep belligerence out of her voice, but she felt a little confrontational.

He shook his head. "We do it my way because I cannot do it any other. I want to be everything you need, Emeline. You do not need this, but I do. In a relationship, there has to be compromise. I must learn modern ways in order to ensure your happiness. In some things, you will have to forgo modern ways to ensure mine."

"Do you care if Blaze goes into battle with Maksim?"

He shook his head. "Blaze is a good warrior. You are not,

nor will you ever be. I see into your mind, *sívamet*. You have compassion for all things. You have determination and courage. You would fight at my side, but the toll on you would be horrific. There is no need to prove to me or anyone else that you're willing to fight. I want you to learn to handle the modern weapons being developed to kill the vampire. I want you adept at using them. What I cannot have is you needlessly putting your life on the line because you think you should."

"Why is your life worth less than mine?"

"It isn't. I have centuries of experience and you cannot hope to catch up. Truthfully, Emeline, you are the other half of my soul. I am what you need and you are what I need. Blaze is what Maksim needs. I cannot have a warrior for a partner. I cannot." He shook his head and his golden eyes were back on hers. Holding hers. Waiting for judgment. Waiting for her to tell him she couldn't live with him the way he was.

Emeline wanted to reassure him, but first, she had to know in her own heart if she could live with the man he was. She would be forever tucked away while he went into battle. He would never stop. Not because he had a lifemate and not when he had children. Fighting the vampire was ingrained in him. He would never stop, and she would always worry.

Would it be better if she fought at his side? She wasn't like Blaze. She never had been. She didn't like confrontation and she certainly, despite being taught by Blaze's father, didn't like to fight. Still, to know Dragomir was in danger and she could do nothing . . . If he was injured and she was locked away, she would go crazy.

She shook her head. "We have to find a compromise, Dragomir. I'm fine with not going into battle. I don't want to face a vampire ever again. I don't. On the other hand, I have to be able to defend my children, my life and yours if necessary. I can't be a little mouse sitting at home waiting for my big bad warrior to return."

"I have never thought of you as a little mouse," he denied. "I want you to be able to defend yourself, the children and me, if necessary. What I don't want is for you to make a rash decision because, like last night, things look grim. You would have to give me your word you would look to me for guidance in a situation."

"Then you would have to give me your word you would call to me if help was needed even in the worst situation."

"Do you understand what happens to the male Carpathian if his lifemate dies?"

She shook her head slowly. Something about the way he asked the question made her heart beat faster. She was fairly certain she wasn't going to like his answer.

"We have two choices. We suicide, or we turn vampire. It happens fast. One can't take the sudden change, from light to complete darkness. Everything gone after having everything beautiful. Can you imagine what kind of vampire I would be with the knowledge stored in my head? I would wreak havoc on the world, Emeline. That is one of my greatest fears. It always has been. That's why I chose the brotherhood. Living in the monastery when I reached the point of no return rather than chancing turning vampire."

"You wouldn't."

"If you were gone, I would."

She heard the conviction in his voice. Why was she throwing up arguments? "I'm not Blaze. I don't want to fight vampires. I just want you to understand that I have to make my own choices. You need to explain to me the things you need to make you happy. I have to be the one to make the choice. You can't force me. That's a dictatorship, not a partnership."

291

"I understand the kind of man I am, Emeline."

Again, she could hear sorrow in his voice. He didn't believe she could accept who he was. He believed she would reject him. Her breath rushed out of her lungs. She understood that feeling. She'd had it all her life. She'd lived without acceptance. He had given her unconditional acceptance to be who she was.

She detested fighting. She always had; as far back as she could remember, she'd had to fight off men, fight for food, fight for the right to be educated. Dragomir knew all those things about her, because unlike her, he'd looked into her memories and taken those things into consideration. She'd been a coward and hadn't considered his memories. She hadn't wanted to see the stark ugliness of his life, but if she'd bothered to learn everything she could about him, she would know what he needed.

She took a deep breath. Whatever commitment she made, he would expect her to keep. If she gave her word, she should expect to keep it as well. Could she? If there was danger, as there had been the night before, to the children, to the other women, to *him*, would she be able to stay in her house and let him—and any others—go into battle without her?

"I want to give you my word. I know you need that from me."

"But you can't."

"Not yet," she admitted reluctantly. "I need to get to a place where I know how all this works before I can give you my word of honor."

"Can you accept me putting you in a safe position, Emeline? Because I will. Make no mistake about it, I will safeguard you every single battle until I have your word that you will do so yourself."

She heard the implacable resolve in his voice. He would lock her up. He would take the decision out of her hands.

She either had to accept that or . . . what? Lose him? That was unacceptable. She bit at her fingertips nervously. "For now, when something happens, safeguard me, Dragomir, but leave me a way out in your mind so I can get to you if you're injured and I need to do that."

Relief crept into the gold of his eyes. He nodded slowly. "Thank you, Emeline. I realize it is difficult for you to give me that and it is all the more appreciated that you would. I will use your consent with care and as sparingly as possible."

She leaned into him to kiss him. She'd been fixated on his eyes, but his mouth was equally as intriguing to her. He tasted wild. She loved that about him. He tasted dangerous. He was both those things and yet, he was hers. She had to be brave enough to look into his mind and see those terrible memories—the emptiness that drove men of honor to become the worst monsters on earth.

He kissed like sin. Like heaven. She indulged because she'd hated that look in his eyes, the one that said he thought she wouldn't want him as he was. She indulged because he was just sexy and his kisses were hotter than the most out-of-control firestorm imaginable.

She laid her head over his heart. "I love you, Dragomir."

"I know you think you do, Emeline. I know you're my lifemate and you said I was your choice, but I'm not an easy man. I swear to you, I'll give you everything I can, everything you want or need, but I cannot give you the right to fight at my side when I battle vampires. I will never be that man."

She didn't think she would ever be that woman. She was more the kind of woman who flung herself into danger without thinking it through because a child was in need. "There were so many on the streets, Dragomir. Kids, without homes. Boys. Girls. There was always some kind of trouble. Most of the time I ran, just like the others did, but sometimes, someone was caught and if I didn't go back and help . . ." She trailed off, trying not to think about the dangers of being a child on the street. "It isn't in my nature to want to fight, but it is to protect children."

He smiled for the first time that evening and she realized she'd been waiting for it. Hoping for it. Needing it.

"Everyone, Emeline. You go out of your way to protect everyone. You may not want to fight physically, but you can't help rushing in when others are afraid."

He said it with admiration and that was a soothing balm when she knew he wouldn't think twice about putting her somewhere safe if the situation ever came up again—and she was certain it would.

"What are we going to do about Amelia?"

She knew he changed the subject deliberately because there was nowhere to go with it, so she let him. "I don't know if I can reach her, Dragomir, but if you take me to her, I'll try."

He got to his feet in that fluid, sexy way he had, pulling her up with him. He'd dressed her, and it was a long dress again, one that swirled around her ankles. It was an empire-waisted gown with bold black piping, a balloon hem and petal sleeves. The neckline was a vee, and not too low. She loved the way it felt on her, swirling around her ankles.

"Do you stay up all night looking in catalogues for dresses?" she teased.

He frowned, puzzled by what she asked. "I don't know what that means, but I look into your mind and see images you have there."

She burst out laughing. She'd been the one to look in catalogues. She had all her life because she couldn't afford the kind of clothes she wanted. She didn't need to afford them now, she could make them the way Dragomir did, although she rather liked that he was choosing dresses for her.

"I like this one," she acknowledged, smoothing her hand down the fabric. "Why gray? I would have thought that was the one color you would avoid."

"I thought so as well," he agreed, taking her hand. "But the image in your head was gray, and it didn't look the same as the shadowy world I lived in. This gray is vibrant, and against the black accent quite beautiful. I knew it would look beautiful with your hair and eyes." He ran his hand down her side, over the curve of her hip. "I want you to always feel beautiful, Emeline. You have a list of favorites."

"I do?" She'd forgotten she'd done that. It seemed so long ago. Everything had happened so fast.

"You do. You keep adding to that list for me. If it's in there, I'll use it."

They stepped out her front door, and she was shocked to see everything looked the same. The lawn was green with no gopher holes. The flower beds were intact. There were no dead birds in the yard. The play yard was there, with swings, slides and climbing equipment. The stone dragons sat in there waiting for the children. The lake was as beautiful as ever.

"It must be nice to be Carpathian and be able to clean everything up after a battle with a wave of your hand."

He laughed softly and brought her hand to his mouth, nibbling on her fingertips. "Emeline, you're Carpathian. Everything I can do, so can you. Picture it in your mind and you can do it. We'll work on the things you want most."

She'd forgotten that. Color swept up her neck into her face, but she didn't care. She loved the idea that she could do so many things by thinking of them. "I want to fly and then fly a dragon. The minute we have some breathing room, teach me."

"I should have known that would be first on your list. Of course. That's easy enough."

"I thought the children lived in the house over there." Emeline indicated the smaller house close to the water.

Dragomir shook his head. "Tariq and Charlotte want them living with them now. They've officially adopted them in the human world. In our world, they were already theirs. I think Tariq believes they're going to have to convert Amelia soon. He doesn't think she can get through this otherwise. The trauma has been too much for her mind. First the terror of what Vadim did in the underground city and then his using her to harm those she loves. They want the children close to them."

Emeline shook her head. "She won't convert as long as Bella remains human. We talked about it several times. She's been looking after her little sister since the day she was born. She doesn't want someone else to do it now."

Dragomir shrugged. "I am not Tariq. These are his children and he has the right to do as he sees fit."

"What does that mean?" She looked up at him, the knots in her stomach tightening.

"Just that I do what is best for my child regardless of what she believes she wants. If she needs to be converted, I would do so in a heartbeat. If Bella were mine, I would convert her as well. That way, when I rest, so do they, and I don't have to worry they are up to no good."

"And Danny?"

There was a small silence. "Danny is a problem. I wouldn't have thought so, but I look at Gary and realize turning a male isn't the same as turning a female. The male must be imprinted with the ritual binding words. The ancestors must accept him. The line must go back centuries. Danny would have to be accepted by Tariq's ancestors. There would be a risk to him. It isn't a small one."

"What kind of risk?"

"I told you what happens to the male Carpathian when he loses his lifemate. All emotion and color is ripped from him. Going from that light to the ugliness of darkness so fast, without all the years of fading gently, causes a thrall. Insanity. That happened to the healer. From what the others have told me, it took the prince of the Carpathian people and his second-in-command, Gregori, to keep him from turning."

"You think that could happen to Danny?" The thought was terrifying. "He's only a boy."

"I don't know what would happen. In my day, there was no question of converting humans. It wasn't done. I've never heard of a male child being converted. Our children remain so until they are fifty years. Danny is a baby in our world. He would have to die and be reborn Carpathian. His soul would split, and somewhere in the world a child would be born with the other half of his soul. If I was Tariq I would be consulting the prince and any other who might have knowledge to share on what would happen to the boy."

"I can't imagine Amelia converting if she knew any of this. She would stay with him."

"Again, I wouldn't give my child the choice. I would do what was best for her."

Emeline pressed her hand over her stomach protectively. She would do the same for her child. Wouldn't every parent? She sighed. Amelia was human, and Tariq and Charlotte were Carpathian. If they converted all the female members of the family, but not Danny, what would happen then? Eventually there would be a division.

"Don't think about it, *sívamet*. Tariq is a wise man. The reason the others follow him, the reason I stayed when I knew I should go, was because of Tariq. There is something compelling about him, and I found myself wanting to protect him and what he's trying to build here. He's intelligent and he's found a way to bring the Carpathian people into this century. He is loyal to our prince and makes certain to keep in touch with him at all times. Trust him to find the solution for his family, just as we will find solutions for ours."

She liked that. She liked that he felt respect for Tariq and that a part of him wanted to stay and protect him and the others. With Dragomir came the brotherhood. They were loyal to him and to one another.

"I don't understand why Vadim doesn't just give up and go away when there are so many ancient hunters here. Tariq has an army of humans with weapons that can kill vampires. Why doesn't Vadim find another empire where there aren't any hunters?"

Dragomir opened the door and stepped into the foyer. She hung back. "We should knock."

"I called ahead and let Tariq know I was bringing you. He said to go inside and up the stairs to the first bedroom."

She found herself smiling. She wasn't certain she would ever get used to the Carpathian telepathic way of communication. "I would like to buy land near here. Bordering Tariq and Charlotte's. Maybe even on the lake, although the water scares me."

His gaze jumped to her face. "Why?"

She shrugged, unwilling to sound like a frightened child. "Dreams. Bad dreams since I was a child. I blamed not learning to swim on opportunity, but Blaze's father would have taught me. I didn't want to learn because that meant getting into the water."

Dragomir stepped in front of her on the stairs, reaching behind him for her hand. He did that a lot, sheltering her. She wasn't used to it, but she liked it. She had always tried to imagine what it would be like to have a man want to protect her. To love her. To put her first. No one had ever done that.

298

Blaze and her father were wonderful to her and she loved them both, but always they had each other. She knew if she wasn't perfect, Blaze's father wouldn't have thrown her out, but she still feared it and went out of her way to always be on her best behavior.

Tariq paced in the hall, a small frown on his face. He swung around as they reached the top of the stairs. "Emeline. Thank you for coming. Not even Gary can reach her. We thought for certain Liv would be able to, but she said Amelia had gone too far. I'm not certain we'll get her back. If you can't do it, then I'll have no choice but to convert her. Gary isn't certain if that will work, either."

"I'll do anything I can to help her, Tariq, but I'm no healer. I don't know how to do the things all of you do to heal one another. It's a tremendous gift, but I'm not certain I can do it."

"I'll be with you," Dragomir assured.

Emeline wasn't certain that would be the best thing for Amelia. The teenager was afraid of Dragomir. All the children were. She knew Amelia in particular was because they'd discussed it. Once, when he had stridden by, his long hair flowing like a waterfall to his waist and his golden eyes alive with heat and danger, Emeline had waited to speak until he took to the sky, using two running steps and then he was gone. He had been breathtaking. Her body had reacted despite the pain racking her, and she'd turned to find Amelia staring at the same spot where he had taken to the sky.

They'd stared at each other and then laughed, agreeing he was hotter than hell and someone to stay away from. She had seen the shy admiration in Amelia's eyes, but also the fear. He was big and bad and just plain scary. He scared Emeline, too, so she hadn't tried to persuade Amelia to feel any differently.

"Let me just sit with her for a few minutes," Emeline said. She started past Tariq, but Dragomir caught her hand and pulled her back to him.

"What scared you about the water, *stvamet*?" he asked softly.

Her stomach rolled. Knotted. She felt slightly nauseous. Forcing a smile, she shook her head. "I was a child, Dragomir."

He looked as if he might object and force her explanation, but in the end, he caught her chin in his fingers and forced her head up. "Kiss me."

She would anywhere, anytime. She leaned her body into his and gave herself up to his kiss. He always was hungry. Commanding. He tasted like sin and sex and love. So much love. She kissed him again and again, wishing they were alone, and then abruptly pulled away to glare at him. "You're distracting me."

"So you're thinking of something you love rather than something you fear. Go be strong for the both of you. You were born for me," he said, "but also for this. For children like Amelia who need a strong, courageous woman to guide them when they're lost. Do what you do best."

She hadn't thought she did anything best, except maybe dance. But that wasn't something others needed. She looked at Tariq, at the lines of worry in his face. Charlotte came out of the bedroom, her eyes red from crying, her arm around Liv, who also was in tears. Valentin was their shadow, his features grim. Hope had been lost. She could see that.

They're all counting on me. What if I can't do this? She reached out to the one person she knew was always going to be there for her.

It isn't about them or for them. This is between you and Amelia. What happened to you, happened to her. Vadim and his pawns violated both of you. She's a child. Barely fourteen. Traumatized. Afraid. Vadim put parasites in you, but he put a splinter of himself

300

*in her. He forced her to inject her three-year-old sister with para-
sites. He tried to make her kill Liv. Do you know that she fought
him? A master vampire. There under the water, with Liv drowning, knowing he would kill her, she tried to fight his influence.
That's magnificent, Emeline. And, sívamet, it's also you. She did
what you would have done.*

She took a breath and let it out, looking up at his beloved
face. He always made her feel brave and perfect. In his eyes,
maybe she was. She wanted to be. She had to get Amelia to
see that she was brave and perfect as well. She had to find a
way to guide her back to them. "I love you," she said softly,
wanting the others to hear. To know. Because her man was
brave and perfect and he always knew the right thing to
say to her.

She walked into the bedroom, hesitated and then closed
the door. There were things that were private, things others
didn't need to know—not about her and not about Amelia.
She sank down onto the chair by the bed and took Amelia's
hand. The teenager looked so pale she was nearly gray. It was
disconcerting to see that her eyes were wide open. Glassy. She
was gone. There was no Amelia in that shell.

She stood a long time, looking down at the teenager. She
had once been beautiful, just as Emeline had. Vadim had hurt
both of them until neither felt or looked that way. Dragomir
had intervened for Emeline. Amelia had her. The healer,
Tariq, Charlotte and Liv had all tried the Carpathian way of
retrieving her. No one had tried reaching out and connecting.
That was all Emeline had. The truth and the obscene way
they were connected. God knew, she didn't want to relive one
moment of that time, but Amelia was stuck there and there
was no other way to get her back.

Emeline took another deep breath, set her shoulders and
drew on every ounce of courage she had. "Baby," she greeted

softly. "I know you're locked away from us, somewhere safe. Somewhere monsters can't get to you. I know, because I've gone there a time or two myself. It's all right to go there; we all need that respite once in a while. It isn't cowardice, it's self-preservation. Just know, you can't stay there."

She stroked caresses down Amelia's arm. "I know, Amelia. Vadim's horrible vampires surrounded me and held me down. They ripped my clothes off. Some of them licked me with their tongues. Their tongues were black and bumpy with parasites wiggling on them. When they touched my skin I felt filthy."

She watched Amelia closely. The body never moved. Her skin was cool to the touch. Had those lashes fluttered, or had Emeline just wanted them to do so? Could she do this again? Relive it all for Amelia? She had to, because it was what Amelia was escaping—what she couldn't face—and she had to know that she wasn't alone.

"When I told Dragomir about it, I left out details like that because I didn't want him to know. I didn't want anyone to know. The way it felt when Vadim grabbed my ovaries, when he put his fingers in me." She choked on that. A shudder went through her body. She almost reached for him but she knew this was between her and Amelia. A child. A young girl the vampire had treated the same way.

"*Inside* me, Amelia. His hand was inside me. I felt so filthy. I felt as if I could never get him out." She threaded her fingers through Amelia's and held on. When she looked up at the girl's face, there were tears running down her cheeks and this time, her eyes were closed, not open staring vacantly.

"It hurt so bad." She whispered the truth. "I knew he wanted it to hurt. He made me hurt because my pain caused him pleasure. My fear gave him even more pleasure, but even knowing that, I couldn't stop crying. I couldn't stop fighting him. He made me feel weak and helpless. He made me feel filthy, and unworthy. I didn't want anyone to know, but I knew. I knew how they touched me, the things they said."

A sob escaped Emeline, and Amelia's sob matched it. Amelia's fingers tightened around hers.

"Then he put that needle in me. Nothing ever hurt like that did. It was so thick and long and when he pushed that plunger and emptied the contents into me, it was so terrifying and painful I couldn't quit screaming. They all laughed, and he took my blood. He just sank his teeth into me and it felt so horrible. I wanted to go to that place, Amelia, the one I knew I would be safe in, but I couldn't get there. Not even when he forced me to drink his blood." She whispered the last admission because it shamed her. It sickened her. That black, acid blood with the parasites wiggling on her tongue and down her throat.

"Then he made me drink more blood from a cup. There was some on my face and lips and the other vampires fought to lick it off. He did. Vadim. He waved his hand and none of them could move, and he licked it off me."

Her body shuddered. She knew tears ran down her face. She looked at Amelia to find the girl looking back at her. They stared at each other, a shared horror in their eyes.

"You're the only one I can tell the entire awful thing to," Emeline said. "You're the only one who would understand what I felt. What I still feel."

"Like you can never be good again," Amelia whispered. "He took everything and then he made me hurt people. Dragomir. He fought for you and then he fought for me, and Vadim made me hurt him." She closed her eyes again. "And Liv."

"You didn't hurt Liv or Dragomir. Even had you managed, it wasn't you, it was Vadim. Understand that, Amelia. I had to understand when I knew I was carrying a baby and there were parasites in me . . . "

"Bella. How could he make me do that? How could I have followed his instructions?"

"Vampires can take our will. Vadim's particularly powerful, yet you still fought. Dragomir said you were courageous like me. He thought you were magnificent. He actually used that word—*magnificent*."

"He did?" Amelia's voice said she didn't believe it.

"He did," Emeline assured. "I know it's difficult to face others, but, honey, it's our own fear and guilt, not what they feel about us. It's what he planted in our minds. He wants us to feel fear and guilt. He doesn't want us to have any kind of life because that means he loses. I want him to lose. You have so many people who love you. They want you to be with them, not lost in a world with none of them in it. Not somewhere you had to go to escape Vadim. Tariq and Charlotte want you as their daughter."

"I'm . . . unclean."

"Am I unclean?" Emeline looked her straight in the eye.

She looked confused. "No. You're amazing. I want to be like you, Emeline. You're beautiful and brave."

"He did the same to me that he did to you," Emeline pointed out. "If I am not unclean, neither are you. Dragomir said we're alike, and he should know."

There was a small silence. Amelia closed her eyes on the fresh flood of tears. "I'm so afraid, Emeline," she whispered. "I don't know if I'm strong enough."

"Baby, I'll be here with you. Tariq and Charlotte will be with you. Dragomir will stand with you as well. You have Danny and Liv and little Bella and Lourdes. Genevieve has hardly left your side. I want you to think about this. We're alike, you and me. We've been touched by monsters, but we're

304

still standing. We're going to grow so strong that if he comes at Bella or Lourdes, if he goes after Liv or Danny, we'll be there to stop him. We'll learn how to wield those new weapons and how to kill vampires if we have to. We'll be that last line of defense for them."

Emeline held out her hand. "Come on, Amelia. We can do it together."

She hesitated but then nodded, clasping Emeline's hand hard.

15

So far, Vadim has been the aggressor every time," Tariq said, looking around the circle of ancients, the men he trusted with his family. "I think it's time we struck back and struck back hard. I know many of you have been out looking and scanning all around San Diego and the surrounding parks and hills, but so far, we've got nothing."

The ancients looked at one another, shaking their heads. "Not a thing," Tomas reported. "They head out toward the water and we lose them there. I've checked ships. We all have. The wharf, docks, storage, they disappear without a trace."

"Even the newer vampires," Lojos added. "We deliberately targeted them because they tend to leave such a mess behind making them easier to find. We've noticed they have another vampire with them, one that's been at it longer. Vadim isn't taking chances with his recruits."

"That's worrisome in itself," Tariq said with a sigh. "No

master vampire has ever concerned himself with lesser vampires. They've always been pawns to sacrifice."

Dragomir watched Gary's face. He had the knowledge of so many centuries of battles, of experiences. Gary turned and looked at him with his strange, ice-blue eyes, so rimmed with silver it was difficult to tell what his eye color really was. He shook his head. "If a master vampire has ever had similar behavior, I have no knowledge of it."

Sandu drummed his fingers on the table. "What is the draw here? Is it really Dragomir's lifemate? Emeline? She is carrying a female child. That child would be useless to him, and he has already tried to kill it. Amelia is of no more use to him. What does he hope to gain by staying in this place? His underground city is destroyed—" He broke off and exchanged a long look with Dragomir. "Have we kept an eye on it?"

"When last we checked, it was completely destroyed," Mataias answered. "Vadim brought the thing down after we discovered it. He didn't want us to find his secrets, although we managed to get most."

Dragomir shook his head. "Vadim is cunning. He wouldn't leave behind anything he thought would lead you to him. Or anything of value to him. The things he allowed us to recover were of no more use to him."

Afanasiv leaned across the table toward Tariq. "If Vadim brought down the ceilings of his city, he could just as easily have resurrected them. Or disguised them so we take a cursory look and see what he wants us to see."

Tariq nodded. "I have to agree. Vadim Malinov has always been highly intelligent. All the Malinovs were good at strategy. Once they became vampires, we tended to put them in the category of the unthinking—every negative emotion drives them. But that isn't so with the Malinovs. They stuck together and they had a plan."

307

"Vadim is different from the master vampires I've tracked and destroyed," Dragomir added. "Using his vanity against him doesn't work. Taunting him doesn't work. Nor does compulsion. He stays in control for the most part."

Tariq leaned forward in his chair. "I don't understand why he sacrificed Amelia. His spy in our camp. He couldn't have known we were onto him. We already know he's patient. He could have waited and instructed her to kill the children one by one. He could have had her go after Genevieve. We were watching for that. So why didn't he?"

"He's testing our strengths and looking for weaknesses," Nico suggested. "We've come through with little damage because there are so many of us. But so far, we haven't seen what he's fully capable of. The worst attack was when he was trying to reacquire Emeline and he came himself. He brought so many for his protection."

Silence fell, broken only by the drumming of Sandu's fingers on the table. At home, in the Carpathian Mountains, the war council would have been conducted in the privacy of the sacred warriors' caves where their ancestors would have listened and weighed in on decisions. Here, in the newer world, where technology reigned and they had to fit in with the humans surrounding them, they sat at an oblong table made of thick oak.

Tariq let his breath out in a long slow hiss. "I can't figure out what he's up to, but whatever it is, it must have something to do with San Diego. No vampire has ever stayed in a place where so many experienced hunters have gathered."

Dragomir heard the frustration in his voice. It echoed a similar frustration gathering inside himself. He glanced at his fellow ancients from the monastery. In some ways, they were lucky they could no longer feel. They understood Tariq's frustration but did not share it, and it didn't affect them one

308

way or another. They hunted. That was their life. They hunted individually or in packs. It made little difference how they caught their prey, only that they did.

"I want the waterfront watched," Tariq said. "Tomas, Lojos and Matias, you've been patrolling the wharf, can you continue?"

"Of course," Tomas answered for them.

"We should extend the areas where we've been looking over the water and along the shore," Tariq continued. "Spread out along the sea to encompass as much as we can."

"I'll take that," Nicu volunteered.

"I will aid you," Afanasiv added.

"Good. The two of you work out a schedule. Vadim and his army know we're watching for them, so go unseen. Even if you spot them, don't let them know you have. We need to follow them back to their lair and find out what they're up to," Tariq advised.

"I'll take another look at the underground city," Dragomir said. "If Vadim is hiding something there, we need to know."

Tariq nodded. "Chances are, if he is still using the underground, he'll have more than one vampire guarding it. If he is using it, we need to know why and what he's doing. I think I'll go with you ..."

"No." Gary stated the denial firmly.

The others shook their heads and shifted uncomfortably, as if they might surround Tariq and force him to stay where he was. Tariq looked shocked. He studied the ancients facing him and then slowly looked around the circle.

"What is this?" The question was directed at Gary.

"You have to be protected. We will hunt."

"I have always hunted," Tariq said. "Granted, there are many at this table considered stronger and faster, but I have managed, these centuries, to stay alive. I will do what I have always done for our people."

Dragomir cleared his throat to bring Tariq's attention to him. "We are in a new world. An environment the rest of us are struggling to understand and catch up with. You are familiar with this world. You've shared your knowledge with us, but where we are still trying to process and learn to fit in, you do so naturally. You fit and move in this century with humans as if you are one of them. You understand their technology, and more, you look ahead, anticipating. We need you. All of us. We cannot afford to have anything happen to you or Charlotte."

Tariq frowned. "Maksim"—he turned to his partner—"you are as familiar as I am."

Maksim shook his head. "Not so, Tariq. You'd chosen to live among humans long before I came along. You instructed me for several years. I live among them, work among them, but I still feel as if I am moving just out of step. You are at ease. Completely so. If we are to survive, we have to be like you. All of us."

"If our lifemates are human, and it appears many will be, then we need to understand them," Afanasiv added.

"The technology of this century is so advanced, it is a threat to us," Sandu pointed out. "We have to be aware of cameras everywhere."

"Software recognition," Tomas said. "The perils of this century."

"All of it," Ferro said. "It isn't simple, especially for those of us who've been locked away for a couple of centuries."

Tariq pushed his fingers through his hair in agitation. "I am sorry. I should have worked with each of you more. You all seemed to be learning so fast. I have no problem sharing information—you have only to ask. I can't just push my way into your minds."

"No one here thinks you have shirked your duty to our

people," Gary said. "To the contrary, you are the leader here, one we all accept, so you must remain safe."

Dragomir suppressed a groan. He understood how difficult it was for ancients to process emotion, but they'd been well on their way to convincing Tariq until Gary used the word *safe*. Safe was what they wanted for their women and children, not a hunter of Tariq's caliber.

Tariq's eyes flashed with a kind of fire. That fire smoldered in him, deep, suppressed maybe, but always there. He glared at Gary. "I am no leader. We have a prince. His name is Mikhail Dubrinsky, and I have sworn my allegiance to him. He is the leader of our people."

Gary nodded. "Most of us have sworn our allegiance to him." He looked around the room, his gaze touching the members of the brotherhood. "There are a few exceptions, but for the most part, everyone acknowledges Mikhail as our leader. When he sends out orders, those who have sworn allegiance to him can do no other than obey."

Those odd-colored eyes pinned Tariq. The Daratrazanoff line had produced renowned warriors and through the centuries, some had strange eyes. The ice blue rimmed with silver had significance, but Dragomir wasn't certain what it was.

"Is this not so, Tariq?" Gary pressed.

"Of course we would obey Mikhail," he said. "I send him daily updates on all urgent matters, which these days encompasses just about everything. I am hoping he has ideas as to why Vadim is behaving the way he is."

"He has sent a message to you. I received it last rising, but we were under attack and you needed my skills as a healer. Unfortunately, I was too fatigued to deliver it to you." Gary pushed a piece of paper across the table to him.

Tariq drew it to him reluctantly. Very slowly he picked it up and read it. His expression darkened. He frowned and shook his head. "I don't understand. He sent you to me for what purpose?" His blue eyes focused on Gary. "I have no need of a bodyguard or second-in-command. I am not in command. I own a nightclub with Maksim. I have this property, and hope those of you who want to remain will, and that you'll purchase the properties around mine. Some of them I own and can allow you to buy; others need to be acquired."

Gary shook his head. "You are deliberately not understanding what Mikhail is saying. It is an order, Tariq. He isn't asking."

Tariq tossed the thin parchment onto the table and leapt up, all restless energy. He shook his head. Gary didn't move, not even when Tariq paced close to him, looking threatening. The Carpathian was always elegant in his attire. Now, he looked what he was, a predator pushed close to the edge of control.

"He's got this wrong. He can ask someone else."

"Order, Tariq. This is an order from the prince of our people," Gary corrected. "He sent me to assess the situation here in the States. It is dire. Vadim is not the only master vampire here. We need more hunters. We need a stronghold and a way to protect our families and the humans around us. You've already thought of that and begun the process."

"I was here," Tariq said.

Gary shook his head. "You anticipated this happening long before it did. You are going to become a target. I suspect you are already the biggest target. Vadim knows it is your mind going up against his. You are the appointed leader in the United States. You answer only to Mikhail. All hunters coming here are bound by your orders ..."

Tariq snarled and leapt at Gary, landing inches from him. "I do not give orders to my fellow hunters."

Gary didn't flinch. "You have no choice in this matter.

None. Look around you. Long before Mikhail sent me, you already had those ancients following where you led. Mikhail recognized your abilities just as everyone at this table has."

Tariq snarled again, whirled around and paced across the room. The Carpathian had wide shoulders, but already, Dragomir could see weight settling there.

"I am here to protect you. Mikhail sent you a Daratrazanoff to keep you alive. I will do so whether you wish it or not."

Dragomir's head went up. "I was there, Gary. In the monastery. Surely you told the prince that your lifemate was in Paris."

Gary sent him a quelling look. "She is no more than an infant. When there is time, I will search, but there are many years between now and then. As Valentin knows, it is not easy to have a child for a lifemate. It can be a special kind of hell. I know when she was born, and that she is alive, and that is more than most know. I also know it will be years before I can claim her." His strange eyes returned to Tariq. "In the meantime, I have my orders and I intend to carry them out."

Maksim patted the chair Tariq had vacated. "Quit prowling like a tiger and sit, old friend. Everyone but you knows you were born to lead. We need your skills to figure out what Vadim is up to. Sit down and show us your brain power."

Tariq did a slow perusal of each ancient's face. "I think you're all a little crazy, but Maksim is right. We must figure out what Vadim is up to. I don't like that he gave Amelia up. The sliver is destroyed. He no longer has a spy in our camp, and what real damage did she do?" He leaned his hands on the table and shifted his gaze to include them all. "I keep going back to that. What real damage did he do?"

Dragomir had wondered that all along. If Vadim had so senselessly sacrificed Amelia, then she had never been important to his plans. She was merely a pawn. A diversion.

"He has to have someone else here, someone who can feed him information, someone he isn't willing to sacrifice or use to kill so he can receive vital information when he needs it. If he knows Tariq is his greatest enemy, then it has to be someone who would have contact with him in a more adult way. Someone Tariq might talk in front of."

Frustrated, Tariq slapped his palm on the table, almost glaring at Dragomir. "But who? How? We've checked everyone. My entire security force was checked. I did it myself. The Waltons, although they had no real contact with Vadim or his army. Genevieve? She immediately offered to have us check her and we did. She was fine. So who else? What are we missing?"

Dragomir turned the problem over and over in his mind. "Who did he have access to? Emeline and Amelia for certain. We know he had Liv. Her blood was taken, and she was given first to Valentin to use for food and then Vadim's puppets. Where was Danny?"

"He was never in the same room with Danny," Tariq said.

"Bella?" Dragomir persisted.

"She was put in a cage in the same room with Liv."

"So he could have put something in her as well."

"We checked her," Tariq pointed out, his head turning toward Gary for confirmation. "We checked her. You did. She had parasites and you got rid of them."

"The parasites were injected into her that rising," Gary said. His tone was strictly neutral. "Once we knew the parasites were in her body, I got rid of them. I didn't check for anything else, and even if I had, if there was a second splinter, I most likely wouldn't have found it."

"*O köd belső*," Tariq swore. "She's three years old."

"She isn't the only one we have to consider," Dragomir said reluctantly. "Emeline was with Vadim the longest. He could have put a splinter into her. Or the baby. Is that

314

possible, Gary? When he impregnated Emeline, could he have also given the baby a splinter? If he killed the baby, what would happen to the splinter? Because he definitely wanted to kill Carisma."

Again, there was silence as the ancients looked to Gary for answers. Dragomir felt as if he had betrayed Emeline and his daughter. Each time he fed Emeline, his blood went to their child, turning her more and more to his. Her organs and brain developed with the nutrients of his ancient blood. *I'm sorry, sívamet, but we have to know.*

She never quite left him, or he, her. Emeline had gone through too much and there was a part of her that just refused to believe he was real. She didn't want to be lied to, or kept from knowing what was happening around her. He gave her that because she needed it.

He knew she wasn't the only one who needed reassurance. He had never been an easy man. Others often avoided him. He was ruthless when it was needed, implacable in his resolve, and he knew that his woman would always be that—his. To cherish and protect. To make happy. To love and respect. Above all, he would keep her safe. Those weren't qualities in men, as far as he could see, that modern women appreciated. They wanted to be the same as a man, with all the same rights and responsibilities. He didn't know how to make that happen.

He knew Emeline would never have the ability he had to fight a vampire. She could—and would—defend her home, children and herself if she needed, but to seek out a vampire in his lair was dangerous. Seeking a master vampire could be suicide. No, he wasn't ever going to let that happen. He would take her choice away, and that was something a modern woman couldn't live with. He didn't know how to resolve that issue.

Another man might have just let her make her choices and live with the consequences, but he wasn't that man. He'd never be that man.

Stop, Dragomir. We talked about this. I am your lifemate. You told me I am and I believe you. I feel the ties connecting us with every breath I take. That means you respect me and see to my happiness. It also means I do the same for you. I know it won't be easy staying in the house when I think I need to run outside to scoop up a child, but if you assure me you have it covered, and the others are watching over you, I'd only get in the way.

He knew it was the best concession she could give him and he loved her all the more for it. His heart felt painful it was so full. Emeline. His heart and soul. There was no way to express to her the feelings he had for her.

Thank you. I am sorry about discussing Vadim's slivers without first talking to you. I hadn't considered it fully yet. It had been nagging at him. If Vadim gave up Amelia, his eyes and ears in the camp, he had to have another fully entrenched, one he didn't believe anyone would ever consider.

I would want to know, too. There is no betrayal.

I should have spoken first with you.

He felt a wave of warmth pour over him. His woman. Perfection. She didn't see it in herself, not the way he did, but he vowed that one day she would.

"Emeline? Or the baby?" Gary spoke softly, clearly giving it thought. "It is very possible, of course, that either has a splinter. If he killed the baby, the splinter would simply move to a new host. That host would be Emeline, but we inspected the baby's brain for anomalies and there were none. We could have missed it, splinters are tiny, but I doubt it."

"He didn't want any of the vampires to kill Emeline, nor did he try when he had the opportunity," Dragomir said. "I thought it was because of the baby, or that he wanted her for another purpose. Could it be that she is host to a sliver of Vadim? If so, how do we find it without tipping him off? If he knew we were aware of it, he would move quickly to kill both the baby and Emeline. He would have to kill her to leave her body and find a new host."

"We would have to outsmart him," Tariq said. "Emeline would have to be ill. She'd need a healer to look at her. He would have to inspect every part of her and, if he did find the splinter, not give that away."

The idea was repugnant to Dragomir. Vadim had done so much to Emeline already. She had gone to Amelia and talked to the girl. He'd heard every word. More, he'd heard and felt the emotions she felt. Not only her, but Amelia as well. Emeline had relived those memories in order to connect with the teenager and bring her back to them.

"Are there any others who Vadim was with long enough to implant a splinter?" Tariq asked.

"Me," Valentin said. "He was with me a very long time. I do not believe he thought I would ever get free, so the chances are slim, but I would very much like the healer to check. I want Liv checked as well."

"At any time were you unaware?" Gary asked.

Valentin nodded. "I was in and out sometimes after he tortured me. He kept me starved and often took my blood. I was weak most of the time. It could have been done."

"I need some others to go with Dragomir to the underground city," Tariq said. "Remember, this is to gather information only. Don't engage unless you have to. Once we assess the situation, we can put together a comprehensive plan of action. In the meantime, Gary, we'll need you and Dragomir to examine the victims for any sign of Vadim."

"There's a feel to him," Dragomir stated.

Gary nodded. "The longer the splinter is in someone,

even if he isn't using it—and I suspect he can't help himself, he has a toy and he'd want to play with it—the taint grows. Dragomir has felt him as well. I think, between the two of us, we should be able to rule out his victims or at least narrow our suspect list."

"Start with me," Valentin insisted, looking not to the healer or Dragomir but instinctively to Tariq. "And then Liv."

Tariq nodded. "And then I want Bella cleared."

Dragomir shook his head. "We need others looking as well. Sandu is capable. So is Andor or Ferro. I want to check Emeline and the baby."

"I go with you," Sandu said. "I am no healer."

Dragomir glared at him, but Sandu just shrugged. There was no changing his mind once it was made up. *Köd jutasz belső.* "Shadow take you" was a Carpathian curse, but Sandu looked as impassive as always when Dragomir hissed it on their private telepathic path. *You know how to heal. You just don't want to do it.*

Look what has come of Tariq taking responsibility. Now he has no choice. The healer will not allow him to hunt the vampire. At least he already has a song . . .

Veridet peje, you heathen. Dragomir continued to curse him.

Sandu lifted an eyebrow, but only shook his head. *You do realize you could take your woman and go. We would follow you and protect the two of you. Vadim will follow or he won't. Either way, we will be away from the madness of this place. Humans are beyond comprehension, and human women are insane with their demands.*

Dragomir wasn't about to admit he halfway agreed with that last statement, not with his woman listening to them.

"Dragomir, I realize you want Emeline tested immediately, but she has been harassed and prodded enough. If we can spare her, I would prefer that." Tariq's tone was gentle.

Dragomir closed his eyes. Was he so selfish that another man had to tell him what would be best for his lifemate? He had wanted to make certain no vestige of Vadim was left in her. Not one single trace.

I share your need, Dragomir. Perhaps I even drove it. The thought that Vadim might still have some small part of him in me or Carisma was more than I could stand. I wanted you to check me immediately. It's okay, though. I can wait. Bella is a baby. She should be examined first. It makes sense to look at Valentin and Liv first as well. I am fine.

She wasn't. He could tell. She felt, once again, apart from everyone. She had been sitting quietly with Amelia, but now she wanted to go lock herself up in her house, away from everyone, just in case Vadim was using her as his eyes.

I am coming to you.

No, don't. Stay and check the others. I'm going to sit on the porch and listen to the night. It makes me feel better.

He made her feel better. His lifemate came first. Before all else. Before the warrior's council. Before finding Vadim's spy. He stood. "My lifemate needs me. I will take care of her. That includes looking for any evidence that Vadim created a second splinter."

Gary rose as well. "I will go with you. I believe she has need of a healer. When I am finished there, Valentin, I will return immediately and check you. I do not think Vadim would put a part of himself in you. It would be too risky. You are a hunter with a hunter's instincts. It wouldn't take long before you suspected and eventually discovered him. No, a human and female would much more suit him. He's bold, but he's also extremely intelligent. He needs someone of the light, someone who would never suspect the evil he's capable of."

Dragomir didn't wait for the rest of the conversation. He sped out of the house and across the yard to the house where he knew Emeline paced. She looked as if she might be wearing a hole in the wood floor. She wore the flowing gray dress and it swirled around her as she paced. Her hair was intricately braided and as he strode into the room he studied it, determined to be able to reproduce it by human means.

She turned as he approached and practically threw herself into his arms. A little sob escaped, tugging at his heartstrings. "I can't believe this, Dragomir. It must be me. You know that's why he didn't try to kill me. That never made sense. Once he knew the baby was female and he was willing to kill her, I really was of no more use to him."

"You know better. You're upset, but I'm in your mind and you know your ability to dream the future is of huge use to him. There are other things in your mind you fear as well, that he can use you to do." Dragomir pressed a kiss to her forehead. "We will get through this together, as we've done everything else."

She took a deep breath and nodded, her gaze clinging to his.

I am at your door, Dragomir. Invite me in. I think she is of great use to him and in her mind is the key to why he is staying here in this area. When I was in her before, I caught glimpses of strange things.

Dragomir had, too. He'd been in her mind now often. He moved around, looking for ways to understand her. That meant looking at her memories, the times with Blaze and her father. The times on the streets. Those saddened and angered him. Even further back, to her childhood.

She dreams. Her dreams often are grounded in reality.

She is the key to all of this, Dragomir. Sandu and the others are out here. They are like a pack of wolves, restless for the hunt. They want direction. We need to point them so they can do what they do best.

It was more than that. The members of the brotherhood were far more predatory and dangerous than wolves, and living among sheep wasn't helping to take the edge off.

"I invite you into my home, healer. Please enter of your own free will." He turned the tables on Gary with just a rearrangement of words. Gary would have power coming in but if he entered of his own free will, that swung the balance of power back to Dragomir. It was an old, ancient balance of power. A vampire or Carpathian had to be invited into a home, if it was closed to them, but if they entered of their own free will, the owner of the house had the power.

"Sandu, Andor, Ferro, just come in," he added. He should have known they would follow him. They thought he had a lead. Maybe he did.

He wrapped Emeline securely in his arms and brushed a kiss on top of her head. "We'll both go in and look for this sliver."

She shook her head. "You protect the baby. Let the healer look."

"Who will protect you? Without you, the baby won't survive. I protect you."

"I can help the healer look," Sandu said.

Dragomir glared at him. "Now you're willing to own up to your healing abilities?"

Sandu shrugged, clearly unrepentant. "Now we're not talking about sidelining our hunters if they have other useful skills. Let's just do this. I'll be the child's shield. You find the *kuly* and destroy it once and for all. It will weaken him even more."

"You all think the sliver is in me, don't you?" Emeline said.

"There is a good chance," Dragomir said. "You would be the best option for him."

She pulled out of his mind abruptly and he felt the loss

321

instantly. He gripped her forearms and waited until she looked up at him. It took a while and her gaze kept sliding from his.

"Don't do that. We're in this together. It doesn't matter if the sliver is there. We know what Vadim is doing and we're countering his every move. He can't make you less than you are. He simply can't."

"He knows what we're doing. Those moments we talk, or you're ..." She broke off, shaking her head. "If I leave the house, he's watching the children. My friends. You. He can hear what you say to one another. What we say to each other." Her voice broke.

His heart clenched hard in his chest. "That's not the way it works, Emeline. Just because he put a slice of himself into you, or someone else, that doesn't mean he knows what everyone is doing. He would have to reach for it. Leave his body and go into the splinter. That's always dangerous to him. Just as when we're healing someone, the body is unprotected. If he is attacked or another vampire decides to kill him, he's in trouble."

"You set a trap for him using Amelia. How could you know he was listening?"

"Even if he wasn't, he would go through her memories, but when he is active, there is a taint of evil. She had it," Dragomir explained. "You do not."

"He directed Amelia," she said. "He directed her to hurt others."

"His body was safe somewhere when he orchestrated that attack. He would never have gone that long outside his body without being safe," Dragomir assured. "We have to know. I'm going to keep you safe. Let the healer move through you and search. I will do the same. Sandu will protect Carisma." He nuzzled her hair, slid his nose down hers and found her mouth.

She was very aware of the men in the room with them and she didn't kiss him back, but she clung to him.

"Emeline?" If she wasn't convinced, he would take more time.

She nodded and closed her eyes, burying her face in his chest. He sank onto the couch, pulling her down with him. He kept his arms around her, even as he shed his body to become pure healing spirit. Gary was just as fast and the two entered her a split second before Sandu.

Dragomir and Gary moved through her body, streaming straight to her brain. Vadim had a pattern he repeated because it worked for him. That gave the healers an idea where to search. The splinter in Amelia had been found hiding in a crevice in the cerebrum. Vadim had chosen the cerebrum because the neurons there initiated movement, coordination, hearing, vision, judgment and everything else Vadim needed to control the host.

Once they reached Emeline's cerebrum, the two healers split off and began to carefully examine Emeline's brain. Dragomir knew Sandu was doing the same to the baby. He hadn't lied to Emeline. Had she asked, he would have told her the ancient would have to clear their child. The splinter had to be found. Getting rid of it might be easy if Vadim wasn't aware. He would feel the heat of their spirits and he might not be able to resist checking to see what was happening, especially if thought he was in danger of being discovered.

Your woman is very confused. I lived a human life, Dragomir. You think only in terms of Carpathians and Carpathian women. She knows nothing of our culture. She doesn't understand the lifemate bond.

Dragomir heard a warning in Gary's voice. *Tell me what you want to say.*

She lived a life on the streets. Homeless. Thrown away by her family. Like these children Tariq has taken as his own, she doesn't feel as if anyone can want her. Or love her. That's ingrained in her. The fact that she was pregnant with Vadim's child ...

My child.

Yes, she is wholly your child now, but she was Malinov's and part of her will always be Malinov. That isn't necessarily a bad thing. Ivory Malinov is a great warrior and a wonderful woman. The point is, Emeline believes she entered the compound under false circumstances. She carried Vadim's child and was host to his parasites. That alone, having those creatures in her bloodstream, made her feel filthy. She looked on them as a sexually transmitted disease.

That's ludicrous.

That's human thinking.

Dragomir detested that for Emeline. He didn't want her thinking she was less than him. Less than anyone.

Now, we tell her that she has a piece of Vadim in her somewhere. That he can control her actions through that little sliver. He can force her to betray you and everyone in the compound.

She was resistant to his compulsions.

She doesn't see that. She sees that time and again, she isn't good enough. She will want to run. For your good. For the good of the Carpathian people. For the children.

Dragomir nearly lost his ability to stay pure spirit. The thought of his woman wanting to leave him shook him. *Lifemates cannot be apart.*

She is not Carpathian and does not understand that concept. You must remember she thinks like an abandoned human. She will convince herself it is for your good.

Dragomir let his spirit spread light through Emeline, bathing her brain in warmth and love. He wanted her to know how he felt about her. How the others felt about her. Didn't she realize that ancients like Sandu would never have actively sought her out to aid her if they didn't respect her? If they didn't see her as part of their community?

Here it is. Vadim has hidden himself very well, but I can see the darkness against her light. He cannot stamp out her light. I had hoped, for her sake, he was not here.

Dragomir hadn't realized how much he had also wanted Vadim's splinter to be found in someone else. He would have taken it from her if he could. Gary was right in that Emeline was already thinking herself unworthy. He had to find a way to counteract that feeling, to show her that the Carpathian community embraced her. Welcomed her and the baby. The baby . . . It hit him then, the real problem wasn't just the way Emeline felt about herself—she didn't think Carpathians would accept her daughter, not even with Dragomir's blood flowing in the child's veins. That was something he could combat. He knew exactly what to do. Reaching out to the prince and other Carpathians wasn't something he was comfortable with since he hadn't yet sworn allegiance to the prince, but for Emeline, he would do it.

16

Emeline stared out the window. Dragomir and the others had gathered together to figure out the best way to get rid of the splinter Vadim had left in her. Her heart was so heavy she thought it might just shatter into a million pieces. There was no going back from this. It was the last straw. The very last. She'd done everything she knew how to do to make things right with Dragomir and the others, but no matter what she did, there was always more.

"Emeline."

She closed her eyes. She was certain Tariq had sent Charlotte and Blaze to assure her everything would be all right—but it wouldn't. She would always be that girl from the streets. She could change species, but she couldn't shed who she was inside. *That* girl.

She touched her fingers to her face and was shocked to find bloodred tears tracking down her cheeks. She stared for a moment at the blood smearing the pads of her fingers, not comprehending. Her tears were blood? She sat there feeling frozen inside. She didn't answer the door. She just couldn't bear to see their faces, Charlotte's and Blaze's, looking at her with pity.

She was that girl who got food from a Dumpster. The one carrying the child of a vampire. The one with a vampire controlling her through a splinter of himself he'd put *inside* her. *In her brain.* Where she thought. Reasoned. Where she shared her dreams with Dragomir.

She lifted her face to stare out the window again at him—her man. He was the most perfect man in the world, and he deserved better. So much better. She watched him, her heart pounding, love swamping her. He protected her. He watched over her. He treated her as if she were a queen.

He turned and looked at her, his gaze mesmerizing even through the glass. Love hurt. It hurt so much. She'd always tried to be a decent person. Even when she was dancing on a pole, it was to help Blaze get to the men who had murdered her father. She hadn't told Dragomir about dancing in a strip club.

I want to see this dancing you do. Privately. Just for me.

She would like that, but it wasn't going to happen. She couldn't saddle him with a woman so tainted. He was too good a man.

Answer your door.

His voice. So gentle. Even commanding it was gentle. She shook her head and found drops of blood on the windowsill. She *had* to stop crying. She wasn't even a good Carpathian. They could will themselves to do things, but she couldn't even stop the tears from flowing.

Sívamet. You are my life. Answer the door and allow your friends to talk with you, or I will be forced to leave the warriors circle and come to you.

He would. He would leave the other men in a heartbeat and come to her. The others would know what a needy baby she was. Dragomir wouldn't care, but she didn't want them to think he was lifemate to someone so weak he had to leave an important meeting. A meeting they had to hold away from her. Just in case Vadim decided to listen in on what the Carpathians were planning. And they were planning something big.

"Emeline." The voice was Blaze's this time. Of course they'd asked Blaze to come. Blaze had been her only friend through the years. "Please open the door and invite me in. You know how stubborn I am. I'm not going away. Charlotte is with me. We just want to talk to you."

Emeline kept her gaze on Dragomir. She knew he heard every word spoken in that circle of warriors, but it looked as though his entire focus, all his attention, was on her. Her body hurt, every muscle exhausted as if she'd run a marathon. Her mind hurt from trying to puzzle out what to do. She was tired of being afraid, but the truth was, this nightmare was never going to end. When she'd been alone in her house with the parasites tormenting her night and day and the baby inside of her screaming in agony, she had come to that same conclusion. Now, after having hope, it was worse to know there was none. Vadim had marked her in ways she could never get rid of.

Open the door to your friends. Vadim programmed you to believe you were born to betray the Carpathian people. He told you that you were his lifemate. He said it over and over when he was raping you. The rape was mental and emotional as well as physical. He whispered it to you day and night, using the parasites as his way to keep his connection with you. He deprived you of sleep and kept you sick, weak, unable to eat. Emeline, you have been systematically taken apart and made to believe the things Vadim wants you to believe.

328

She lowered her lashes, unable to meet his gaze, not even through the window. Did he not realize *he* was a big part of the problem? He was so good to her. He was such a good man. He might believe he lived in a different century, but what man could be sweeter? More supportive? She felt like such a fraud. What had she given him in return? Vadim's child. More pain and suffering. Survival of attack after attack. Was it ever going to end? She shook her head. She knew Vadim wouldn't stop. Not ever. Sooner or later Dragomir wouldn't be fast enough and the vampire could kill him.

A sob welled up and she jammed her fist in her mouth. Where could she go?

To the door. Go to the door and allow your friends to come into the house to visit with you while I am away. I am the man you can trust. You've given yourself into my keeping. You have to have faith, Emeline. I know you want to be independent and you think you should be to be worthy, but that is not how I think. I believe partners lean on each other when they need to. It isn't weakness, it is strength. For this time in your life, when the world feels like it is ending, lean on me. Choose my way, sívamet. Do this for me.

Of course she would do as he asked. What else was there for her when his voice stroked caresses in her mind and righted her tilting world? She forced her stiff body to respond. Very slowly she got to her feet, her eyes on him. She smoothed her hand down the beautiful dress he'd created for her and took a deep breath.

For you, Dragomir, because I'd do anything for you.

Love surrounded her. His love. It poured into her like a healing balm. It spread through her mind, rushing to encompass her heart. The emotion went deeper, finding her soul and wrapping it up in him—in his love. His love was

329

deep and abiding and endless. Unconditional. She saw it and felt it and it made her ashamed that she wasn't stronger for him. Still, if he wanted her to lean on him, to choose his way in this time of madness, she would follow him. She would do it even when she felt it would be better for him if she left him.

I wouldn't survive you leaving me. I am weak in ways you cannot imagine. You are my strength. My light in a world of darkness. You just haven't realized it yet.

She wrapped her arms around her middle as she made her way to the front door. He made her feel extraordinary. In her worst moments, even knowing Vadim hid inside her, a monster waiting to activate his spy, Dragomir still managed to make her feel as if she was beautiful, innocent and amazing. She didn't know how he did it, but right then she didn't care. She didn't care that others might see her as weak. She would lean on him just as he asked, and she would trust him to stay.

I have blood on my face. Smeared. I look awful.

Now you are clean. All you do, sívamet, is picture what you want, in this case a clean face, and you have it. I did it for you, but when you're alone, practice.

Thank you. She opened the door and Blaze and Charlotte stood there, big grins on their faces and packages in their arms. She stepped back and waved them inside. "I'm sorry it took so long to get to the door."

"No matter," Charlotte said. "We've brought some awesome things. They arrived this evening, flown in from Paris, as well as from the Carpathian Mountains."

Blaze flung her arms around Emeline, hugging her tightly, forgetting all about personal space. "I am so excited to see what a prince would send you."

"Dragomir sent word that you were pregnant. He wanted Ivory Malinov to know she had blood kin, so to speak."

Emeline's breath caught in her lungs until she felt as if she were burning for air. *You told the other Carpathians about Carisma?*

I am proud that our daughter will one day be the lifemate to a warrior. More than likely she will be a warrior herself, defender, like you, of her children and home. Her aunt Ivory is legendary. She hunts with a pack of wolves and her lifemate is Razvan. At one time, he was the most despised man in Carpathian history. Now he is renowned.

A defender of children and her home? Emeline was torn between laughter and tears. Already he was choosing for his daughter.

Look to your gifts.

Emeline wasn't positive how to feel about what he'd done. *Perhaps you should have discussed this with me.*

I wanted to surprise you. Carisma is our child, Emeline, but she belongs to all the Carpathian people, and they deserve the chance to welcome her. I knew they would send gifts.

Gifts? She looked at the packages. "Gifts?" she murmured aloud.

"Genevieve is coming as well," Charlotte said. "She needs adult company. She said if she stayed with the children one more hour she would begin blubbering like a baby."

Emeline couldn't help the smile. It was small, but genuine. She pressed a hand to her belly. She was very small to be pregnant, but already the conversion and Dragomir's care were showing. Her skin and hair looked a thousand times better. She wasn't in pain, and that took away the lines in her face.

"Dragomir sent word to the Carpathian Mountains, to the prince, that I was pregnant." She stood, one hand on the door, waiting for Genevieve to get there. She was hurrying up the path.

"And now look. Gifts. I can't wait to see what they sent," Charlotte said. "Tariq talks to the prince all the time, and he said Mikhail and Raven were very excited to know you are carrying a girl. We need them desperately."

Genevieve hurried in, a little breathless but smiling. "Lourdes was upset and didn't want to take a bath. Thank God for Amelia. She has a way with children." She hugged Emeline briefly and followed that up with hugging Blaze and Charlotte.

Amelia. Emeline was so glad Amelia was going to be all right. There was no changing the things that had happened to her, but now, at least, she could begin the healing process.

"She is wonderful with children, isn't she?" Emeline mused. Amelia had been used by Vadim. Her sliver hadn't lain dormant, Vadim had actually directed her to spy on and harm those within the compound. Emeline had told her she wasn't responsible. She was a victim.

Her teeth sank into her bottom lip. Had she been lying to Amelia? Did she secretly despise the girl for the things that had happened to her? Things out of her control? No. Of course not. What was wrong with her that she could say those things and mean them to Amelia, but not apply them to herself?

Do you ever get tired of my feeling sorry for myself?

Dragomir's soft laughter warmed her heart. She loved to hear him laugh. She knew it didn't happen often and she felt it was a great victory every time she made him laugh—even it if was at her expense. *Hän sívamak.*

He stroked the endearment along the walls of her mind. Caressing her with it. *Beloved.* She loved how he called her that. Or his heart. Sometimes it was keeper of his soul. But she loved *beloved.*

Pesäd te engemal.

I don't know what that means.

It means you are safe with me. Do you feel safe? Do you know that I would do anything for you? Pesäd te engemal. You are safe with me.

She loved him so much she was overwhelmed with the emotion. She wanted to run to him, fling her arms around him and hold him tight. Just hold him, so he knew he was just as safe with her. She wasn't going anywhere. If Amelia could face the Carpathian world, holding her head high without an extraordinary man like Dragomir standing beside her, then certainly Emeline could do it.

I love you so very much, Dragomir.

That is a good thing, since I am not giving you up.

"Stop talking to your man and come have girl time," Charlotte said, taking the door from Emeline's hand and closing it firmly. "Sheesh."

"How do you know I was talking to him?" she asked, striving for a little dignity.

"You have that goofy look on your face every time you look at him and it's so much worse when you talk to him," Charlotte said.

"I don't have a goofy look," she denied, although she knew she probably did.

"Yeah you do," Blaze said. "All mushy and starry-eyed." She caught her hand and pulled her to the couch. "When we were kids, we'd make fun of some of the women who would look all googly-eyed at their men. We'd giggle about it and vow we'd never be like that."

Emeline glared at her. "I hope you're not implying that I'm gaga over Dragomir."

"Not implying it, babe, I'm stating a fact," Blaze said. "Your eyes go dreamy and you smile this beautiful, but very goofy, I'm-so-in-love-with-you sort of smile."

"I refuse to dignify that with an answer." Emeline sank down onto the cushions of the sofa.

The three visitors laughed, and she couldn't help joining in. She did feel goofy when Dragomir was anywhere near her, let alone talking to her in that velvet-soft voice of his.

"I want to see what a prince sends," she said. But she was more interested in Ivory's reaction. Would she accept Carisma as blood kin?

Charlotte handed her a large carefully wrapped package. Emeline took it, and the moment she put her hands on it, she felt the power of it, even wrapped. Whatever had been sent had safeguards embedded deep. She bit her lip and looked up at her friends. "I can already feel the energy coming off it." Good energy. Powerful.

She removed the wrapping paper without tearing it, revealing a quilt, one that would go over a crib. Squares of bright material, each stitched with obvious care, made up the blanket. She picked up the letter and scanned it quickly.

"Each individual square has been created by a Carpathian couple from the prince's stronghold."

Raven and Mikhail were represented by a forest, a raven and a crown. She touched the square and instantly felt a burst of strength and reassurance as well as the presence of safeguards. Strong ones. Shea and Jacques, the prince's brother, had contributed a square depicting the forest as well, but with a sense of peace. When she touched that square, the stars gleamed silver and glittered like diamonds.

Gregori, the prince's second-in-command, and Savannah, the prince's daughter, had also contributed a forest scene to the quilt, but in theirs the leaves had a silver sheen, and as Emeline touched it, she swore she could hear the sound of laughter. Four small owls peeped through the branches of trees at her touch. She did it twice and the others leaned forward to listen to the childish laughter.

Emeline held the quilt to her chest, once more feeling the burn of tears. It was a beautiful, thoughtful gift and she would spend a long time looking at the various squares the Carpathian people had put together to make it. No wonder it was so powerful. Each couple had embedded safeguards and soothing, peaceful messages to the baby. Her baby. No, *their* baby. Dragomir had done this; he was the reason they'd sent such an incredible gift.

He had sent word to the prince. She knew he hadn't yet sworn allegiance to Mikhail, but he had still contacted the prince to let him know of the newest addition to the Carpathian family. That had been answered with a beautiful welcome. Her heart hurt it was so full. Dragomir loved Emeline and Carisma, and he showed it in everything he did. She rubbed her palm over her little baby bump. Carisma kicked her, a small little brush of her foot, much like the brush of Dragomir's voice when he spoke to her telepathically.

"This is beautiful," Blaze said, smoothing her hand over the squares she could see.

"The safeguards are strong," Charlotte said. "She'll be safe while she's sleeping aboveground."

"I can't feel safeguards, but it is gorgeous," Genevieve added. "I've never seen anything so beautiful. When you touch it, it feels so soothing."

"Tariq and Dragomir must have sent them the measurements of the crib they're making. Tariq likes to work with wood. He uses his hands, not magic, but there is magic in his work. He embeds safeguards as well. Dragomir asked him to help him make the crib with his own two hands. I loved that so much. I told Tariq that when we have a baby, I want him to make our crib with his own hands."

Dragomir had asked Tariq to help him build a baby crib. For her. For Carisma. He'd done that without saying one word to her. It was so like him.

"He's so . . . " She struggled to find the right words. There were none. He was incredible, but even that didn't describe him, or what she felt about him.

"He told Tariq you love the dragons and he wanted to incorporate dragons into the design. I thought that was very cool," Charlotte went on. "Did you talk about it with him? About the dragons? He was very specific."

Emeline shook her head. "Specific in what way?"

"The headboard is the male dragon with his wings outspread. The footboard is the female dragon with her wings spread. He wanted the feeling of the baby being held by both, protected by both. Loved, he said. The carvings are beautiful, and both Tariq and Dragomir are weaving strong safeguards into the wood."

Emeline set the quilt carefully on the small end table and stood up to walk to the window. She touched the glass, staring out at Dragomir. He was talking, shaking his head, the others listening. Tariq said something, and Dragomir nodded. Suddenly he turned his head and looked straight at her. His features had been stone, cold, expressionless. The moment his gaze touched her, he warmed.

You have need of me?

Just looking at the man I love. Her heart was so full she knew it was overflowing. So what if Vadim stuck a splinter of himself in her? Dragomir would take it out. Dragomir could move mountains.

He smiled at her, that small, barely there smile, but it was for her alone. She owned that smile and it was more precious to her than any treasure. She touched the glass in a little salute and turned back to her friends. She discovered that Dimitri and Skyler had not only contributed a square to the crib quilt but sent a small stuffed wolf to put in the crib with the baby. The wolf had magical properties woven into it, but Emeline wasn't certain what they were—or what they did. She would have to ask Dragomir.

Another package was from Paris, from Gabriel and Francesca. Francesca was famous for her quilts, and she'd sent a beautiful blanket. This one looked embroidered, although Emeline could see it wasn't, it was actually quilted with material. The intricate scene had been handstitched using tiny pieces of material for every hill, rock, forest and stream. Wolves peered out of the forest, birds peeked through the trees, dragons dipped their muzzles into water as others sat with folded wings on rocks.

Every movement of the blanket brought the images to life. She knew Francesca was renowned for knowing what was the most appropriate thing for a client; she was famous enough that she was written up in magazines. Looking at the quilt, she saw, once again, the theme of dragons and wolves. She loved it, but more, she loved the power and peace woven into it. She felt the love that had gone into every stitch and she knew Carisma would feel it as well.

"I can't believe he would think to do this. To have the Carpathian people welcome our daughter as they have. It means everything to me."

Charlotte smiled at her. "Your man is a force of nature, Emeline. Tariq says it's like trying to tame a hurricane or tornado. He wants him to stay here with us, but it's all about you. Dragomir doesn't care where he is, as long as you're happy. He made that very clear. He also made it clear that everyone had better make you happy."

Emeline couldn't help herself. She burst out laughing. It would be like him to try to command the world to make

337

her happy. "He makes me happy." She was telling the wrong people. *You make me happy.*

"The prince also sent protections and blessings," Charlotte added, holding up the letter. "I think Ivory is going to come for the birth. I hope she isn't planning to tattoo the baby."

Emeline's head came up and she scowled at her. "What?"

"Ivory looks as if she's covered in wolf tattoos, but they're immortal wolves, permanently a part of her pack. When she needs or wants them, they come alive, showing themselves, protecting her. It's really cool, Tariq said, but what would we do with wolves in San Diego?"

Clearly she was going to have to communicate with Ivory and find out what kinds of gifts she planned for Carisma when she came.

We're ready for you.

Emeline pulled the quilt to her, held it tightly against her body. The sense of fun was gone just like that. They were ready for her. They would lock her in that safety room, as they had Amelia, and they would try to destroy the splinter without it harming her or the baby. Sandu would be there. Gary. Dragomir. All would be at risk. For her—again. She licked her lips and tasted fear.

"They want me now."

Blaze frowned, spinning around to stare out the window at the circle of men. "For what, Emeline? What do they want you for?"

They hadn't told anyone. She glanced at Charlotte. No, she knew. Tariq had told her. "Vadim isn't finished with me. Just as Amelia had a splinter of Vadim in her, there is one in me. He hasn't used it yet, at least it doesn't appear as if he has, but we have to remove it." She kept her head up, refusing to be ashamed. Dragomir loved her just as she was and she refused to stay a coward. She refused to give Amelia advice and then fail to apply it to herself.

338

"Oh, honey." Blaze reached out and caught her hand. "That vampire needs killing."

It was such a Blaze statement. She always went to the final scenario, cutting straight to the kill.

"Yes, he does," she agreed. "I've had enough of him in my life and I want him gone. I also want the other children searched, just to be sure."

"It was done last night," Charlotte said. "None of them have even a tiny sliver of Vadim in them. When we get this one from you, then he's gone completely and can't access the compound. Once again, it will be safe."

Her stomach knotted, and she put her hand carefully over her baby as if she could protect her. A cloud passed over the moon, an ominous sign. Even the wind chose that moment to kick up leaves and twigs against the window. "I think, no matter what, as long as Vadim lives, we should all be on alert, even here in the safety of the compound."

She squared her shoulders as Dragomir broke away from the group and started toward the house. She refused to give the appearance of cowering inside. She immediately put down the quilt, stroking her hand over it to collect courage and peace as she hurried to the door. She was halfway down the outside steps when Dragomir got there. He swept her up, his hands at her waist, lifting her off her feet and swinging her around to set her on the ground.

The small, dizzying dance warmed her. She slid her arm around his waist and looked up at him. "Your supersecret meeting is over?"

He narrowed his eyes at her. "Are you giving me a hard time about our strategy meeting?"

"Is that what you call that? I'm not certain I believe it was all about strategy. I think chest thumping went on."

Now his eyebrow went up. "Chest thumping?"

She nodded. "You know—I'm the coolest. I'm the baddest badass in town. That sort of thing. Laying it out and measuring."

"Laying it out and measuring? I presume you are now talking about cocks."

There was a hint of a promise of retaliation for all her teasing, but that only sent a thrill of anticipation down her spine, rather than deterring her. Who could be deterred when it sounded like so much fun getting in trouble?

She let her hand slip from his waist to his hip, her fingers caressing the line of his trousers and inching toward the bulge developing there. "Just hearing that word makes me hungry."

"You're going to get yourself in trouble."

"I like being in trouble," she admitted, batting her eyelashes at him.

His hand slipped from the small of her back to the curve of her butt. Rubbed. Stroked. Massaged. She hoped no one was walking behind them, but of course his shadows would be there. Sandu. Andor. Ferro. She didn't protest, even though she knew she should. His hand felt too good. Heat spread through her body, pushing the cold out—the cold fear brought. Now there was only Dragomir, with his hard body and amazing hands. She couldn't think about anything else but that fire beginning to smolder so deep in her body.

They walked toward the main house where Tariq and Gary waited. She was aware of every step Dragomir took with her. The way his body sheltered hers, every ripple of muscle and the strength in his arms. Most of all she was aware of his hand, massaging her bottom. Then his fingers were around her thigh, under the hem of her long dress, his fingertips caressing bare skin.

"Someone will see."

"They can't see. I would never let them see your body. It is mine. It belongs only to me. I love the way your skin feels. So soft. I've never felt anything so soft, not in all my centuries of existence." The pads of his fingers swirled over her thigh. "My name should be right here." He ran his thumb down the inside of her thigh. His knuckles brushed her slick entrance. "So hot for me, already, *sívamet*? I love that."

Before she could reply he pulled his hand from her thigh and wrapped his arm around her waist, waving his fingers in a circle to create a breeze. She swung her head around and saw Amelia hurrying toward them. She'd been so caught up in Dragomir and the magic of his hands that she hadn't thought of anything else. Grateful he was still aware of their surroundings, she rubbed her face along his chest.

You're amazing. She poured love into her voice.

I'm hard as a rock, and willing it to go away hasn't worked yet. I need to come up with a spell. Dragomir sounded pained.

She burst out laughing. *You get right on that. I'll come up with a counterspell.*

"I was worried about you," Amelia greeted. "You looked so sad."

Dragomir halted so the teen could hug her. She swept her hand down Amelia's hair. "They found a splinter in me. Just like the one they found in you. I think it's our fate to have similar lives."

Amelia's breath caught in her throat, but then she forced a small smile. "You found Dragomir, and he makes you happy. I can tell. If I find someone like him, maybe I can find happiness, too."

"You'll find a man who will make you happy one day,"

Dragomir confirmed. "In the meantime, you have us. We will look after you and ensure your happiness until he comes along."

Emeline liked that. Liked that he was all but saying they would stay there and help protect the children. She'd saved them and she was invested in them. She wanted them to be happy and healthy. She wanted to be a part of their lives.

"You won't take Emeline away from us?" Amelia's voice was tinged with fear, but she tried to keep the emotion from her face.

"We're family. Part of a circle. We might purchase land for ourselves and set up a home, but it would only extend the compound so you would have twice the area to play," he assured.

"I'd like that," Amelia said. "Are you going to take out the sliver?"

"Yes," he said. "Right now. I'll keep her safe."

Amelia stopped walking with them and just nodded her head as they continued toward the house, watching with that same fear in her eyes, but refusing to acknowledge it.

"She's very brave," Emeline said as Tariq opened the door for them.

"The place we want to go is accessed from the great room," Tariq said.

He waved them from the foyer into the large beautiful room. Emeline caught a glimpse of high wood ceilings and hardwood floors as he ushered them through to the longest wall. He waved his hand and an entrance opened into another smaller room. She stepped inside.

She knew it was much like a panic room, but it was built to keep out vampires, not humans. Maybe both. The room reminded her of a huge vault. For a moment, she forgot how to breathe. Dragomir's arm circled her waist, and he pulled her back against his solid body. Leaning down, he whispered in her ear, his mouth moving against her earlobe, yet he spoke telepathically, making his communication intimate.

Think only of me, of what I wish to do to you. I do not care if the others are close. I want to slowly remove this dress, slip the buttons from their holes and allow the dress to slip from your body and pool at your feet. Feel me. So hard for you. I am always like that now.

It was impossible to think about anything else when he spoke like that to her.

Think of me when I'm inside you. When I am a shield and a destroyer. Think of only me, Emeline. Do this for me.

She nodded. *I'll try.* It shouldn't be that hard. His body was pressed so tightly against hers, the fullness of his cock reminding her how it felt when he was inside of her.

He pulled her down on top of him, his body hard beneath hers, his arms around her waist, his chin on her shoulder. Just that fast he shed his body, Gary following him. Sandu and Ferro followed suit. To her shock, Andor joined them.

She tried not to think about why they needed five men to go after Vadim's splinter if he wasn't there to defend himself. It took a moment to realize that when Dragomir left his body, he also pulled out of her mind. He'd left behind the feeling of his mouth and hands on her, of his body moving gently in hers, but he'd taken care to remove his mind from hers.

She took a deep breath. He was up to something, that man of hers—something dangerous, or he wouldn't have completely left her like that. He never did. Sometimes he moved in and out of her mind, but for the most part, since he'd claimed her, he had stayed just close to the surface. She pushed gently into his mind, her touch subtle, barely there, so she was able to see what they were doing.

He had moved to her brain very quickly, Gary following. Sandu positioned himself in front of the baby, ready to shield her if Vadim became aware and attacked. Ferro and Andor positioned themselves on either side of her brain, right where the sliver was located. She saw it through Dragomir's eyes. It was a dark crescent-shaped shadow lying in a crevice. She would never have noticed it, but all of a sudden it took on an ominous, vile appearance.

Then Dragomir's light began to fade until it was so dim she could barely make it out. How did one do that? His spirit shone bright. What was he doing to make himself diminish? Then she knew, his heart and lungs slowed. He was more vulnerable than ever. She held her breath. Knowing. Wanting to scream a protest, but afraid it would alert Vadim and further endanger Dragomir. He was so reckless, willing to put himself in harm's way. They'd talked about it, but nothing could prepare her for the things he insisted on doing.

He moved so gently into the splinter, barely a touch, his spirit merging, traveling. A long way. She felt his spirit drawn from them to a distance. Then she was hearing the sound of the sea. The boom of a wave crashing over rock. She felt the ground moving in a swelling rhythm. Again, the sea. Dragomir moved closer, and she could suddenly see the water. It was dark and frightening in the long expanse. There was a ship ahead, anchored in the water. Waiting for Vadim and the others. She felt his glee.

There were men and women on the ship. Several children. As the vampires swept in from the night sky, panic erupted. Screams. She closed her eyes, but she refused to separate herself from Dragomir. If he had to see the carnage, the least she could do was hear it. For what seemed an eternity, Dragomir stayed in the background, hearing and feeling what Vadim was. Watching the sickening massacre. Then Vadim was soaring over the ocean again, back toward San Diego. Twice he plunged into the water, stayed underwater near a long, thick cable and then he was back in the air. Her heart jumped. She recognized that cable. She'd seen it before.

Dragomir withdrew very slowly and then stepped back to give Gary room to work. Gary was very precise. He had done this twice already and he knew exactly how to destroy the splinter. He hit the sliver hard with laser precision, running up its back, incinerating layers of cells quickly.

Vadim jumped into the sliver, throwing up a shield, halting the attack, having learned from the last two. He sliced deep into Emeline's brain. Excruciating pain radiated through her head. She screamed, jerking in Dragomir's arms, trying to throw herself clear so she could run from it.

Andor leapt into action, inserting his spirit between the sliver and Emeline so that the next slice never touched her. Vadim abandoned her brain, throwing himself into her deoxygenated bloodstream so that he was quickly carried toward her heart. He began jabbing at her vein as he did so, driving holes through the three layers of tissue making up the tubing. Ferro was there, his spirit nearly blinding the master vampire as it burned through another layer of cells, incinerating them. Vadim was forced to stop damaging the vein in order to survive. He leapt to the heart. She could feel his triumph.

Dragomir and Gary were already there waiting. While Ferro and Andor had chased him from the brain, they had moved surreptitiously into the heart. As Vadim entered, their combined spirits hit him, white-hot light incinerating the cells too fast. The sliver dissolved into ash, curling into itself to try to protect even a few cells. Vadim had already

345

lost the other two slivers and a piece of his heart. He fought
to protect what he had left, even though it was only a few
cells. He tried to make it to the lower chamber, desperate
to get to the fetus via the umbilical cord. Andor was there,
blocking the way. Dragomir was behind him, Gary and
Ferro on either side. The four together incinerated the
remaining cells, destroying the splinter.

17

The sea rocked gently back and forth, a cradle holding vast amounts of salt water. Beneath the black, glassy surface, great long arms of kelp reached first one way as the water tugged them, and then the other. The arms reached up from the ocean floor so that only the top of the canopy showed, and then only briefly.

As she swam, Emeline caught glimpses of hidden sea life when the kelp opened the lanes. Near the surface schools of fish moved in and out of the stalks, sometimes with a barracuda or yellowtail tuna pursuing them. It was the explosion of color that made the scene so beautiful, although oftentimes, over the years, she was never certain whether or not she was adding to the vivid colors.

Curious sea lions rocketed through the long blades, and sometimes she stopped to watch them play. Most times she swam along the rocky reef below, where pastel sea fans swayed back and forth with the surge and so many sea creatures made appearances. There were lobsters moving in and out of cracks, and octopus and moray eels peeking out of crevices. Bat rays rested in the sand, although it was night, and feeding time, so most were beginning to stir.

The kelp forests were generally between thirty and eighty feet deep, but these went down even farther, their air-filled bulbs planted in the uneven floor. She had been here countless times and knew the way as if it was her own home. She had been exploring the kelp forest from the time she was very young. She dove down into that wondrous world, glancing sideways to ensure Dragomir was with her. She wasn't afraid; this—dreaming—was her forte. She knew exactly what she was doing—and she knew what she had to show him.

Other than his initial shock when she'd first taken him with her, sharing her dream, he had remained silent, content to allow her to lead the way. She stayed close to the ocean floor, moving in and out of the stalks straight to the large round pipes that stretched out for miles. The pipes were very large, tall enough that a man could easily stand in them. Wide enough to allow several men to walk side by side inside of them.

Instead of following the pipes out to the sea, staying on the floor of the ocean, she headed back toward San Diego.

Wait, I need to follow this out. Find out what is going on.

She stopped, turned back to him and caught at his arm, shaking her head. She'd done that already so many times. Recalling a dream, she could change the details, and she had, night after night, ever since she was a child. She had explored all the way to the end of the pipes.

It is like the catacombs ahead. People lying in wait to be taken by the vampires. There was horror in her voice—in her mind. She couldn't do anything to save them. Or rescue them.

She knew, because she'd spent months, years, trying to discover a way. In the end she'd given up and continued her explorations, trying to determine what the vampires no one believed in were up to or even—when she was so young—if they were real.

There is nothing to be done for them. But this is where I think is most important for you to see. I thought it wasn't real because I've dreamt it for so many years, but ... Follow me. She attempted to pour demand into her voice. She didn't have the dominant trait that allowed him to speak so softly yet command everything and everyone around him. She had to be emphatic, insistent, to get her way. She should have known better. It took her pointing in the direction she wanted to go and a quick shake of her head. He was already swimming toward her, following her lead.

God, she loved him for the way he trusted her. She loved that everything she said or did mattered to him. She wasn't positive she'd ever fully get used to it.

She led him along the pipes through the vast kelp forest back toward the mouth of the river. Once she was there, they found the narrow opening that ran underground and connected to the river. She swam through it and then began to swim along the bottom of the river with Dragomir right behind her.

She was aware of him in the way she always was aware of him. It didn't matter that this was a dream that she was sharing with him, her reactions to him were the same. Every single cell in her body alerted to him. She felt beautiful. She felt sexy. She felt safe. That was all new. In her previous dreams, she'd never felt any of those things—especially safe. She'd learned even dreams could be dangerous.

She showed him the arteries that ran beneath the ground. Deep canals that led all over the city, that led to the lake

349

where Tariq had built his fortress. Those deep canals led to the underground city where she had helped to rescue the children from Vadim.

Show me the lake access.

She hesitated and knew he was aware of her reluctance. *He sets traps for me.*

She felt his shock. His fingers shackled her wrist, and he brought her up against him. One arm circled her waist and he tugged until her body was pressed tight to him. *What do you mean, he sets traps for you? Vadim knows you dream of these waterways? This is his method of traveling beneath the city?*

She nodded. *I was too young to recognize the importance of hiding from him when I first dreamt of these waters. I didn't know where they were or what the significance was. The map is in my head now, and I can draw it out. I've explored far more than he has. I've been to places all over, places that connect from one part of the ocean to vast amounts of land.*

Why didn't you tell me immediately? Why didn't you tell Tariq?

She winced at his tone. It was a lash, and part of her felt she deserved it. Maybe she should have told Tariq, but then she wasn't certain. She hadn't made the connection between the pipeline and the lake. She had the underground city, but not the lake. She hadn't realized the extent of Vadim's empire beneath the ground.

I was a child when I accidentally discovered the kelp forest. It was a wonderland to a child without a home. A place I could escape. I dreamt of it as often as possible. When I first discovered the pipeline, I ignored it. Then I followed it. I had uncovered the catacombs, the dead suspended beneath the sea, in long rows of clear chambers beneath the pipes. It was something out of a horror film. I was around ten or eleven. I wasn't certain it was real.

Sívamet. Just that one word of endearment. All the anger was gone from his voice, leaving it a purring caress.

She loved the sound of his voice and the way it brushed over her skin, on the inside of her mind, poured into her body.

I don't know why I kept going back. I was drawn there. Every night I told myself I wouldn't go, but I couldn't stop myself. I would explore the ocean floor over and over, swim all along the pipeline, and then one day, when I was about fourteen, I saw him. He was in the chamber below the pipe. It was the first time I ever saw anyone alive. I was elated, thinking, at last someone that isn't lying there dead. I almost came out from behind the rocks where I was hiding. Honestly, Dragomir, I'd been dreaming it for so long, I didn't know if I made it up.

Her voice shook. She couldn't help it. She would never forget those moments of her life. It was a dream, yet, for the first time she'd feared it was real. She'd known, as she'd walked the streets in San Diego, that just out from shore, where tourists dove and paid good money for locals to take them exploring along the kelp forests, a monster had begun to build a vast empire.

No one would have believed her had she told them. She'd tried to tell Sean McGuire, Blaze's father, that there were vampires, and he'd told her she was having nightmares. That much was true, she couldn't deny it, but the fact that she'd *dreamt* it hadn't helped her cause.

Keep going. I need to understand.

I watched as he waved his hand and awakened a woman. I thought her dead, but she was sleeping. He smiled at her and held out his hand. Her fear was so strong it radiated all the way to me. I could feel her fear and his ... delight. He needed her fear. He fed it. Amplified it and drank it in. I swear it was like an aphrodisiac to him. When he smiled again, I saw his teeth. He grabbed her and pulled her to him. She couldn't fight him physically, but I felt her struggle. He felt it, too, and that made him ecstatic.

She shuddered and tasted fear in her mouth the way she

351

always did when she thought of that night. She'd watched him sink his teeth into the woman's neck and drain her blood. *When he lifted his head, there was blood all over his lips and teeth. He left it there. He turned to go and then suddenly turned back and looked straight at me. I didn't move. He strode to the glass and continued to look out. When he waved his hand, the kelp parted away from the surge, not with it. We stared at each other.*

Dragomir stroked her hair, his hands as steady as his reassuring heartbeat. *So he saw you. He knew what you looked like.*

He was like a bloodhound sniffing my scent through the glass. He tried to force me to go to him, I could feel the pull of his commands, but I resisted. That shocked him. More, it aroused his curiosity. I don't think many people had resisted his compulsions.

You would be correct. The fact that you were only fourteen would have really caught his attention. And you were in a dream. Controlling the dream. I can see why he searched for you.

She shivered again and pressed her face to his chest. To the steady rhythm of his heart. Her anchor. *I backed up and got out of there. But I couldn't stop going back.*

He drew you back.

She bit down on her lip. *Perhaps. I considered it. Eventually I began to see that he had access to so many places. I set out to find them all. Several years went by before I figured that out.*

You mapped out the underground passageways, the arteries of his highway. You know where all his underground cities are. There's more than one, isn't there?

She nodded. *When I came back from France to help Blaze find Sean's killers, I considered going to the authorities, but of course, they would have thought me crazy, and Vadim has some sway with a few of them. He'd gotten in pretty deep with some of the crime families and was developing his own using male human psychics.*

Why didn't you tell Tariq?

I was taken to his compound after Vadim had me. I was terrified he would find out that I was pregnant. Vadim kept whispering to me that Tariq and all the other Carpathians would reject me. I was terrified to leave the compound. I knew if I left, Vadim would get me. I barely knew Tariq or any of the others, only Blaze, and I hid from her as much as possible.

Dragomir tipped her chin up. *Why didn't you tell me?*

I was going to. I needed to figure out what it all meant. I can't get that piece as much as I try. Day after day I would go out and find every passageway I could to try to find just how large his holdings were. I tried to stop dreaming at night.

He went very still. *Tried? You still dreamt at night?*

Sometimes, I couldn't help it.

Did you have other encounters with Vadim?

I would see him in the dream, close it down and the next time avoid that area. So yes, there were a few encounters, but I always woke up immediately if I saw him.

Did he know about Sean McGuire and Blaze?

She didn't like where the conversation was going. *I don't know what he knew about me, only that when we would meet in the dream there was always an exchange of something, I didn't even know what. I just knew I could feel him before he was there, stronger and stronger after each encounter. But he never got close to me. He certainly didn't take my blood.*

You were afraid of him. He sounded matter-of-fact.

Of course she had been. Who wouldn't be? She wasn't embarrassed or ashamed of being afraid of a master vampire. She nodded, uncertain where he was going with his statement.

Very much. Every time I saw him, I was terrified. I kept thinking he would find a way to trap me.

But he didn't. He let you move through his waterways. His personal highway. Emeline, he didn't create the map, you did. He just watched you explore it all and followed you. You knew the ways to go before he did.

She frowned, shaking her head. *That's not true. I just followed where he'd already gone. The dream ...* She trailed off, suddenly filled with doubt. Her eyes widened and one hand flew defensively to her throat. *Dragomir. Are you saying I helped him?*

No, of course you didn't help him, but he found a way inside your dreams.

And I mapped out an entire city for him. More.

He shook his head. *Don't, Emeline.* He was silent for a moment, and then she saw the dawning comprehension on his face. *He doesn't know. He knows the passages are there, but he doesn't know how to access them. Only you do. He needs you. Vadim has no idea of those places he wishes to go. He knows how to get in and out of the underground city, and perhaps to the lake, although I doubt that, but he needs you for the rest. That's why he's sought you out from the very beginning. He didn't know who you were until you went in for psychic testing.*

My dreams? My ability to map out the ocean floor and connect it to the rivers and lakes? To all the cities? That's what he's after?

It's more than that. You're unusual, even among psychics. You can resist his compulsions, you can command dreams, you are so strong that even his poisonous blood can't kill you. And you can map continents for him.

It would have killed me.

I don't think so, Emeline. I was inside you, in your blood-stream. He kept forcing the parasites to reproduce because you kept killing them off. Your blood. If he hadn't been able to get to the parasites, you would have managed to rid your body of them, not the Carpathian way, but by building antibodies that fought them off.

She frowned at him. *I don't understand what you're saying.*

I'm saying you're of tremendous value to both sides. You know the location of Vadim's stronghold, or at least you do within your dreams,. You can produce antibodies, which, because you've shared blood with me, means I can do the same, so at some point both of us will be immune to his parasites. That means every hunter, woman and child can be made immune. It isn't just that he thought you could produce the child he wanted, you are the ultimate prize for him.

She shook her head. She'd created a map of the arteries and veins that made up the underground rivers. She had found all the passageways beneath the ground so that one could come in by sea and go just about anywhere they wanted. She knew them all like the back of her hand. Over the years she'd gone back nightly to try to find ways to stop the vampire. Find anything that might convince others of them. She'd never even told Blaze about her underwater dream, not after Sean dismissed it as a nightmare.

She'd been looking for a place to sleep one night when she stumbled across two vampires feeding on homeless people in a back alley. Sean had sent her to Paris, and then he'd been murdered. She'd come home to help Blaze find his killers. She'd come home, already knowing Vadim would get his hands on her and she'd be pregnant with his child by the time the others found and rescued her.

Take me to his underground city.

Her heart jumped. She shook her head. *They guard that place. If we go near it, the chances of running into some of them are fairly high. I've tried to slip past the guards. Sometimes I make it. Most times I nearly get caught and have to wake up fast.*

If we get into trouble, you can wake up.

She didn't like it. She was uneasy. The passageway to Vadim's underground city was narrow, an easy place to set up an ambush. She knew Vadim was angry. The moment she'd entered the dream, she felt him in the water. His rage. His need to control her, to reacquire her. She didn't want to lead Dragomir into a trap. She'd wanted to show him the extent of Vadim's stronghold.

She knew Tariq wouldn't abandon San Diego, but once he knew what he was really up against, with the information she could provide, maybe they could find Vadim and plan an attack. She wouldn't be able to fight with the hunters, but she would at least feel as if she'd contributed something. She'd brought Dragomir with her rather than tell him, so that there would be no question whether or not she was crazy and just having nightmares.

She had taken Dragomir to the deep but thin ribbon of water beneath the ground that fed the lake Tariq's compound bordered. She turned to swim back toward the main artery underground. As she turned, Dragomir suddenly caught her by the arm and thrust her behind him. To her horror, a shark, mouth open wide, snapped at him, catching his upper arm, spinning around and streaking through the water with him. At once blood turned the murky water red, so Emeline, rushing after them, swam through a red tunnel.

She didn't dare end the dream with one of Vadim's creatures holding on to him. Dragomir's body was deep beneath the earth safe, but his spirit traveled with hers through the water in her dream. She should have been more vigilant. She knew Vadim had put traps throughout the waterways. This had never happened, but then she'd never taken Dragomir with her before. She wasn't going to get a "do over." She counted on having the dream night after night to correct any mistakes she made, such as triggering a trap.

She put on a burst of speed. One thing dreaming of swimming every night allowed her to do was to become a very fast and strong swimmer. She might not put her foot in the water when she was awake, but in her dream, she was kick-ass all the way. She also had the advantage of knowing the canals, where they were deep or shallow, where they dropped deeper into the earth, turned abruptly or lazily made an *S* before straightening out. She knew a few little veins that were just a trickle, with barely enough water to get through. They were shortcuts connecting one waterway to the next.

She hated losing sight of Dragomir. He was used to relying on his Carpathian powers, but in the dream, he didn't have them. She'd been a young child unknowing of Carpathian powers when she began dreaming about the kelp forests and what lay hidden in them. Cursing herself for ever bringing him into her dream, she took the shortcut, streaking toward the wider underground river that ran out to sea.

She reached down to her leg where she'd strapped a knife. She'd started carrying one after she first saw Vadim when she was a teenager and knew she was hunted. She laid the blade along her wrist, her fist around the hilt. As she swam, the tops of her thighs skimmed the rocks on the floor, scraping skin, but she didn't slow down. She barely felt the burn as she rounded the corner and slashed at the eye of the beast holding Dragomir in its mouth.

She thrust a second time, this time driving the point of her blade right into the eye. The shark opened its mouth, thrashing wildly, nose and tail wreaking havoc in the water. More blood floated away, creating a thin thread much like a bloody worm trailing through the water. Dragomir caught her around the waist and pushed her in front of him. She held tight to his arm and let go of the dream.

Usually she could force her eyes open and the dream ended. It wasn't quite that simple now, not with the sun still in the sky. It took a few moments to open her eyes and then she was completely, utterly panicked. She was buried alive. She had to get out. She *had* to dig her way out. It took forever to get her hands moving, to try to rip away the soil, but already she was choking, breathing loose dirt into her lungs.

Suddenly the dirt over her head opened and she found

herself staring at the ceiling of the basement in her house. Breathing heavily, she tried to roll, coughing.

Breathe normally. There is no dirt in your lungs. It is only your human imagination. Dragomir's voice was gentle and soothing. *Turn your head and see me.*

She didn't want to just in case he was wrong and she was alone, buried in the earth. She was lying a good six or eight feet under the soil. It was pitch-black there under the ground, the floorboards of the basement stacked to one side neatly, waiting for the command to rebuild. She could look all the way up to the ceiling, and see with her enhanced night vision.

Sívamet, this is a simple thing I have asked of you.

It was—and yet it wasn't. Her heart pounded so loudly it sounded like thunder drumming in her ears, but it was Dragomir and she couldn't find it in her to deny him anything. She turned her head slowly. There he was, his strange golden eyes staring back at her. He was beautiful to her with the scars on his face and that strong, male jaw. Even lying in the dark, rich soil, he looked elegant.

Her gaze moved over him. His arm was chewed up, bloody, now that he was awake. She'd done that. *I'm sorry. I should have checked for traps in all the places I was going to take you before I shared the dream.*

You are extraordinary, Emeline, and you don't even know it. You didn't even hesitate facing the shark. You've been mapping Vadim's waterways since you were a child and you know them better than he does. There was pride in his voice. Respect.

She found herself smiling at him. *I can't swim. Not really. I'm afraid to be in the water because I know what's down there.* It was a confession. She was slightly ashamed that she couldn't be like other human beings, swimming on a hot day—or night.

I think you have courage enough for ten people, Emeline. Any

358

more and I would spend an eternity being terrified my woman would do something crazy.

He made her feel whole and happy even in the midst of knowing Vadim and his army could move unseen throughout San Diego. How were they going to destroy him if they couldn't find him? If he had so many exits?

That is the job of the hunters, Emeline. You did your job. You have supplied us with valuable information. We can find and destroy all the places he has built here. There are many of us now, more than he knows. Thanks to you, we have places we can start. From those places, we will find trails to others.

She took a deep breath. *It is close to sunset. Just once, I would like to have a night with you when the children, or someone else, are not in danger. Just one night.*

His laughter was soft in her mind. *I would like that as well. It will happen. We have eternity together. Soon it will be a baby interrupting us at every turn.*

Charlotte told me you are making a crib with your own hands. She said Tariq is helping you.

His sigh was heavy in her mind. Then male amusement. *Charlotte shouldn't have told you. It was my surprise for you. I like to give you things, and the thought of making something as Tariq has done, made by hand, was appealing to me. I thought about what I wanted it to look like as well as what we could incorporate to keep Carisma safe.*

She said dragons.

You like dragons, so that seemed something I could use. The male was easy enough to carve, but the female, making her look beautiful and deadly at the same time, capturing that look in wood has been a challenge.

When are you doing this? You are always with me.

We really don't have quite as many warrior councils as I've led you to believe.

359

She found herself laughing. *Laughing.* It had to be closer to sunset than she realized because the sound filled the basement beneath her home. She licked her lips. "You're terrible."

"You fell for it."

"I thought lifemates couldn't tell lies to each other."

He rolled. Stretched. He looked delicious with his muscles rippling powerfully beneath his skin. "Only, apparently, when surprises are involved."

He bunched her hair in his fist and turned her face fully toward him so he could take her mouth. Heat rolled through her. His mouth was paradise. He knew how to kiss, and she gave herself up to the exquisite beauty of his mouth on hers. Kissing over and over. Igniting a fire in her that couldn't be put out unless his body was in hers.

He gathered her into his arms and then she was floating, his mouth working hers. Commanding. Demanding. So hot she was afraid she'd catch fire and burn before they were on the bed, their bodies clean, his healed. She loved that they could do that. Simply think about being clean and fresh and then they were.

He all but tossed her in the middle of the bed and came down on his knees, his hands on either side of her head. "Did I mention I love you?" Even as he asked the question he leaned down and licked at her nipples. First one then the other, making them peak. His mouth closed over her left breast, suckling, pulling strongly, and then her right.

She was sensitive, and his mouth was merciless, hot enough to scorch. He used the edge of his teeth and instantly her body was spilling liquid heat in invitation. He caught her ankles and twisted, rolling her over onto her stomach. He leaned forward again and bit her left cheek.

"You look lovely and very tasty, Emeline. I don't know whether I want to devour you or be inside that hot, tight body." He caught her hips and yanked her bottom back toward him so that she was on her knees. He pressed her head to the mattress with one hand, fingers circling her nape to hold her in position. She was supporting herself on her forearms, her face pressed tight to the mattress, looking back at him over her shoulder. Her body pulsed in anticipation. He hadn't had to do much—just wake up—and she wanted him.

His hand was there, testing her readiness. She heard his growl of satisfaction. "I love when you're like this. So wet for me."

She pushed back against his hand. "I'm totally wet for you," she whispered. "I want you so much I can barely breathe." That was true. Her lungs burned for air. She felt raw. Exposed. She didn't care that he knew how much she wanted him. She knew he was the same way. She loved the way he held her so easily, his fingers stroking and teasing, bringing her close, moving away so that she cried out in demand, her fists gathering the comforter into her palms. It was a beautiful ache. A hunger that grew and grew. She loved that so much.

Then his mouth was there, his tongue wicked and sinful, stroking, flicking, stabbing deep. He suckled, drew out honey and then raked her clit gently with his teeth.

"Dragomir." She could barely get his name out. A demand.

"Don't know what you want, *sívamet*. You're going to have to be specific."

She loved that, too. More liquid heat spilled out for his tongue to catch. "You in me." She was panting so hard, her breath so ragged she could barely talk.

"My tongue *is* in you," he said and lapped at the fresh wave of honey. "Mmm, you taste so good. Maybe you want my fingers." He replaced his tongue with first one finger, then two, pushing deep into her scorching-hot, very tight sheath.

She gave a groan of sheer frustration. "Not your fingers. I

361

want your cock." She blushed when she said it, but she knew that was what he wanted, and in giving that to him, she found her body hotter than ever.

She couldn't tear her eyes from him as he knelt up, his hand circling the girth of his cock, his eyes on her. She wiggled, pushed back, trying to get him to hurry. He leaned down and bit her again. The shock of that sting sent another fresh wave of honey spilling out so that she was certain her inner thighs were glistening.

"Please, honey," she whispered. "Right now. Hurry."

"You want gentle?" He lodged the head of his cock in her entrance, giving her just enough to make her feel as if he was stretching her, but not enough to fill her.

Frustrated, she pushed back again, trying to impale herself on him. "I'm going up in flames. I need you right now." This time, along with the pleading little sob there was demand.

He laughed and surged into her. Hard. Fire streaked through her. White lightning. At the angle he had her, holding her helpless, he could power deep, his shaft a piston, moving in and out while flames poured over her skin and into her veins. It was good, so good. Better than she could ever have conceived.

She loved that teasing laugh. Almost carefree. She'd given him that. She watched the beauty on his face. Those hard lines and the scars softened, only to be replaced by a mixture of lust and love carved deep. There in the molten gold of his eyes. It was beautiful to see. That tension rising in him just as it coiled in her. Hot and bright, a fierce loving burn.

Then she couldn't think, only feel. He took her up so high, only to stop just short of letting her tip over the edge. Over and over again, until her body was so ready, so coiled. Until tension stretched her beyond her breaking point. She could hear the sob in her voice. The demand. The promise of retaliation. But the look on his face, that fallen angel skating so close to heaven, to paradise, was as much a reward as the desperate hunger in her body.

Tied vogyok, ainaak. Tet vigyázam. Peje míca.

He murmured something. She caught the words *Tet vigyázam* and knew it meant "I love you." She wasn't certain what else he'd said, but the way he'd said it was beautiful. His hair fell around his face like a beautiful Renaissance painting. He stole her breath. Her heart. Her soul. She knew she did the same for him. She didn't know why or how, only that for him, she was special. He made her feel that way every moment.

She couldn't speak, not with her heart so full, not with lightning zinging through her veins and that unbearable pleasure coiling so tightly she thought she might go insane. *I love you, Dragomir, but I need . . .*

I know exactly what you need.

His body kept moving in hers. Hard and fast and so deep she felt so connected to him, felt they lived in the same skin. She kept her eyes on him, her cheek pressed to the mattress, his hand on her neck, collaring her. She felt her heartbeat surrounding him, pulsing and gripping. His heartbeat answered, throbbing like a drum in her deepest core.

His face. That face—her fallen angel. So beautiful to her. She watched the rush come over him. The way his eyes darkened and the gold turned antique. The way the lines of lust and love carved deeper, giving him a look of pure sensuality. His fingers tightened on her neck and hip.

"Now, *míca*. With me now."

His shaft swelled in her, stretching her tight muscles, the burn adding to the terrible, brutal beauty of the friction, of that steel spike moving in and out of her. His command whispered in that silken voice, hot and husky with need, sent her careening over the edge. Hot seed poured into her, bathing the walls of her sheath. She was flung into the sky. Free-falling. Soaring. It was as terrifying as it was beautiful.

Her orgasm went on and on, tearing through her with a force she'd never known. Taking every cell by storm. All the while she watched his face, watched what it did to him. Such perfection. She could only hang on to the comforter with both fists and ride out into the night sky with him.

He was there, surrounding her with his protection. To catch her when she came tumbling down, gasping for breath, heart exploding, so far gone she wasn't sure who she was, where she was. Only that he was there. That face. His hands, stroking her, soothing her. His mouth, whispering to her, kissing his way up her spine. His cock, inside her, tying them together, giving her love with every stroke. Giving her ecstasy. Just simply giving her—everything.

He withdrew, and she cried out as his heavy cock slid over the bundle of sensitized nerves, setting off another strong wave of ripples. His arms went around her and he pulled her down to her side, his body curling protectively around hers. One hand went to her belly, where their child was growing.

"Every time I touch you, it is a miracle." He nuzzled her hair aside with his chin. The brush of the bristles of the shadow on his jaw sent yet another round of heat and ripples careening through her. "Your skin is incredibly soft. I thought of you so many times over the centuries, but the reality is so much better than anything I could ever have conceived of."

"I didn't dare hope to dream of someone like you," she admitted. Her lashes drifted down so she could savor him. Savor the scent of him, the feel of his body against hers and his arms, so strong, surrounding her. She felt safe. In her life, she didn't remember a single time before him when she'd ever felt safe. Now she equated that with him.

He kissed the nape of her neck, gently put her on her back. He stayed on his side, bending over her, waiting until she opened her eyes. His hair fell in long waves around both of them, brushing her skin as he kissed her eyes, brushed her nose, and then his mouth settled on hers, causing the flight of a thousand butterflies in her stomach. He kissed his way down her throat to her breasts, spent a few minutes there and continued to her belly button. His tongue strayed, did a quick foray and then he was whispering to the baby in his own language. Talking to her. Reassuring her.

Love swamped Emeline. So much she couldn't contain the emotion. It filled her heart and soul and spilled over so that she didn't know what to do with so much feeling. She could only stroke his hair with trembling fingers, and vow to herself that as much as he gave her, she would find a way to give him the same.

"You give me as much or more every minute in your company," Dragomir whispered against her skin. He kissed the pooch where the baby nestled. "You've given me a child. What greater gift is there? You've given me your love, your heart and soul. You've given me *you*. There is nothing else, Emeline. You are my miracle."

"This from a man who carves dragons for our child's crib." She didn't want to cry. Blood tears were messy. "I know you have to go to your council thingy, but would you teach me to do the clothing thing? And flying? And maybe cleaning house?"

He laughed and rolled to the side of the bed, keeping her hand. "Just picture what you want to wear in your head. Have the image of you fresh and clean from a shower, your hair washed and dry. The details are the most difficult. Just pay attention to every detail."

Emeline wrinkled her nose. Could it really be that easy?

She pictured herself clean and fresh and added a dress of soft white covered in delicate red roses. It had been one of her favorites in a catalogue she'd looked at almost daily. She chose it because she remembered every detail. She found herself wearing it, the soft material falling around her ankles, flowing in swirls when she jumped up, shocked and excited that it had worked. "I did it. I can't believe I actually did it." She flung her arms around his neck and hugged him. Of course he was fully clothed and looking perfect. "I'm going to clean every room. It's good practice. Then I'm going to talk to Liv about dragons and how to fly them."

He kissed her. "Housecleaning—okay. Talking to Liv about flying dragons—absolutely not. That child is in enough trouble without you helping her get into more." He stalked to the door, that other Dragomir already taking over. The one that was intimidating and scary. The dangerous predator that moved with fluid power over the ground and through buildings. The one that took her breath just as easily as the one that treated her so gently.

He paused at the door and turned back to her. "Before you go outside, *sívamet*, you might want to add undergarments. Personally, I like you without panties and a bra, but I'm not so certain you will be as thrilled when someone else notices."

She watched the door close and then burst out laughing, hugging the baby, knowing she was truly happy for the first time.

18

The breeze stirred the leaves on the ground, throwing them playfully into the air. Dirt, cement and debris were piled high in the alley just behind the deserted building. The entire block of empty stores looked like a ghost town. The slight breeze used the alley as a private playground, lightly touching the debris, rifling through it. The wind slipped across the dirty glass of the windows, as if peering in, looking to see what state the shops were left in when people abandoned their businesses.

Dragomir circled one way, using the breeze to carry him where he wanted to go. Sandu and Ferro moved around the outside of the buildings from the main street, each searching for signs of vampire activity. Andor took the roof. The hunters were traveling in packs, spreading out through the city, following the underground map Emeline had laid out for them. She'd given it to Dragomir, leaving it in his mind after she'd pulled him into her dream.

Tariq and Maksim stayed in the compound surrounded by the human security force. With their women, they began teaching the children, the Waltons, Genevieve and Emeline as well as the security force how best to slay vampires. The drills had begun in earnest. It wouldn't matter that they were children, women or humans, they were in the fight to stay alive and keep others safe. To do that, they needed to know how.

Carpathians had always been hunters. They had other skills, but it was ingrained in each of them that they had to hunt the vampire or any other threat to their people. They were born with the drive. In some it was stronger than in others, but no matter what, they hunted, found the enemy and destroyed him. It wasn't personal. There was no sense of fairness, no rules. It simply was. They locked on to a target and they destroyed it.

Five ancients made up Dragomir's pack. They had hunted together many times and were used to the way one another thought. They had taken one another's blood and could communicate together separately from the common path of the Carpathian people, which gave them an advantage since the vampires couldn't hear them.

It was their good luck that when they put out the call, others from the brotherhood answered. Benedik had joined them. He made up the fifth man in Dragomir's pack. He was as cold as ice, with unique midnight black eyes that never blinked. He made his way around the block, coming in from the other side of the alley.

The second pack was also made up of ancients; all were in the brotherhood or had been at one time. Afanasiv, Nicu and Valentin were joined by Petru and Isia. They made a formidable pack, moving fast, going out to sea.

Tomas, Lojos, Mataias, Andre and Gary made up the last

pack. At present, they were streaming out over the national park, where water ran in rivers beneath the ground. Those rivers connected directly to the lake bordering Tariq's property.

Dragomir dismissed the other packs from his mind, knowing they were strong and could weather any storm sent their way by Vadim. His pack's job was to enter the underground city undetected, observe what the vampires were doing and then permanently destroy any of the undead they found.

He used the wind to aid him. It was natural and would never give the vampires pause. On the outside, the alleyway looked as if no one had been there since a cave-in had destroyed the entrances and hallways inside. He studied the debris piled in front of the entrance from every angle, touching it lightly with the breeze. He felt the taint of evil. It wasn't strong, barely more than a whiff of darkness. Ordinarily, he might have dismissed it as the trace of a vampire that had passed by long ago. Thanks to Emeline, however, he knew the vampires were still using the underground city, which made this faint scent of evil a trail worth pursuing.

He kept moving with the breeze so no alarms could be triggered. His progress was slower than he would have liked, but he felt no frustration. It was his job to hunt the enemy, and sometimes that took patience. The wind slipped into a crevice and found space. Emptiness.

One entrance here, he reported to the brotherhood. *I'm going in.*

Entering the tunnels would be more dangerous than staying outside where the breeze of his presence would seem natural. Now he would have to be a slight draft, cold air seeping in from the outside night.

There is an entrance from the floor of the shop I am in, Sandu reported. *I'm going in.*

Be careful. I am using a faint draft.

No worries, I am creating a nice habitat for the black witch moth. It isn't small, it has a seven-inch wing span, but the undead would not believe a hunter would use such a creature to spy on them. I, however, will have to give my moth at least eight inches to be realistic.

Dragomir nearly choked. Leave it to Sandu. The black witch moth was legendary as a harbinger of death. And eight inches? It was starting. He shouldn't have shared humor with any of them.

Found another entrance here on the street. Ferro this time. *I will go in as a black witch moth. Perhaps I should make my wingspan that little bit bigger as in keeping with my size. Say, nine inches?*

Dragomir would have laughed if his present form allowed it. They might not find humor in the things they said, but they were funny. Now that he had regained his emotions, he shared them automatically with the others. It had been so long since any of them had felt *any*thing, they almost didn't remember what humor was.

If we went by that, I would have to go for a ten-inch wingspan, Andor said, his voice droll. *Sandu, I hope that you do not feel embarrassed.*

Given that much larger than eight or nine inches is going to draw attention and be smashed first by some stubby vampire, I have no reason to feel this emotion—this embarrassment you speak of.

That rules out my twelve-inch wingspan, Benedik grumbled. *I am going in by the back wall three shops down.*

Dragomir's heart clenched hard in his chest. He knew that entrance—or more precisely—exit. Vadim had used it after he had impregnated Emeline. *Be especially cautious. That leads directly into Vadim's private lair.*

He moved into the pile of debris, floating in the steady

breeze down through the crevice and into the hallway of the underground city. Rock and dirt covered the floor in great impassable mounds. One rock blocked the door to the chamber where Bella, Liv and, farther back, Val had been held. Live experiments with children had been conducted there. Children were fed to the flesh-eating puppets Vadim had created. Most of those children had been alive at the time. In hunt mode, he was grateful he'd put some distance from his emotions. As it was, the place turned his stomach and sorrow slipped in. He began to drift away, more than happy that there was no sign of Vadim or his pawns.

He halted abruptly, staying in the steady cool stream of air, but not moving with it. He couldn't overlook anything. It seemed ridiculous to think that Vadim would use the chambers again, but they couldn't afford to take the chance. He slipped out of the breeze and, moving slowly so as not to trigger any alarms, slid into a tiny opening between the rock and the chamber wall.

At first the room appeared empty. He nearly turned to go back, but then air was displaced and figures shimmered for a moment. They appeared translucent, so that anyone looking could see right through them to the dirt-covered ceiling, the blood-stained floor and the dark, ominous scratches in the walls.

Dragomir slipped into a corner and stayed absolutely still as he focused his Carpathian vision on the interior of the chamber. It only took a few moments before the images began emerging into flesh-and-blood apparitions. There was a woman of indeterminate age in the cage. Her hands were tied at the wrist, suspended over her head. She had scars on her neck from rough biting and there were more on her arms and even one up high on her thigh where her skirt was pulled up. Her hair was pulled back in a loose, disheveled ponytail.

He could tell she was tall and very thin, almost emaciated. Her hair was very thick and long, the color dark with a few streaks of silver woven through. Her face and body appeared young, but there was something about her that made him think she was older.

She appeared dehydrated, glassy-eyed and beaten. There were bruises everywhere he could see. Her head was down, but without warning, her gaze shifted toward the corner of the room—the corner where he stayed so still. She took a breath and let it out slowly. Her head moved, her chin jerking slightly toward the second chamber, the one where Valentin had been held.

Telling him something. Warning him, perhaps? *She knew he was there.* She was aware of him even when the vampire was not. What did that say about her? Who was she?

A vampire moved around a long stone table. He muttered to himself and kept casting murderous glances over his shoulder at the prisoner. She had once more dropped her head, looking defeated when Dragomir knew she wasn't. There was fresh blood on the floor and smears of it, small bloody footprints, leading into the next chamber.

Dragomir didn't much like the fact that the woman knew she was no longer alone in the chamber with the vampire so close. He needed to find out what was in that chamber before he made a move against the vampire. And he had to kill the vampire without alerting the underground city.

Vadim had woven a spell over the chambers, one that the Carpathians had already fallen for once. They had examined these chambers once before and believed he had abandoned his city, but it was still in use. He just hid it better now.

Dragomir moved slowly, inching his way through the chamber to keep from moving air. The vampire was engrossed in what he was doing, still muttering to himself, obviously angry at his assigned task—or the orders to leave the prisoner alone. It was the way the vampire alternated between glaring at her and licking his lips hungrily when he eyed her that had Dragomir certain he had been given orders to stay away from the woman.

Without warning the chamber door banged open so hard it hit the rock, bounced closed, swung open a second time with equal force, but this time a large vampire stood framed in the doorway. Dragomir recognized him immediately. Eugen. He had successfully escaped from the cave, but he was covered in scars from his encounter with the sun. He'd burned severely. Half of his face was a flat silver sheet with strange, almost cheesy skin around the borders. As if it were a mask, when the vampire spoke, the skin, already pulled tight, didn't allow for expression.

"Get a move on, Artur, I'm tired of waiting. We don't have all night."

Artur glared at Eugen. "You got to eat. I'm starving. She smells delicious. Her blood must be . . . powerful. I want just one taste. I'm hungry." The last was almost a whine.

"I don't give a rat's ass if you're starving. I'm not going to let you get me killed. Sergey wants the information and I told him I'd get it for him." Eugen glanced behind him, bared his teeth and swung around. "I can see you're anxious for your treatment today," he said to someone behind him.

"I don't have anything to prove to him," Artur snapped, almost gleeful, although he shot a glance toward the door behind him, as if Sergey Malinov might step through at any moment.

Dragomir inched closer to the open door. Inside he could see a second female, and this one looked very young, maybe in her early twenties. She was chained to the wall and hadn't fared any better than the other woman, maybe worse. She'd been severely beaten. Her face was swollen and bruised. Streaks of blood were smeared at her rib cage and along her right arm, where there was a large cut.

Eugen stomped back to the girl and grabbed her throat, his thumb forcing her face up. "If you don't give Sergey the information he wants this time, I'm going to hurt you like you've never been hurt." A malicious smile revealed his spiked, stained teeth. "Or I'll tell him you've deceived him all this time and you don't know how to undo Xavier's spell."

Dragomir had continued floating, inching his way around Eugen, but that brought him up short. Xavier had been one of the most powerful mages ever born. He was wholly evil and had almost succeeded in stamping out the Carpathian people.

There was a stir behind him and both vampires trembled, fear removing the cocky looks on their faces. Eugen had always been a fighter. He was no newly turned vampire. In fact, Dragomir would have thought he was well on his way to becoming a master vampire, yet whoever was coming to the chamber had inspired pure fear. It permeated both rooms. Even the two women looked scared.

Artur quickly began to lay out a tray with instruments of torture. That was purely psychological for the humans. No vampire needed such things to hurt a victim. Dragomir studied the older woman. Her gaze was glued to the door, but he felt a warning, a distinct push to leave the chamber. To leave the women to their fate.

Everything in him stilled when he felt that delicate push. He studied the woman much more closely, moving slowly to the cage. She wasn't human, this one. She was ancient. A Carpathian. The Malinovs had a Carpathian woman in their possession. He couldn't begin to recognize her. He'd been gone far too long to identify her. He'd heard news, of course, of lost women, those who had disappeared, but too many centuries had gone by. He didn't remember who they were or if they'd been found.

Eugen's fingers tightened around the throat of the girl hanging by chains on the wall. He squeezed down hard, cutting off her airway. Immediately the woman in the cage reacted, throwing herself at the bars, kicking at them. She didn't call out or speak, but she made such a ruckus with her body against the bars that Eugen whirled around with a hiss.

"Stop it or I'll kill her."

Instantly the woman in the cage subsided. The girl in chains gasped for breath, coughed, wheezed and then drew in a lungful of air. The outside door to the chamber opened and Sergey Malinov strode in. Dragomir had encountered him several times. In the pack of five brothers, Sergey had never stood out. He seemed to disappear when there was a fight and almost never voiced his opinion, preferring to follow his brothers' lead.

The temperature in the chamber dropped several degrees. Sergey looked handsome, a man made for the present century. He first looked to the woman in the cage. He smiled at her, and bowed slightly, an old-world, courtly gesture. "Good evening, Elisabeta, I trust you slept well."

The woman inclined her head, but didn't speak. Her eyes, on Sergey through lowered lashes, held a kind of terror, yet there was defiance in every line of her body.

Sergey's eyebrows went up. "Really, Elisabeta, I tire of your continued behavior. This girl is not a good influence on you."

Elisabeta seemed to shrink, looking smaller and defeated.

Sergey turned to the vampire standing beside the girl in the second chamber. "Have you gotten the information I require?"

Eugen turned stark white beneath the sallow, grayish skin. "There hasn't been enough time. She is strong and doesn't react to the—"

Sergey raised his hand, one finger apart from the others, his nail a long, thick talon. He slashed down, and Eugen screamed as the good side of his face was torn nearly in two. The master vampire did it casually, with no expression on his face, sending a chill through Dragomir. Sergey wasn't weaker or less dangerous than his brothers. This man was fully in control. Fully in charge. Those in the chamber knew it. Both women had gone utterly still, as if faced with a venomous viper, and neither wanted to draw his attention.

Sergey ignored Eugen to focus on the girl. At once the chains holding her began to smoke. She gasped but didn't cry out. The skin on her wrists where the cuffs held her began to blister.

"I suggest, Julija, that you give me what I want, or you are of no use to me. I have run out of patience." He snapped his fingers, and the chains fell to the dirt floor and slithered there like snakes. He pointed to the stone table behind him and the girl's body jerked and then began to come toward him, one unwilling step at a time.

Sergey had escaped death several times, and watching the casual way he wielded power, Dragomir was reminded of Xavier, and recalled that Sergey had a splinter of the high mage in him. He had obviously utilized it, learning from it. This was a dangerous adversary. Clearly he had been all along, but none of the hunters had recognized that he was far more powerful than his brothers. More cunning—hiding his skills and biding his time. He allowed his brothers to shine, to be the most feared while he worked in the background. That made him the most unusual vampire in the history of Carpathians.

Was he hiding those same skills from his brothers? Dragomir compared him to Vadim. Vadim was always the one in charge. He directed everyone, including Sergey, taking the lion's share of whatever they received for himself. He was always the first to feed and the one to make the decisions. Vadim considered his brother as less than himself—and he was making a big mistake. Sergey was recruiting quietly behind his brother's back. He had a plan, a strategy, and so far, it seemed to be working.

Before Dragomir made a move, he had to determine just what was going on. He needed information. He would have to send for backup in case one of the vampires escaped the chambers, but that required energy and Sergey would feel it. He remained very still. If Sergey tried to kill the girl he would have no choice but to intervene immediately, information, backup or not.

Julija made it to the stone table, her eyes on Sergey the entire way. There was fear, but there was defiance. She was a fighter, this one, and she was angry.

From the cage came waves of soothing peace. The feeling settled over all of them, vampire, hunter and enraged female. Sergey glanced up, his face softening. He smiled at Elisabeta.

"I see you are determined to work your magic on all of us, my dear. You don't have a mean bone in your body. I would give you anything you asked, but this one continues to defy me. We must move you. We must find a way. Vadim wants this part of the city abandoned. If he knew I was returning here, he would know I had a very good reason, and he would find you. I keep you safe from him. The least you can do is be grateful and tell this idiot mage to give us the proper spell. She isn't helping us, Elisabeta, and I cannot have that."

"If you move her, you know you will hide her away some-where the Carpathian hunters will never find her," Julija said. "Giving you the spell will harm her, not help her."

Sergey turned the power of his penetrating glare on the mage girl. Both Eugen and Artur took a step back as if any moment he would explode into violence. "I spent a good many years searching for a direct descendant of Xavier . . . "

"Well, you didn't find one."

The vampire's hand struck like lightning, slapping her face and then catching her arm, turning it over to show the mark on her forearm. "This is the mark of a high mage. You must be born with it. No one can wear such a mark without a direct lineage." He hissed each word. Enunciated as if she were a child and wouldn't understand.

"I am aware I was born with the mark," Julija answered. She didn't touch her reddened cheek. She didn't rub at the blisters circling her wrists. She stared up at the vampire with a calmness that belied her years. "I am the direct descendant of Xaviero. Or perhaps Xayvion." She shrugged. "Maybe I am from Xavier's bloodline. Who knows? I understand they liked to share. At least Xaviero and Xayvion did. In any case, I am far more powerful than you know."

"I am aware of that. I was aware of it when you had the chance to escape and you stayed to help Elisabeta escape. She is precious to me." He changed tactics, his voice softening. "My brother would be cruel to her. Elisabeta and I belong." He lifted his head to smile at the caged woman.

"Because you have emotions when she is near. Xavier imprisoned a Carpathian female in the hopes of children. Vadim is experimenting in the hopes of children. What is it you want? A child? I don't think so." Julija's voice was speculating. "I think you crave the emotions she gives you. It is Elisabeta that allows you to think and plan so clearly. She keeps the negative traits at bay, doesn't she?"

Sergey inclined his head. "Clever girl. I will never let her go. If you cannot help me, you are of no use, Julija, so I suggest you figure out very quickly how to undo the spell that holds her here."

378

She sighed. "It's complicated. You used a spell you chose from Xavier's memories without knowing the consequences."

"I showed it to you."

Again, Dragomir had the impression that Sergey's patience was wearing thin. The moment that happened, that wave of soothing peace filled the room. It wasn't just Sergey affected by Elisabeta's wave of peace. The other two vampires, the mage and Dragomir all felt that peaceful surge moving through them, quieting tempers.

"Yes, Sergey, you did," Julija admitted. "But it wasn't the entire memory. I need more. I have started to unravel it, but it's complicated. Very complex. Xavier put a holding spell on a Carpathian. He held her prisoner for a very long time, just as you have done to Elisabeta, using those same methods, but this spell, this is extremely difficult to undo. I cannot do it without seeing his entire memory."

There was the ring of truth in her voice, and yet, Dragomir had the feeling the girl was either very close or might have figured it out. Clearly there was a spell holding Elisabeta to the underground city, the part Vadim wanted vacated. Sergey couldn't leave his prisoner there, a prisoner his brother wasn't even aware of. That was an added complication for Dragomir. Even if he could kill all three vampires, he wouldn't be able to free Elisabeta unless this girl could actually remove the holding spell.

Without warning Sergey's hand lashed out again, sending Julija tumbling back against the stone table. "You will unlock this spell or die right now." There was no anger in his voice. He was a cold killer. This was the man Elisabeta feared. The one the vampires feared. He raked his talons down Julija's forearms, shoved his fist into the air, which lifted her body and slammed her down onto the top of the table like a human sacrifice.

Elisabeta kicked at her cage frantically, still not speaking, not making a sound. Part of the holding spell had to include being unable to speak. That made sense—Xavier would have needed to keep his victims silent if the Carpathians were close. But what else had Sergey given away? Julija had the chance to escape and she hadn't taken it. She'd stayed, risking her life on the gamble that she might be able to rescue Elisabeta. That said a lot about her character and courage. Dragomir couldn't allow Sergey to kill the mage, no matter the danger of any of the others escaping.

Sergey suddenly lifted his head and looked around the chamber, searching inch by inch. He looked up at Elisabeta, who kept her head down. He smiled at her. "You have earned another lesson, my dear. You know you deserve punishment for what you've done." He uttered the words very softly, his white teeth snapping together. Elisabeta shuddered and kept her eyes to the ground.

He whirled back to the mage lying on the stone table. He slammed one long talon—spiked like a thick ice pick—right through her throat. Leaving it there, pinning her to the rock with one long dagger, he waved his other hand toward Elisabeta.

To Dragomir's horror her body began to dissolve, to become part of the rock her cage rested on.

"Keep her alive or you die," Sergey said to his vampire servants. "If she lives, the rewards are vast," and then he was gone. That fast. So fast Dragomir couldn't see him move. He must have gone under the door of the chamber, or even through it, because he didn't open it. One moment he was there, and the next there was an empty space.

Blood bubbled from the horrendous hole in Julija's throat. She coughed and blood sprayed across the room. Eugen sprang toward her at the same time as Artur. They bumped into each other, but it was Eugen who covered the wound with his hand, applying such pressure that the girl couldn't breathe.

The Carpathian woman was still dissolving, her body melting until there was no way to see her, not even when directly looking at the place she'd been. The cage remained. The hook where her hands had been suspended above her head, but not the woman. The woman had been absorbed by the stone around her until there was nothing left of her.

In this chamber. Sergey fleeing, Dragomir warned the others.

All the vampires are exiting, Ferro reported. *It happened so fast that half of them are already deserting the place.*

Engage. These men are Sergey's soldiers, not Vadim's. What was he going to do about the mage's injuries? Elisabeta's imprisonment? *Gary, I have great need of you.* He had skills. So did Sandu, but Gary's skills were far superior. If he got there in time he might save Julija.

Sandu sauntered into the chamber, Andor behind him. Andor didn't waste time—he flew at Artur, his indigo eyes every bit as piercing as Sergey's talons had been. His inky black hair fell to his waist in a braid as thick as his arm. He blew past Eugen and slammed his fist into Artur's chest. Dragomir materialized behind Eugen and hit him with his fist. A short, powerful punch that crashed through bone, driving straight toward the withered heart.

Eugen twisted, screaming in fear and hatred. He thrashed, sending Julija tumbling from the table. Sandu caught her in a firm grip, his hand covering the gaping wound in her throat as he did so. He took her to the floor, on the opposite side of the table from either of the vampires and the hunters fighting them.

She started to struggle, and he simply waved his hand and her body stilled, but her eyes radiated pure fury. He kept his hand over the wound on her throat and slipped from his own body, right there with two vampires in the room, leaving behind a shell to become pure spirit. He moved through her body quickly, noting all the signs of torture. The woman had endured a lot over time. He saw scarring that indicated she could have been held as long as six months. Maybe even a year.

Sandu bypassed all of it, even the fresh lacerations and tears, to get to the puncture wound on the girl's throat. He had to stop the bleeding. That had to be done or they couldn't leave with her. He closed the wound from the inside out. There was damage to her larynx. The two-inch tube was shredded. If she was going to speak again, he had to at least address that.

It took longer than Sandu expected, and by the time he'd managed to get some of the tubing to stick together in the beginnings of a repair, someone or something hit his body, knocking it sideways, and his spirit abruptly was pulled from the girl back to his own shell. A boot stomped down close to his thigh and even closer to the girl.

He threw himself over her, covering her smaller form easily. The boot narrowly missed his back as the vampire stumbled backward, trying to escape Dragomir.

Dragomir kicked Eugen in the head, driving him farther away from Sandu and Julija. He spared them one glance to ensure they both were alive as he leapt over them, following Eugen. Eugen tried hard to take another form, but Dragomir was on him, preventing the change. He pinned him against the wall and slammed his fist deep, searching for the elusive heart.

Eugen roared and somersaulted, taking Dragomir with him as he rolled across the dirt floor, acid blood pouring over Dragomir and soaking into the ground. He landed on top of the Carpathian so they stared into each other's eyes. Dragomir never wavered, his fingers still digging relentlessly for the heart.

Behind Eugen, Andor loomed above them both, his indigo eyes fierce, his features brutally savage. He slammed his fist through the hole in Eugen's back that Dragomir had originally made. The vampire screamed, throwing his head back in an effort to strike the Carpathian attacking from behind. On the ground, he had no leverage, so he slammed his head forward into Dragomir, hitting him in the skull, trying to crash through it, to shatter the bone. When that didn't stop the hunter, he bit down with all his might, letting the rich ancient blood pour into him.

The moment he tasted that blood, his world went white. Narrowed. He felt nothing but craving. A dark, terrible craving that took hold and refused to release him. He thought of nothing else but getting more. The hole opening inside of him was enormous, yawning open so that the blood could fill it. Rich. Satisfying. The only taste that would ever do.

He was aware of Dragomir extracting his heart, but Andor bunched Eugen's hair in his fist and yanked his head back so hard it cracked bones in his neck. That didn't matter. The only thing that mattered was getting to the blood. He could see it, just out of his reach. Dark rubies. Gems of the purest blood he'd ever tasted. He had to have more.

Lightning arced around the room, jumped to the heart on the floor, incinerating it, turning it to ashes. The white-hot energy bathed away the blood on both Carpathians and then the floor. Sandu had kept his arms and body over the mage but now he slowly released her.

"I stopped the bleeding, but she can't talk yet," he announced, lifting her easily to carry her to the stone table out of the way.

Andor finished the job by incinerating the bodies of the two vampires.

"Gary is on his way," Dragomir said. "Her name is Julija and she's mage, a direct descendant of Xavier or one of his brothers. Sergey is also holding a Carpathian woman named Elisabeta."

Andor's eyes went wide. "There was a young girl, Elisabeta. Traian Trigovise's sister. I would go to her home and somehow she could make me feel lighter, as if I had emotions again. The longer I stayed in her company, the longer the effect lasted. She has been gone for centuries. She disappeared one day and no one knew what happened to her. No one could trace her. I know Traian looked for centuries. She was quite a bit younger than him, younger by at least five hundred years. Maybe more."

"It could be the same woman," Dragomir conceded. "She kept Sergey from losing his temper." *Ferro, Benedik, where are you?*

Sweeping the underground city. The vampires left quickly. We've systematically gone through every room here, and they are all gone.

Sergey had clearly sacrificed two to save his army. The vampire had to have felt their presence. Julija had been deliberately injured, the extent bad enough that the master vampire knew they would have to heal her or she would die.

"The healer is on his way. We can't leave here without figuring out how to save Elisabeta," Dragomir stalked over to the cage and walked around it, studying it from every angle, trying to see what wasn't there. "He made her part of the stone. The rock. I was looking right at her and she disappeared into the walls." He glanced back at the mage. Her eyes were open and she regarded him with suspicion, but there was also a faint trace of hope on her face.

"Can you bring her back? Do you know the spell?"

She visibly took a breath, flinched and started to grab at her throat. Sandu caught her hand and shook his head. "Wait for the healer. You don't want to have permanent damage."

Her gaze shifted to him. She studied him for a long time and then she looked back to Dragomir and nodded.

Relief flooded through him. "Did you work out the spell to reverse whatever is keeping her here?"

He could tell by her face she wanted to protect Elisabeta from all of them. She didn't trust them, and he didn't blame her. She didn't know them. She might think they were part of Sergey's plot to get the information out of her.

Her gaze went to the terrible wound that had coated his neck and shoulder with blood. She frowned and looked back at Sandu.

"She wants me to heal you," Sandu said. "I'm not the healer. I'm a *peje* hunter."

"Stop complaining. You didn't have to stick your arm in acid up to your elbow," Dragomir said.

Where are you? he asked Petru and Isia. *We need to regroup.*

We need to wipe this pipeline out for good. Vadim is using the sea to escape. He's created his own city down here complete with a fresh smorgasbord, Petru answered. *We need to call everyone in and destroy this. Now. Tonight.*

Come back to the underground city. I'm calling the third team back as well. We'll include Tariq and come up with a plan. In the meantime, I've got two women here that need healing. One needs to go directly into the healing grounds. I think we have solved the mystery of the disappearance of Elisabeta Trigovise.

There was silence. Elisabeta had been legendary in the Carpathian world because she could restore emotions to those warriors at the very end of their ability to continue. She hadn't exactly restored them, so much as lightened their burdens for the time in her presence. She'd smiled and the world had seemed filled with joy.

Dragomir hadn't seen her smile, but he felt her peace. That enduring serenity. There was calm in her that spread through the room the moment it was needed. She was clearly conserving strength, and she needed blood. Her hunger had beat at him, but so gently he barely registered it until she was gone, made to be part of the walls of the chamber.

Elisabeta? The name was whispered for all the brotherhood to hear. That magical girl. All of them who had ever crossed paths with her would never forget her. She'd been considered an angel, her gift nothing short of miraculous. The child had grown into a beautiful young woman, still as angelic and as selflessly giving as she'd been as a child.

More than one warrior had crossed oceans to get back to her, to just be in her presence. If they had found Elisabeta, they had found a treasure unsurpassed.

Did Vadim have her? Benedik made the demand.

I do not believe Vadim knew of her existence. Sergey had her. He has had her for some time and has hidden her from his brother. He is much more dangerous than we ever gave him credit for. In fact, I believe he is our true enemy. Vadim thinks he is in charge, but Sergey has quietly built an army, and he's learned much from the splinter of the high mage.

I thought Vadim has a splinter of the high mage as well, Ferro said.

Just because he has it, doesn't mean he uses it, Dragomir pointed out.

Power burst into the small confines of the chamber. Gary Daratrazanoff strode in, his long hair flowing behind him. The muscles beneath his thin shirt rippled in an impressive display of sheer strength. His gaze fell first on the mage, jumped to the injuries on Dragomir and then slowly slid over the wall where the empty cage sat.

"I feel her presence," he said softly. "She is very powerful and a boon to any man such as I. Before we try to bring her back, I will do what I can for the mage and you, Dragomir. I grow weary of you and your injuries."

Sandu nudged him. "I told you to learn to be a little faster."

Dragomir sent a very rude gesture Sandu's way.

19

Dragomir held council in the much larger chamber while Gary worked on healing the young female mage. Tariq had joined them, and all agreed the city inside the pipeline had to be destroyed. The humans Vadim had taken there for sustenance were mostly vegetables, incapable of recovery. He left them just enough sanity to feel fear. The undead needed the rush of their victims' fear. It was the drug every vampire craved.

The task was distasteful, but they had no choice. They spent some time working out the details and then Dragomir returned to the smaller chamber where Gary had worked on the mage and the ancients had supplied him with blood.

"I was able to repair the damage, but she shouldn't speak for a couple of weeks. If she does, she will cause permanent damage to her vocal cords." Gary directed his attention to Julija. "I cannot emphasize that enough. You can write down what you need to say, or better yet, someone should take your blood and exchange with yours so you can speak telepathically."

Julija shook her head adamantly. She glared at the healer.

He shrugged. "It is your choice. If you wish to help Elisabeta, that is the only way. I may have some input, but without your guidance of where to look for answers, I can be of no real help here and should go with the others to take down Vadim's city."

Frustration had Julija's brows drawing together. She drew a question mark in the air and pointed to him.

"Dragomir told me you didn't see the entire holding spell that is locking Elisabeta here to this underground city. I have the ability to access very ancient memories. It is possible one of my ancestors saw something or heard something that will help you."

She pointed to Gary and tilted her neck slightly, although her hands were trembling. She locked them together tightly in her lap.

Gary shook his head. "I will not connect you to me. Dragomir has a lifemate. It is safe for him to connect himself to you, but if I ever turned, you would be in danger. It is impossible for him to turn as long as Emeline lives."

Julija sat for what seemed an eternity. Dragomir was aware of time slipping by. The others had already left to attack the city under the sea, and he was a warrior and should be joining them. Tariq had returned to the compound to ready the healing grounds for Elisabeta if they were successful. If they weren't, Gary was prepared to stay in the underground city to guard her, finding a place to sleep and then working out a plan with the Carpathian woman. *She* had to have seen the spell. Even if it was complicated, between Gary, Dragomir and Julija, they had a chance of figuring it out.

"We can't be here too long. Sergey is not going to give

up his prize so easily," Dragomir told the reluctant girl. "He will launch an assault the moment he hears of the attack on Vadim's sea city. Most of our hunters have gone there, leaving us vulnerable as well as the compound."

Julija's mouth firmed. She pointed to her neck. Dragomir didn't give her time to change her mind. He was careful, respectful and distanced her from what was happening without taking her mind. Even distancing her was difficult. She had a very strong shield. Her consent allowed him to do so. He pointed to his wrist after carefully closing the pinpricks. She took a deep breath, nodded and cleared her throat as if she might speak.

"Don't," Gary said. "You will ruin everything. Do you want him to distance you more?"

She nodded.

"You have to allow him into your mind. Make a conscious choice. He is being careful with you, not taking what you are not willing to give. We both realize you are doing this to help your friend, not to aid you in healing, although, I assure you, his blood will do both."

Julija looked to Dragomir and nodded. He pushed further into her mind and when she opened for him, he took away her ability to register what was happening until it was done. Dragomir closed the laceration he'd torn in his wrist and looked at her.

Are you all right? He included Gary in their conversation. *Not dizzy, or light-headed?*

Julija shook her head and touched her throat. *Still hurts.*

"I'm sorry," Gary said aloud. "The damage was very severe."

She nodded. *Thanks for fixing me up.* She slipped off the stone table and walked over to the cage. *I have to reverse the spell Sergey used. It was one Xavier used to hide Rhiannon. It prevented her from making a sound so that he could hide her in plain sight of a Carpathian. That would maximize her torment, being so close to those who could rescue her, yet being completely hidden from them.*

How do you know this? Dragomir had touched her memories, but he hadn't had time to examine them thoroughly. He tried not to allow suspicion to spill over into his mind where she would read it.

Sergey often told the story to Elisabeta. He wanted her to see how much better he was treating her. He didn't let Vadim or his other brothers see her. Not ever. He was careful. She told me about Rhiannon and how Xavier had children by her and then killed her. She said Sergey never tried to force her to have his child.

That was a revelation. He exchanged a long look with Gary. *He has the greatest treasure of all time,* Gary said. *Of course the Malinovs knew of her. Sergey wanted her exclusively for her abilities, not for children. He kept her to himself.*

Elisabeta was trusting. She knew the brothers well, and after their sister, Ivory, disappeared, they went to her often. She didn't think anything of it when Sergey came to her alone and asked her to go with him to a place he'd built in memory of his sister.

Julija walked around the cage, studying it, the wall behind it and the floor under it from every angle. Dragomir saw her stumble, almost go down, and then she straightened her shoulders and put her hands in the air.

Can you do this sitting?

She frowned at him. *I have to concentrate. I only saw this spell the one time. After that he waved his hand and she disappeared into the rock.*

It won't help if you fall on your butt, Dragomir chided. *Answer me.* He poured steel into his voice.

She gave him another frown, but this time she shook her head. *I am shaky,* she conceded, *but I have to mimic his movements exactly in reverse. He was standing, and he moved around the cage as he cast.*

Just know, if you start to go down, I'll be holding you up. If I have to reach for you, I don't want you to think I'm going to harm you.

Her gaze moved over Dragomir's face. *When you came into my mind, I looked into yours. There is only room for one woman. She consumes you. You will fight and die for her. You would never harm me or attack me unless I threatened her in some way. If I start to fall, by all means, keep me from hitting my head.*

Both men moved back behind her and the young woman once again lifted her arms. She began a very complex weave in the air. Gary waved his hand and the weave sprang into the air, the thin lines twisted and looping around and through one another. It was complicated, but the mage worked at it steadily. Sweat dampened her brow. Little beads rolled down her face and dotted her skin. Dragomir felt the pounding in her head. The words she had to reverse were dark and ugly, so dark that speaking them kept the ground moving beneath their feet. Her lips moved, but she didn't utter the words aloud, only pictured them in her mind, but the intimacy of that made them worse.

Slowly the weaves began to unknot. When one line was free, she erased it with a flick of her fingers. She walked back and forth while she worked, then around from one side of the cage to the other. She didn't falter, not even when her knees buckled and Dragomir had to catch her around her waist to hold her up. He held her with strong fingers, but kept a light touch so she could move in any direction she needed to without hesitation.

Several times Dragomir caught sight of Elisabeta huddled

inside the cage. Her arms were raised over her head, chained to the ceiling. She would be there one moment and then she'd be gone again. He realized the second time he caught a glimpse of her that she had heard every word and knew they were trying to help. Although they hadn't been able to see her, she could see them. Bloodred tears tracked down her face.

He couldn't imagine what he would have done if that had been Emeline. Just looking at Elisabeta made him feel sick and angry. Sergey had kept her prisoner for so long. What harm had all these centuries of imprisonment done to her? Freeing her would be merciful, but after so long, what had been done to her mind? He wanted to hold the woman close and comfort her, as if she were his own sister instead of Traian's. He glanced at Gary's expressionless features. Even he had his eyes on the Carpathian woman. There was something magnetic about her. Something that drew warriors and soothed their tattered souls.

The last line fell to Julija's determination. She erased it and slumped. Dragomir lifted her before she fell and placed her on the stone table. "Just rest for a minute. We will get the chains off Elisabeta and then figure out the next spell. You need blood. You're very weak. I'll give you mine." He turned to Gary. "You're going to have to donate to Elisabeta."

Elisabeta didn't say a word. Dragomir wasn't certain she could speak. She kept her eyes cast down, her long lashes veiling her expression. Gary moved to the cage, waved his hand and the lock fell to the ground. He looked at the chains, and they fell away. Elisabeta's arms dropped as if made of lead. She made no attempt to lift them, or rub at her hands to get the blood flowing.

Gary frowned and very gently took her hand, his thumb sliding over her pulse. "Elisabeta? I'm Gary Daratrazanoff.

This is Dragomir Kozel. We'll take you out of here and get you to the healing soil. You need blood." With each word, when there was no response, his voice got softer, more persuasive.

Using his fingernail, he cut a long, thin line in his wrist and held it out to her. She blinked, looked at the blood and then slowly lifted her lashes until she was not quite looking into his eyes.

"I want you to take my blood," Gary said, his voice firming. When there was no response he gave her a definite order, his tone leaving no argument. "Elisabeta, you will take this blood immediately."

She took a breath and then, keeping her hands in her lap, leaned into his wrist. Her mouth moved over the ruby line, her tongue touching the ancient blood. He pressed his wrist deeper into her mouth and then, as if because he'd given his permission or made a demand, she fed. Her movements were almost childlike, delicate and slow.

Dragomir watched her, worry clouding his mind. It was Gary who told her to stop and she did instantly. Once again she sat without moving, her eyes downcast. He looked to Julija for answers.

After hundreds of years of being his prisoner, she's trained to do as she's told. The consequences of not obeying were severe. Julija sighed. *She fought him for me. To keep me alive. He hurt her, but she didn't stop. She'll come back from this if I can get her out of here. The holding spell was one Xavier created and it was extremely complicated. I tried to reverse it several times when Sergey and the others weren't around, but I couldn't.*

Dragomir narrowed his gaze, studying her face, the lines of strain there, the signs of torture. "You could have gotten free at any time, couldn't you?"

She shrugged. *She told me to leave, to get myself free, but I couldn't leave her. Everyone she ever cared about is dead ...*

"That isn't true," Dragomir denied. He turned toward the woman in the cage. "Look at me," he commanded her, using his firmest tone. He waited until Elisabeta raised her gaze to his. Again, she didn't look him in the eye directly, instead fixing her gaze just below his eyes.

"It isn't true that everyone you love is dead. Your brother, Traian, still lives and he has found his lifemate. He searched for you, but there has been no trace. Others have searched. Your gifts are needed now more than ever, Elisabeta. Many warriors have waited centuries for their lifemates and cannot find them. We have no women. It is difficult to continue hanging on. With your gifts, you can bring comfort to those waiting, extend their ability to hold out against the darkness. Your people need you. They want you home. We want you home with us, Elisabeta."

Her gaze flicked from his face to Julija and then back again. She took a deep breath and nodded, but she didn't speak. Once again, tears tracked down her face, tiny ruby drops of blood. The sight made Dragomir's stomach knot.

"Show me," Gary demanded of Julija. "In your mind, let me see the spell he cast to keep her locked in this place. Every detail in your mind. Dragomir is connected to me and I will be able to see what you picture."

Julija didn't hesitate. Dragomir's head was filled with images of Sergey walking back and forth in front of the cage holding Elisabeta. His feet tracked a complicated arrangement around the cage, while his hands moved in an extremely difficult configuration in the air. To do both, one had to be extremely coordinated. All the while, Sergey uttered commands of dark magic, words that should never have been made, let alone spoken.

"A sacrifice was made long ago to seal this spell," Gary said. "In Xavier's chamber, he sacrificed a young mage."

How could you possibly know that? Julija demanded, her suspicion back.

"When it was discovered that Xavier had turned against our people, one of my ancestors took part in the investigation. They uncovered many disturbing things in Xavier's home. He left hastily and in doing so, left behind years of memories within the walls of the ice caves where he conjured most of his spells. That image, because he sacrificed a human being, was very vivid."

Are you saying that the things we do in this room can be imprinted on the walls? Julija asked, shocked.

Gary nodded. "Of course. The more violent, the deeper the etching. These walls are screaming with their burden. Someone gifted would be able to read all that was done here."

For the first time, the skeptical suspicion left Julija's face. *We really might be able to do this, Elisabeta,* she said, jumping up, forgetting how weak she'd been before Dragomir had given her his blood.

Dragomir found himself smiling. "You exchanged blood with Elisabeta. That's how she's included in our circle. All this time I thought you were afraid of a blood exchange."

I know how this Carpathian lifemate crap works. I'm not going to say a word around anyone that doesn't already have a lifemate and I'll exchange blood with the women if necessary, but not the men.

He found himself smiling, thankful to Emeline that she'd given him back a sense of humor. The little mage would lead someone a terrible dance if she proved to be a lifemate to a Carpathian.

Do you think you can access the memory in the cave? he asked Gary on their private telepathic path.

I have located it in the memory of my ancestor, Gary assured. *Whether she can reproduce it, I have no idea.*

"Let's do this," Dragomir said. A shadow slipped into his mind, making him leery. He wanted to get back to Emeline.

Julija took a deep breath and lifted her arms. Concentration was in every line of her body. She looked at Elisabeta. *We will do it this time, my friend, and you will be free.*

I cannot comprehend such a thing.

The voice that spoke in his mind was the most beautiful one Dragomir had ever heard. Just the sound of it could stop a war, stop a kill, perhaps even make a vampire forget he'd chosen to lose his soul, if only for a few moments. Elisabeta was a powerful treasure. No wonder Sergey had kept her to himself. She would be able to persuade every vampire to join his cause. He could use her voice as leverage, as a gift to his most trusted, giving them a few minutes in her company to feel again. To think again without a chaotic brain. She would become a drug they would all be addicted to.

Dragomir glanced at Gary and knew he felt it, too. Knew the man was aware of just how important she was to Sergey and his plans. If he lost his drug, just what would he be willing to do to get her back? Anything for a voice like that. Anything for a gift like that. Anything to keep his army in line. They would want her back as well—every single one of them that had ever known the blessing of her voice.

Julija continued moving her feet in the complicated dance pattern while her hands waved gracefully in the air, completely separate from what her feet and legs were doing. All the while she moved her lips, the dark, ugly words at odds with the beauty and elegance of her body's movements. Dragomir shuddered as the vile spell was uttered softly in his mind. He had closed himself off completely to Emeline and was glad that he had. She didn't need this ugliness in her mind on top of what Vadim had put there.

Julija unraveled the majority of the spell before she

397

faltered, glancing toward Gary. At once, the vision of Xavier, the high mage, was in their minds, the movements and words fed by some unseen ancestor's memories that were now a part of Gary's remembrances. Julija slowed, but she kept moving, her eyes closed now as she turned inward to feel, see, hear and mimic the dark magic spell in reverse in order to free Elisabeta.

Each placement of hand and foot was deliberate and slow so as not to make a mistake. The weight of the spell pressed down on her. It didn't matter that she erased it line by line, that she was undoing something dark and sinister, that slime coated her mind, their minds. Dragomir felt it, so how could she not? His respect for the mage grew. She didn't falter. Not once. No matter how bad it got, and all of them knew the exact moment the spell had been sealed in innocent blood.

Elisabeta cried out and pressed her hand to her mouth, the first sign of real spontaneous movement on her part. Julija's face went pale, so pale she looked nearly translucent and her shoulders pressed down as if she could barely carry the weight of that sin. Tremors racked her body, but her hands never faltered and her legs held her up. Her mind and Dragomir's were melded firmly, two people determined to take Elisabeta from the prison she'd been in for so long. She'd been a young woman, barely twenty summers when she disappeared.

Sergey had shaped her life. Shaped who she was. Dragomir realized she would be very fragile and would have to be handled with care. Her lifemate could be long gone from the world, and she would live a lonely existence, revered by the Carpathian people, but perhaps in her own kind of hell.

He shook his head. He couldn't think about that. Emeline

398

hadn't given up under the worst of circumstances. The fact that Elisabeta had fought her captor to save Julija, knowing he would punish her, told Dragomir the woman was resilient. Women had shown themselves to be unbelievably strong.

You've got this, Gary whispered when Julija slowed even more, her body trembling to the point of shaking.

Dragomir moved up behind her, placing both hands on her waist to keep her from falling. He had to concentrate and follow those intricate steps so that she could move freely. Even with his help, she was exhausted. Without his blood, she never would have made it through to that last move. When the thread unknotted and she erased it, she would have collapsed if he hadn't been waiting for it. He caught her in his arms and took her to the stone table.

"You need blood," he said, making it a command. All the while he watched Elisabeta. They all did. Waiting.

Elisabeta remained on her knees in the cage, eyes cast down for the longest time. Gary stepped close to the metal bars and held out his hand. "You may leave the cage now, Elisabeta."

Her eyelashes fluttered. She took a deep breath and reached slowly for his outstretched hand. Her entire body was racked with tremors. Gary closed his fingers around her hand and slowly began to exert pressure, a silent demand that she obey him. She stretched out her legs as if afraid that at any moment Gary would reprimand her. When he kept up the pressure on her hand, she let him pull her to the front of the cage until her legs hung outside of it.

She gasped and almost retracted her legs, but Gary shook his head. "That's good. See, you can leave the cage. I want you to leave it."

She swallowed visibly. Her breathing was rapid. Panicked.

How long has he kept her in that confined space? Dragomir demanded.

Julija shook her head. *I don't know. A long time. She's terrified out in the open.*

Dragomir assessed the situation. Elisabeta wasn't a modern woman. She would expect a Carpathian male to take charge in a situation she was unfamiliar with and afraid in. He did so immediately, not only to spare her, but because the shadow in him had been growing.

Elisabeta, I am going to carry you to the safety of the healing grounds. If the night sky is too open and scary for you, close your eyes and put your head on my chest so you can't see. Trust me to keep you safe. My lifemate will be in my mind to hold you as well. Do you understand me?

He reached for Emeline. *I have need of you. We have found a woman who has been held captive for hundreds of years. She's terrified. I need you to help me steady her while I take her to the compound.*

Of course, Dragomir. Whatever you need. She gave him her response immediately, before he showed her the terrible conditions Elisabeta had been living in. At once he felt her—his other half. The best part of him. She was there, soft and soothing, reaching for Elisabeta to hold her fragile mind in hers while he physically took charge.

He put his arms around Elisabeta and indicated for Gary to lift Julija into his. Before the mage could protest, he pulled Elisabeta all the way out of the cage and then they were moving fast, going through the thin crack, Gary transforming Julija and Dragomir doing the same for Elisabeta so they could fit.

The moment Dragomir had lifted her wholly out of the cage, Elisabeta tensed as if she might fight him, but instead, she buried her face against his chest. He knew she was crying, but she forced herself to remain still, her body shuddering uncontrollably.

We've got you, Emeline crooned softly. *Dragomir is strong. He won't drop you.*

Too open. Too open, Elisabeta chanted, her voice a sob of pure fear.

Her breathing was so rapid, her heartbeat so wild, Dragomir feared they might lose her before they had a chance to put her in the healing soil. She was so used to obedience that she didn't fight, when every cell and instinct urged her to do so. Emeline did her best to surround her mind with hope and peace.

Dragomir shifted his arms, putting one over her head to cage her in. *Is that better? Feel the night breeze. Think of the things you saw as a child that you loved so much.*

It's too much for her, Emeline said. *She's going to have to start small. I'm with you, Elisabeta. I'm Emeline. Vadim took me prisoner for a short time.*

Elisabeta stilled. *I know you. You saved the children. I saw you. I couldn't warn you that Vadim had planned a trap for you. Sergey took my voice.*

Dragomir was grateful to Emeline as she kept Elisabeta's mind off the flight and on her story. Emeline told her all about the children and what they were doing. He made it to the compound while Emeline was telling her about how the children had tried to fly their dragons when they shouldn't have. Somehow, in the retelling, Dragomir found a little humor in the story.

Tariq had the soil open, and Dragomir took Elisabeta deep in the earth, where the dirt richest in minerals and healing properties had been selected for her. Gary placed Julija gently on the surface and floated down to crouch close to Elisabeta's head. "I am going to attempt to heal you

401

before you are placed in the ground. Lie quietly and allow me to do this."

Elisabeta nodded, but she didn't look at him or Dragomir. Her eyes were on Julija's. Julija smiled at her. *We did it. I told you we would find a way.*

You're going to leave me.

Not for long. When you wake, I will return. That's a promise. The healer says three weeks.

Three weeks it is, then. These are good people, Elisabeta. Let them help you. I know it is new and scary, but you can do this. You're Carpathian. Sergey is a vampire. He's evil. There is nothing you can do to change that.

I tried.

He has no soul.

Abruptly Gary returned, throwing a quick glance at Julija, indicating he'd heard every word exchanged. No doubt he'd been in Elisabeta's head, trying to help her recover faster. He waved his hand, and just that fast, Elisabeta was asleep, far from Julija, far from all of them. He closed the soil over her.

"I'm Tariq Asenguard," Tariq introduced himself to Julija as they walked through the house, back to the outside. "You're welcome to stay."

Julija shook her head. *I have things to do. Important things. I'll be back, though, if you don't mind.*

Dragomir gave Tariq her answer.

"We would welcome you anytime," Tariq said.

Julija held out her hand to Dragomir. *It was a pleasure to meet you.* She did the same for Gary. *Both of you. I would never have been able to free her on my own.*

They watched her leave, walking away, no car, no backpack, just a woman looking frail and battered. Their every instinct was to go after her, but she'd made it clear she wanted to be alone, that she had something of great importance to do, and they had to respect her wishes.

Dragomir couldn't wait to get to Emeline. He saw her on the porch, talking with Genevieve and Amelia, but her gaze was on him.

Tariq, the city is destroyed but most of the vampires were not here, Afanasiv reported. *They were not in the underground city. Nor in the park. We are on our way back.*

Tariq immediately looked toward the high tower where Matt Bennet, the head of his security force, was stationed. Waiting. *Be alert. Have your men ready.*

Dragomir took a careful look around. That shadow in his mind had grown to full-blown dread. *Emeline, send the children to the safe rooms. Have Amelia take them in now. You and Genevieve get inside.*

She didn't question him, just leaned over to talk to Amelia and calmly gesture to Genevieve. He was proud of her. Proud that she looked normal if anyone was watching. Amelia stepped off the porch and sauntered over to Danny. Slinging an arm around him, she laughed while she talked. The two of them scooped up Lourdes and Bella, putting them on their backs, and called to Liv to play with them. Liv ran over and they raced to the main house, laughing and calling out to one another as they went. They disappeared behind the door just as Maksim and Blaze arrived. Charlotte followed the children into the house.

The boom of Donald Walton's new gun reverberated through the night. The night sky lit up with a fiery orange glow. Maksim was in the air immediately, heading toward the lake. The gun from the tower answered, one single shot, a fiery spinning missile fired toward the lake.

They're coming in from under the water. The underground rivers Emeline showed us, Dragomir said. *He has found a way to render safeguards useless in the water.* That was a blow. A huge one. The spell had to come from accessing Xavier's mind. *That's why the attacks always came from underneath us.*

Dragomir launched himself, taking to the air, streaking toward the lake just as Donald's gun and then Mary's sounded. Both were loud, echoing across the wide expanse of water.

Dragomir could see creatures climbing out of the black, shiny water. Some shot out of the water into the sky. Matt and his team took aim from the relative safety of the blinds hidden throughout the compound. They could move freely to and from them via the tunnels Tariq had created for them.

Don't go in the water, Tariq cautioned. *I have a surprise for Vadim's army.*

Tariq spotted Vadim emerging, a dark figure, using two others as a shield. They didn't call attention to themselves, but rather tried to move in the deeper shadows to shore. Dragomir realized Vadim was locked on to Emeline's house. He was certain all the ancients were gone, hunting his cities, and lairs, chasing his army out to sea and leaving the compound unprotected.

Dragomir streaked across the lake, coming at Vadim from behind. He caught him, once again, by the play yard. He struck Vadim from behind, slamming his fist right through his back, utilizing his strength and power, breaking bones and tunneling through tissue to get his fingers around the heart. As if recognizing him as the one who had had the other piece of it, the organ leapt toward him.

Vadim shrieked in fear and fury. He whirled, shouting orders, caught off guard. His shrieks drowned out the sound of gunfire. The two vampires guarding him swung around just as Dragomir extracted the heart and flung it to one side. Lightning forked across the sky, lighting up Vadim's shocked features. The attack had happened too fast, a blitz he hadn't expected.

One of the vampires tackled Dragomir, knocking him back from Vadim. Lightning hit the ground just to one side of the vampire's heart. The second vampire dropped protectively to the ground beside the fallen master. Dragomir recognized Sergey.

Sergey Malinov regarded his brother with sorrow on his face. Surreptitiously he reached out and covered Vadim's heart with one hand while he wrapped his arm around his brother with the other. "I'm sorry, Vadim. We didn't see him coming at us from behind. It's too late now. He has your heart. Give me Xavier's sliver and I may find a way to defeat him. Maybe even stop him from incinerating you." He kept his voice soft and persuasive, gentle, kind even. Filled with grief.

Vadim shrieked and thrashed. Black blood spilled everywhere. Another scream produced a torrent of spittle. With it came a silver-gray splinter. Eagerly the small piece of the high mage recognized that the other vampire had another small section inside him. It entered him easily via his ear, sliding inside to find the brain, to find that other slice left of such a powerful man.

"That is good, Vadim. Let me try to stop him," Sergey said. He kept his sorrowful look, even when triumph spilled through him like water over a dam. He looked up and beckoned one of Vadim's idiot pawns closer. Glee filled him. His plans were coming together nicely.

The vampire hurried to his side.

"I need help with my brother. With Vadim," he said softly, making certain that Vadim heard. "Dragomir has taken his heart and I must get it back, no matter the cost to me. You watch over him."

Sergey stood, slipped away and then returned, coming up behind the vampire, who looked left and right, but paid no attention to what was behind him. He slammed his fist deep, extracted the heart, tossed it to one side and called down the lightning himself. He incinerated the heart and then the body before lifting his brother. He immediately employed a vanishing spell over both of them.

Now he had only to get his most prized possession back. He'd possessed her for hundreds of years. She belonged to him. She was probably terrified without him telling her what to do.

He shifted, molecules in the air, moving slowly so as not to call attention to himself while the battle raged around him, Vadim's idiot army doing the bidding of a man already gone, already under Sergey's rule, although they wouldn't know it. He'd sent three of his best to kill Dragomir and their new healer, Daratrazanoff. That family was always sticking their noses in where they didn't belong. He reached for Elisabeta, trying to connect with her. There was only emptiness. A void. He nearly panicked. She had to be there, somewhere in the compound.

There was no entering the house. He could feel the safeguards from a distance away. If she was in there, he would have known. She was part of him. They'd been together for centuries. He took care of her. She wouldn't be able to function without him. He had no choice but to leave, but he would find her.

⁓

Dragomir felt teeth rip down his shoulder and arm. Talons tore chunks of flesh from his chest. He and the vampire tumbled across the ground, hit one of the stone dragons and came to an abrupt stop. Out of the corner of his eyes, he saw a vampire, Sergey, trap Vadim's heart under his hand, then Dragomir was fighting for his life as a second vampire joined the one trying to kill him. The second one didn't try to wear him down; he went straight for the chest, slamming his fist over and over, creating holes that bled profusely, weakening him.

He sank his teeth into the first vampire's neck, ripping his jugular out, snapping the bones there before turning to face the second one. Catching the fist as it came out of him, he jerked the vampire hard toward him. At the same time, he snapped a hard punch deep into the chest. The momentum of the vampire's forward lurch helped drive Dragomir's fist deep. His fingers found the heart. As he extracted the wizened organ, the first vampire attacked again, leaping on him, raking with teeth and talons, pounding at his back with desperate fists.

Suddenly, the vampire was gone and Gary Daratrazanoff was there. He hurled the vampire from Dragomir and followed it up, not fast or slow, just a steady, relentless pursuit. Dragomir incinerated the heart and then the vampire. He looked toward Sergey and Vadim. The air crackled with electrical energy. In the air over the lake. Over the playground. Gary called for it. Lightning lit up the sky, turning the night into day. Dragomir could see ashes where Vadim had been. He knelt there on one knee, studying the ground, trying to make sense of it. Sergey had covered his brother's heart and then incinerated both the heart and Vadim. He'd made his play and taken the crown.

Dragomir looked around carefully. Gary joined him. "Tariq has lit up the lake and electrocuted every vampire in it. Maksim and the security team destroyed the ones who made it to shore. Vadim must have grown so weak after losing those three splinters and a piece of his heart that he couldn't think clearly and made poor judgments." Dragomir gestured toward the ashes, already blowing away. "Sergey has taken leadership."

"We knew it would happen." Gary glanced toward the house and the healing grounds that lay underneath. "I reinforced the safeguards, above, below and all around her. Sergey can't get to Elisabeta."

"He's trying."

"He'll keep trying. He's addicted to her." Gary sighed and shook his head. "You realize that Vadim had a splinter of Xavier in him. No way would the high mage allow himself to die by lightning. It's in Sergey now. Two of them. He'll have more memories and skills to draw on. He's going to make an even more relentless and powerful enemy than he did when he had Vadim with him."

Dragomir nodded. "We'll just have to make it too difficult for him to continue to snoop around looking for Elisabeta. The woman deserves peace. You don't think he can wake her and call her to him, do you?"

Gary shook his head, a slight smile curving his hard mouth. "I thought of that when I put her in the ground and commanded her to sleep. He can't break that spell, not even if the high mage was working fully with him. She will get her rest. But when she rises, Dragomir, she will have problems you cannot imagine."

Dragomir glanced toward the house where his lifemate waited at the window. She'd done what he'd asked of her and he knew it had cost her, but even with the brief battle they'd been prepared for, she'd stayed clear of his mind, allowing him to fight the vampire without having to divide his attention two ways. He was grateful to her and respected her strength even more.

I love you. He took a step toward the house.

Gary put a hand on his shoulder just as Emeline replied. *Allow Gary to heal you. You're a mess, and getting bloodstains off the floor is becoming difficult.*

The love in her voice always did him in. He gave her a small salute and went with the healer.

20

D on't cheat," Dragomir said.

"I have a blindfold on," Emeline protested laughing. "How could I possibly cheat?"

"You could look *through* the blindfold, but you'd better not," he cautioned, making his voice growl to show her he meant business. He led her down the path, making certain every uneven spot was smoothed out for her. "A surprise means you don't get to see until I'm ready for you to see."

"You give me surprises nearly every night," she pointed out. "You're spoiling me."

"You spoil me." He leaned close to her ear, his warm breath stealing into her, pushing a tendril of desire spiraling with heat through her veins. "Every time you get down on your knees in front of me and swallow me down, your eyes locked with mine, my world turns into pure paradise. Then you do that thing with your tongue, and I'm completely lost."

She couldn't help the soft laughter that spilled out or the

liquid heat between her legs responding to his seductive whisper. "I especially like to lick you clean. You always get that amazing look on your face." Deliberately, she was as wicked as possible.

He groaned. "Don't talk about that. We're out in the open and I'm fairly certain there are dozens of pairs of eyes on us right this minute. Otherwise, I'd lift you up, have you wrap your legs around me and I'd take you right here and now."

He made her crazy when he said things like that. Now she couldn't think about anything but wanting him. The hand on the small of her back guiding her slid down to her bottom, caressing her right through her skirt. It was thin, but not thin enough. She wanted to feel him skin to skin, not with clothes separating them.

"I'm giving you a different kind of surprise," he said. "So behave."

She laughed again and this time she stopped, turned to face him and slid her hand up his chest to find his face. Her fingertips traced the curve of his lip. She didn't want to miss his smile—and she knew he was smiling. She *loved* when he smiled. She did that. She gave him that. Nothing made her happier.

"You're the one who started this. You've got your hand on my butt." She leaned in to brush a kiss over that perfect bottom lip. "And you're rubbing."

"I'll be spanking in a minute," he murmured, but already his hands were in her hair and he was kissing her.

Kissing her. Like there was no tomorrow. His kiss consumed her. Devoured her. Fed her crazy addiction to him. He had so many kinds of kisses. Sweet. Tender. Gentle. Hard. Wet. Commanding. She loved every one of them. She especially loved these because they were the kind she got lost in immediately. If she was strictly honest, she got lost in all his

411

kisses, but she loved these the best. She gave herself to him when he kissed her like this.

Her body melted into his and she circled his neck with her arms, leaning into him, letting him take her weight. She was blindfolded, but it didn't matter, she knew he had her. He *always* had her. She was safe with him. Her heart was safe with him.

Dragomir lifted his head, rubbed his chin over the top of her head and then trailed his lips down the side of her face to the pulse beating in her neck. "I love the way you smell, Emeline. And the way you taste. Sometimes I can't get enough."

His tongue slid over her pulse and then his teeth scraped back and forth as if the temptation was too much to resist. Everything in her responded with a wicked invitation. She wanted that bite, so erotic. So beautiful. He'd taken her blood, given her his. They'd made love twice that evening, tangled together on the sheets in her bedroom, sharing the same skin. Worshiping each other.

"Keep your arms around my neck," he whispered. "Hold tight."

That was all the warning she got, and then she was cradled in his arms and they were moving through the air. She laughed and buried her face against his chest. She loved his surprises, although, truthfully, he was spoiling her far too much. She couldn't keep up with him. He was good at picking her wish list right out of her head and giving her item after item. She tried to do the same, but most of his wants were about making her happy or keeping her safe, or were very intensely sexual.

Every evening he talked to the baby, his hands around the little bump, his mouth pressed to her bare skin. He whispered that she was loved and that they couldn't wait to see her.

To hold her in their arms. Emeline loved him all the more for that. She never once found a single doubt in his mind. He wanted the baby and thought of her as his. With all the blood exchanges between them, she knew his blood ran in Carisma's veins.

I still have trouble thinking he's really gone. She knew Dragomir would know who she was talking about just by the trepidation in her voice. *He ruled my life for so many years. I was afraid for so long, I keep thinking he set us up, pretended to die just so we'd let our guards down.*

Carpathians don't let their guards down, Emeline. His brother killed him. I saw the ashes.

Could it be a trick, Dragomir? Sergey killed another vampire and Vadim is still alive?

There was a small silence. Her heart thundered in her ears. She bit down hard on her lip. She wanted reassurance, not silence, but he didn't lie to her. Not ever. It was a blessing and a curse. *Dragomir?*

I am thinking. Is it possible? I took his heart and then was attacked. I saw his brother close to him. Then Sergey wielded the lightning, and Vadim was incinerated. Did I see that it was Vadim? No. I assumed it was. What reason would Sergey have for keeping Vadim alive? There is no feeling between the brothers. They are vampires.

But Sergey could feel something. Elisabeta gave him emotions and control, didn't she? He has a plan. You said he was actually the one behind Vadim. Now she was terrified. She wanted to pull off the blindfold and look all around her. They were no longer in the safety of Tariq's compound. Dragomir had taken her a distance.

He set her feet on the ground, but prevented her from removing the blindfold. "Vadim is not going to ruin our lives. I have you, Emeline. If he's still alive, he'll reveal that in time.

We can weave safeguards that will not fail to protect our own. Gary found the spell they used to come through the water. They cannot do so again. We will be vigilant. We have a baby coming. We have Tariq and Maksim as neighbors, and the brotherhood is close."

"Neighbors?" She'd caught that. "What have you done?"

He pulled her into his body, her back to his front, his arms wrapped around her. "You can remove it now."

She forced her mind away from the thought of Vadim being alive and reached her hands up to untie the knot at the back of her head. Slowly she brought the cloth down. Straight in front of her was a large sprawling house. It was Mediterranean-style, U-shaped so that there was a large courtyard surrounded on three sides by the house. Trees were abundant as the terrain rolled upward toward the hills.

"What do you think?"

"I think you take my breath away," she admitted. "Just when I think you can't get any better, you do. This is perfect. *Perfect*. When I dreamt of a house, this is what I dreamt. One story, but large, so I could have a big family but still have privacy with my man. I can't wait to see inside."

"We have a good bit of forest. I need that, Emeline. I need wild country. Tariq fits here. He dresses the part and looks like a wolf in sheep's clothing, but I can't be that man. I need freedom. My brothers need the wild as well."

"Will they stay?" She held her breath, waiting for the answer. She wanted them to stay. It was selfish. Each of them needed to go out into the world and find their lifemate, but they added protection. She had the baby to think about.

"For a while. Until they know we're safe. With Elisabeta here, they'll make certain Sergey can't get to her."

"He'll always try, won't he?" She shuddered. "Just the way Vadim won't leave me alone."

"The underwater pathways have been found and are closed to them," Dragomir assured. "Vadim has always been the brother that wanted to work with science and technology. He needed you for his experiments, but now that his cities have been taken from him, he will have to rebuild. You are not as important."

"You're talking as if you believe he's still alive."

He shrugged. "I have no way of knowing. I had thought him dead, but when I touched those ashes, I didn't feel anything. A master vampire would have left behind something of himself, some taint I would have felt as the wind took him. On some level, I registered that but didn't let the significance sink in. Like you, I wanted him dead. The loss of three splinters and that small piece of his heart diminished his power drastically. I don't know how long, if ever, it would take to recover from something like that. In any case, this will be our home, if you approve. It borders Tariq's property, and we'd just expand the safeguards. That allows the children and Genevieve to safely go from Tariq's to Maksim's and now this property. They could fly their dragons. So could you."

She tilted her head back to look up at him, suddenly suspicious. "My dragon?"

His smile was back, that beautiful curve to his lower lip. "You have to have your own dragon, *sívamet*."

Excitement sent adrenaline rushing through her veins. "Where?" she demanded.

He caught her hand and tugged, leading her around the side of the house to the large courtyard. There was an entertainment patio, and a play yard for children. Sitting to one side of the play yard were two dragons made of stone. One was large and golden with emerald eyes.

Her hand went to her throat and she stopped moving, went completely still, her lungs fighting for air. He had done this.

For her. Given her a golden dragon because she'd said she wanted to fly a dragon. *God*. Dragomir. Her man. "I don't think you're real," she whispered. She turned her head to look at him. "I don't. You can't be real, honey. Who does this?"

His answer was not in words. He bunched her hair in his fist, yanked her head back so that there was a bite of pain in her scalp and kissed her. Hard. His tongue warred with hers. His teeth bit down on her lower lip, tugged, and then his tongue soothed that bite. "I'm real, Emeline. Very real."

She laughed when she really needed to cry, joyful tears burning behind her eyes. Her beautiful man. He caught her hand and tugged until both were practically running toward the golden dragon. When they got close, she saw the second one. This was purple, a soft lavender, and was small. She turned and flung her arms around his neck. "You made her one, too."

"Yes." His mouth was raining kisses all over her upturned face.

There was heat. Fire. Hot molasses in her veins. She nipped his chin and kissed her way down his chest, her hands at the waistband of his trousers.

"Where is your dragon?" She had his trousers open and his cock out. She let out her breath as she cupped his heavy sac. "You're so beautiful."

"I *am* the dragon, Emeline," he said and put his hand on her shoulders, exerting pressure so that she knelt in the thick grass. He waved his hand, and she didn't have a stitch on. "I prefer you naked when your mouth is on my cock. I love watching you. Looking at your body. Seeing your mouth stretched over me and your eyes on mine. That gives me more pleasure than you can imagine."

She knew it did. She was in his mind when she licked up his shaft and took him deep. She was in his mind when his body moved in hers. Fast. Slow. It didn't matter. It all gave him pleasure.

Whether Vadim was alive didn't matter. Not then. Not when she was with her man, taking the control, watching the helpless passion carve lines of pure sensuality into his scarred face. Not when desire darkened the gold of his eyes to liquid and his hand gripped her hair and his hips moved so carefully into her. Dragomir was hers. She had everything with him. Everything. It wasn't the home he'd given her, or the dragon, or even the acceptance of the Carpathian people that he'd asked for her and their child. It was Dragomir. She had him, and she knew that would always be enough.

APPENDIX 1

Carpathian Healing Chants

To rightly understand Carpathian healing chants, background is required in several areas:

1. The Carpathian view on healing
2. The Lesser Healing Chant of the Carpathians
3. The Great Healing Chant of the Carpathians
4. Carpathian musical aesthetics
5. Lullaby
6. Song to Heal the Earth
7. Carpathian chanting technique

1. THE CARPATHIAN VIEW ON HEALING

The Carpathians are a nomadic people whose geographic origins can be traced at least as far as the Southern Ural Mountains (near the steppes of modern-day Kazakhstan), on the border between Europe and Asia. (For this reason, modern-day linguists call their language "proto-Uralic," without knowing that this is the language of the Carpathians.) Unlike most nomadic peoples, the Carpathians did not wander due to the need to find new grazing lands as the seasons and climate shifted, or to search for better trade. Instead, the Carpathians' movements were driven by a great purpose: to find a land that would have the right earth, a soil with the kind of richness that would greatly enhance their rejuvenative powers.

Over the centuries, they migrated westward (some six thousand years ago), until they at last found their perfect homeland—their *susu*—in the Carpathian Mountains, whose long arc cradled the lush plains of the kingdom of Hungary. (The kingdom of Hungary flourished for over a millennium—making Hungarian the dominant language of the Carpathian Basin—until the kingdom's lands were split among several countries after World War I: Austria, Czechoslovakia, Romania, Yugoslavia and modern Hungary.)

Other peoples from the Southern Urals (who shared the Carpathian language, but were not Carpathians) migrated in different directions. Some ended up in Finland, which explains why the modern Hungarian and Finnish languages are among the contemporary descendents of the ancient Carpathian language. Even though they are tied forever to their chosen Carpathian homeland, the Carpathians continue to wander as they search the world for the answers that will enable them to bear and raise their offspring without difficulty.

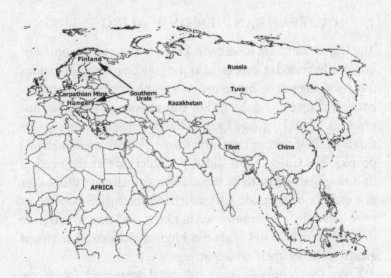

Because of their geographic origins, the Carpathian views on healing share much with the larger Eurasian shamanistic tradition. Probably the closest modern representative of that tradition is based in Tuva (and is referred to as "Tuvinian Shamanism")—see the map on the previous page.

The Eurasian shamanistic tradition—from the Carpathians to the Siberian shamans—held that illness originated in the human soul, and only later manifested as various physical conditions. Therefore, shamanistic healing, while not neglecting the body, focused on the soul and its healing. The most profound illnesses were understood to be caused by "soul departure," where all or some part of the sick person's soul has wandered away from the body (into the nether realms), or has been captured or possessed by an evil spirit, or both.

The Carpathians belong to this greater Eurasian shamanistic tradition and share its viewpoints. While the Carpathians themselves did not succumb to illness, Carpathian healers understood that the most profound wounds were also accompanied by a similar "soul departure."

Upon reaching the diagnosis of "soul departure," the healer-shaman is then required to make a spiritual journey into the netherworlds to recover the soul. The shaman may have to overcome tremendous challenges along the way, particularly fighting the demon or vampire who has possessed his friend's soul.

"Soul departure" doesn't require a person to be unconscious (although that certainly can be the case as well). It was understood that a person could still appear to be conscious, even talk and interact with others, and yet be missing a part of their soul. The experienced healer or shaman would instantly see the problem nonetheless, in subtle signs that others might miss: the person's attention wandering every now and then, a lessening in their enthusiasm about life, chronic depression, a diminishment in the brightness of their "aura" and the like.

2. THE LESSER HEALING CHANT OF THE CARPATHIANS

Kepä Sarna Pus (**The Lesser Healing Chant**) is used for wounds that are merely physical in nature. The Carpathian healer leaves his body and enters the wounded Carpathian's body to heal great mortal wounds from the inside out using pure energy. He proclaims, "I offer freely my life for your life," as he gives his blood to the injured Carpathian. Because the Carpathians are of the earth and bound to the soil, they are healed by the soil of their homeland. Their saliva is also often used for its rejuvenative powers.

It is also very common for the Carpathian chants (both the Lesser and the Great) to be accompanied by the use of healing herbs, aromas from Carpathian candles and crystals. The crystals (when combined with the Carpathians' empathic, psychic connection to the entire universe) are used to gather positive energy from their surroundings, which then is used to accelerate the healing. Caves are sometimes used as the setting for the healing.

The Lesser Healing Chant was used by Vikirnoff Von Shrieder and Colby Jansen to heal Rafael De La Cruz, whose heart had been ripped out by a vampire as described in *Dark Secret*.

Kepä Sarna Pus (The Lesser Healing Chant)

The same chant is used for all physical wounds. "Sívadaba" ("into your heart") would be changed to refer to whatever part of the body is wounded.

Ku´nasz, nélkül sívdobbanás, nélkül fesztelen löyly.
You lie as if asleep, without beat of heart, without airy breath.

Ot élidamet andam szabadon élidadért.
I offer freely my life for your life.

O jelä sielam j~orem ot ainamet és soŋe ot élidadet.
My spirit of light forgets my body and enters your body.

O jelä sielam pukta kinn minden szelemeket belső.
My spirit of light sends all the dark spirits within fleeing without.

Paj´nak o susu hanyet és o nyelv nyálamet sívadaba.
I press the earth of our homeland and the spit of my tongue into your heart.

Vii, o verim soŋe o verid andam.
At last, I give you my blood for your blood.
To hear this chant, visit: http://www.christinefeehan.com/members/.

3. THE GREAT HEALING CHANT OF THE CARPATHIANS

The most well-known—and most dramatic—of the Carpathian healing chants is *En Sarna Pus* (The Great Healing Chant). This chant is reserved for recovering the wounded or unconscious Carpathian's soul.

Typically a group of men would form a circle around the sick Carpathian (to "encircle him with our care and compassion") and begin the chant. The shaman or healer or leader is the prime actor in this healing ceremony. It is he who will actually make the spiritual journey into the netherworld, aided by his clanspeople. Their purpose is to ecstatically dance, sing, drum and chant, all the while visualizing (through the words of the chant) the journey itself—every step of it, over and over again—to the point where the shaman, in trance, leaves his body, and makes that very journey. (Indeed, the word *ecstasy* is from the Latin *ex statis*, which literally means "out of the body.")

One advantage that the Carpathian healer has over many other shamans is his telepathic link to his lost brother. Most shamans must wander in the dark of the nether realms in search of their lost brother. But the Carpathian healer directly "hears" in his mind the voice of his lost brother calling to him, and can thus "zero in on" his soul like a homing beacon. For this reason, Carpathian healing tends to have a higher success rate than most other traditions of this sort.

Something of the geography of the "other world" is useful for us to examine, in order to fully understand the words of the Great Carpathian Healing Chant. A reference is made to the "Great Tree" (in Carpathian: *En Puwe*). Many ancient traditions, including the Carpathian tradition, understood the worlds—the heaven worlds, our world and the nether realms—to be "hung" upon a great pole, or axis, or tree. Here on earth, we are positioned halfway up this tree, on one of its branches. Hence many ancient texts referred to the material world as "middle earth": midway between heaven and hell. Climbing the tree would lead one to the heaven worlds. Descending the tree to its roots would lead to the nether realms. The shaman was necessarily a master of movement up and down the Great Tree, sometimes moving unaided, and sometimes assisted by (or even mounted upon the back of) an animal spirit guide. In various traditions, this Great Tree was known variously as the *axis mundi* (the "axis of the worlds"), Ygddrasil (in Norse mythology), Mount Meru (the sacred world mountain of Tibetan tradition), etc. The Christian cosmos, with its heaven, purgatory/earth and hell, is also worth comparing. It is even given a similar topography in Dante's *Divine Comedy*: Dante is led on a journey first to hell, at the center of the earth; then upward to Mount Purgatory, which sits on the earth's surface directly opposite Jerusalem; then farther upward first to Eden, the earthly paradise, at the summit of Mount Purgatory; and then upward at last to Heaven.

In the shamanistic tradition, it was understood that the small always reflects the large; the personal always reflects the cosmic. A movement in the greater dimensions of the cosmos also coincides with an internal movement. For example, the *axis mundi* of the cosmos corresponds with the spinal column of the individual. Journeys up and down the *axis mundi* often coincided with the movements of natural and spiritual energies (sometimes called *kundalini* or *shakti*) in the spinal column of the shaman or mystic.

En Sarna Pus (The Great Healing Chant)
In this chant, ekä ("brother") would be replaced by "sister," "father," "mother," depending on the person to be healed.

Ot ekäm ainajanak hany, jama.
My brother's body is a lump of earth, close to death.

Me, ot ekäm kuntajanak, pirädak ekäm, gond és irgalom türe.
We, the clan of my brother, encircle him with our care and compassion.

O pus wäkenkek, ot oma ´sarnank, és ot pus fünk, álnak ekäm ainajanak, pitänak ekäm ainajanak elävä.
Our healing energies, ancient words of magic and healing herbs bless my brother's body, keep it alive.

427

Ot ekäm sielanak pälä. Ot ombo'ce päläja juta alatt o jüti, kinta, és szelemek lamtijaknak.
But my brother's soul is only half. His other half wanders in the netherworld.

Ot en mekem ŋamaŋ: kulkedak otti ot ekäm ombo'ce päläjanak.
My great deed is this: I travel to find my brother's other half.

Rekatüre, saradak, tappadak, odam, kaŋa o numa waram, és avaa owe o lewl mahoz.
We dance, we chant, we dream ecstatically, to call my spirit bird, and to open the door to the other world.

Ntak o numa waram, és mozdulak; jomadak.
I mount my spirit bird and we begin to move; we are under way.

Piwtädak ot En Puwe tyvinak, e'cidak alatt o jüti, kinta, és szelemek lamtijaknak.
Following the trunk of the Great Tree, we fall into the netherworld.

Fázak, fázak nó o 'saro.
It is cold, very cold.

Juttadak ot ekäm o akarataban, o sívaban és o sielaban.
My brother and I are linked in mind, heart and soul.

Ot ekäm sielanak kaŋa engem.
My brother's soul calls to me.

Kuledak és piwtädak ot ekäm.
I hear and follow his track.

Sayedak és tuledak ot ekäm kulyanak.
Encounter I the demon who is devouring my brother's soul.

Nenäm ´coro, o kuly torodak.
In anger, I fight the demon.

O kuly pél engem.
He is afraid of me.

Lejkkadak o kaŋka salamaval.
I strike his throat with a lightning bolt.

Molodak ot ainaja komakamal.
I break his body with my bare hands.

Toja és molanâ.
He is bent over, and falls apart.

Hän ´caδa.
He runs away.

Manedak ot ekäm sielanak.
I rescue my brother's soul.

Alədak ot ekam sielanak o komamban.
I lift my brother's soul in the hollow of my hand.

Alədam ot ekam numa waramra.
I lift him onto my spirit bird.

Piwtädak ot En Puwe tyvijanak és sayedak jälleen ot elävä ainak majaknak.
Following up the Great Tree, we return to the land of the living.

Ot ekäm elä jälleen.
My brother lives again.

Ot ekäm we´n´ca jälleen.
He is complete again.

To hear this chant, visit: http://www.christinefeehan.com/members/.

4. CARPATHIAN MUSICAL AESTHETICS

In the sung Carpathian pieces (such as the "Lullaby" and the "Song to Heal the Earth"), you'll hear elements that are shared by many of the musical traditions in the Uralic geographical region, some of which still exist—from Eastern European (Bulgarian, Romanian, Hungarian, Croatian, etc.) to Romany ("gypsy"). These elements include:

- the rapid alternation between major and minor modalities, including a sudden switch (called a "Picardy third") from minor to major to end a piece or section (as at the end of the "Lullaby")
- the use of close (tight) harmonies
- the use of *ritardi* (slowing down the piece) and *crescendi* (swelling in volume) for brief periods
- the use of *glissandi* (slides) in the singing tradition
- the use of trills in the singing tradition (as in the final invocation of the "Song to Heal the Earth")—similar to Celtic, a singing tradition more familiar to many of us
- the use of parallel fifths (as in the final invocation of the "Song to Heal the Earth")
- controlled use of dissonance

- "call and response" chanting (typical of many of the world's chanting traditions)
- extending the length of a musical line (by adding a couple of bars) to heighten dramatic effect
- and many more

"Lullaby" and "Song to Heal the Earth" illustrate two rather different forms of Carpathian music (a quiet, intimate piece and an energetic ensemble piece)—but whatever the form, Carpathian music is full of feeling.

5. LULLABY

This song is sung by a woman while a child is still in the womb or when the threat of a miscarriage is apparent. The baby can hear the song while inside the mother, and the mother can connect with the child telepathically as well. The lullaby is meant to reassure the child, to encourage the baby to hold on, to stay—to reassure the child that he or she will be protected by love even from inside until birth. The last line literally means that the mother's love will protect her child until the child is born ("rise").

Musically, the Carpathian "Lullaby" is in three-quarter time ("waltz time"), as are a significant portion of the world's various traditional lullabies (perhaps the most famous of which is "Brahms' Lullaby"). The arrangement for solo voice is the original context: a mother singing to her child, unaccompanied. The arrangement for chorus and violin ensemble illustrates how musical even the simplest Carpathian pieces often are, and how easily they lend themselves to contemporary instrumental or orchestral arrangements. (A wide range of contemporary composers, including Dvořák and Smetana, have taken advantage of a similar discovery, working other traditional Eastern European music into their symphonic poems.)

Odam-Sarna Kondak (Lullaby)

Tumtesz o wäke ku pitasz belső.
Feel the strength you hold inside.

Hiszasz sívadet. Én olenam gæidnod.
Trust your heart. I'll be your guide.

Sas csecsemõm; kuñasz.
Hush, my baby; close your eyes.

Rauho joŋe ted.
Peace will come to you.

Tumtesz o sívdobbanás ku olen lamt3ad belső.
Feel the rhythm deep inside.

Gond-kumpadek ku kim te.
Waves of love that cover you.

Pesänak te, asti o jüti, kidüsz.
Protect, until the night you rise.

To hear this song, visit: http://www.christinefeehan.com/members/.

6. SONG TO HEAL THE EARTH

This is the earth-healing song that is used by the Carpathian women to heal soil filled with various toxins. The women take a position on four sides and call to the universe to draw on the healing energy with love and respect. The soil of the earth is their resting place, the place where they rejuvenate, and they must make it safe not only for themselves but for their unborn children as well as their men and living children. This is a beautiful ritual performed by the women together, raising their voices in harmony and calling on the earth's minerals and healing properties to come forth and help them save their children. They literally dance and sing to heal the earth in a ceremony as old as their species. The dance and notes of the song are adjusted according to the toxins felt through the healer's bare feet. The feet are placed in a certain pattern and the hands gracefully weave a healing spell while the dance is performed. They must be especially careful when the soil is prepared for babies. This is a ceremony of love and healing. Musically, the ritual is divided into several sections:

- **First verse**: A "call and response" section, where the chant leader sings the "call" solo, and then some or all of the women sing the "response" in the close harmony style typical of the Carpathian musical tradition. The repeated response—*Ai Emä Maye*—is an invocation of the source of power for the healing ritual: "Oh, Mother Nature."
- **First chorus**: This section is filled with clapping, dancing, ancient horns and other means used to invoke and heighten the energies upon which the ritual is drawing.
- **Second verse**
- **Second chorus**
- **Closing invocation:** In this closing part, two song leaders, in close harmony, take all the energy gathered by the earlier portions of the song/ritual and focus it entirely on the healing purpose.

What you will be listening to are brief tastes of what would typically be a significantly longer ritual, in which the verse and chorus parts are developed and repeated many times, to be closed by a single rendition of the final invocation.

Sarna Pusm O Mayet (Song to Heal the Earth)

First verse

Ai Emä Maye,
Oh, Mother Nature,

Me sivadbin lañaak.
We are your beloved daughters.

Me tappadak, me pusmak o mayet.
We dance to heal the earth.

Me sarnadak, me pusmak o hanyet.
We sing to heal the earth.

Sielanket jutta tedet it,
We join with you now,

Sivank és akaratank és sielank juttanak.
Our hearts and minds and spirits become one.

Second verse

Ai, Emä maye,
Oh, Mother Nature,

Me sívadbin lańaak.
We are your beloved daughters.

Me andak arwadet emänked és me kaŋank o
We pay homage to our mother and call upon the

Põhi és Lõuna, Ida és Lääs.
North and South, East and West.

Pide és aldyn és myös belső.
Above and below and within as well.

Gondank o maɣenak pusm hän ku olen jama.
Our love of the land heals that which is in need.

Juttanak teval it,
We join with you now,

Maɣe maɣeval.
Earth to earth.

O pirä elidak weńća.
The circle of life is complete.

To hear this chant, visit: http://www.christinefeehan
.com/members/.

7. CARPATHIAN CHANTING TECHNIQUE

As with their healing techniques, the actual "chanting technique"
of the Carpathians has much in common with the other shamanistic traditions of the Central Asian steppes. The primary mode of
chanting was throat chanting using overtones. Modern examples

of this manner of singing can still be found in the Mongolian, Tuvan and Tibetan traditions. You can find an audio example of the Gyuto Tibetan Buddhist monks engaged in throat chanting at: http://www.christinefeehan.com/carpathian_chanting/.

As with Tuva, note on the map the geographical proximity of Tibet to Kazakhstan and the Southern Urals.

The beginning part of the Tibetan chant emphasizes synchronizing all the voices around a single tone, aimed at healing a particular "chakra" of the body. This is fairly typical of the Gyuto throat-chanting tradition, but it is not a significant part of the Carpathian tradition. Nonetheless, it serves as an interesting contrast.

The part of the Gyuto chanting example that is most similar to the Carpathian style of chanting is the midsection, where the men are chanting the words together with great force. The purpose here is not to generate a "healing tone" that will affect a particular "chakra," but rather to generate as much power as possible for initiating the "out of body" travel, and for fighting the demonic forces that the healer/traveler must face and overcome.

The songs of the Carpathian women (illustrated by their "Lullaby" and their "Song to Heal the Earth") are part of the same ancient musical and healing tradition as the Lesser and Great Healing Chants of the warrior males. You can hear some of the same instruments in both the male warriors' healing chants and the women's "Song to Heal the Earth." Also, they share the common purpose of generating and directing power. However, the women's songs are distinctively feminine in character. One immediately noticeable difference is that, while the men speak their words in the manner of a chant, the women sing songs with melodies and harmonies, softening the overall performance. A feminine, nurturing quality is especially evident in the "Lullaby."

APPENDIX 2

The Carpathian Language

Like all human languages, the language of the Carpathians contains the richness and nuance that can only come from a long history of use. At best we can only touch on some of the main features of the language in this brief appendix:

1. The history of the Carpathian language
2. Carpathian grammar and other characteristics of the language
3. Examples of the Carpathian language (including the Ritual Words and the Warriors' Chant)
4. A much-abridged Carpathian dictionary

1. THE HISTORY OF THE CARPATHIAN LANGUAGE

The Carpathian language of today is essentially identical to the Carpathian language of thousands of years ago. A "dead" language like the Latin of two thousand years ago has evolved into a significantly different modern language (Italian) because of countless generations of speakers and great historical fluctuations. In contrast, many of the speakers of Carpathian from thousands of years ago are still alive. Their presence—coupled with the deliberate isolation of the Carpathians from the other major forces of change in the world—has acted (and continues to act) as a stabilizing force that has preserved the integrity of the language over the centuries. Carpathian culture has also acted as a stabilizing force. For instance, the Ritual Words, the various healing chants (see Appendix 1) and other cultural artifacts have been passed down through the centuries with great fidelity.

One small exception should be noted: the splintering of the Carpathians into separate geographic regions has led to some minor dialectization. However, the telepathic link among all Carpathians (as well as each Carpathian's regular return to his or her homeland) has ensured that the differences among dialects are relatively superficial (e.g., small numbers of new words, minor differences in pronunciation, etc.), since the deeper, internal language of mind-forms has remained the same because of continuous use across space and time.

The Carpathian language was (and still is) the proto-language for the Uralic (or Finno-Ugric) family of languages. Today, the Uralic languages are spoken in northern, eastern and central Europe and in Siberia. More than twenty-three million people in the world speak languages that can trace their ancestry to Carpathian. Magyar or Hungarian (about fourteen million speakers), Finnish (about five million speakers) and Estonian (about one million speakers) are the three major contemporary descendents of this proto-language. The only factor that unites the more than twenty languages in the Uralic family is that their ancestry can be traced back to a common proto-language—Carpathian—that split (starting some six thousand years ago) into the various languages in the Uralic family. In the same way, European languages such as English and French belong to the better-known Indo-European family and also evolved from a common proto-language ancestor (a different one from Carpathian).

The following table provides a sense of some of the similarities in the language family.

Note: The Finnic/Carpathian "k" shows up often as Hungarian "h." Similarly, the Finnic/Carpathian "p" often corresponds to the Hungarian "f."

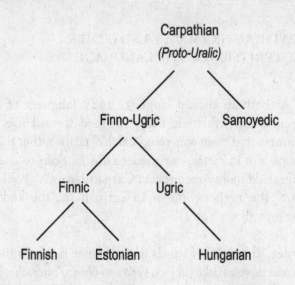

Carpathian
(Proto-Uralic)

- Finno-Ugric
  - Finnic
    - Finnish
    - Estonian
  - Ugric
    - Hungarian
- Samoyedic

Carpathian (proto-Uralic)	Finnish (Suomi)	Hungarian (Magyar)
elä—live	*elä*—live	*él*—live
elid—life	*elinikä*—life	*élet*—life
pesä—nest	*pesä*—nest	*fészek*—nest
kola—die	*kuole*—die	*hal*—die
pälä—half, side	*pieltä*—tilt, tip to the side	*fél, fele*—fellow human, friend (half; one side of two) *feleség*—wife
and—give	*anta, antaa*—give	*ad*—give
koje—husband, man	*koira*—dog, the male (of animals)	*here*—drone, testicle
wäke—power	*väki*—folks, people, men; force	*val/-vel*—with (instrumental suffix)
	väkevä—powerful, strong	*vele*—with him/her/it
wete—water	*vesi*—water	*viz*—water

441

2. CARPATHIAN GRAMMAR AND OTHER CHARACTERISTICS OF THE LANGUAGE

Idioms. As both an ancient language and a language of an earth people, Carpathian is more inclined toward use of idioms constructed from concrete, "earthy" terms rather than abstractions. For instance, our modern abstraction "to cherish" is expressed more concretely in Carpathian as "to hold in one's heart"; the "netherworld" is, in Carpathian, "the land of night, fog and ghosts"; etc.

Word order. The order of words in a sentence is determined not by syntactic roles (like subject, verb and object) but rather by pragmatic, discourse-driven factors. Examples: *"Tied vagyok."* ("Yours am I."); *"Sívamet andam."* ("My heart I give you.")

Agglutination. The Carpathian language is agglutinative; that is, longer words are constructed from smaller components. An agglutinating language uses suffixes or prefixes whose meanings are generally unique, and which are concatenated one after another without overlap. In Carpathian, words typically consist of a stem that is followed by one or more suffixes. For example, *"sívambam"* derives from the stem *"sív"* ("heart"), followed by *"am"* ("my," making it "my heart"), followed by *"bam"* ("in," making it "in my heart"). As you might imagine, agglutination in Carpathian can sometimes produce very long words, or words that are very difficult to pronounce. Vowels often get inserted between suffixes to prevent too many consonants from appearing in a row (which can make a word unpronounceable).

Noun cases. Like all languages, Carpathian has many noun cases; the same noun will be "spelled" differently depending on its role in a sentence. The noun cases include: nominative (when the noun is the subject of the sentence), accusative (when the noun is a direct object of the verb), dative (indirect object), genitive (or possessive), instrumental, final, suppressive, inessive, elative, terminative and delative.

We will use the possessive (or genitive) case as an example to illustrate how all noun cases in Carpathian involve adding standard suffixes to the noun stems. Thus expressing possession in Carpathian—"my lifemate," "your lifemate," "his lifemate," "her lifemate," etc.—involves adding a particular suffix (such as "-*am*") to the noun stem (*"päläfertiil"*) to produce the possessive (*"päläfertiilam"*—"my lifemate"). Which suffix to use depends upon which person ("my," "your," "his," etc.) and whether the noun ends in a consonant or a vowel. The table below shows the suffixes for singular nouns only (not plural), and also shows the similarity to the suffixes used in contemporary Hungarian. (Hungarian is actually a little more complex, in that it also requires "vowel rhyming": which suffix to use also depends on the last vowel in the noun; hence the multiple choices in the cells below, where Carpathian only has a single choice.)

person	Carpathian (proto-Uralic)		Contemporary Hungarian	
	noun ends in vowel	noun ends in consonant	noun ends in vowel	noun ends in consonant
1st singular (my)	-m	-am	-m	-om, -em, -öm
2nd singular (your)	-d	-ad	-d	-od, -ed, -öd

	Carpathian (proto-Uralic)		Contemporary Hungarian	
person	noun ends in vowel	noun ends in consonant	noun ends in vowel	noun ends in consonant
3rd singular (his, her, its)	-ja	-a	-ja/-je	-a, -e
1st plural (our)	-nk	-ank	-nk	-unk, -ünk
2nd plural (your)	-tak	-atak	-tok, -tek, -tök	-otok, -etek, -ötök
3rd plural (their)	-jak	-ak	-juk, -jük	-uk, -ük

Note: As mentioned earlier, vowels often get inserted between the word and its suffix so as to prevent too many consonants from appearing in a row (which would produce unpronounceable words). For example, in the table on the previous page, all nouns that end in a consonant are followed by suffixes beginning with "a."

Verb conjugation. Like its modern descendents (such as Finnish and Hungarian), Carpathian has many verb tenses, far too many to describe here. We will just focus on the conjugation of the present tense. Again, we will place contemporary Hungarian side by side with Carpathian, because of the marked similarity between the two.

As with the possessive case for nouns, the conjugation of verbs is done by adding a suffix onto the verb stem:

Person	Carpathian (proto-Uralic)	Contemporary Hungarian
1st (I give)	-am (andam), -ak	-ok, -ek, -ök
2nd singular (you give)	-sz (andsz)	-sz
3rd singular (he/she/it gives)	— (and)	—
1st plural (we give)	-ak (andak)	-unk, -ünk
2nd plural (you give)	-tak (andtak)	-tok, -tek, -tök
3rd plural (they give)	-nak (andnak)	-nak, -nek

As with all languages, there are many "irregular verbs" in Carpathian that don't exactly fit this pattern. But the above table is still a useful guide for most verbs.

3. EXAMPLES OF THE CARPATHIAN LANGUAGE

Here are some brief examples of conversational Carpathian, used in the Dark books. We include the literal translation in square brackets. It is interestingly different from the most appropriate English translation.

Susu.
I am home.
["home/birthplace." "I am" is understood, as is often the case in Carpathian.]

Möért?
What for?

csitri
little one
["little slip of a thing," "little slip of a girl"]

ainaak enyém
forever mine

ainaak sívamet jutta
forever mine (another form)
["forever to-my-heart connected/fixed"]

sívamet
my love
["of-my-heart," "to-my-heart"]

Tet vigyázam.
I love you.
["you-love-I"]

Sarna Rituaali (**The Ritual Words**) is a longer example, and an example of chanted rather than conversational Carpathian. Note the recurring use of *"andam"* ("I give"), to give the chant musicality and force through repetition.

Sarna Rituaali (**The Ritual Words**)

Te avio päläfertiilam.
You are my lifemate.

Éntölam kuulua, avio päläfertiilam.
I claim you as my lifemate.

Ted kuuluak, kacad, kojed.
I belong to you.

Élidamet andam.
I offer my life for you.

Pesämet andam.
I give you my protection.

Uskolfertiilamet andam.
I give you my allegiance.

Sívamet andam.
I give you my heart.

Sielamet andam.
I give you my soul.

Ainamet andam.
I give you my body.

Sívamet kuuluak kaik että a ted.
I take into my keeping the same that is yours.

Ainaak olenszal sívambin.
Your life will be cherished by me for all my time.

Te élidet ainaak pide minan.
Your life will be placed above my own for all time.

Te avio päläfertiilam.
You are my lifemate.

447

Ainaak sívamet jutta oleny.
You are bound to me for all eternity.

Ainaak terád vigyázak.
You are always in my care.

To hear these words pronounced (and for more about Carpathian pronunciation altogether), please visit: http://www.christinefeehan.com/members/.

Sarna Kontakawk (The Warriors' Chant) is another longer example of the Carpathian language. The warriors' council takes place deep beneath the earth in a chamber of crystals with magma far below it, so the steam is natural and the wisdom of their ancestors is clear and focused. This is a sacred place where they bloodswear to their prince and people and affirm their code of honor as warriors and brothers. It is also where battle strategies are born and all dissension is discussed as well as any concerns the warriors have that they wish to bring to the council and open for discussion.

Sarna Kontakawk (The Warriors' Chant)

Veri isäakank—veri ekäakank.
Blood of our fathers—blood of our brothers.

Veri olen elid.
Blood is life.

Andak veri-elidet Karpatiiakank, és wäke-sarna ku meke arwa-arvo, irgalom, hän ku agba, és wäke kutni, ku manaak verival.
We offer that life to our people with a bloodsworn vow of honor, mercy, integrity and endurance.

448

Verink sokta; verink kaŋa terád.
Our blood mingles and calls to you.

Akasz énak ku kaŋa és juttasz kuntatak it.
Heed our summons and join with us now.

To hear these words pronounced (and for more about Carpathian pronunciation altogether), please visit: http:// www.christinefeehan.com/members/.

See **Appendix 1** for Carpathian healing chants, including the *Kepä Sarna Pus* (The Lesser Healing Chant), the *En Sarna Pus* (The Great Healing Chant), the *Odam-Sarna Kondak* (Lullaby) and the *Sarna Pusm O Maγet* (Song to Heal the Earth).

4. A MUCH-ABRIDGED CARPATHIAN DICTIONARY

This very-much-abridged Carpathian dictionary contains most of the Carpathian words used in the Dark books. Of course, a full Carpathian dictionary would be as large as the usual dictionary for an entire language (typically more than a hundred thousand words).

Note: The Carpathian nouns and verbs below are word **stems.** They generally do not appear in their isolated "stem" form, as below. Instead, they usually appear with suffixes (e.g., *andam—I give*, rather than just the root, *and*).

a—verb negation (*prefix*); not (*adverb*).
aćke—pace, step.
aćke éntölem it—take another step toward me.
agba—to be seemly; to be proper (*verb*). True; seemly; proper (*adj.*)
ai—oh.

aina—body (*noun*).

ainaak—always; forever.

o ainaak jelä peje emnimet ŋamaŋ—sun scorch that woman
   forever (*Carpathian swear words*).

ainaakä—never.

ainaakfél—old friend.

ak—suffix added after a noun ending in a consonant to make
   it plural.

aka—to give heed; to hearken; to listen.

aka-arvo—respect (*noun*).

akarat—mind; will (*noun*).

ál—to bless; to attach to.

alatt—through.

aldyn—under; underneath.

alə—to lift; to raise.

alte—to bless; to curse.

amaŋ—this; this one here; that; that one there.

and—to give.

**and sielet, arwa-arvomet, és jelämet, kuulua huvémet ku
   feaj és ködet ainaak**—to trade soul, honor and salvation
   for momentary pleasure and endless damnation.

andasz éntölem irgalomet!—have mercy!

arvo—value; price (*noun*).

arwa—praise (*noun*).

arwa-arvod—honor (*noun*).

arwa-arvod mäne me ködak—may your honor hold back the
   dark (*greeting*).

arwa-arvo olen gæidnod, ekäm—honor guide you, my
   brother (*greeting*).

arwa-arvo olen isäntä, ekäm—honor keep you, my brother
   (*greeting*).

arwa-arvo pile sívadet—may honor light your heart
   (*greeting*).

aš—no (*exclamation*).

ašša—no (before a noun); not (with a verb that is not in the imperative); not (with an adjective).

aššatotello—disobedient.

asti—until.

avaa—to open.

avio—wedded.

avio päläfertiil—lifemate.

avoi—uncover; show; reveal.

baszú—revenge; vengeance.

belső—within; inside.

bur—good; well.

bur tule ekämet kuntamak—well met brother-kin (*greeting*).

ćaða—to flee; to run; to escape.

čač3—to be born; to grow.

ćoro—to flow; to run like rain.

csecsemõ—baby (*noun*).

csitri—little one (*female*).

diutal—triumph; victory.

džinõt—brief; short.

eći—to fall.

ej—not (*adverb, suffix*); *nej* when preceding syllable ends in a vowel.

ek—suffix added after a noun ending in a consonant to make it plural.

ekä—brother.

ekäm—my brother.

elä—to live.

eläsz arwa-arvoval—may you live with honor; live nobly (*greeting*).

eläsz jeläbam ainaak—long may you live in the light (*greeting*).

elävä—alive.

elävä ainak majaknak—land of the living.

elid—life.

emä—mother (*noun*).

Emä Maγe—Mother Nature.

emäen—grandmother.

embɛ—if; when.

embɛ karmasz—please.

emni—wife; woman.

emni hän ku köd alte—cursed woman.

emni kuŋenak ku aššatotello—disobedient lunatic.

emnim—my wife; my woman.

én—I.

en—great; many; big.

en hän ku pesä—the protector (literally: the great protector).

en Karpatii—the prince (literally: the great Carpathian).

enä—most.

enkojra—wolf.

én jutta félet és ekämet—I greet a friend and brother
     (*greeting*).

én maγenak—I am of the earth.

én oma maγeka—I am as old as time (literally: as old as
     the earth).

En Puwe—The Great Tree. Related to the legends of
     Ygddrasil, the axis mundi, Mount Meru, heaven and
     hell, etc.

engem—of me.

és—and.

év—year.

évsatz—century.

ete—before; in front of.

että—that.

fáz—to feel cold or chilly.

fél—fellow; friend.

fél ku kuuluaak sívam belső—beloved.

fél ku vigyázak—dear one.

feldolgaz—prepare.

fertiil—fertile one.

fesztelen—airy.

fü—herbs; grass.

gæidno—road; way.

gond—care; worry; love (*noun*).

hän—he; she; it; one.

hän agba—it is so.

hän ku—prefix: one who; he who; that which.

hän ku agba—truth.

hän ku kaśwa o numamet—sky-owner.

hän ku kuulua sívamet—keeper of my heart.

hän ku lejkka wäke-sarnat—traitor.

hän ku meke pirämet—defender.

hän ku pesä—protector.

hän ku pesäk kaikak—guardians of all.

hän ku piwtä—predator; hunter; tracker.

hän ku pusm—healer.

hän ku saa kuć3aket—star-reacher.

hän ku tappa—killer; violent person (*noun*). Deadly; violent (*adj.*).

hän ku tuulmahl elidet—vampire (literally: life-stealer).

hän ku vie elidet—vampire (literally: thief of life).

hän ku vigyáz sielamet—keeper of my soul.

hän ku vigyáz sívamet és sielamet—keeper of my heart and soul.

hän sívamak—beloved.

hängem—him; her; it.

hank—they.

hany—clod; lump of earth.

hisz—to believe; to trust.

ho—how.

ida—east.

igazág—justice.

ila—to shine.

inan—mine; my own (*endearment*).

irgalom—compassion; pity; mercy.

isä—father (*noun*).

isäntä—master of the house.

it—now.

jaguár—jaguar.

jaka—to cut; to divide; to separate.

jakam—wound; cut; injury.

jälleen—again.

jama—to be sick, infected, wounded or dying; to be near death.

jamatan—fallen; wounded; near death.

jelä—sunlight; day, sun; light.

jelä keje terád—light sear you (*Carpathian swear words*).

o jelä peje kaik hänkanak—sun scorch them all (*Carpathian swear words*).

o jelä peje emnimet—sun scorch the woman (*Carpathian swear words*).

o jelä peje terád—sun scorch you (*Carpathian swear words*).

o jelä peje terád, emni—sun scorch you, woman (*Carpathian swear words*).

o jelä sielamak—light of my soul.

joma—to be under way; to go.

joŋe—to come; to return.

joŋesz arwa-arvoval—return with honor (*greeting*).

joŋesz éntölem, fél ku kuuluaak sívam belsö—come to me, beloved.

jotka—gap; middle; space.

454

jotkan—between.

juo—to drink.

juosz és eläsz—drink and live (*greeting*).

juosz és olen ainaak sielamet jutta—drink and become one with me (*greeting*).

juta—to go; to wander.

jüti—night; evening.

jutta—connected; fixed (*adj.*). To connect; to join; to fix; to bind (*verb*).

k—suffix added after a noun ending in a vowel to make it plural.

kać3—gift.

kaca—male lover.

kadi—judge.

kaik—all.

käktä—two; many.

käktäverit—mixed blood (literally: two bloods).

kalma—corpse; death; grave.

kaŋa—to call; to invite; to summon; to request; to beg.

kaŋk—windpipe; Adam's apple; throat.

karma—want.

Karpatii—Carpathian.

karpatii ku köd—liar.

Karpatiikunta—the Carpathian people.

käsi—hand.

kaśwa—to own.

kaða—to abandon; to leave; to remain.

kaða wäkeva óv o köd—stand fast against the dark (*greeting*).

kat—house; family (*noun*).

katt3—to move; to penetrate; to proceed.

keje—to cook; to burn; to sear.

kepä—lesser; small; easy; few.

kessa—cat.

kessa ku toro—wildcat.

kessake—little cat.

kidü—to wake up; to arise (*intransitive verb*).

kim—to cover an entire object with some sort of covering.

kinn—out; outdoors; outside; without.

kinta—fog; mist; smoke.

kislány—little girl.

kislány kuŋenak—little lunatic.

kislány kuŋenak minan—my little lunatic.

köd—fog; mist; darkness; evil (*noun*). Foggy, dark;
  evil (*adj.*).

köd alte hän—darkness curse it (*Carpathian swear words*).

o köd belső—darkness take it (*Carpathian swear words*).

köd elävä és köd nime kutni nimet—evil lives and
  has a name.

köd jutasz belső—shadow take you (*Carpathian
  swear words*).

koj—let; allow; decree; establish; order.

koje—man; husband; drone.

kola—to die.

kolasz arwa-arvoval—may you die with honor (*greeting*).

kolatan—dead; departed.

koma—empty hand; bare hand; palm of the hand; hollow
  of the hand.

kond—all of a family's or clan's children.

kont—warrior; man.

kont o sívanak—strong heart (literally: heart of the warrior).

kor3—basket; container made of birch bark.

kor3nat—containing; including.

ku—who; which; that; where; which; what.

kuć3—star.

kuć3ak!—stars! (exclamation).

kudeje—descent; generation.

kuja—day; sun.

kule—to hear.

kulke—to go or to travel (on land or water).

kulkesz arwa-arvoval, ekäm—walk with honor, my brother (*greeting*).

kulkesz arwaval, joŋesz arwa arvoval—go with glory, return with honor (*greeting*).

kuly—intestinal worm; tapeworm; demon who possesses and devours souls.

küm—human male.

kumala—to sacrifice; to offer; to pray.

kumpa—wave (*noun*).

kuńa—to lie as if asleep; to close or cover the eyes in a game of hide-and-seek; to die.

kuŋe—moon; month.

kunta—band; clan; tribe; family; people; lineage; line.

kuras—sword; large knife.

kure—bind; tie.

kuš—worker; servant.

kutenken—however.

kutni—to be able to bear, carry, endure, stand or take.

kutnisz ainaak—long may you endure (*greeting*).

kuulua—to belong; to hold.

kužõ—long.

lääs—west.

lamti (or lamt3)—lowland; meadow; deep; depth.

lamti ból jüti, kinta, ja szelem—the nether world (literally: the meadow of night, mists, and ghosts).

laña—daughter.

lejkka—crack; fissure; split (*noun*). To cut; to hit; to strike forcefully (*verb*).

lewl—spirit (*noun*).

457

lewl ma—the other world (literally: spirit land). *Lewl ma* includes *lamti ból jüti, kinta, ja szelem*: the nether world, but also includes the worlds higher up *En Puwe*, the Great Tree.

liha—flesh.

lõuna—south.

löyly—breath; steam. (related to *lewl*: spirit).

luwe—bone.

ma—land; forest; world.

magköszun—thank.

mana—to abuse; to curse; to ruin.

mäne—to rescue; to save.

maɣe—land; earth; territory; place; nature.

mboće—other; second (*adj.*).

me—we.

megem—us.

meke—deed; work (*noun*). To do; to make; to work (*verb*).

mić (or mića)—beautiful.

mića emni kuŋenak minan—my beautiful lunatic.

minden—every; all (*adj.*).

möért?—what for? (*exclamation*).

molo—to crush; to break into bits.

molanâ—to crumble; to fall apart.

moo—why; reason.

mozdul—to begin to move; to enter into movement.

muonì—appoint; order; prescribe; command.

muonìak te avoisz te—I command you to reveal yourself.

musta—memory.

myös—also.

m8—thing; what.

na—close; near.

nä—for.

nâbbŏ—so, then.

ŋamaŋak—these; these ones here; those; those ones there.

nautish—to enjoy.

nélkül—without.

nenä—anger.

nime—name.

nókunta—kinship.

numa—god; sky; top; upper part; highest (related to the English word *numinous*).

numatorkuld—thunder (literally: sky struggle).

ńůp@l—for; to; toward.

ńůp@l mam—toward my world.

nyelv—tongue.

nyál—saliva; spit. (related to *nyelv*: tongue).

ńiŋ3—worm; maggot.

o—the (used before a noun beginning with a consonant).

ó—like; in the same way as; as.

odam—to dream; to sleep.

odam-sarna kondak—lullaby (literally: sleep-song of children).

olen—to be.

oma—old; ancient; last; previous.

omas—stand.

ŏrem—to forget; to lose one's way; to make a mistake.

ot—the (used before a noun beginning with a vowel).

ot (or t)—past participle (*suffix*).

óv—to protect against.

owe—door.

päämoro—aim; target.

pajna—to press.

pälä—half; side.

päläfertiil—mate or wife.

päläpälä—side by side.

palj3—more.

palj3 na éntölem—closer.

partiolen—scout (*noun*).

peje—to burn; scorch.

peje!—burn! (*Carpathian swear word*).

peje terád—get burned (*Carpathian swear words*).

pél—to be afraid; to be scared of.

pesä—nest (*literal; noun*); protection (*figurative; noun*).

pesä—nest; stay (*literal*); protect (*figurative*).

pesäd te engemal—you are safe with me.

pesäsz jeläbam ainaak—long may you stay in the light
  (*greeting*).

pide—above.

pile—to ignite; to light up.

pion—soon.

pirä—circle; ring (*noun*). To surround; to enclose (*verb*).

piros—red.

pitä—to keep; to hold; to have; to possess.

pitäam mustaakad sielpesäambam—I hold your memories
  safe in my soul.

pitäsz baszú, piwtäsz igazáget—no vengeance, only justice.

piwtä—to seek; to follow; to follow the track of game; to
  hunt; to prey upon.

poår—bit; piece.

põhi—north.

pohoopa—vigorous.

pukta—to drive away; to persecute; to put to flight.

pus—healthy; healing.

puwe—tree; wood.

rambsolg—slave.

rauho—peace.

reka—ecstasy; trance.

rituaali—ritual.

sa—sinew; tendon; cord.

sa4—to call; to name.

saa—arrive, come; become; get, receive.

saasz hän ku andam szabadon—take what I freely offer.

sas—shoosh (*to a child or baby*).

saɣe—to arrive; to come; to reach.

salama—lightning; lightning bolt.

sarna—words; speech; song; magic incantation (*noun*). To chant; to sing; to celebrate (*verb*).

sarna hän agba—claim.

sarna kontakawk—warriors' chant.

sarna kunta—alliance (literally: single tribe through sacred words).

śaro—frozen snow.

satz—hundred.

siel—soul.

sieljelä isäntä—purity of soul triumphs.

sisar—sister.

sisarak sivak—sisters of the heart.

sisarke—little sister.

sív—heart.

sív pide köd—love transcends evil.

sív pide minden köd—love transcends all evil.

sívad olen wäkeva, hän ku piwtä—may your heart stay strong, hunter (*greeting*).

sívam és sielam—my heart and soul.

sívamet—my heart.

sívdobbanás—heartbeat (*literal*); rhythm (*figurative*).

sokta—to mix; to stir around.

sõl—dare, venture.

sõl olen engemal, sarna sívametak—dare to be with me, song of my heart.

soŋe—to enter; to penetrate; to compensate; to replace.

Susiküm—Lycan.

susu—home; birthplace (*noun*). At home (*adv.*).

szabadon—freely.

szelem—ghost.

ször—time; occasion.

t (or ot)—past participle (*suffix*).

taj—to be worth.

taka—behind; beyond.

takka—to hang; to remain stuck.

takkap—obstacle; challenge; difficulty; ordeal; trial.

tappa—to dance; to stamp with the feet; to kill.

tasa—even so; just the same.

te—you.

te kalma, te jama ńiŋ3kval, te apitäsz arwa-arvo—you are nothing but a walking maggot-infected corpse, without honor.

te magköszunam nä ŋamaŋ kać3 taka arvo—thank you for this gift beyond price.

ted—yours.

terád keje—get scorched (*Carpathian swear words*).

tõd—to know.

tõdak pitäsz wäke bekimet mekesz kaiket—I know you have the courage to face anything.

tõdhän—knowledge.

tõdhän lõ kuraset agbapäämoroam—knowledge flies the sword true to its aim.

toja—to bend; to bow; to break.

toro—to fight; to quarrel.

torosz wäkeval—fight fiercely (*greeting*).

totello—obey.

tsak—only.

t'śuva vni—period of time.

tti—to look; to see; to find.

tuhanos—thousand.

tuhanos löylyak türelamak saɣe diutalet—a thousand
  patient breaths bring victory.

tule—to meet; to come.

tuli—fire.

tumte—to feel; to touch; to touch upon.

türe—full; satiated; accomplished.

türelam—patience.

türelam agba kontsalamaval—patience is the warrior's
  true weapon.

tyvi—stem; base; trunk.

ul3—very; exceedingly; quite.

umuš—wisdom; discernment.

und—past participle (*suffix*).

uskol—faithful.

uskolfertiil—allegiance; loyalty.

usm—to heal; to be restored to health.

vár—to wait.

varolind—dangerous.

veri—blood.

veri ekäakank—blood of our brothers.

veri-elidet—blood-life.

veri isäakank—blood of our fathers.

veri olen piros, ekäm—literally: blood be red, my brother;
  figuratively: find your lifemate (*greeting*).

veriak ot en Karpatiiak—by the blood of the prince
  (literally: by the blood of the great Carpathian; *Carpathian
  swear words*).

veridet peje—may your blood burn (*Carpathian
  swear words*).

vigyáz—to love; to care for; to take care of.

vii—last; at last; finally.

wäke—power; strength.

wäke beki—strength; courage.

wäke kaða—steadfastness.

wäke kutni—endurance.

wäke-sarna—vow; curse; blessing (literally: power words).

wäkeva—powerful; strong.

wara—bird; crow.

weńća—complete; whole.

wete—water (*noun*).

Do you love fiction with a supernatural twist?

Want the chance to hear news about your favourite
authors (and the chance to win free books)?

Keri Arthur
Kristen Callihan
P.C. Cast
Christine Feehan
Jacquelyn Frank
Larissa Ione
Darynda Jones
Sherrilyn Kenyon
Jayne Ann Krentz and Jayne Castle
Lucy March
Martin Millar
Tim O'Rourke
Lindsey Piper
Christopher Rice
J.R. Ward
Laura Wright

Then visit the Piatkus website
www.piatkus.co.uk

And follow us on Facebook and Twitter
www.facebook.com/piatkusfiction | @piatkusbooks

piatkus